# EXODUS OF SPIES

## Also by Brian Landers

*Empires Apart: The Story of the American and Russian Empires*

The Dylan Series:

*Awakening of Spies*
*Families of Spies*
*Coincidence of Spies*

# EXODUS OF SPIES

## BRIAN LANDERS

Red Door

Published by RedDoor
www.reddoorpress.co.uk

ISBN 978-1-913062-43-9

Cover design: Rawshock Design

Typesetting: Jen Parker, Fuzzy Flamingo
www.fuzzyflamingo.co.uk

Printed and bound in Denmark by Nørhaven

# AUTHOR'S NOTE

Operation Argon and the Democratic International are both real events from the twenty-seven-year-long Angolan civil war. They are depicted here as accurately as possible. Some of those involved – Captain Wynand Du Toit, Jonas Savimbi and Lieutenant Colonel Oliver North – are real people.

Most other characters are fictional and any similarity to real people and events is largely, but not entirely, coincidental.

# PROLOGUE

The killing of Adam Joseff stunned his friends and former colleagues.

Even after all these years I can still remember the shock and disbelief when my wife Julia phoned.

'Adam's dead. He's been shot. In Antigua.'

He had been killed by two shots to the back of the head fired at close range. There were signs of a struggle but his wallet had been found untouched. The house itself had not been ransacked and nothing appeared to be missing. To many of us that made the initial police assumption of a bungled robbery seem very wide of the mark. Adam had been around long enough to know that if someone is pointing a gun at you the only sensible response is to put your hands up. Adam Joseff had been executed.

Because he had been a pillar of the Intelligence Establishment for so long there were inevitably calls for the Security Services to use their resources to investigate his death. But the reality was that he had retired nearly eight years earlier and his death seemed to have no current security implications. My own Service could not get involved.

Why, we all asked ourselves, would anyone want to kill Adam? Collecting early postage stamps, rather than anything in his no doubt murky past, was what obsessed him now. And what was he doing in Antigua? Adam's only known connection with the Caribbean had been a best-forgotten operation in Trinidad many years ago.

The local police did ask for assistance and two Metropolitan Police detectives flew out to the Caribbean. They spent a week in Antigua but nothing new emerged. I was told they had produced a voluminous report but it was not until later that I had a chance to read it. The case remained unsolved. Back in London interest waned.

'Joseff was one of the best,' I heard Colin Asperton remark to one of his team. 'But very much old school. Put out to grass long ago.'

I wouldn't have described Adam as 'old school' myself. I remembered him poring over computer printouts when I joined the Defence Intelligence Staff, at a time when most of our colleagues were still coming to terms with electric typewriters. And I certainly didn't like the expression 'put out to grass'. I had transferred from the Defence Intelligence Staff to MI6 before Adam retired but I knew his contrarian thinking was sorely missed.

Not that Adam had cut himself off entirely from our world. He and a couple of others had set up what he called a 'strategy consultancy', which seemed to be moderately successful. My wife had joined him for what she expected to be a part-time role; it had proved to be far more than that. He remained in touch with an astonishing network of contacts like a one-man LinkedIn app. Many of them speculated at length about his murder but to no avail.

Adam's death would have remained one more mystery to be filed away and then forgotten but for the discovery of the second body.

Only then did we realise that the killing of Adam Joseff

had everything to do with the Security Services. His death, it became clear, was the result of a long chain of apparently unconnected events that went right back to a commando raid in Angola nearly three years earlier, Operation Argon.

# PART 1

# LUANDA, ANGOLA, 21 MAY 1985

Salvador da Silva Pinheiro, head of the Angolan security police, was expecting the raid that the South Africans had named Operation Argon. He cursed only that he had received the details too late to do more than send a warning to the army commander in Cabinda on the very evening that Captain Wynand Du Toit and his men were going ashore. His mood was not improved when he heard that most of the South African raiding party had escaped.

'Have you heard the news from Cabinda?' demanded the Russian colonel who barged into Pinheiro's office the next morning.

Pinheiro turned. 'Please knock before you enter.'

The Russian merely nodded to acknowledge he had heard the reprimand. He wasn't about to apologise.

'The South Africans have attacked the storage tanks in Cabinda,' said the Russian.

'Tried to attack. They were intercepted. Our forces captured one and killed two.'

'And the rest escaped.'

'The rest? You think there were more?'

'Of course. They will be back inside Zaire by now.'

Pinheiro said nothing. Why should he tell this arrogant pig that he knew for a fact that the raiding party had indeed been larger and that some did unfortunately seem to have escaped? And if the Russian wanted to believe they had crossed the frontier from Zaire let him. There was no point in telling him that he was wrong. The commandos had come by sea all the way from Saldanha Bay in South Africa's Cape Province.

The Angolan turned away. The Russians seemed to think that he should gratefully accept the crumbs of information that they were willing to pass him. But he no longer needed to rely on them. Now he had his own man in the enemy camp and he was not about to share him with anyone: not with his subordinates, not with the Russians, not even with his party comrades here in Luanda. Only one other person needed to know, and she could be trusted.

# I

The European powers carving up Africa at the Conference of Berlin in 1885 had done so by simply drawing lines on maps. Cabinda was a leftover that had to be tidied up, an enclave of less than 3,000 square miles jammed between the bits of the Congo delta given to France and Belgium. The Conference decided to give Cabinda to Portugal. Eventually the Portuguese lumped it into their colony of Angola despite the fact that the two territories shared no common border. Cabinda was separated from the rest of Angola by a strip of what, at the time of Operation Argon, was called Zaire and is now, with a fine sense of irony, called the Democratic Republic of the Congo.

There was no way the nineteenth-century map makers could have guessed that their casual creation would achieve the importance it eventually achieved. The discovery of the world's largest offshore oilfields changed Cabinda for ever.

Cabinda's oil storage facilities, owned by Gulf Oil, were the intended target for the nine South African Special Forces commandos who approached the Cabinda coast on the night of 20 May 1985.

The moon was hidden by heavy cloud and a gentle swell was all that stirred the sea. 'Ideal conditions,' commented one of the commandos but already the mission was not going entirely to plan. The boats had been launched further out than the mission commander, Captain Wynand Du Toit, had hoped. There were further delays when a fishing boat appeared close to the planned landing site.

Nevertheless the initial landing went well and Du Toit was confident they could make up lost time. After hurriedly hiding their boats the South Africans set off inland. The familiar smells of Africa were a welcoming comfort after long days at sea. They successfully skirted around a small village but after that soon got lost. Operation Argon was running well behind schedule when the raiders reached the heavily wooded lying-up position that had been identified for them by South African Intelligence.

The aerial photographs used in the planning sessions back at the South African Military Academy in Saldanha appeared to show that the surrounding area was uninhabited. They were wrong. When daylight broke, the commandos discovered that their hiding place was surrounded by camouflaged encampments of Angolan troops. It seemed that a major Angolan Army base was hidden in the jungle little more than half a mile away.

From their hiding place the commandos watched in alarm as an Angolan Army patrol appeared, apparently following the tracks they had left during the night. The patrol stopped before it reached the undergrowth where they had hidden and then disappeared in the direction of the base. Du Toit breathed a sigh of relief but that relief was short-lived.

The patrol returned with reinforcements. Then another group of soldiers arrived and started to fire rocket-propelled grenades in the general direction of Du Toit's hiding place. This was not at all what had been planned.

Du Toit ordered his men to retreat back towards the

beach. But more Angolan troops were arriving from the west. Machine-gun and RPG fire was coming from all sides.

Two of the South African commandos were hit.

Ahead the South Africans saw a heavily wooded area that might provide refuge. The only way to get there was by crossing a wide expanse of waist-high grass. Du Toit ordered his men to take cover. He and two NCOs would cross the grass and head into the trees. From there they could provide covering fire while the other six commandos, including the two wounded, followed.

It was a desperate plan and it didn't work. As soon as they broke cover the three men were spotted. Bullets screamed at them from every direction.

Corporal Liebenberg was killed almost immediately. Du Toit and Sergeant van Breda, both badly wounded, fought on until their weapons were red hot. The entire engagement was over in much less than an hour.

When the undisciplined Angolan troops finally descended on the two soldiers they found Du Toit too badly wounded to carry on and his sergeant dead. Du Toit was beaten mercilessly and then carried off, the Angolans keen to parade their prisoner in a display reminiscent of the triumphal celebrations of the ancient Romans. But the Romans wouldn't have missed the surviving six South Africans who managed to evade the distracted Angolans and escape to their boats.

They were the lucky ones. The badly injured Du Toit was thrust before the world's cameras to admit that his target had been three enormous oil storage tanks on which the Angolan economy depended. The raid had been a fiasco and Operation Argon made newspaper headlines around the world. To many it symbolised the global struggle between right and wrong, black and white, weak and strong. Of course in the Cold War climate of the period who was right and who was wrong, who was weak and who was strong was a matter of opinion. The only thing everyone could agree on was who was black and who was white.

It was a massive propaganda coup for the Angolan regime in the midst of a vicious civil war. Here was proof that the thousands of Cuban soldiers and Russian advisers in the country were needed not to crush internal rivals, as the United States and Britain alleged, but to fight off the threat of foreign invasion. Du Toit spent more than two years in solitary confinement before being exchanged for 133 Angolan soldiers and two political prisoners. Throughout that time he remained a constant reminder of, as the world's media put it, the day that 'Apartheid troops invaded black African nation on failed sabotage mission.'

Part of the media's outrage arose because they had previously been reporting, with more or less confidence, that hostilities between South Africa and Angola were coming to an end.

The first South African troops in any great numbers had entered Angola in 1975 and during the next ten years there had been numerous 'incursions', 'invasions', 'raids' and partial 'occupations' but that now seemed to be over. Talks in the Zambian capital Lusaka had eased tensions. Just a month before, a ceremony had taken place on Angola's southern border to mark the departure of the last South African soldier. Angolan and South African representatives had shaken hands and expressed the wish that South Africa would never again feel the need to send its troops north.

Much of the press may have taken the Lusaka agreement at face value but those of us more closely involved thought differently.

I remember the period well because just two weeks earlier I had been promoted. I was now Thomas Dylan, Acting Deputy Saddo. By then I had spent more than a decade in one or other of the Intelligence services and had reached that stage in my career where I wanted to move on not just to gain wider experience but to demonstrate progress up the ladder. There had been a sudden crisis when one of the Desk Officers, the Service's legendary Africa specialist Giles Smith, suffered a heart attack on a flight back from Accra. He could be off for months. The SAD, the Subsaharan Africa Desk, needed a new Desk Officer, a role invariably and inevitably referred to in the jargon of the Service, as the Saddo.

'Things are hotting up in Africa,' Colin Asperton told me when I was called in to see him. 'That's where the Cold War is now. Russian advisers all over the shop and half the Cuban Army deployed in Angola. We can't afford to leave the Desk understrength. Smith's Deputy, John Darwyn, will act as Saddo for now and you will take over from him as Deputy Saddo.'

I may not have responded as enthusiastically as he expected; after three years in London I had been hoping to go back into the field. 'You are ideal,' he assured me. 'You understand the Russians from your time in Moscow and you speak Portuguese, precisely the skills we need to stay on top of events in Southern Africa.'

To be appointed Deputy Desk Officer, even on an acting basis, on one of the big Desks at the age of thirty-three was unusual and I was flattered. Subsaharan Africa was not a region I had any special interest in but promotion was promotion, even on a temporary basis.

'How long do you expect me to be there?' I asked.

'That depends on how long before Smith is fit to return, if he returns. It's an area where a few changes may be needed whatever happens.'

I soon discovered what he meant. Smith and his Deputy John Darwyn had both been born and bred in Africa and had an instinctive feel for the continent. They were steeped in its history at a time when our lords and masters had decided that history no longer mattered.

As Asperton himself put it, 'Ministers don't want to hear about squabbles between the Kikuyu and Luo in Kenya, they just want to know what the hell the Russians are doing in Angola and Mozambique.'

What Ministers weren't so interested in is what the South Africans were doing there. For our political masters Intelligence cooperation with the 'apartheid regime' in South Africa was something to be encouraged in private but ignored in public. They would rather not know how closely our Service was involved in the darker games being played in the region. In the case of Operation Argon we hadn't told Ministers that MI6 had been forewarned and in the subsequent inquiry we made sure they didn't find out. Better to let Ministers think that we had been as ignorant as everyone else than to let them discover we knew the raid was going to take place but hadn't thought it sensible to alert Sir Geoffrey Howe, the Foreign Secretary.

He didn't know what was planned, but I did.

## II

Back in May 1985, at the time of Operation Argon, the Secret Intelligence Service, MI6, was still headquartered in Century House, a suitably anonymous tower block on Westminster Bridge Road. It was obvious that we needed somewhere more secure and better able to house the technology on which we were starting to depend but it would be another nine years before we moved to the futuristic headquarters at Vauxhall Cross featured in the later James Bond films.

Just two weeks before Operation Argon hit the headlines I moved into a cramped and windowless office at the back of Century House. I was still trying to convince myself that my new Acting Deputy Desk Officer role was the job I really wanted. Until then all my attention had been focused on 'the enemy', the Soviet Union and its satellites. I had joined the Defence Intelligence Staff, DIS, straight from university to analyse Soviet military dispositions. When I married a colleague the powers that be decided that married couples working in the same section could not be allowed and so one of us had to leave. Julia's uncle pulled some strings and Julia remained with DIS, I transferred to the Secret Intelligence Service, MI6, and we were both posted to Moscow. Married couples working in the same embassy apparently could be allowed.

After an extended tour in Russia, a very brief stint in

Poland and a much delayed six-month introduction to Service tradecraft at Fort Monckton I joined the Soviet Operations Desk, the SOD, my first spell in Century House. Now in the parlance of the Service I would be rotating from the SOD to the SAD.

I was sorry to be leaving the Soviet Operations Desk. Gorbachev was shaking things up in the Soviet Union and the first signs were appearing that the eastern bloc really might start to fracture. I had handled the London end of two of the Service's more successful operations behind the Iron Curtain and Justin Brasenose, my sponsor, had been fulsome in his praise. I was expecting my next posting to be in the field somewhere, probably one of the smaller stations behind the Iron Curtain or, if I was really lucky, one of the more important stations, perhaps back to Moscow or to Washington or Paris. The prospect of an accompanied posting to somewhere like Paris was very attractive. On the other hand with a three-year-old daughter in my life I wasn't overly excited at the prospect of touring African hotspots instead.

Asperton soon put me straight on that.

'I really don't see the need to go gallivanting around Africa propping up bars like Graham Greene in his heyday,' he told me. 'We have people on the ground to tell us what the locals think is happening. Your job is to put the pieces together and make the big picture clear. The only people worth flying down to talk to are the South Africans and fortunately they have some really decent hotels.'

I still wasn't as enthusiastic as I should have been but Asperton seemed to have no doubts.

'Play your cards right and you could be Desk Officer yourself in a couple of years.'

He was right. I considered myself a 'field man' but the truth is that, as in so many organisations, the quickest way to the top is to stay close to head office. This was promotion and I would have been stupid to turn it down. I threw myself into understanding the byzantine and violent politics of the region. John Darwyn, my new boss, delighting in his promotion to Acting Saddo, heaped file upon file on to my desk with the vague incantation, 'Better digest these.'

Darwyn was a breed of Englishman which has now disappeared. His father had spent his entire adult life as a colonial civil servant in one part of Africa or another. John had been bundled off to one of the less expensive boarding schools back home where I suspect repeated bullying had caused him to retreat into his books, praying for the moment he would be released back to Africa for the summer holidays. He was too young for the war but after national service, which he somehow managed to do with the King's African Rifles, he joined the Secret Intelligence Service. Without an Oxbridge degree he stood apart from most of the Service but his ability to quote Horace and Virgil at length, gained no doubt in long solitary hours at school, persuaded the powers that be that he was nearly 'one of us'.

'Start with Angola and Mozambique,' he suggested on my first day. 'The Portuguese made a complete mess of everything there.'

I had spent many of my school holidays in Lisbon with a Portuguese penfriend and thought I knew what he meant. The 'Carnation Revolution' that ended Portugal's decades of dictatorship produced a new government who announced they were not interested in continuing the country's colonial wars in Africa. Unusually they meant what they said: the

Portuguese simply sailed away. Angola and Mozambique were left to collapse into civil war, made far worse by the vast quantities of modern arms shovelled in from outside.

As Asperton had said, the Cold War had now arrived in Subsaharan Africa and the Russians seemed to be winning.

Long before the Portuguese left Angola, the United States and the Soviet Union had chosen sides in the so-called 'Liberation Struggle'. The Russians had no difficulty finding a Marxist guerrilla group to support. For the Americans, life was not so straightforward. Portugal was a member of NATO and their Lajes airbase in the Azores was an important asset for the US Air Force. Nevertheless it was clear that the Portuguese Empire in Africa was doomed so the CIA chose to back another of the groups fighting for independence. For twenty years they intermittently funded guerrilla leader Holden Roberto, but they had chosen the wrong side.

When the Portuguese left, the two superpowers called in their surrogates. Troops from US ally Zaire were met by forces arriving from Russia's ally Cuba. The American-backed faction was crushed.

Just to complicate matters South African forces invaded from the south and captured Benguela and other key cities. Their troops were within 600 miles of the Angolan capital, Luanda, when they realised that with the Americans having thrown in the towel and the Soviets flying in massive reinforcements they had better retreat.

That left the Americans and South Africans faced with the prospect of a Russian satellite controlling one of the richest countries in Africa. Luckily there was another guerrilla group available, UNITA, with its charismatic leader Jonas Savimbi.

Savimbi had been trained in China but managed to reconcile his professed Maoism with a willingness to turn to South Africa and the United States for military assistance. A man who turned out to be one of the most vicious psychopaths in Africa found himself being paraded as the champion of western values. The stage was set. In Angola on the western side of the continent and Mozambique on the eastern, Russian-backed governments fought American-backed rebels in civil wars of unremitting barbarism.

The position of Her Majesty's Government was unambiguous. Russia could not be allowed to usurp Britain's historical position in Africa. The Prime Minister, Margaret Thatcher, denounced Russia's 'brazen intervention' in Angola. What this meant in practice was less clear. Military action was ruled out, but what was expected of us? Was MI6 to be witness or participant?

I put that question to Colin Asperton. He raised an eyebrow at my naïveté.

'The role of the Service is to provide intelligence, nothing more, to ensure that Ministers are fully up to speed at all times. Of course if in doing this we are able, in cooperation with our allies, to further HMG's broad policy objectives in the region we should clearly do so.'

A hint of what that meant came a few days before the ill-fated Operation Argon.

It had been announced that there were to be changes at the top of the Service. Justin Brasenose, with whom I had worked closely, was off to join the Joint Intelligence Committee in the Cabinet Office. As one office wit put it the JIC was where good spies went when they died, 'All the prestige, none of the pressure.'

Before leaving Brasenose called a late afternoon meeting to update himself on operations in Southern Africa. John Darwyn and I were invited and Colin Asperton sent along a South African-born but English-schooled former Guards officer named Turk Rowbart. Rowbart had just finished some sort of attachment to our Station in Pretoria. I was surprised to find someone else present: an old colleague, Richard Mendale.

When I had joined the Defence Intelligence Staff the Deputy Director General had been Adam Joseff and Richard Mendale had been the Director, Operations. Following Joseff's retirement Mendale had become Deputy DG but he hadn't survived a major reorganisation and found himself posted to the Embassy in Washington. Now Mendale too was about to retire but before doing so he had been invited to give a guest lecture at the South African Military Academy in Saldanha. While there, he told us, he had observed preparations for an imminent raid on Cabinda.

'What they're calling Operation Argon is quite a risk,' he started. 'It's a hell of a long way from Saldanha to Cabinda. The South African Navy have raided that far north before but they still have to hope the Russians don't spot them.'

'The real risk will be getting back after the raid,' interrupted Brasenose. 'The Soviets will be looking for them and if they happen to have a killer submarine down there who knows what will happen. Do we know if the Russians have anything south of Luanda at the moment?'

'Well the Americans have apparently reported no hostile activity in the area.'

'So the Americans are involved?'

Mendale nodded. 'A Company man popped up while I

was there, Frank Cato.' By 'Company' he meant CIA.

'I hadn't come across Cato before,' Mendale continued, 'Africa's never been my patch.'

Brasenose said nothing, he clearly knew Cato but then he knew everybody worth knowing in our secret world.

'Cato's senior,' confirmed Turk Rowbart. 'Knows what he's doing. Special Ops.'

I didn't think to ask Rowbart where he'd come across the CIA man and Mendale continued.

'This isn't a Company operation. This is purely SADF, South African Defence Force. Chap named DeSmid is in charge, Colonel. He's using the Recces.'

'Recces?' I asked, not afraid to show my ignorance.

'South African Special Forces. There will be a nine man team from Number 4 Reconnaissance Regiment based at Langebaan, headed by a Captain Wynand Du Toit.'

'They seem to have been pretty open with you,' Brasenose commented.

'Probably more open than they've been with their own people,' suggested John Darwyn. 'I bet the Cabinet in Pretoria haven't been told. Pik Botha and his people at Foreign Affairs are trying to calm things down and here's the military playing war games.'

The conversation moved on to a discussion of the state of South African politics and in particular the clashes between the velvet glove of Foreign Minister Pik Botha and the iron fist of Defence Minister Magnus Malan. Darwyn was clearly a velvet glove man while Turk Rowbart equally clearly was not. But as Brasenose pointed out, the whole point of a velvet glove was to hide the iron fist inside, you needed both.

After the meeting, Brasenose invited Mendale up to his

office and I was surprised when he called me twenty minutes later.

'Ah Thomas, you're still there. I was hoping you hadn't left the building yet. Could you pop up here for a quick farewell drink with Richard?'

After phoning Julia to warn her I might be late home, I climbed the stairs to Brasenose's office wondering who else might be there. The answer was no one. Brasenose and Mendale were seated, glasses in hand, in front of a small coffee table bearing another glass and an opened bottle of Lagavulin.

'Sit down, Thomas. We were just discussing Richard's plans. Seems we're all off to pastures new. Quite an exodus.'

I sat down and poured myself a drink. Despite having worked closely with Brasenose this was the first time I had been into his office when he wasn't seated behind the protective barrier of his desk.

'Richard has a new project.'

'Not mine really, Adam Joseff's.' Mendale turned to me. 'You see much of Adam?'

'Off and on,' I replied. 'When we're down in Cornwall he sometimes pops over to see Julia's uncle.'

'When he's in the country I suppose,' Mendale commented. 'He seems to spend more of his time on planes than he did in Defence Intelligence. He was just off to Luanda of all places when I saw him. Chasing some sort of rare stamp. I told him to keep well away from Cabinda. The point is when he's not philatelising, if there is such a word, he's keeping his ears to the ground. Nothing much gets past Adam, and he seems to be making a business out of it. He's managed to get people to pay him to tell them what's not in the newspapers.'

'Private intelligence,' put in Brasenose. I thought I detected a hint of disapproval in his voice. 'Security consultancy I believe it's called.'

Mendale smiled. 'Not quite. You know Adam. This is brain without brawn. Nobody's going to hire a one-legged pensioner to act as a bodyguard or break into somebody's safe. No, he uses his experience and his contacts to explain what's really happening in parts of the world other people don't understand. What are the chances of a coup in Bolivia, who's going to win the next election in India, will I get paid if I sell a fleet of cars to a particular state governor in Nigeria? That sort of thing.'

'The sort of questions our Embassies are there to answer,' Brasenose suggested.

'Perhaps, but it's always useful to get an independent view. And of course most of Adam's customers aren't British. I gather his first client was an Italian coffee magnate.'

'And now Richard is going to join him,' interrupted Brasenose, turning to me, 'and he thinks you can help.'

'Me?'

'Not you,' corrected Mendale, 'your wife, Julia. Adam has a proposal he wants to put to her and as I was here today I thought I might forewarn you, warm you up as it were.'

He looked at me but I was too surprised to respond.

'The thing is,' he said. 'Adam's found a gap in the market. It's not going to make anybody rich but it will pay the bills and it's better than just fading away. But it needs a bit of organising. We can't rely on what Adam and I happen to pick up. There has to be some proper desk work, the sort of research where we can quote sources. We need to produce regular, credible reports we can show prospective clients. We need what is called these days a brand. At the moment we just have a name: Exodis.'

'Clever that,' admitted Brasenose. 'Ex-DIS. Although I doubt that an Italian coffee merchant will catch on, the great virtue of the Defence Intelligence Staff is that nobody's ever heard of it.'

Mendale just smiled. His potential customers wouldn't recognise the DIS connection but his informants would. Joseff and Mendale were no doubt planning to call in a lot of old favours.

'And as well as the research,' Mendale continued, 'we need someone to answer the phone, or at least to pick up any messages. Someone to provide cover when we're away and manage the accounts. But the research is the important part, that's what we need someone experienced to handle. It probably won't be full-time, not at first anyway. A couple of days a week perhaps. Adam said he spoke to Julia recently and thinks she's keen to get back to work. And of course she's ex-DIS herself.'

I could imagine Julia in that sort of role, as long as it really was research and analysis not just answering phones and making tea. But I knew Julia too well to try to answer for her. She would undoubtedly be annoyed that Mendale had spoken to me first.

'Obviously you'll have to speak to my wife yourself. She might well be interested.'

'Oh we will. Adam has already arranged to meet her when he gets back from Luanda. Like I say, I just wanted to warm you up first.'

It could have been my turn to be somewhat peeved, Julia had said nothing to me about meeting Adam Joseff to discuss a possible job. But I knew my wife well enough to know that there must have been a reason she hadn't mentioned it.

As it turned out Joseff had not been entirely open with Julia.

'He didn't say anything about working with him,' she explained when I arrived home. 'He phoned me a couple of days ago and said that my uncle had mentioned we were coming down for a long weekend. Apparently Adam's got a very rare stamp he wants to show me and he invited us over. I knew you wouldn't be interested so I suggested I come over on my own.'

'I wouldn't have thought you would be interested in his stamps.'

'You know perfectly well I'm not. But Adam's all on his own in that funny little cottage and he's a good friend of Uncle Gordon's. We should make an effort to see him. He was very good to us when we joined DIS. You don't have to come.'

'Oh I'll come but I'm not sure he's the lonely recluse you seem to think he is. Richard Mendale was telling me that Adam is constantly hopping on and off planes. I got the impression he doesn't spend much time in Cornwall.'

Julia raised a questioning eyebrow. 'Well when he is down there it must be pretty lonely, especially on a winter's night. He's even less likely to have many local friends if he's always dashing off here and there.'

I had only been to Joseff's cottage near St Mabyn once but I could imagine that, as Julia said, it was lonely on a winter night. It was quite a way from the village and the sense of isolation had been total.

I had that same almost palpable feeling of isolation some

three years later standing, looking at another cottage. Despite the heat and the vivid colours around me I had suddenly seen in my mind's eye Joseff's grey stone cottage and the bleak countryside of North Cornwall: it had been a shock to look up and realise that the pale green building in front of me was not where Joseff had lived but where his life had been suddenly extinguished.

# III

Two weeks later on a Friday evening we bundled our daughter Eveline into the child seat in the back of the Saab and set off for Cornwall. Ostensibly we were visiting family, my mother and Julia's aunt and uncle, but I suspect that for Julia the real reason was her desire to get behind the wheel of her ancient but beloved red MG and race like a lunatic over Bodmin Moor. She kept the car in a disused stable at her uncle's house.

'Stupid to have two cars in London,' she always insisted and always regretted.

We would also be visiting Adam Joseff.

When I joined the Defence Intelligence Staff straight from university Julia's Uncle Gordon had been the Director General but it was Adam Joseff who held the organisation together. His enormous office with its government issue metal desk, characterless metal table and chairs, flip charts and scattered papers always carefully locked away at night was the hub around which everything else revolved. Behind the apparent chaos was method, discipline and an obsession with detail. My first operational mission in Holland had been a disaster and it was Joseff who had handled the painful debriefing with coldly forensic skill. It was also Joseff who afterwards set about identifying and rectifying the gaps in my training that my own Director had done nothing to address.

The Defence Intelligence Staff in those days was an organisation in which civilians like me were expected to know their place. It was also almost entirely, and unapologetically, male. Although Adam Joseff had spent most of his working life in that environment his own values were quite different. He was no feminist but he judged people as individuals and his attitude to new recruits was more paternal than patriarchal. He was loyal to the organisation and all who joined his team. When doubts were expressed about Julia and I working together after we married he vehemently opposed the suggestion from some that Julia, as the woman, should be the one to resign and instead helped engineer our transfers to the Embassy in Moscow.

Now we faced another decision about Julia's future. She had left DIS and resigned her RAF commission when Eveline was born but, despite pressure from her lovely, but slightly old-fashioned, Aunt Anne, Julia had no intention of giving up on a career. The problem was my career. I could be posted anywhere in the world at any time and one thing we agreed on was that Julia and Eveline would come with me. That made finding a career for Julia difficult. Something like teaching English seemed the only option but I couldn't imagine Julia doing that for long. Joseff and Mendale's proposal might be a perfect way out. Presumably if I were posted somewhere with good communications, like Paris or Washington, we could just pack up the Exodis office and take it with us. A posting to Moscow or Mogadishu would be more difficult.

Julia had known Adam Joseff and Richard Mendale from the old days and liked working with them both. She wasn't surprised to hear that they were not planning to retire into obscurity.

'Do you really think they'll be able to make a go of something like Exodis?' Julia asked after we had stopped in a lay-by to swap drivers. 'Who is going to employ two ageing spooks?'

'Joseff seems pretty confident. His first client was an Italian coffee trader, but apparently what he's really looking for is a few contracts with some of the big players, banks, insurance companies, oil companies and the like.'

'But what is he going to sell them?'

'Well Mendale called it intelligence.'

'But they can't sell anything really secret, and in any case any secrets they have will be out of date in no time at all.'

'He doesn't mean copies of secret messages or details of the next nuclear submarine. He's talking about political intelligence. What may or may not be going to happen. You know how it works. Not that much different from most of the reports DIS produces.'

Over a second whisky and then a third in Brasenose's office Mendale had become increasingly enthusiastic about the Exodis project. Islay single malts can have that effect on some people. I could even sense Justin Brasenose warming to the idea.

'Apparently,' I explained to Julia, 'Joseff has accumulated a whole archive of materials down in Cornwall and he's going to bring all that up to somewhere they are planning to rent in Chiswick. That's for the basic research and they will want you to keep it up to date. Joseff and Mendale will tap into the network of contacts they have built up over the last twenty years. Imagine one of their clients reads something in *The Economist* and wants more background. The first step will be to see if you can find any obscure but relevant articles filed away in Joseff's archive. Then if say it's about French interests in Libya they'll phone friends in Paris and try to find some juicy titbits they can use to flesh the files out.'

'And you think their friends will talk to them?'

I had asked that myself. 'It seems to me that if whoever they speak to is really in the loop and knows anything secret they will just clam up, but that in itself says something. But if they don't know anything truly secret they will want to talk because everyone wants to pretend they still have access.'

'But if they don't know anything secret what are they going to talk about?'

'That's the point. It will be speculation. But it will be informed speculation and Adam is astute enough to put that together with anything else you can find and produce a report that someone will pay for.'

Julia nodded knowingly. 'And no doubt he'll tailor the story to whoever is receiving it. If one of these American think tanks asks him for a report on the civil war in Angola he's not going to say that the Cubans are sure to win even if that's what he believes. He will say that the Cubans are going to win unless the United States does XYZ, knowing full well the United States won't do XYZ.'

'Something like that.'

Julia was silent after muttering something to herself about the ethics of it all. After a moment she changed the subject.

'Are the Cubans going to win in Angola?'

'I've no idea. The new chap in Asperton's office, Turk Rowbart, is convinced they can be stopped, Brasenose agrees they ought to be stopped but isn't sure they will be and I really think John Darwyn doesn't care as long as his appointment as Saddo is made permanent. Now that Reagan's won his second term in the White House there's a lot of pressure building up for the Americans to really unleash the dogs of war.'

'Let slip,' responded Julia. 'The phrase is let slip the dogs of war.'

We grinned at each other, playing the pedant was something we both enjoyed.

We said nothing more about Angola, my mangling of Shakespeare or Julia's potential job offer until we reached Penelowek, Julia's family home in Cornwall. No sooner had we arrived, than Julia's Aunt Anne announced that we had all been invited to dinner at Adam Joseff's on Saturday evening.

'Adam says he wants to return our hospitality, he's always popping in here. And,' she added unenthusiastically, 'he's got some new stamps to show us.'

'That's kind,' Julia responded. 'We had planned to see him anyway, if we can arrange a babysitter.'

Anne had already thought of that. My mother, who had been coming over for Sunday lunch, would be happy to stay over on Saturday night and babysit while we were at Adam Joseff's pretending an interest in philately.

'It's all arranged,' said Anne brightly without noticing her niece's glance in my direction. While I was pleased my mother would be able to spend more time with Eveline, I knew Julia had been planning for the two of us to leave Eveline with Anne and have Sunday morning to ourselves. Now one of us would be expected to accompany my mother to church.

Saturday was a glorious day without a cloud in the sky. Despite that, when we reached Adam Joseff's home, which he insisted on calling a cottage, it seemed as grey and bleak as I had remembered. Trees permanently bowed down by the winter winds turned their backs on a house sprawling haphazardly in every direction. The heavy stone walls and steeply sloping slate roof seemed to suck up any heat that remained from the day.

Julia and I had gone on ahead to discuss the Exodis proposal. She had a host of practical questions for Joseff, not least how much he could afford to pay her, but I could tell that she was attracted to the idea. If it panned out as he and Mendale hoped, the role would answer many of the dilemmas that had been facing us.

Julia wanted a career but even more she wanted the time with our daughter that she had not had with her own mother. Her own parents had died tragically young and in any event had already sent her from Singapore to prep school on the other side of the world. That was not going to happen to Eveline. But Eveline was nearly three, she would be going to nursery in another year. Julia had shone on the Defence Intelligence Staff and wanted to shine again. She had been seconded to DIS from the RAF only because her uncle had pulled the right strings but I had seen how Joseff and Mendale quickly came to depend upon her. I could imagine them working well together again.

There was still one major, massive question. Did Exodis have a future?

Adam Joseff was now approaching seventy. I remembered him as being remarkably fit and active despite having lost half a leg, but as he greeted us I couldn't help thinking he had aged since his retirement. Richard Mendale was younger but could they really drum up enough business to pay Julia's salary and for how long could they continue to do so? Mendale had told me that he would ensure that his contacts became Julia's contacts and that he was confident that she would develop new sources and new clients herself. But the reality, I suspected, would not be like that. Joseff and Mendale had a reputation in the Intelligence world that a relative newcomer like Julia could not achieve overnight, despite Mendale's suggestion that she use her maiden name in her new role. Grimspound was still a name commanding respect in Intelligence circles even though her uncle was no longer head of the Defence Intelligence Staff.

Exodis was not a long-term career. Julia was betting on a race that might be called off at any moment. Taking up Joseff's offer could be like thrusting her hand into a lucky dip only to find that all the prizes had already gone.

Joseff did his best to persuade her that his plans for Exodis had solid foundations. When it came to business I discovered that he was very much on the ball. I shouldn't have been surprised as he had always been a detail man, someone who planned for every eventuality.

'You should read this,' he said when we arrived, 'while I make us a cup of tea.'

He handed us an eight-page document headed 'Exodis Business Plan'. Knowing how he worked I suspect that he had bought a business school textbook and found a suitable template. The plan started with 'Objectives' and ended with 'Medium-term Cash Flow'. It was impressive and ambitious. It all seemed perfectly reasonable if, and it was a big if, if the business Joseff thought was out there was really out there. Were there really companies who were willing to spend money to hear the views of retired spies?

'What do you think?' Joseff asked, putting mugs of tea in front of us.

Julia seemed to have been reading my thoughts. 'Where is the business going to come from?'

'Where it's already coming from. This is what I've been doing for the last five years. That business plan is about ramping things up not doing anything dramatically new. With Richard coming on board, and hopefully with you, we can start to put everything on a proper footing. And I'm sounding out someone else who might join us. Right now I'm producing one-off reports on this or that but there are people out there who would be happy to pay a subscription for regular reports, annual or even quarterly. What I want to call the *Exodis Bulletin*. That will give us a steady income to supplement our instant responses to particular developments.'

'What sort of people?'

'All sorts. Your uncle introduced me to the chairman of an insurance company who wanted me to advise on their plans for Latin America. I've worked for banks, defence contractors, governments.'

'Governments?' Julia sounded surprised.

'Yes governments. For example in the last eighteen months I've organised three in-house seminars for the security services of one of our smaller allies. They can't afford to station people all around the world but they want to know what's happening out there. There will be other opportunities like that.'

'And these are all contacts you made at DIS?'

'Not at all. I've just mentioned your uncle introducing me to someone. And I met a man named Abrahão Raposo Taravares at the Mercado da Ribeira stamp market in Lisbon, his son is now one of my biggest clients. In fact I bought a very special stamp from Abrahão, which I'll tell you about when Anne and Gordon arrive.'

Julia kept pressing him but she had just agreed to 'give Exodis a try' when we heard the sound of her uncle's car outside.

Joseff disappeared into his cellar. He had lost half a leg in the war but it had never seemed to bother him; now for the first time I noticed him limping as he returned with a bottle. Without asking he poured out five glasses of Beaujolais. The wine was an expensive Morgon. An expert would probably say it should be served at just below room temperature but I wasn't sure that they would consider the temperature in Joseff's cellar 'just below'.

Before we could settle down he led us into what he termed his library. The furniture in the other rooms was traditional heavy brown wood. In the library there were two such wooden chairs and a large table but in addition three of the walls were lined with identical grey metal fire-proof cabinets. His office at DIS had been lined with similar cabinets. I remembered that the only sign of individuality back then had been a single poster depicting an old postage stamp bearing the head of some continental monarch and a gold table lighter presented to him for unspecified services by colleagues at GCHQ. The table lighter now stood on one of the cabinets but the four briar pipes that used to stand in their rack next to it had disappeared. Joseff had given up smoking on the day he retired from DIS.

He unlocked one of the cabinets and brought out three blue albums, which he placed carefully on the table.

Adam had become a philately bore. He claimed to have

the most complete collection of stamps from Spain, Portugal and their colonies in the country.

'Look at this,' he said, opening one of the albums.

As we crowded round I could see that the album contained stamps from Angola. On the first page was a simple set of stamps each with a crown in the centre surrounded by a border and the word ANGOLA in a cartouche at the top. There were a variety of colours each with a different value at the bottom. The values were in réis, the currency used in Portugal until the monarchy was overthrown in 1910.

'These are the very first stamps used in Angola in 1870,' Joseff explained before opening the second album.

It seemed to me the second set of stamps were very similar to the first. It was only when Julia moved aside and I could take a closer look that I could see that these were not from Angola. Instead of ANGOLA in the cartouche at the top the word CORREIO had been inserted and MOÇAMBIQUE had been inscribed in the border around the crown.

'And these were the first stamps used in Mozambique in 1877,' said Joseff. 'I have some wonderful examples of both of these sets, some really perfect covers sent from the colonies back to Portugal or out to India or Timor.'

'Beautiful,' agreed Julia's aunt with an enthusiasm I suspect she was far from feeling.

'But the ones here in my stock-book are really special,' he said, opening the third and much smaller album. 'Look at these.'

At first glance the two stamps he showed us in their plastic pockets looked remarkably like the previous ones.

'You see what's happened?' Joseff asked, looking at Julia's uncle who merely shook his head.

The design seemed very similar to the other two sets. These were from Mozambique as the cartouche at the top had the name MOÇAMBIQUE squeezed into it.

'Are they forgeries of some kind?' I asked.

'Not at all, although that's exactly what I thought at first. No, look here,' he pointed at the black 5 réis stamp. 'The meandros goes all the way round the crown.'

'The what?'

'The meandros. The Greek key pattern. On the stamps I showed you just now in the other album the meandros is broken so that Moçambique can be inscribed above the crown. But here the name of the colony is in the cartouche at the top, in the same way as the Angola issue, even though it doesn't really fit there. They've had to make the letters far too small. It's really ugly.'

'Is that important?'

Joseff gave me the sort of look Julia might give someone who said 'less' when they meant 'fewer'.

'Of course it's important. These two were prototypes, first editions. When they decided to produce stamps for Mozambique someone in Lisbon simply took the Angola engravings and replaced Angola with Moçambique in the cartouche. They then shipped them out to Africa. But they didn't reach Mozambique. When they arrived in Luanda the authorities must have had second thoughts. They would have realised how awful the new stamps looked. See here how small they had to make the characters so that the ten letters of Moçambique could fit into the same space as the six letters of Angola. The authorities stopped the stamps going on to Mozambique.'

'So the two stamps you have here were never used?'

'Never. And they are almost certainly unique. I have the only examples of these values.'

'And you're sure they're not forgeries?'

'Quite sure. There's documentation. Correspondence ordering all the stamps to be sent back to Lisbon to be destroyed and telling the designers to try again. They came up with a better design. You've seen what they did. MOÇAMBIQUE was inscribed above the crown and a shorter word, CORREIO meaning post, was found to put in the empty cartouche. It was another bodge. The next series in 1886 was much better, they dropped the word Correio completely.'

'If all the stamps were destroyed how did you find these two?'

'All those sent back to Portugal were destroyed. But they weren't all sent back. One set remained in Luanda.'

'And you bought one of them from the man whose son is now your client?' I asked.

'Abrahão Raposo Taravares, yes.'

'And the other one?'

'Oh that's from Abrahão as well.'

'Such a shame,' said Anne, 'that such pretty stamps have been lost. That they've all been destroyed.'

'Except for these,' Joseff said. He turned away before adding, 'And of course for the rest of the set. I only have these two low values but whoever saved them would surely have saved the whole set.'

'What happened to the higher values?' I asked.

He smiled to himself. 'If only I knew.'

As he locked the albums away, Julia asked the question we probably all wanted to ask.

'Are they valuable?'

'To a real collector, yes. Finding errors is the holy grail of all philatelists.' Joseff's eyes positively sparkled. 'In 1855 the first Swedish stamps were issued and somehow on one occasion a stamp that should have been green was printed in yellow. There's only one example known but that three skilling yellow is worth millions of dollars today. I know collectors who would kill for that stamp. Of course my two stamps are different. They never actually went into circulation. And they weren't true errors, just bad design. Nobody's going to kill for stamps like these.'

# IV

The next morning my mother astonished us by announcing that this Sunday she would not be going to church. As Anne Grimspound would be busy in the kitchen she would stay and look after Eveline.

'It will be a joy. And you two need a break,' she told Julia. 'Go for a nice long walk.'

Instead we took the MG for a spin and arrived back to something even more unexpected. My mother, having been entirely teetotal while my cider-quaffing father was alive, with the one exception of consuming a thimble of champagne at my wedding, was seated with Julia's uncle sipping hesitantly at a glass of sherry.

'Reverend Lovelock says the Lord changed water into wine for a purpose,' she explained. Reverend Lovelock was the new young minister who had presided over my father's funeral the year before.

'I thought you couldn't teach an old dog new tricks,' I remarked to Julia on the way back to London. 'I can't believe my mother would succumb to a temptation she has fought all her life.'

'It just shows how little we know about those closest to us,' Julia replied thoughtfully.

I thought it best not to respond to that. I was lucky that, to use a very trite cliché, I had married my best friend. I was confident that by now there was nothing important that we had not learned about each other.

I sat back and tried to decide how we should celebrate Julia's new job which, she had agreed with Adam Joseff, would start on the 3rd June. Unfortunately when I arrived at Century House next morning I discovered that I wouldn't be in London on that date. I would be in a mud hut 4,500 miles away.

Colin Asperton had called John Darwyn and me into his office for what he called a conference. With him was Turk Rowbart whom Asperton now introduced as his PPS. I wasn't aware that Asperton was entitled to his own Principal Private Secretary. By civil service standards the hierarchy of the Secret Intelligence Service had an unusual degree of opacity. Rank was often signalled primarily by the quality of the tailoring from Asperton's bespoke Saville Row to Darwyn's off the peg Marks & Spencer. Turk Rowbart didn't quite fit the usual mould; not many men wore Armani in the corridors of Century House, even if matched with the dark red and blue striped silk tie of the Brigade of Guards.

Having told me that my new role wouldn't involve exploring the remote corners of Africa, Asperton now reversed himself.

'You're off to see democracy in action,' he announced. 'We need a presence at the Democratic International next week.'

My heart sank. John Darwyn had already briefed me on what he clearly regarded as little more than a joke. He had referred to it as the Jamba Jamboree.

In 1985 the Cold War was reaching its climax. President Reagan, starting his second term after winning a landslide

37

victory the previous year, had famously described the Soviet Union and its allies as the 'Evil Empire'. He was determined to destroy the Communist menace wherever it appeared. To do that the forces of freedom had to learn the lessons of their enemies, to be eternally vigilant, to fight terror with terror and above all to organise globally. And they needed one other thing: a public relations coup.

The result was the Democratic International. Freedom fighters would gather from all across the globe at Jamba in a remote corner of Angola and present their case to the world. Darwyn and I were going to join them. It seemed that our Station Chief in South Africa had unexpectedly resigned and would not therefore be attending.

'This is our chance to go on the offensive,' proclaimed Rowbart. 'To use the lessons from Vietnam, Afghanistan, Nicaragua to put some spine into Jonas Savimbi and his people. Officially Savimbi and UNITA are hosting the whole event; as you know Jamba is now his headquarters. The Americans are backing this big time.'

'But not officially,' put in Darwyn. 'They won't be sending anyone from the State Department.'

'Frank Cato will be there from the Company and a big wheel from the National Security Council, Lieutenant Colonel Oliver North, is throwing his weight behind it. This is about fighting the Communists not talking to them. We don't need politicians. It's time to stop the press going on about apartheid and show them where the real threat comes from.'

'And what is our role?' I asked.

It was Asperton who replied. 'Just to be there. The Prime Minister is determined to ensure that Soviet aggression in

Angola is stopped and the Cuban troops are sent home. We must be seen to stand with the Company on this one. And of course we would wish to continue the Service's longstanding support for Mr Savimbi.'

'But not officially,' Darwyn repeated.

'None of this is official,' Rowbart responded evenly. 'The Democratic International is the brainchild of patriotic and wealthy Americans determined to root out Communism wherever it strikes. That also happens to be the policy of the British government and as far as I am aware has been so for a very long time. Your role at Jamba is to find ways to ensure that this policy succeeds. I suggest you start to pack.'

We did as we were told with Darwyn muttering to himself not too discreetly. I caught a reference to 'PPS' and 'overstepping his station' and hoped that Rowbart had not heard.

Darwyn was old school. Although he lacked the smooth public school charm of most of the Service's old-timers, he shared their intellectual curiosity and cultural tastes. It was typical of Darwyn that four days later when I found myself looking down on the African veldt from a creaking Douglas DC-3 Dakota he sat calmly reading a volume of early-nineteenth-century poetry, not even Shelley, Byron or Keats but Felicia Hemans. He only looked up when I wondered under my breath which idiot had decided to hold the event in somewhere like Jamba.

The Israeli and South African governments had both offered to act as hosts but had been deemed too much of a public relations risk. The South Africans had however provided an escort of two Mirage fighters, just in case there were any Cuban-piloted MIGs in the area. One of Julia's responsibilities in Moscow had been keeping an eye on Soviet air capability, I felt sure that if it came to a dogfight her money would not have been on the ageing Mirages.

The Dakota came in low over the savannah and a few scattered trees, setting down on to a runway that until recently had been little more than a bare strip. Now there was evidence of construction everywhere with sophisticated radar and anti-aircraft systems already in place. Despite the new defences and two men in jungle fatigues standing nonchalantly beside the plane with a Stinger surface-to-air missile the pilot was clearly nervous.

'Time for you to go,' he shouted, pointing at three battered US-made M-151 jeeps waiting for the plane. 'The less time we sit on the ground the better.' As we clambered out of the plane two stretchered figures were carried on board and the Dakota was already back on the runway by the time we had been bundled into the right jeep. We heard it take off as we were driven away.

So this was the real Africa. My first thought was that it was a lot colder than I had expected. I should not have been surprised, the pilot had mentioned that our destination was a thousand metres above sea level. Winter in Jamba seemed to be only a degree or two above the early summer I had left behind in London, but with a lot less rain.

I knew that the little town of Jamba had doubled in size since the arrival of UNITA but it soon became clear we were not heading for the town. The Jamboree was elsewhere. We had been stuck in Johannesburg for two days as the flights were full and nobody and nothing was going to Jamba by road. When we finally reached the camouflaged UNITA headquarters the event had already started. The contrast with the relative calm of and sophistication of Johannesburg could not have been greater.

Armed men were everywhere, most wearing a motley collection of vaguely military garb. Here and there smartly dressed white men hurried past, uniformed South African Special Forces and, looking curiously conspicuous in civilian clothes, their Israeli and American opposite numbers.

Despite the jungle fatigues we were a thousand kilometres south of the nearest jungle. Buildings straggled away in every direction. Barracks, offices, huts and tents jumbled together. There were none of the mud huts I had been half expecting, brick and corrugated metal seemed to be the preferred building materials. Despite the brown and green paint and the camouflage netting there was no way the enemy could be ignorant of just where Savimbi had located his headquarters.

Women and children milled around and the smell of cooking filled the air. A table loaded with pots of *funje*, the tasteless cassava flour porridge, which I was to discover accompanied every Angolan meal, stood next to a French-made Roland surface-to-air missile system. Beside that someone had strung up a banner proclaiming 'Freedom Starts Here' in English above a pile of discarded Coca-Cola packaging.

We were hurried to a newly built stadium.

In front of selected members of the world's press, all carefully vetted by the organisers, the leaders of four US-backed guerrilla groups were explaining why they were joining together in this new anti-Communist crusade. The four leaders could not have been more different. The representative of the Afghan jihadists, at that time fighting the Russian Army, came in national dress, the leader of the

Nicaraguan Contras looked, said one journalist, as if he was off to play golf while the third, from Laos, was so short special steps had to be provided for the group photos.

The proceedings were dominated by the gun-toting host Jonas Savimbi, a man later described by one American diplomat as the world's most charismatic homicidal maniac. Savimbi was well known to our Service. He had long paraded around Africa in a Hawker Siddeley 125 executive jet nominally belonging to the British company Lonhro and lent to him by Lonrho's chief executive Tiny Rowland. It was an arrangement facilitated, Darwyn assured me, by an earlier Subsaharan Africa Desk Officer.

As the translation facilities failed, most of the press had no idea what the Afghan and Laotian speeches were about and therefore homed in on Savimbi who gloried in the attention. Press attention was further guaranteed by the phalanx of young women in blue skirts and orange shirts that accompanied him, all clearly too poor to afford bras.

I glanced across at the solitary white woman present who appeared singularly unimpressed. Standing at the back of the hall she was in her late forties, five foot six, heavily built but fit, no make-up or jewellery, dark shirt, camouflage pants and heavy boots.

'Who's that?' I asked Darwyn.

'No idea,' he replied. 'Why don't you find out? We're here to work, remember. We have to be seen. That South African colonel who Mendale said was behind Operation Argon is here somewhere, I'm going to find him.'

The woman left the hall and I did the same. I don't usually approach people and announce myself as coming from MI6 but it seemed appropriate this time as she was wearing a badge proclaiming her to be Robbie Perez, Central Intelligence Agency, COBJ.

'What's COBJ?' I asked when we had shaken hands.

'Chief of Base, Jamba.'

I was surprised. I had assumed she was a Langley desk warrior who had flown in to mind the press. In those days the Company were better at employing women than we were but there weren't many in the field, and certainly not in Africa.

'You're stationed here?' I asked.

'I spend a lot of time here. There's a lot going on. How about you, you based in London?'

'I am now. For my sins I'm the Acting Deputy Saddo.'

'What the hell's that?'

'It means I'm way down the pecking order but not right at the bottom. I'm supposed to look after British interests in Subsaharan Africa.'

'You fly a Desk.'

'You could say that.'

'Not sure I could handle that.' She smiled and her face unexpectedly softened. 'This is where the action is. Every day we push out the frontiers of freedom and every night we discover we're right back where we started.'

I wasn't sure what to make of that but before I could respond a man leaving the hall spotted us and came striding over. About the same age as Robbie Perez but six inches taller and similarly well fed. He was wearing a camouflage jacket with no insignia. He too wore a name badge proclaiming Central Intelligence Agency, this time with no indication of his title.

'Frank Cato,' he announced, perfunctorily shaking my

hand. 'You're Dylan, I've seen your file. Glad you could make it. I'm sorry about the mix-up in Jo'burg but we needed the aircraft for the film crews.'

He gestured back towards the hall from which came a round of half-hearted applause. 'Put yourself about, these guys need to know you people are on board.'

'I intend to.'

'Good. Robbie show our friend around, make introductions.'

'Yes sir,' she replied but Cato was already off. She turned to me. 'I don't suppose you want to meet the grunts who are actually doing the fighting.'

'Then you suppose wrong.'

She gave me a wry smile and turned away. I followed her to her jeep and we shot off. I wasn't prepared for her next comment.

'I guess you've never been in the field before,' she said. 'Don't get me wrong but sitting behind a desk analysing and strategising is not what this business is about.' I was about to make a tart response when I remembered my own casual assumptions when unexpectedly finding a woman here. 'What you have to remember is that the natives here deserve a better life and that's worth fighting for. There is so much wealth in this country, diamonds, oil, coffee but what the Communist Party bosses in Luanda don't take the Russians will, nothing ever reaches the people who really need it. That's the only reason I'm here.' She paused for a moment, sliding the jeep into a bend and then gunning it out. 'To someone like you I'll just be a name on a report, a necessary evil. The gunslingers Cato calls us. For now we are relying on the Jonas Savimbis of this world to do our killing for us. But sometimes we have to be willing to pull the trigger ourselves. You're lucky you'll never need to do that.'

I wasn't going to put up with condescension like that from anyone. 'That's quite a speech. Do you use it often?'

Her face tightened. 'What's that supposed to mean?'

'It means don't patronise me. I've been there too. I just don't feel a need to flaunt it.'

She clearly didn't believe me. 'You've been where? The smell of the battlefield stays with you for ever and you don't have it. You've never had to shoot anyone.'

She was wrong but I knew what she meant. Company field agents all seemed to bear the scars of Vietnam. That war had been a rite of passage for a generation of Company men and, I was now discovering, at least one woman. I wondered what she had been doing there and how much it had killed the sensitivity I thought I had detected before Cato appeared.

There's a Memorial Wall at the CIA headquarters in Langley with a gold star for every agent killed in action. Three of those were for men I had been close to when they died but I wasn't going to tell her that. I didn't need to prove myself to anyone, least of all to a woman for whom killing someone seemed to be a badge of honour.

We continued in silence and five minutes later she left me in the company of a UNITA commander.

Lusiano Nambala had the sleek, well-fed appearance of a prosperous businessman. While his men lounged around in a motley collection of dirty uniforms, jeans and T-shirts, Nambala himself wore brand new olive green jungle fatigues with enormous blue epaulettes. The three stars on the epaulettes were repeated on the front of his bright red beret.

The money spent on his matching olive silk scarf would have kept the average Angolan fed for a year.

He shook my hand, his gold-ringed fingers crushing mine.

I addressed him in Portuguese but he responded in South African accented English.

'Welcome to Free Angola.'

This was followed by a speech I suspect he had spent the last couple of days repeating for visiting VIPs and journalists, the gist of which was that UNITA's victory would be assured if only they had sufficient funds.

'What can we do to help?' I asked, remembering Asperton's instructions that we find ways of assisting Britain's 'wider policy objectives'.

'I need wages for my men and weapons.'

'What sort of weapons?'

'Tanks. We need tanks. The Americans will give us Stingers to shoot down the Communist jets but the Cubans have tanks. England makes tanks. Tell Mrs Thatcher to send me fifty tanks and they will carry us all the way to Luanda.'

It seemed an improbable request but I made a show of writing it down.

'Perhaps better,' Nambala added, 'to send dollars. We can buy tanks with dollars.'

I saw Robbie Perez again the next morning. She came to find me. Frank Cato had shown her my file.

'Seems I misjudged you. You've been in some pretty hot spots. And your Monckton scores are pretty good too. But you misjudged me: I don't flaunt what I do.'

'Point taken. Let's start again.' We chatted for a few minutes and then she was off.

I was intrigued by her mention of my file. There was nothing special about Cato having a file on me, he would no doubt have a file on everyone here. I had come into contact with Company operations before – in Brazil, Italy, Poland – and the Company's voluminous record system in Langley would undoubtedly be able to kick out the details if asked. But Perez had also mentioned the scores from my more recent training at Fort Monckton, that could only have come from inside the Service and I was surprised it had been shared with the Americans.

Perez made one other casual comment that seemed odd at the time. It was to seem far more significant later, when the truth about Adam Joseff's murder began to emerge and people started to ask whose side Robbie Perez was on.

I asked her about someone Turk Rowbart had mentioned back in London and who the Americans here seemed to hold in awe. Lieutenant Colonel Oliver North was the Deputy Director for Political-Military Affairs at the National Security Council. This was well before North hit the headlines for his role in the Iran-Contra affair but he was already known as President Reagan's hard man.

'Have you met North?' I asked.

'I sure have. I was called back to Washington just for North to tell me how important Jonas Savimbi and UNITA are in the battle to preserve civilisation.' She gave a bemused smile. 'He's a true believer. He really does think that if we don't stop the Soviets here they will take over the world.'

'Today Africa tomorrow America.'

'That's right.'

'And you don't agree?'

'Oh we have to win and we will, but is this the way?

47

The Russian economy right now is a basket case. They're in an arms race they can't win and the more they spend trying to catch us up the bigger their economic crisis becomes. We simply have to be steadfast and wait. There's no need to bankroll warlords all over the place. We're just making future enemies. The truth is none of the leaders in this country give a damn about the peasant woman stepping on a landmine that some callous bastard has deliberately planted in her field. Both sides think that maiming a woman like that is a legitimate way of stopping the enemy growing food and making them use up their precious medical supplies to keep her alive. For the warlords it's all about making themselves rich. And it's the same for all these super-patriots.'

She pointed at a man chatting to a group of South African officers. 'You've seen GI Coley strutting around.'

'The oil man?'

'Yeh that's him. Likes to pretend he's a real GI Joe. But GI my ass, he's no more been a GI than I've been a ballet dancer. When we had men dying in Vietnam he got five draft deferments, four for college and one, would you believe, for having bad feet. Now he's funding this jamboree in the name of freedom. You can be sure that if Savimbi wins Coley will be first in line when the oil concessions are parcelled out. But,' she added, 'Oliver North is different, he doesn't see it like that. When he says we're here to save Africa from the Communists he really believes it. I sometimes think there are only two people in the whole of this goddamn charade who honestly think they're fighting for the salvation of the Angolan people: Ollie North in Washington and Fidel Castro in Havana.'

It was not a remark I ever expected to hear from anyone

in the CIA. On that note we went our separate ways. Perez had mentioned that her brother Larry worked for Citibank in London and I told her to look me up if she was passing through, not really expecting her to do so.

The Democratic International lasted two days and ended with me covered in insect bites and the organisers issuing a communiqué affirming solidarity with all the world's 'freedom movements'. The participants concluded by pledging to 'cooperate to liberate our nations from the Soviet imperialists'.

'What the hell does cooperate mean?' Darwyn sniffed. 'Does anyone really think the Mujaheddin are going to turn up here once they've managed to boot the Russians out of Afghanistan?'

Darwyn and Perez it struck me had the same odd combination of dedication and cynicism. Determined to fight the good fight even when the good became indistinguishable from the bad.

In many ways Darwyn had been in his element at Jamba. He loved Africa, he loved intrigue and he quickly fitted in with the assorted spooks, soldiers of fortune and guerrilla fighters huddling conspiratorially in dark corners. He might show his cynicism to me but by the time we left he was firm friends with Colonel DeSmid, who had planned the ill-fated Operation Argon, and GI Coley, the American oilman Perez had been talking about. Darwyn, it struck me, was the perfect spy. I soon found out that others disagreed.

# V

Colin Asperton had asked for flash reports from each of us. We hurriedly scribbled them on the flight back to Johannesburg and gave them to one of our local people waiting at Jan Smuts airport. In return we received a press digest.

In the United States the press and TV coverage of the Democratic International had been everything the organisers could have hoped for, with *Time* magazine predicting that Congress would now provide far more money for groups like UNITA and the Contra guerrillas. Ten years before, with Jimmy Carter in the White House, Congress had passed the 'Clark Amendment' prohibiting US funding of groups like UNITA, forcing the CIA to find more circuitous routes for its money. Now things were changing. Within a year the Clark Amendment would be repealed, Jonas Savimbi would be a guest at the White House and President Reagan would be announcing 25 million dollars of military aid to UNITA.

The British press was less enthusiastic. The *Observer* merely describing the Jamba Jamboree as a Who's Who of the world's extreme right.

An attached note from Rowbart commented that we didn't appear to have succeeded in getting our message across to the British press contingent.

I was about to remark to Darwyn that press 'contingent'

was rather an exaggeration when I saw his expression change. He had been reading a note from Colin Asperton.

'The Saddo's died,' he said hoarsely. 'Giles has gone.'

He was clearly shocked, he and Giles Smith had worked together for twenty years.

We hardly exchanged another word on the way back to London. By the time I had retrieved my luggage at Heathrow Darwyn had disappeared.

Julia and Eveline were happy to see me when I got home and I hardly gave a thought to the implications of Giles Smith's death.

'So your Deputy Saddo appointment will be made permanent,' Julia commented.

'I suppose so. John Darwyn and I get on well enough, he'll be good to work for.'

When I arrived at Century House the next day I immediately discovered that I would not have John Darwyn as my boss. The Saddo office had been transformed. The desk was the same but everything else had gone. Giles Smith's easy chairs and coffee table had been removed and six upright wooden chairs were set around a polished rectangular table. The painting of sunset over the Serengeti which used to hang behind the desk had been replaced by a photograph of the English Rugby Team dated 9th June 1984. Smith's African prints had been replaced with military photographs, which I realised all featured Turk Rowbart. The man himself sat at the desk.

'Come in, Dylan,' he said, more order than invitation.

'What's happening?' I asked.

'We are making some changes. As I keep saying, Africa is the front line now and we need to treat it that way. I'm taking over as Saddo and I hope you'll stay on as Deputy for the time being, although I must say your flash report from Jamba was a little disappointing. I hope you haven't been infected by Darwyn's reluctance to engage fully with what's happening down there. UNITA is the only thing standing between the Russians and South Africa and Savimbi must have our unqualified support. Remember in Africa you don't choose your friends, your enemies choose them for you.'

I said nothing for the moment, taking in the implications of the palace revolution that had clearly taken place.

'There's a lot to do right now. I have some special plans for you but we'll discuss them next week when you've finished your full report on Jamba, and when all the changes here have been announced.'

'What's happening to John Darwyn?'

'He's up with Asperton right now and then off to Lagos, he's to be Station Chief there. Nigeria's just the sort of place where his experience will prove invaluable. Tribal tensions and so on, military coups. The Station Chief there will transfer down to fill the vacancy in Pretoria.'

I wondered how Darwyn would take that. It didn't take long to find out. Twenty minutes later Darwyn came striding past my office, a look of thunder on his face and, briefcase in hand, stormed out of the building. He returned after lunch and went straight up to Asperton's office before leaving once again.

Asperton and Rowbart spent the rest of the afternoon in conference and this time it was Rowbart who descended red-faced. He slammed the Saddo office door behind him and I decided today was definitely a day for me to leave on time.

Asperton had decided on a compromise which, like

52

so many compromises, left everyone feeling dissatisfied. Rowbart was confirmed as Saddo and Darwyn would leave for Africa but as Station Chief in Pretoria not Lagos and with some sort of vague promise for the future. As Station Chief roles went, South Africa was regarded as a plum posting but it wasn't what Darwyn wanted and certainly Rowbart didn't want him there.

I would have preferred Darwyn as my boss but I didn't think it would make much difference. I was wrong. Rowbart had used the opportunity to bully Asperton into making a further change: there were to be two Deputy Saddos. I was to share the responsibilities.

'Africa's close to collapse,' Rowbart told me. 'The dominoes are falling down. If the Russians consolidate their grip on Angola the way is open to the Cape. That's why having the right man as Pretoria Station Chief was so important. Darwyn's good on the nitty-gritty but he still doesn't see the bigger picture. The result is that I need an extra pair of eyes right here in the office, a second Deputy.'

'That's quite unusual.'

'It is but it shows how important this Desk is. And don't worry there's plenty for you to do. In fact I have something special for you, some real cloak and dagger stuff.'

Rowbart introduced me to my new colleague and by the time I arrived home that evening I had a lot to tell Julia.

One of the mantras banged into everyone in the Service from their very first day is that our work is secret and secret means secret.

'If you feel the need to discuss your work with your wife,' I remember one bumptious training officer telling me, 'find another job. Or another wife.'

It was nonsense of course, there was even a short course at Fort Monckton for wives of agents about to be posted abroad under cover. It was the only Service rule I ever completely ignored. Julia and I discussed everything. I told myself that she had joined the Intelligence world before me, had been vetted on numerous occasions and had proved herself time after time. But the truth is that I would have talked to her even if she had never been part of our world. I trusted her totally.

'I'm going back to university,' I announced when I got home. 'Turk Rowbart wants to identify the next generation of African terrorists so he expects me to mount a "shallow cover" operation.'

'You're not serious?'

'Yes I am. He's convinced that students from Southern Africa must either support one of the guerrilla groups we don't like, in which case I'm to watch them, or be on our side, in which case I'm to recruit them.'

As I wasn't going under deep cover there would be no new identity to learn or back story to invent. I would simply be a civil servant who had decided he needed a change of direction after ten years of tedium negotiating trade deals in various parts of the world. I was therefore going to be enrolled for some sort of part-time postgraduate qualification that would allow me, in theory, to get to know African students in London without arousing suspicion.

Julia was not impressed. 'And what happened to the Deputy Saddo job?'

'Oh that's still my main job. Going undercover is just part-time, a day or two a week. But he's appointed another Deputy as well, a woman.'

Julia raised an eyebrow. 'That's a first.'

'No, the Russia desk has three Deputies.'

'That's not what I meant as you very well know. What's she like?'

'Not like you.'

'What does that mean?'

'She doesn't dress as well and she's taller.'

Julia replied, with the hint of a smile, 'That tells me nothing.'

I wasn't so sure. I suspected that the way my new colleague dressed said quite a lot about her. Julia had read and dismissed the fashion bible of the time, a best-seller entitled *Dress For Success*, but Felicity Macnamara clearly subscribed to what was known as power dressing: tailored suits, severe jackets with padded shoulders and knee-length skirts, all in dark blues, greens and blacks. These were invariably matched with roll-neck sweaters and a single strand of pearls. She emphasised her 5'9" height by wearing 2½" heels.

I soon discovered that Macnamara combined two characteristics not always seen together in the Service: ambition and ability. She had a phenomenal appetite for hard work and turned out to be exactly what Rowbart said he didn't want: someone who loved detail. A couple of years older than me, probably approaching forty, she had at one stage been posted to Nairobi but had spent most of her Service career in the Far East. At some point she had been attached to the British Council and had acquired a wealth of useful contacts in the world of academia. We agreed she would set up the flimsy cover-story I needed.

After establishing that my Modern Languages degree had included six months at the University of São Paulo in

Brazil she disappeared into her office with a stack of contact cards and the phone glued to her ear. When she re-emerged she was smiling broadly.

'It's all arranged,' she informed me. 'Right up your street. You're conducting research on the parallels and divergences in the development of the Portuguese language in Brazil and the former Portuguese colonies in Africa. Nominally you'll have two research supervisors: a specialist in Brazilian Portuguese at King's College and a Professor at SOAS, the School of Oriental and African Studies. We know them both. By being based at two institutions you'll be able to mix freely with other students but nobody will be surprised if they don't see you for a while.'

In case anyone queried how a minor civil servant was able to afford to take on a part-time research degree Macnamara suggested I should describe my wife as a management consultant. Management consultants were known to be grossly overpaid.

SOAS, the School of Oriental and African Studies, was regarded by the government as an important part of Britain's 'cultural hegemony' and for that reason alone the Foreign Office used it extensively for language training. In the early 1980s the School went through a tough period but the training facilities that the Foreign Office had used in Beirut for many years suddenly became unavailable and many Foreign Office Arabic specialists found themselves moving to SOAS. Consequently the School seemed to be awash with relatively pampered Foreign Office types. I didn't want to be mistaken for one of their elite club and decided to concentrate on King's College first.

Rowbart disagreed. 'Start at SOAS,' he told me. 'A

couple of students there are already on our radar.' He passed over a stack of files that had been sitting on his office table. Most of our own files by then were stored on floppy disks but paper was still the norm when it came to material sourced elsewhere. Macnamara helped carry the bulging folders into my office.

'I'll leave you to it,' she said and wisely disappeared.

The files were all arranged in the same way. The first few pages contained a 'Person Of Interest' summary from our friends across the river, MI5, sometimes with attachments from Special Branch or GCHQ. At the back of each file were the visa and immigration details. All but one of the subjects were what Rowbart would call non-white. In between, and forming by far the largest part of each file, came a miscellaneous collection of typed and handwritten documents, all photocopies, and most originating within one or other of the South African police and security agencies.

I spent nearly a week wading through these files, taking notes and cross-referring to the material already in our registry. Rowbart's files all had one thing in common, all the MI5 'Person Of Interest' summaries bore the security classification NDT – No Domestic Threat. With that classification, and with so much of their resources being focused on the IRA, it was not surprising that MI5's own input was skimpy.

I divided the folders into two piles. The first contained students from South Africa and what is now called Namibia. In those days the one-time German colony was known as South West Africa and was controlled by the South Africans. This pile contained the fewest files but they were by far the thickest. I marvelled at the amount of information the

South African security services had managed to accumulate but very little of it struck me as surprising. The only thing the students had in common was that they all seemed to be guilty of not liking apartheid; most British students probably felt the same way although with less reason.

Only three of the students in the first pile had any alleged links with Umkhonto we Sizwe, the armed wing of Nelson Mandela's African National Congress, or with its opposite number in South West Africa, SWAPO. One of the three had left London by the time his file reached us.

The second pile consisted of students from other countries, particularly Angola, Mozambique and Zimbabwe. These files were thinner but again the bulk of the reports had come from South African intelligence. There were also half a dozen memos or reports bearing the logo of the Central Intelligence Agency. Two were marked 'From the Office of Frank Cato', the CIA Director I had spoken to at the Democratic International. A report on a student named Marco Mutorwa bore the reference RP/COBJ which could only be Robbie Perez, Chief of Base, Jamba.

My part-time shallow cover role began in the late summer of 1985, in time for me to be established before the start of the academic year, and ended more than two years later when a bomb exploded just yards away from me.

# VI

Looking back now those two years were among the least satisfying in my career. Partly this was because I felt that in career terms I was treading water. Deputy Desk Officer was certainly a promotion but the way it had turned out it didn't feel like that. Sharing that role was, if I am honest, a disappointment and being given what seemed to me a half-baked part-time shallow cover mission wasn't really what Desk Officers were supposed to do. In Moscow I had been handling a mole we had inside the office of Andrei Gromyko, the Soviet Minister of Foreign Affairs. I had been up against professionals, usually much more experienced than me. Now I was supposed to be targeting a bunch of students who probably thought a Moscow mole was a vodka and ginger beer cocktail.

I had joined MI6 to serve my country. I wasn't sure my new mission qualified. It was clearly in Britain's interest to promote stability in Africa and to ensure that governments in the region were favourably disposed towards us. Russian meddling in Africa was bad news for everyone. However it was hard to see how getting to know twenty-three students in London was going to advance British interests.

Rowbart seemed to come to the same conclusion and was soon happy for me to spend more and more of my time in Century House. The situation in Southern Africa was deteriorating. Not only was the war in Angola dragging on but in South Africa itself widespread protests had led to a nationwide state of emergency being declared in July 1985 with hundreds of arrests.

Our Service was committed to Mrs Thatcher's policy of 'constructive engagement' with what some of the British press had taken to calling the 'apartheid regime'. Rowbart spent much of his time in South Africa but who he was constructively engaging with and to what end remained unclear. I assumed he still had relations there but as he never spoke about his family I couldn't be sure. I discovered that the photo of the June 1984 English Rugby Team which he had positioned in pride of place behind his desk had been taken at Ellis Park in Johannesburg. I wondered if it was the score that Rowbart was commemorating, South Africa had won 35–9, or the fact that this was the last team of any sort to break the Commonwealth's sporting boycott of South Africa agreed at Gleneagles seven years earlier.

Rowbart's enthusiasm for the land of his birth was not shared by John Darwyn but, to many people's surprise, Darwyn had thrown himself into his new role as Pretoria Station Chief. Just as he had at the Jamba Jamboree he soon knew everyone worth knowing. Even Rowbart was impressed by the factual quality of his reports on the sometimes bloody intrigues within Nelson Mandela's African National Congress. But the two men were never going to get on.

The South Africans were obsessed with what they called 'Die Rooi Gevaar', the Red Threat. An invasion of South Africa by Russia's African allies was imminent and had to be stopped. Rowbart was incensed that Darwyn wilfully refused to take Die Rooi Gevaar seriously. When Leonid

Brezhnev had been Russian leader the threat had been clear cut. Russia's willingness to pour vast amounts of weaponry into the African continent to arm anyone willing to proclaim their anti-imperialist credentials only made sense if the ultimate Soviet goal was to control the sea routes around the Cape. But with Gorbachev now struggling with a moribund economy at home and too timid to let the Red Army crush Solidarity in Poland, Russian intentions were less clear.

'Have you seen Darwyn's latest report?' Rowbart demanded marching into my office one day. 'The bloody man still doesn't understand. Listen to this.' He read from a report which I could see was covered in scribbled comments and exclamation marks.

'Those responsible for the failure of Operation Argon are now asserting that the enemy must have known that Du Toit and his men were coming. There is as yet no evidence to support this suggestion. The Angolans had not previously been thought to have any effective intelligence sources within South Africa, let alone within the South African Defence Force. The assertion that the Angolans received prior warning of the attack would seem to be an attempt to distract attention from what was plainly a failure of South African intelligence to correctly assess Angolan troop dispositions in Cabinda.'

'You don't agree with Darwyn's assessment?' I asked.

'No I don't. Do you really think the Recces, the cream of the country's Special Forces, could have been outsmarted in a firefight by a bunch of African conscripts? They were ambushed. DeSmid tells me the Angolans were all ready and waiting, there were Cubans with them. Du Toit's men were completely surrounded. That can't have just happened. The Angolans were forewarned.'

'But South African security is red hot, you've said that yourself. How would the Angolans get hold of the plans for something as secret as Argon?'

'Not the Angolans, the Russians,' said Rowbart scornfully. 'Doesn't anybody here understand what's happening down there? It's the Russians who are pulling the strings. That's what Darwyn simply doesn't get.'

He clearly put me in the same camp as Darwyn and disappeared to find a more sympathetic ear in Felicity Macnamara.

I'm not sure Rowbart was impressed with much of what I was doing. He had grandiosely designated my shallow cover assignment as Operation Studio, and to people outside our Desk boasted that one of his team had now gone 'undercover'. In fact the only cover I had was a spurious ID card from the DTI, the Department of Trade and Industry. Anyone trying to check up on me would soon guess that all was not as it was intended to appear. That's the essence of shallow covers: they're shallow.

Rowbart dismissed any concerns I might have. 'The kids you're monitoring aren't going to make any checks. And if you're blown we'll just start again. This is a sideshow remember, just getting to know the enemy.'

I wasn't reassured by being told that my new assignment was just a sideshow but Rowbart was right not to be worried. Even those students who were convinced that everyone was spying on them all the time didn't seem to suspect me in particular.

Right at the beginning of my assignment I had a meeting with a grey-haired Home Office civil servant who appeared to have some sort of liaison role between MI5, Special Branch and various Whitehall departments such as the Department of Education and Science. When I explained my mission he nodded non-committally.

'Frankly,' he told me, 'most students from developing countries are here either to get away from their families or to gain a qualification that will make them a lot of money when they get back home. Not many of them are political.'

He was very largely right.

Rowbart regularly produced new files for me to add to my target list but despite my best endeavours in just over two years I didn't find a single potential terrorist and the only future spy I recruited was the son of a Nigerian government minister who wasn't on my list and who agreed to work for us on his return home only because Turk Rowbart threatened to tell his father that he was gay.

The Angolans I met divided into two groups. Committed students being sponsored by one of the many Protestant church missions in the country, or children of the local elite for whom Lamborghini and Mercedes meant more than Lenin or Marx.

Marco Mutorwa, the man whose file contained a report from Robbie Perez, the Chief of Base, Jamba, was one of the latter, although somewhat more serious than most. I decided to make him my first target. Perez's report was brief and merely recorded the appearance of Marco Mutorwa at Jamba ten months before the Democratic International. With the bureaucratic attention to process that is the hallmark of the CIA Perez recorded the details of every official visitor to her base at Jamba on a printed form. Mutorwa had arrived, she reported, in the company of his uncle and stayed overnight before leaving the next day. Perez had been introduced to him and recorded that his English was passable but not fluent and that she was surprised to hear that he was hoping to study in London. 'His uncle's position and access to funds will no doubt help,' Perez had written.

The uncle's name was given as Lusiano Nambala, the UNITA commander I had met at Jamba. I remembered the smartly, and expensively, dressed guerrilla commander who had asked me to tell Mrs Thatcher to send him fifty tanks.

There was nothing to say why Marco Mutorwa was in Jamba but Perez had clearly not been impressed. In her neat handwriting she had added her own dismissive comment at the bottom of the form: 'war tourist'.

One of my contacts, a junior lecturer, buttonholed Mutorwa after a lecture and I casually joined them. Mutorwa seemed pleasant enough. He looked younger than I expected and at 5'6" lacked the physical presence of his uncle. He smiled easily, his long, narrow face lighting up. A wispy moustache struggled to be seen below his broad nose. When I told him I was researching Angolan Portuguese he expressed a polite interest. I suggested we might go for a drink some time and left it at that. Better to be pulled than to push was one of the Fort Monckton mantras. We met up a few times after that but I learned nothing useful.

'Come on man,' insisted Rowbart. 'He's a student in London, thousands of miles away from home, he must be doing something disreputable. Women, drugs, there has to be something we can use if you dig enough. You haven't even established what he's going to be doing when he goes home. He's Lusiano Nambala's nephew and Nambala's a big player, if we could get something on him that might prove very useful.'

'I thought Nambala was on our side, he's close to Savimbi.'

'He is now, but who knows. Savimbi's a slippery bugger and so's Nambala. If they fall out we might need to exert some pressure somewhere along the line. It's all about having options.'

I hadn't been able to find out what Mutorwa's plans for the future were because he didn't seem to have any. All I could say was that he showed no desire to return to Angola. Marco Mutorwa was happy to talk about the peculiarities of the Portuguese language used in the highlands where he grew up, and I was fascinated to find Brazilian terms that had originated in Angola, but when I touched on contemporary politics he clammed up claiming to be disinterested. His people, the Ovimbundu, formed the core of Savimbi's UNITA guerrillas but I couldn't get him to open up about his own contacts with the group.

'Have you been affected by the civil war?' I asked in one of our early meetings.

'Of course. Everyone has. It's crazy. All that killing for nothing.'

On another occasion I was more direct. 'I've been reading about a place called Jamba down in the south. Apparently someone is claiming that's where the Samba dance originated.'

'That's rubbish. There's nothing in Jamba, there never has been.'

'Have you been there?'

'No,' he lied, 'but I'm telling you the Samba may have come from Africa, I don't know, but nothing ever came from Jamba.'

I was no more successful in gaining much of an insight into his private life. In London he seemed to have no particular friendships, perhaps that's why he let me befriend him. But he did have a girlfriend in Lisbon and regularly disappeared there. He talked about quitting his course and moving back to Portugal but his family, who were funding him, would have objected.

Just before Christmas I happened to bump into him in Russell Square. He was with a girl of perhaps eighteen or nineteen.

'I can't stop, Tommy,' he explained. 'I've been showing my friend around the School. Now we're off to the British Museum.'

He didn't introduce his companion and they hurried away hand in hand. If that had been the girl from Lisbon the relationship clearly cooled after that. He still disappeared for long weekends but when I asked about her he just shrugged his shoulders.

'People change. The head must rule the heart.'

Some of the people on Rowbart's list were more approachable than others and over the two years of Operation Studio I was able to establish myself as an accepted part of the student scene, albeit never a real insider. After Rowbart's admonition I tried to stay close to Mutorwa but he seemed to have withdrawn into himself when his love interest vanished. There were a couple of hard-drinking King's College students on Rowbart's list but when I suggested to Mutorwa that he join us at the Princess Louise pub he was always busy.

On one occasion I happened to see Mutorwa using the phone box in Byng Place near the School. He turned away as he saw me approach and instinctively covered the mouthpiece with his hand as if scared I would overhear the conversation through the glass. It was such an odd thing to do that I had the call traced. He hadn't called anyone; he had been called. Why, I wondered, would he arrange to be called at a public phone box when I knew he had a phone in his flat? I eventually established that the call had originated from a public phone booth at the airport in Lisbon, which did nothing to make his actions seem less suspicious. But, I thought, if that was the most suspicious thing I was able to discover about him, Operation Studio really was a complete waste of my time.

I reported the call to Rowbart who immediately demanded that we place a tap on the line but Asperton ruled out bugging public phone boxes. He did however agree to a tap being placed on the phone in Mutorwa's Highgate flat. That produced nothing at all.

I didn't know it then but Marco Mutorwa was going to occupy a great deal of my Service's time in the future, and not only my Service's. The police and MI5 would be shining a much brighter light on his life than Rowbart or I had ever contemplated. But it would be Mutorwa's former girlfriend who proved to be the most important contact I made in my whole two years posing as a research student. And when I met her again nearly a year later the introduction came not from Marco Mutorwa but from Julia's boss, Adam Joseff.

# VII

Exodis, the consultancy set up by Adam Joseff and Richard Mendale, proved more successful than either Julia or I had expected. People were willing to pay for an independent view and Joseff could always be relied upon to provide that. My very first encounter with Joseff, when I had joined the Defence Intelligence Staff eleven years earlier, had been at a meeting called to discuss who might be responsible for a theft from a US Navy research facility. The Russians, Chinese, French and Israelis were all considered but Joseff had insisted the South Africans be added to the list without, as far as I could see, any evidence or any support from anyone else. Lord Grimspound called him the 'DIS Contrarian' and meant it as a compliment. I wasn't so sure. In the case of the US Navy theft he had been entirely wrong.

Joseff persuaded a recently retired Treasury mandarin, Sir Jonathon Craverse, to join Exodis ostensibly to provide economic analysis but more importantly to tap into his extensive network of contacts. Mrs Thatcher's 'Big Bang' had opened up the City of London to foreign competition signalling what was later described as the 'Death of Gentlemanly Capitalism'. As foreign banks poured in and started amassing profits they created a ready market for consultancies like Exodis which soon had a reliable base of well-paying clients. That justified hiring an office assistant to handle all the admin, to Julia's great relief.

'Adam nearly brought someone else into Exodis when Jonathon Craverse joined us,' Julia mentioned one day. 'Your man John Darwyn.'

'Darwyn? But he's in Pretoria.'

'Yes. But before he left he contacted Adam Joseff and asked if Exodis had a role for him. Apparently he was really keen but we aren't big enough yet to have a full-time Africa specialist. They agreed to keep in touch in case anything comes up.'

I wasn't surprised. Darwyn, I thought, had been pretty shoddily treated by the Service. But he had clearly decided that the role of Pretoria Station Chief would allow him to prove his detractors wrong. Even Rowbart boasted about the intelligence Darwyn had been able to gather from inside the African National Congress camps in Angola. Rumours had been circulating about mutinies at the Pango camp but Darwyn was the first to confirm their scale and detail the subsequent torture and execution of leading mutineers. The time might yet come when the Desk Officer role he so coveted would be his.

Julia had similarly thrown herself into her role at Exodis. She was working closely with Richard Mendale and Jonathon Craverse. Adam Joseff, having set the business up, seemed to be losing interest. Adam still contributed fully to the 'product' but the hunger for new business was no longer there. The passion for order and routine that had characterised his time at Defence Intelligence was deserting him and Julia complained that much of the time nobody knew where he was. On one occasion she had thought he was in Lisbon but discovered he was at a stamp fair in Goa. Another time she expected him in the office to finalise a report but learned that he was with a client in Cape Town.

Exodis was establishing a healthy reputation for its distinctive reports. Julia found that while what she called the 'old timers' were happy to gather intelligence and socialise they were more than pleased to leave crafting the regular client reports to her. A combination of gossip from the secret world sprinkled over the sort of news that could easily be gleaned from *The Economist*, *L'Express* or publicly available CIA digests seemed to be producing something people would pay surprisingly large sums for. Julia produced the product, Craverse flashed his knighthood at bemused American bankers and Mendale captivated new clients with tales of spies and spying. Joseff concentrated on keeping his old customers happy, principal among them was Cristóvão Taravares.

I first met Taravares sometime in 1986 when he was visiting London. I remember the South Africans had just mounted their most spectacular mission of the entire war, Operation Drosdy Teams of Recces infiltrated the port of Namibe and sank three Russian and Cuban freighters, as they were unloading military supplies. The port was out of action for months.

Adam Joseff had invited Taravares and Julia to dine at his club, the Reform, and had suggested Julia bring me along.

Taravares arrived late. He made an impressive entrance. The Reform was not the stuffiest of the London clubs, it had just been the first to permit women members, but its male members invariably dressed in that expensive but slightly shoddy way that a particular sort of Englishman considers 'appropriate.' Taravares on the other hand was quintessentially continental: a beautifully tailored and unmistakably Italian Zegna wool suit in dark blue, preppy shirt, silk tie, tanned skin and not a hair out of place. In his mid-forties and just under six foot tall he was a man accustomed to being looked at. What in others might have been arrogance, in him simply signalled absolute confidence.

He greeted Julia as if he had known her all his life although she had only met him the previous day.

'You are a lucky man,' he told me after kissing Julia's hand.

I had been introduced merely as Julia's husband. Joseff, I was confident, had been in Intelligence long enough not to divulge any unnecessary detail about me.

The evening was relaxed although Joseff was looking tired. Taravares was happy to be the centre of attention. His business, Mercantaravares, was the most successful trading company in Italy he proclaimed, although he himself was not of course Italian. Without prompting he then proceeded to regale us with his life story.

'I was born in Uíge in the northwest of Angola, in the highlands where the coffee beans were grown. In those days Angolan coffee was renowned the world over. The wealth of the old coffee traders, like my ancestors, made the capital, Luanda, one of the most beautiful cities on the continent. It was known as the Paris of Africa.' He spoke as if the city's former glories were produced by his own personal efforts. 'We Portuguese had been there for hundreds of years, since 1576. Luanda isn't some upstart twentieth-century city like Nairobi or Johannesburg. My family have traded coffee for generations. The Bairro do Café, the coffee neighbourhood, was famous. Did you know that when I was born half of the country's foreign exchange came from coffee? Of course that all changed in 1961.'

'What happened then?' Julia asked.

Taravares paused. By now I knew enough about Angola's recent history to answer but I waited for Taravares to respond.

'The cork exploded from the bottle. You probably thought that slavery was abolished long ago. Perhaps it was, but in the Portuguese colonies it was simply replaced by forced labour. By conscription. Natives taken from their villages and put to work perhaps hundreds of miles away. In the second half of the twentieth century that could not continue. What your Prime Minister Macmillan called 'the winds of change' were sweeping through Africa. In the spring of 1961 the revolution began, first in Luanda and then suddenly in the coffee fields. It was a bloodbath. In a few days hundreds of whites were massacred. They say eighteen hundred whites were killed before it was all over, and of course far more Africans. The war that still continues today, twenty-five years later, started then. I was at university in Lisbon. My father was in Lisbon also. We had left my mother and my brothers behind. They were all killed.'

'It was an awful period,' said Joseff, who had obviously heard the story before. 'Like the Mau Mau in Kenya.'

I glanced across at him in surprise. The Mau Mau uprising was on a far, far smaller scale and his comment seemed an unfeeling response to a man who had just revealed that almost his entire family had been butchered.

Taravares himself seemed unconcerned. After a brief hesitation he continued his story.

'My father and I decided to rebuild our lives in Portugal.

We set up Mercantaravares importing coffee beans from Angola. But the market was disappearing. And when Angola's independence came ten years ago it vanished completely.'

The businessman in him took over, he might have been reading from a company prospectus. 'In 1974 Angola exported 5.2 million sacks of coffee, last year, just eleven years later, exports were less than 300000 sacks. After independence ninety per cent of the European population fled the country. The coffee industry collapsed. The agronomists and managers emigrated to Brazil. For years the new regime tried to live off the coffee left behind by the Portuguese. Since independence they've sold 4 million sacks but the last of the colonial stocks was sold in 1983 and now the coffee trade has virtually disappeared. So Mercantaravares had to develop contacts elsewhere, Brazil, Colombia, Ivory Coast. I set up an office in Italy, in Trieste.'

'The coffee trading capital of Europe,' I put in. 'Julia and I have holidayed there.'

'Yes your wife told me. A beautiful city. And Mercantaravares has prospered. We started to trade in tea also and then other commodities. We trade all over the world.'

'That's why you need Exodis,' said Julia.

Taravares looked towards Joseff. 'That's right. When my father met Adam he thought here is a man I can do business with and I thought the same.'

He raised his glass. 'We should drink a toast to Dona Ana's stamp.'

I must have looked perplexed.

'You know the story of my father's meeting with Adam?' Taravares asked.

'Yes I do. Adam mentioned buying a Mozambican stamp from him. But who is Dona Ana?'

'Dona Ana Joaquina Noreto Taravares was my grandmother. The matriarch of the family. The women in my family have always been strong.' He smiled at Julia. 'My own grandmother's grandmother, also Dona Ana Joaquina, was brought to Luanda from the highlands as a child slave. She had a brain as well as beauty and married her owner, not as unusual as you may think, there were not many white women in Luanda in those days. The first Ana Joaquina created a trading empire, not in coffee of course, in slaves. Slaves brought long distances from the interior and then shipped to São Tomé, to Brazil, even to Cuba and on to the United States.'

There was unmistakable pride in his voice. For him she was a trader first and foremost, that she traded in human misery was forgotten.

'And the stamp?' I asked.

'Ah yes. Dona Ana's stamp. My grandmother was what do you say, an *açambarcador*.'

'A hoarder.'

'A hoarder, yes. She kept everything. My aunt Joana was the same, and one thing she kept was the stamp my father sold to Adam.'

'For a fair price,' interjected Joseff.

'Of course for a fair price.'

Joseff changed the subject by going off on a familiar tangent: his stamp collection. This time it was about the stamps of the old Spanish colony of Río de Oro in North Africa, a subject on which he was clearly passionate. He had just found a stamp that completed a set he had spent years searching for. I tried at one point to bring the conversation around to the state of Angola today but Taravares would only comment that corruption was everywhere. The meal was nearly over when Joseff turned to me.

'There is a favour Cristóvão would like to ask of you.'

'Of me?'

'Yes, something connected with your studies, your research. Cristóvão needs a spy.'

I felt myself tense. Had Joseff told a casual business associate that I worked for MI6? That would be unforgivable. If Taravares really wanted to contact British Intelligence, and I couldn't see why he would, there were 'proper channels' as Joseff would know perfectly well.

Taravares spoke before I had a chance to respond. 'It is a family matter, a sensitive family matter.'

'I mentioned to Cristóvão that you are a research student,' put in Joseff, 'at the School of Oriental and African Studies. I suggested you might help a young cousin of his who has come to study in London.'

'Help in what way?'

'Help to keep her safe,' said Taravares. 'There is a young man involved. A very unsuitable young man. He is studying at the School Adam mentioned. Mariana has promised not to see this man again but her father is worried.'

'We just want you to keep an eye on her,' said Joseff. 'Nothing more. She arrives tomorrow morning, Cristóvão and I will meet her at the airport. Once she's settled in I will introduce her to you and Julia. Just look out for her Thomas, please. Let us know if she is seeing this man again.'

Put like that it didn't seem so worrying, although I didn't like the idea of spying on young lovers.

'Can't her father simply stop her coming here? There must be lots of other universities. How old is she?'

'She's twenty years old.' It was Joseff who replied. 'You know what it's like with young girls these days. Their fathers have no authority, even in Africa.'

'She's African?'

This time Taravares answered. 'Of course. She is the granddaughter of my father's sister, Joana. Aunt Joana married a teacher in Luanda, a Mbundu. Mariana has been studying accounting in Lisbon. She will return to Angola when her studies are finished. I thought my cousin had forbidden her from coming to London but he has changed his mind, Mariana can be very persuasive. She wants to learn English.'

'We'll look after her,' said Julia. 'Of course we will. But we won't be interfering in her love life.'

I expected Taravares to respond but he seemed happy to leave things to Joseff.

'Cristóvão doesn't want you to interfere, just let him know if this young man is hanging around. His name is Marco Mutorwa.'

That of course was a name I knew well: Robbie Perez's war tourist and nephew of the UNITA leader I had met in Jamba, Lusiano Nambala. Quite a coincidence.

Looking back on that evening I wondered if it was indeed a coincidence. Did Joseff know I was already keeping an eye on Mutorwa? If he did then someone inside the Service must have told him because I hadn't mentioned the name to Julia.

When we had said our farewells to Taravares Joseff took my arm. 'There's one favour you could do for me Thomas. I gather you're on the Africa Desk now. A bit irregular but I do need to make sure Exodis is protected from any possible embarrassment. That's in all our interests. The girl we talked about earlier, Mariana, I want to make sure there's nothing untoward about her. I just want to know if she's on our radar as it were. I don't expect details of course, nothing like that. But is there any reason we should steer clear of her?'

He wrote her full name on the back of one of his visiting cards. 'As I say if you could just check she's not what we used to call a "person of interest" I would be really appreciative. I checked on Cristóvão of course when we started to do business together and he's completely above board but you never know with these youngsters. Nothing official of course.'

'I'll see what I can do,' I replied, not quite sure what I would do if I did find anything.

'What's that all about?' I mused in the taxi home.

'Just Adam being cautious,' Julia replied. 'He's been getting that way lately. Not paranoid but certainly suspicious. I told you he's started fixing his own travel.'

I glanced at the card Joseff had given me. On it he had written Mariana Pinheiro. I was sure I didn't know her but there was something familiar about the name. When I asked Registry to check our files the next day they found no mention of her. As much as I liked Joseff I wasn't inclined to make any more active enquiries and I told Julia to let him know that we had no interest in Miss Pinheiro.

A week later Julia told me that Mariana Pinheiro would be coming to lunch at the weekend. It would be interesting to see, I thought, whether she mentioned Marco Mutorwa.

On the Friday afternoon before I was to meet Mariana Pinheiro, Turk Rowbart came into my office and dropped a file on to my desk.

'Pretoria has just sent this through. Someone coming to study in London. Quite a juicy prospect. If we can get anything on this one we could be on to a winner.'

I picked up the file. The photocopied page of an Angolan passport fell out. The photograph could have been anybody but the description was plain enough.

Mariana Efigenia Vasconcelos da Silva Pinheiro.

Date of birth: 28th November 1966.

Place of birth: Moscow.

# VIII

Cristóvão Taravares hadn't mentioned that. In the recitation of his family history from nineteenth-century Angola to Portugal and Italy today he had said nothing about a Russian connection. And neither had Adam Joseff.

Suddenly I realised why the name of Mariana Pinheiro had struck a chord in my memory. Mariana might not have been in our files but another Pinheiro certainly was and I should have recognised the name. Salvador Pinheiro was one of the most important figures in the Angolan regime. Salvador Erasmo da Silva Pinheiro was the governing party's head of security, effectively the head of the Angolan secret police.

Before going home I combed through the Registry's voluminous files catalogued under the heading DISA. The Direção de Informação e Segurança de Angola had officially been abolished six years ago in one of the numerous reorganisations of the Angolan regime's security apparatus but DISA was the term everyone still used. The name Salvador Pinheiro came up time after time. Rowbart was right, if we could turn Pinheiro's daughter it would be a massive coup.

'You're late, is everything OK?' asked Julia when I arrived home.

'Something unexpected came up. Something we need to talk about: Mariana Pinheiro.'

'Well let's wait. I've just put Eveline down. Go and read her a story and then we can prepare supper.'

It was an hour later with a bottle of wine on the table in front of us when Julia raised the subject I had wanted to discuss.

'Mariana Pinheiro is coming for lunch on Sunday. Is there something I need to know about her before then?'

'She was born in Moscow.'

'Is that important?'

'Not in itself. The point is that her parents were living there, they were in exile. Her father is, or was, a hard-line Communist. Rowbart wants me to turn her, get her on to our payroll.'

'You'd better explain. Who is her father? Was he with the guerrillas who kicked out the Portuguese?'

'The guerrillas didn't kick out the Portuguese.'

I had no hesitation in talking to Julia about my secret work but we had a tacit agreement that I wouldn't usually do so. She obviously knew about my trip to Jamba and about my cover at SOAS and King's College but we'd never talked about the intricacies of Angolan politics. Now I needed to explain some of the background before Mariana Pinheiro's visit.

'When the dictatorship in Portugal collapsed the new democratic government in Lisbon just walked away from their colonies. Almost literally overnight. The Communists took over. They had a guerrilla wing but the real power lay with the party leadership who were nearly all in exile. The exiles came home, many of them now with European wives, and just took over. Don't be confused by these people calling themselves Communists. The returning exiles were a worldly-wise elite who simply grabbed what the Portuguese had left and divided it up among themselves.'

'And Mariana's father was one of those returning with a European wife?'

'Almost, he had married before he left Angola. His wife had accompanied him into exile and died there.'

'That was Mariana's mother?'

'That's right, Adelina Taravares Vasconcelos. The cousin of your client Cristóvão Taravares.'

'What does Mariana's father do now?' Julia asked.

'He imprisons, tortures and kills people.'

When Julia looked shocked I explained. 'After the Communists took power the economy collapsed. Slum dwellers in the capital saw their new leaders living in luxury and joined forces with disaffected guerrillas still fighting UNITA in the bush. The Russians had to decide whose side they were on: the corrupt elite they had installed or the downtrodden masses and heroic freedom fighters they claimed to be fighting for. They chose the men they knew, men like Pinheiro. After Cuban troops put the uprising down he became the regime's hatchet man. There was a bloodbath, Salvador Pinheiro made sure anyone suspected of being part of the plot was butchered.'

'Not a nice man.'

'But a man whom Cristóvão Taravares and Adam Joseff want us to do a favour for.'

'But we can't. We can't spy on this poor girl for a man like that.'

Julia was horrified. I tended to agree but we were both also conscious that Salvador Pinheiro was a key player in the Russians' plans for Southern Africa. Any way I could get at him had to be pursued.

Julia changed tack. 'Adam must have known what sort of man Mariana's father is.'

I had been thinking the same thing and gone further. Adam Joseff had spent most of his life in the Intelligence world. Not only would he have known exactly who Salvador Pinheiro was, he would have realised just what a priority the man was bound to be for my Service. Why hadn't he alerted us as soon as he found out that Pinheiro's daughter was planning to study in London?

'Are you going to tell Adam that your Service now knows who Mariana is and you've been asked to watch her?'

'No. Adam's not inside any more.'

'Will you tell Rowbart about Adam's interest in her?'

That was more difficult. 'Not at this stage. Adam's a friend. No need to have Rowbart stirring things up around Exodis. Let's just see what happens.'

Julia nodded. 'It will be interesting to see what sort of person Mariana Efigenia Vasconcelos da Silva Pinheiro turns out to be.'

The first indication of that came on Sunday when a brand new Mercedes 500SL convertible drew up outside our terraced house and out stepped Mariana Pinheiro. She was clearly not a typical student.

I had seen her before, nearly a year ago with Marco Mutorwa in Russell Square. She looked different now, although I was hard pressed to say in what way.

'We met,' I reminded her. 'When you were here last year with Marco Mutorwa.'

She looked confused and it was clear that I had made no impression on her.

'Oh yes. I came over to visit the British Museum.'

The UNITA leader Jonas Savimbi had taken to describing the regime in Luanda as 'mixed race mongrels' but there was little sign of the white Taravares ancestry in Mariana Pinheiro. She was as African as Savimbi himself, a comparison she would surely find abhorrent. Her long thin face was framed by straightened black hair and brashly coloured hoop earrings. She wore a giant turtleneck sweater, Calvin Klein jeans and Nike trainers. Our visitor was smaller than Julia and she looked younger than her twenty years but, I soon discovered, acted older. I wondered how old she had been when her mother died. She had certainly grown into an independent, self-confident woman.

Her English, while not perfect, was excellent. It was far from obvious that she needed more tuition.

Mariana spent two hours with us and in that whole time said very little of interest. Our house was 'charming'. The roast beef was 'very good'. The weather was 'very bad'. London was 'interesting'. She answered our questions with a smile but asked none of her own. When I commented on her car she declared that the convertible was more 'suitable' than the car preferred by her father, but 'too heavy'. Even four-year-old Eveline failed to break through her shell. Only when discussing shopping did she come alive. Bond Street she enthused was 'enchanting'. I couldn't imagine her making a special trip to London to visit the British Museum.

Julia asked about life at home in Angola.

'The war is everywhere,' she replied.

'When will you return?'

'Who knows? Until the South Africans leave there cannot be any peace. It is not safe to travel outside the capital.'

'What does your father do in Luanda?' I asked.

'Mr Joseff didn't tell you? My father works for the government. He is a functionary. An important one. But it is not safe there even for him.'

There was an unmistakable note of pride in her voice.

'You must miss him,' Julia said.

'Perhaps. He is a very busy man. We are not close.'

I waited for her to continue but she said nothing more on the subject.

I tried another tack. 'I'm sure Cristóvão told you that I used to study in Brazil and now I'm doing research on the Portuguese language. I've met a couple of Angolan students recently at King's College. I could introduce them to you if you wish. And of course you already know Marco Mutorwa who's been helping with my research.'

'Marco? I didn't know he was still in London. The Embassy arranged a meeting last night for Angolan students over here. He wasn't there but then he's not one of us.'

'One of us?'

She looked away. 'There is a civil war in my country, people take sides.'

It was clear that she wanted to change the subject.

When the lunch was over Julia insisted that if there was anything that Mariana needed she should get in touch. Perhaps we could go shopping one day.

'Yes,' said Mariana. 'That would be nice.'

'That could be an expensive shopping trip,' I said to Julia when our guest had gone.

'Don't worry, she won't call. For her this has been a duty visit. I wonder why she's in London. It's certainly not just to improve her English. She didn't once mention the course she's supposed to be on.'

'Marco?'

Julia smiled. 'You're a romantic Thomas, but no I don't think so. There was no warmth in her eyes when you mentioned his name.'

I wasn't convinced, when I had seen them in Russell Square they certainly seemed to be more than friends. If they had broken up I wondered which of them had decided to end the relationship. My money was on Mariana.

'Adam seemed sure she had followed Mutorwa to London. It's bizarre that she should say she hadn't even known he was still here. That doesn't sound right.'

Whatever the reason for Mariana Pinheiro's presence in London I had to tell Rowbart I had made contact. When I arrived at Century House the next morning Rowbart was already on the case.

'We must find out where Pinheiro is staying and get our friends over the river to move their arses over there,' he announced.

'She's got a flat in South Kensington. I have the address.'

Rowbart looked startled. 'How the hell did you find that?'

'She gave it to me.'

I explained that Mariana had a Portuguese cousin who by pure coincidence was a client of Julia's firm. The cousin had asked Julia to look out for Mariana while she was in London.

'But I got the impression she doesn't want anyone looking out for her. She's a confident young lady. She says she's not close to her father but he's certainly given her access to his credit card, we're not going to be able to bribe her.'

'We'll see,' responded Rowbart. 'The first step is to make sure we know what she's doing.'

He disappeared from the office to engage in an interdepartmental battle that would continue on and off for weeks. MI5 had better things to do than keep Mariana Pinheiro under surveillance after an initial 'inspection' of her flat produced nothing of interest. The most they were willing to do was place a tap on her phone and send across the recordings of any conversations for us to listen to. It occurred to us that if she was doing anything sensitive for her father she might route any messages through the Angolan Embassy in Dorset Street. GCHQ as a matter of routine were intercepting and recording encrypted messages from the Angolan Embassy and agreed, on a random basis, to go one step further and actually decrypt them.

Even that degree of cooperation disappeared after six months when we had found nothing. It seemed to be clear to most people that Mariana Pinheiro had no interest in anything political, was doing nothing that might open her to blackmail and, as I had suggested, seemed to have unlimited funds.

'Where's the money coming from?' one of the MI5 watchers asked. 'Russia?'

'No, Texas.'

'Texas?'

'The Russians are happy to arm the regime but they expect someone else to pay. Texas oil money is pouring in through the front door and most of it goes right out again through the back door. No doubt Mariana's father has his own numbered account in Zurich.'

It seemed that, like his daughter, Salvador Pinheiro enjoyed spending that money. A few months later, and with only a few weeks' notice, we learned that he was coming to

London for hastily arranged discussions at the Foreign Office and for his daughter's twenty-first birthday. And primarily, according to South African Intelligence, for some Christmas shopping.

Peace negotiations were yet again underway in Angola, this time under the auspices of an American diplomat Chester Crocker. The reality of Angola's civil war had always been that it was not a civil war. Although nominally between the government and UNITA rebels, most of the strings had been pulled by Russians, Cubans, South Africans and Americans. Now some of those strings were looking frayed. Gorbachev was desperately trying to revive the sclerotic Russian economy and South Africa was facing the double onslaught of riots at home and increasingly effective sanctions from outside. Cuba could no longer count on Russia to prop up its economy in the face of US sanctions and, although Castro was content to keep fighting, somebody had to pay. Only the United States remained resolute but resolute to do what? Latin America was the priority not Africa and when it came to Angola US strategists came to fixate on the Cubans.

The outlines of a deal were starting to appear. Providing the Cuban troops were sent home the United States would switch support from the UNITA rebels to the existing supposedly-Communist government. And providing the government stopped supporting 'freedom fighters' in South West Africa the South Africans would do the same. The government, with both American and Russian support, could then open up its economy and everyone would be happy, except for Jonas Savimbi and UNITA who would have to accept some sort of vague reconciliation process.

It seemed an optimistic prospect but the Foreign Office

were throwing their weight, such as it was, behind Crocker's plans. Discussions with Salvador Pinheiro were part of an ambitious bid to hold the final signing ceremony in London.

Rowbart was not impressed.

'They're mad,' he insisted to anyone who would listen. 'Gorbachev won't last and as soon as he's gone the Russians will be back in there. They'll want the oil. If we sacrifice Savimbi and UNITA there's nothing to protect South Africa. We'll have a bloodbath on our hands. What's Pinheiro really up to in London? Who's he seeing?'

'No doubt our friends across the river will be keeping their eyes open,' Felicity Macnamara assured him.

'Bollocks. All they think about these days is the IRA. I'm going to make sure we know exactly what he's doing.' He turned to me. 'You keep close to his daughter. If either of them do anything we can use I want to know about it.'

Keeping close to Mariana Pinheiro was not easy. Julia had tried but after the first lunch at our home the most Mariana Pinheiro could find time for was an occasional coffee. Her English lessons, she reported, took up all her time, although I knew from our on-and-mainly-off surveillance that she was a far from conscientious student.

We put the watchers back on to Mariana Pinheiro full time. The only thing they saw that was in any way suspicious occurred a week before her father arrived. She took a taxi from her flat in Kensington to the Habitat in Tottenham Court Road. After spending just five minutes in the store she walked down Torrington Place to the phone box in Byng Place that I had seen Marco Mutorwa using some months before. A few minutes later she received a short call and then made a longer one.

Our friends traced the calls. The first came from another phone box only a mile away. Her own call was to a number in Italy, the office of Mercantaravares in Trieste. She then caught a taxi back to Kensington.

'What do you make of that?' I asked Julia when I got home. 'Rowbart says it stinks. He's demanded that Mercantaravares be investigated urgently. He thinks they must be some sort of Russian front and Mariana is a Russian courier being given instructions to pass on to her father when he arrives.'

'I can't see Cristóvão Taravares as a Russian spy.'

'No, Rowbart's barking up entirely the wrong tree. Salvador Pinheiro must be surrounded by Russians in Luanda. If they wanted to give him a message they would just knock on his office door, they wouldn't use a cousin in Italy.'

'But Mariana's behaviour is more than odd,' said Julia. 'If she wanted to receive a phone call why not use the phone in her flat, why such an elaborate pantomime?'

'And why call Cristóvão from the same phone? Again why not make the call from the comfort of her own home? Was it really so urgent she couldn't wait?'

'She obviously thinks somebody might be listening in to calls from her apartment.'

'Which raises the question what is so secret that she doesn't want anyone hearing? And who does she think is listening? Her father or her father's enemies?'

Mariana Pinheiro was an enigma but not, I thought, an important enigma. We were interested in her father not her. Mariana's potential value was as a way of finding out more about her father. But even then, as she was in London and he was in Luanda, there didn't seem to be much she would be able to tell us. In any event she clearly had no intention of telling anyone anything and we had discovered nothing that might persuade her to change her mind.

The one factor that niggled away at the back of my own mind was the part being played by Adam Joseff. It even occurred to me that the dinner with Cristóvão Taravares at the Reform might have been arranged solely so that he could ask me to keep an eye on Mariana Pinheiro. Her father, Adam had claimed, was worried about his daughter's supposed relationship with Marco Mutorwa but as far as I could tell that relationship was over by the time she came to London. Did Adam have another reason for wanting me to look out for her? Did he perhaps have reason to think somebody might tap her phone?

I remembered what Adam had actually asked me at the very end of the meal. Just as we were leaving he had casually asked whether Mariana was a 'person of interest' as far as my Service was concerned. Was that the reason for inviting me to dinner? He wanted to know if we were likely to put her under surveillance. Did he worry that we might tap her phone? Perhaps that was also the suspicion that Mariana Pinheiro harboured. Was she using a public call box rather than the phone in her own flat not because she was afraid her father, or one of her father's enemies, might be listening in but because she thought British Intelligence might be? And if she did believe that, was she just being paranoid or was she, as Rowbart insisted, up to something she wanted to make sure we wouldn't discover?

Julia had been following another line of thought. 'There's another question,' she suggested. 'Why Byng Place? Why somewhere so far from her flat?'

'Because she didn't want to be observed?'

'Perhaps. Or perhaps because whoever called her had suggested Byng Place because they knew the number of the phone there. And they knew that because they had used it themselves for the same sort of reason.'

'Marco Mutorwa.'

Julia nodded. She was right, it was too much of a coincidence to think that of all the phone boxes in London both Mariana and Marco Mutorwa would both happen upon the same one, especially as Mariana had to take a taxi to get there.

'If we're right,' said Julia, 'it was probably Mutorwa who phoned Mariana. He passed on a short message and then she phoned her cousin in Italy. Perhaps Rowbart does have a point. Something's going on. At the very least relations between Mariana, supposedly on one side of a civil war, and Marco, supposedly on the other, are not as cold as they both pretend.'

Julia paused for a minute before continuing. 'You know Thomas this creates a potential problem for me. Mercantaravares is a big client for Exodis and Adam Joseff is very close to the Taravares family. What does Rowbart mean when he says he wants them investigated? Should I warn Adam?'

'You can't do that. I shouldn't have told you about any of this.' Another thought occurred to me. 'Has Adam asked how we are getting on with Mariana? We were supposed to be guarding her from a young man her father disapproved of.'

'No he hasn't. As we agreed I let him know your Service didn't regard her as a person of interest after that dinner at the Reform, but since then Adam has hardly mentioned her.'

I nodded. I was starting to regret telling Adam that we weren't interested in Mariana Pinheiro. If I had known at the time who her father was I wouldn't have said anything. She was certainly a person of interest now.

I would have left it at that but the very next morning Julia called me.

'Can you manage a quick drink at lunchtime? Adam wants to talk to you. He'll come over to you.'

'What's it about?'

'He wouldn't say, just a quick word.'

# IX

We met at a pub behind Waterloo station. When I arrived Joseff was sitting at a table with two whiskies in front of him. He pushed the smaller one towards me.

'I thought you wouldn't want a double at lunchtime.'

He was right but I wondered when he himself had started drinking at lunchtime. He had been fairly abstemious in the old days.

'You wanted to see me.'

'Yes just to catch up. Haven't seen you for a while. See Julia, of course. She's a wonder. Exodis depends on her. Doing well you know, the business, Julia must've told you.'

'She has, but that isn't why you wanted to see me.'

'No, no, of course. It's Cristóvão Taravares' cousin Mariana, you know I mentioned her before.'

'That's right. You see much of her?'

'Me no. Not at all. The young, they don't want an old codger like me around.'

He smiled to himself. I didn't smile with him, Adam Joseff had never been an old codger and he wasn't now.

'Come on Adam, what's this all about?'

'Cristóvão is still worried about her. Her father is coming over here.'

I interrupted, 'Cristóvão Taravares told you Mariana's father is coming to London?'

'No, he didn't know. I told him.'

'But the visit hasn't been announced.'

'No of course not, but come on Thomas, word gets around. I keep my ear to the ground.'

'Mariana told you.'

'No, I don't see Mariana. They're not a close family but when I told Cristóvão that his cousin was coming over here he just said he was worried. He is very protective towards Mariana. Salvador Pinheiro is a dangerous man and he has his enemies. He probably won't even see his daughter while he's here. The security surrounding his visit will be very tight, it's a really sensitive time, politically. But she could get caught up in it all. This new man of yours, Turk Rowbart. He's a wildcard. Is he getting Mariana involved in some way?'

'What do you mean involved?'

Joseff paused. I couldn't remember ever seeing him so hesitant. 'Thomas I'll come to the point. Mariana has spoken to Cristóvão. She thinks someone is watching her, tapping her phone even. Her father's people perhaps or us. She's frightened. I said I would make enquiries. Nothing official of course. Is she under observation?'

'I don't know Adam. But even if I did I couldn't tell you. You must realise that. If MI5 are watching her, which I doubt, I couldn't let you warn her.'

'Oh I wouldn't do that. No, if this is official I'll just go back to Cristóvão and tell him I couldn't find anything. But if she's not I could reassure him. We could do something. Persuade her nobody's watching her. Perhaps find her a psychiatrist.'

I looked at him, uncertain what to say. I didn't believe a word he was saying, which saddened and surprised me. What was Adam Joseff really up to?

He emptied his glass. 'Another?'

'No thanks, one is enough.'

He stood up and went to the bar, returning with another whisky, a single this time.

I decided to confront him. 'Listen Adam,' I said. 'None of this adds up. When you first mentioned Mariana, why didn't you tell us who her father was? You must've known.'

'No I didn't, Cristóvão never talked about him. I just knew that Mariana was the daughter of a cousin. I assumed he was talking about his other cousin Martim. I met him once at Abrahão's house in Lisbon. He's in the oil business. Abrahão thought he might want to use Exodis but nothing came of it.'

'So it's pure chance that you asked me to make some enquiries about a girl with the same surnames, da Silva Pinheiro, as the head of the Angolan security police?'

'Of course it is. It turns out Martim had an older sister, Adelina, who died some years ago. Adelina married Salvador Pinheiro, Mariana is their child. I didn't make the connection. Africa has never been my beat. I don't know Angola at all. You remember me, strictly a Cold War warrior.'

'But you've been there. Richard Mendale told me you were there back around the time of that South African raid Operation Argon.'

'Oh that was philately,' he explained. His tone changed. 'A chap was selling stamps from the Portuguese Congo. They're very hard to get hold of. They stopped issuing them in 1920.' I detected a hint of the old enthusiasm in his voice but I wasn't reassured.

'Portuguese Congo? That's Cabinda now. Were you in Cabinda when the South Africans attacked?'

'No of course not, I didn't go anywhere near Cabinda. Far too dangerous. I didn't know anything about the raid until I landed back home. Look there's nothing sinister here. When Cristóvão told me Mariana's father was Salvador Pinheiro I was horrified, I didn't want to get involved. I didn't want Exodis involved. Julia told me Mariana didn't seem keen to see the two of you again and I was relieved. But now Cristóvão is worried. The least I could do is have this quick chat. Just to reassure him. But if it's going to put you in a difficult position let's drop it. I've been around long enough to know that discretion is the better part of valour and all that. I was just thinking you could tip me the wink if there is anything the family should know.'

'I'll see what I can do,' I said, non-committally. 'But I can't promise anything.'

We left it at that. I was disappointed. When I had joined the Defence Intelligence Staff, Adam Joseff had been the rock on which the organisation was built. Even though formally he was only the Deputy Director General the reality was that his office was the point around which everything else revolved. Now he was playing games with me. His claim that he had thought Mariana was the daughter of cousin Martim rather than of Martim's sister Adelina was nonsense. He had given me her name: Mariana Pinheiro. Portuguese surnames can be far more intricate than English, with considerable flexibility on what surnames are used, but there was no way Martim Vasconcelos would give his daughter the family name of his sister's husband. Adam Joseff might be no great linguist but he must have been able to work that out.

I thought Julia might throw some light on Adam Joseff's

behaviour, after all she was working with him, but she had no more idea than I had.

'It's pretty clear that Adam had only one thing in mind,' I said. 'He wanted to know if we were keeping Mariana under observation. But why? I don't buy him doing Cristóvão Taravares a favour. In any case Cristóvão didn't strike me as a doting uncle. How close is he really to Mariana? Not very. She's his father's sister's grandchild.'

'Extended families mean more in some cultures than in ours,' suggested Julia.

'Perhaps.'

I suppose I should have mentioned my conversation with Joseff to Rowbart but I didn't.

Working with Turk Rowbart was a challenge. He was unlike anyone else in the Service, indeed he seemed more like the various Americans from partner agencies who would suddenly pop up in Century House for weeks or even months only to disappear without warning back across the Atlantic. He took what we were doing very seriously. Of course most people in the Service were serious but it was considered almost bad form to show it. At times he was more than serious, he was messianic. He had the total certainty I remembered Robbie Perez attributing to Oliver North and Fidel Castro.

All his energies were devoted to what we were trying to achieve. He rarely spoke about anything else and when he did he could be abrupt to the point of being offensive.

Felicity Macnamara told me that when she had casually asked him if he was married he had replied, 'Of course.' That in itself seemed to me a fairly odd response but according to Felicity he had then added, 'And before you ask, I don't do affairs.'

He was self-consciously blunt with no time for prevarication. When one of our Minister's pet projects was clearly going nowhere and needed to end, Rowbart wanted to simply notify the Minister's office that the operation had been 'aborted'. Colin Asperton stepped in quickly to suggest that it might be better to simply 'play the ball into the long grass' until a suitable opportunity arrived to let the Minister know that it might be 'time to draw stumps'. The classic civil service mantra that 'compromise is less an expedient than a principle' was totally alien to Turk Rowbart.

He was a man of ups and downs and those ups and downs always seemed to be driven not by events close at hand but by whatever was happening in Africa. When Thomas Sankara, the man labelled by the liberal press as the Che Guevara of Africa, was assassinated, Rowbart was smiling for days. When the same press trumpeted another success of those campaigning for sanctions against the 'apartheid regime' in South Africa his secretary would know to keep out of his way. But he never lost control completely. It was like watching a man with a too-tight shirt, always expecting a button to pop but it never happened.

If Justin Brasenose hadn't moved over to the Cabinet Office I would have spoken to him about the encounter with Adam Joseff but I didn't have the same sort of relationship with Colin Asperton. I was worried that if he or Rowbart started investigating Joseff and Exodis he was bound to drag in Julia at some stage.

'Pinheiro's up to something,' Rowbart announced when MI5 reported that Mariana Pinheiro had travelled halfway across central London to use the same phone box in Byng Place that Mutorwa had been seen using. 'I knew it. I bet she and Mutorwa are cooking up some scheme with the Soviets. Mutorwa must have had a bust-up with his uncle and he's changed sides. Go and rattle his cage.'

This last comment was directed at me.

I did what I was told and arrived at the SOAS campus just after midday. I thought I might find Mutorwa having lunch. In fact I located him in the Philips Building, the concrete edifice designed by the brutalist architect Denys Lasdun to house the SOAS library. Mutorwa was seated head down at one of the library desks, a pile of journals in front of him. Every so often he would scribble a note on a yellow legal pad. It occurred to me that compared to some of the African students I had come to know Mutorwa was particularly studious. I remembered the enthusiasm on his face when I bumped into him taking Mariana Pinheiro to the British Museum. It wasn't just that he had seemed so clearly in love with the beautiful girl on his arm but he was enjoying life in a way that seemed to have left him now.

It was hard to imagine Marco and Mariana as a couple. I could understand why he would be attracted to her, she was beautiful and rich although I suspected he was still young enough to be smitten by the former more than the latter. What had attracted Mariana to him? He was a couple of years older than her but she seemed the more worldly. Perhaps the fact that he had so deeply fallen for her was enough. Perhaps she was rebelling against her father by consorting with the enemy. It struck me that I still didn't really understand either of them. After two years on the Subsaharan Africa Desk I was starting to understand the world these two had come from but I didn't have the instinctive feeling for the place and the people that someone like John Darwyn had. I was still very much an outsider looking in.

Mutorwa hadn't seen me. I didn't want to try to talk to him in the library so I chose a desk at the back. I found the journal *Portuguese Studies* which had just been started by Helder Macedo of King's College and would fit with my cover. I didn't get far. Mutorwa stood and started clearing his desk.

I approached him as he left the building. He didn't seem pleased to see me.

'Hi Marco,' I greeted him.

He merely nodded in return.

'I was hoping to bump into you,' I continued. 'Something odd has come up.'

He stopped. 'What do you want Tommy?' A hint of resignation in his voice.

I decided to take the bull by the horns. 'I wanted to ask you about your girlfriend Mariana Pinheiro. My wife is a friend of her uncle and he seems to think you've been upsetting her.'

'Well I haven't. Mariana Pinheiro is not my girlfriend. I don't know her.'

'But you introduced me, last year, you were taking her to the British Museum.'

'That was a long time ago. We are no longer friends.'

'Well her uncle Cristóvão seems to think you are.'

Mutorwa turned to look directly at me. 'What's this about Tommy? What are you trying to do?'

'I just thought I might be able to help out. My wife says Cristóvão Taravares is really concerned about his niece.'

Mutorwa shook his head. 'That's not true. You're a

spy Tommy. I know you are. Your wife has no interest in Mariana.'

'A spy!' I tried to sound shocked. 'Why would you say that?'

Marco just shook his head again. 'I know who you are Tommy. You work for the police. You spy on us Africans. But you picked the wrong man. I'm not political. And Mariana Pinheiro is not my friend.'

He spoke calmly, matter-of-factly. No anger. No sudden lashing out at something I had said. No sense of feeling betrayed. It was as if he was merely telling me that rain was on the way or that the book he wanted wasn't in the library. There was an absolute certainty in his voice. It was said as a statement of fact. You're a spy. And suddenly I realised: he knew. Something had happened to convince him. And it couldn't have been something I had done because I had done nothing. Someone had told him.

He turned away. I put my hand on his arm but he brushed it off. Without another word he hurried off towards Malet Street.

Marco had been perfectly relaxed with me when he first arrived in the UK. What had happened since then? I could only assume that his uncle Lusiano Nambala must have mentioned my being in Jamba. But that seemed highly unlikely.

That evening I told Julia what had happened. 'Why,' I asked, 'would a guerrilla leader in the middle of Africa bother to send his nephew the name of someone who he had met a year or so before for just a few minutes?'

'Whom he had met,' corrected Julia with a twinkle. 'Perhaps he wanted Marco to find out what happened to those tanks you were going to ask Mrs Thatcher to send.'

I decided not to repeat that to Turk Rowbart, Julia's humour would not go down well with him.

'It's worrying though,' I said to Julia. 'My cover story was not that feeble and I thought I played it well. I took things slowly, made sure I never seemed overly keen approaching people. I've been there more than a year and nobody else has reacted that way. What went wrong?'

'Like you said, somebody told him. And it wasn't some guerrilla leader in the middle of Africa.'

'But who?' I asked.

'Mariana Pinheiro.'

'Mariana?' I couldn't keep the surprise out of my voice. 'Why her?'

'She and Marco seem to be closer than either of them admit. I don't think there's anything romantic going on, at least from Mariana's point of view. But if you're right about those phone calls there's something they don't want us to know.'

'But why would she suspect I was a spy? Did she see something when she came to lunch? I never have anything official in the house.'

'Perhaps someone told her.'

'That brings us back to square one. Who told her?'

Julia was silent for a moment. 'There's one person who definitely knows you're in the Service and who seems very keen to ensure that the Service isn't spying on Mariana Pinheiro. Someone we both know well.'

Even then I wasn't entirely sure what Julia was getting at.

'Adam? You think Adam Joseff might have told Mariana that I work for MI6?'

That was the one thing nobody in his position would ever do. If Adam had ever married I suspect he would not even have told his wife what he really did for a living.

'Not tell Mariana directly perhaps but tell Cristóvão Taravares. Cristóvão is really important to Adam. His first big client. Remember what Adam said when the four of us had dinner at the Reform: 'Cristóvão wants a spy.' Suppose that when Taravares said he wanted someone to keep an eye on Mariana, Adam had replied that he happened to know a man who might be able to help, someone he'd worked with in the past. A chap called Thomas Dylan who just happened to be enrolled at SOAS.'

But I still couldn't believe it. 'Adam's been in Intelligence almost all his life. He simply wouldn't tell a foreign business associate that I was a serving MI6 officer. It's treason, he would never do that. It's second nature. You can't believe he's getting that senile.'

Again Julia hesitated. 'No he's not senile, far from it. He's getting a bit disorganised maybe but no, his brain is all there. But he might have just hinted at something, he would have wanted to impress Cristóvão. It's just a suggestion. I could be wrong, I hope I am.'

It was another theory that I was not going to suggest to Rowbart. In the event, when I reported my conversation with Marco Mutorwa to Rowbart he brushed my concerns aside.

'Mutorwa is just paranoid,' he said. 'Keep on him. I want to know what he and Mariana Pinheiro are up to.'

I wasn't sure they were up to anything, using the same phone box to receive calls was hardly evidence of some grand conspiracy. And if there was a grand conspiracy my casual mixing with a few dozen students wasn't going to uncover it.

Julia had been typically straightforward the previous evening. 'It was a bloody silly idea putting you in there in the first place. If Turk Rowbart really thought that any of those students were terrorists he should have let Five or Special Branch handle it.'

I agreed. My assignment had been less about uncovering any security risk to the UK than it had been about the Service demonstrating to the South Africans that we were taking their concerns seriously. Staying close to Colonel DeSmid and the various South African intelligence agencies had always been a priority for both Asperton and Rowbart. Rowbart had wanted me to produce a monthly summary of my findings to pass on to Pretoria. He wasn't impressed by my own compositions and soon gave the task to Felicity Macnamara who had a remarkable talent for sexing up my own insubstantial efforts. As the military situation in the region developed, Rowbart focused his own attention on what he referred to as the Border War.

Anyone with a casual interest in military history might believe that there were two wars going on in Southern Africa towards the end of the twentieth century. One was the twenty-seven-year-long 'Angolan Civil War', pitting the government that had seized power after independence against the UNITA guerrillas. The other was the twenty-three-year-long 'Border War' in which the South African army and police fought to maintain control over what today is called Namibia. The reality however is that there was only ever one war. The only differences between the Angolan Civil War and the Border War were the dates at which they were deemed to have begun and finished.

Rowbart understood that better than most. South

Africa's future depended on the destruction of Angola's Marxist government and he expected Darwyn to make the war in Angola his main priority.

The situation inside South Africa was becoming bloodier by the day. Bombs in shopping centres and casinos, landmines left on roads near white farms, almost daily assassinations, gun battles between police and insurgents. John Darwyn's reports had been full of the depressing detail as well as his analysis of the political implications. Sanctions were really starting to bite and in response the government were tentatively moving away from their previous hard-line stance. The laws that insisted that non-whites in white areas had to carry passes showing that they were allowed to be there had just been relaxed.

'I can find all that stuff out from the newspapers,' insisted Rowbart. 'What I want to know is what the Russians were doing in Moçâmedes?'

Rowbart had just returned from a flying visit to South Africa where he and John Darwyn had obviously exchanged angry words.

'He wants Darwyn replaced,' Felicity Macnamara told me.

Turk Rowbart had said nothing to me. 'Why?' I asked.

'The South Africans are stewing over another raid they planned on the harbour at Namibe which had to be aborted.' Namibe was the new name for the port Rowbart still called by the Portuguese colonial name of Moçâmedes. 'When the submarine with the Recces on board got there this time they found a couple of Russian warships waiting for them.'

'What's that got to do with John Darwyn?'

'John hadn't said anything about it to London. It turns

out he knew all about it, he even knew the raid was being planned, but he didn't put it in his reports. He claimed there were so many raids going on that it wasn't worth detailing every one. Turk's theory is that John has a source in the South African military and he doesn't want anybody else working out who it is.'

I could understand John Darwyn wanting to keep the name of any source to himself but that wouldn't make him friends back in London. Turk Rowbart was close to the DMI, the South African Directorate of Military Intelligence. He wouldn't hesitate to pass on the name of John's source if he thought he could gain something valuable in exchange.

Felicity wasn't finished. 'And then there's the issue of those diamonds being intercepted.'

That I knew about. Three months earlier UNITA were bringing a consignment of diamonds down to Jamba when the convoy was ambushed by Angolan troops.

'But John Darwyn reported that,' I replied. 'He told us the diamonds were going to be flown up to Zaire and exchanged for arms. He was in Jamba when it happened.'

'Yes John reported that. What he didn't report is that the Russians organised the attack. There were Russian officers there.'

'There are always Russian officers there. The Angolan Army is useless. We all know that. The Russians and Cubans have been involved in every success they've ever had.'

Felicity just shrugged her shoulders. 'I know you like John Darwyn but Rowbart's right. The more we learn about how the Russians operate down there the better. That's what we're here for.'

I couldn't disagree with that. The problem was that I

couldn't disagree with Rowbart about anything. Like so many who have never been tested he had total faith in his own judgement and therefore had nothing to gain by listening to the opinions of others.

He certainly didn't want to hear the views of junior staff. He told a departmental meeting bitterly that the British press just didn't understand how black governments in Africa work.

'They're all just in it for themselves,' Rowbart insisted. 'Sitting in their fancy offices while ninety per cent of the population struggle to survive.'

'Just like the whites in South Africa,' one of the secretaries mumbled to herself, but not quietly enough. We never saw her in the building again.

His objective as a Desk Officer, Rowbart kept telling us, was to get things done. Action was the priority. On the Soviet Operations Desk every piece of intelligence had been pored over, dissected and had its meaning debated. Even junior members of the SOD were expected to analyse the evidence and then articulate their own conclusions. No question was invalid, no answer infallible. The one thing to learn from Hegel and Marx I was told was that wisdom comes from the synthesis of thesis and antithesis. To Rowbart such a view was incomprehensible. A thesis was either right or wrong, wisdom comes from selecting the right and discarding the wrong.

That difference in approach coloured every aspect of our work. SOD operations had been planned in minute detail and endlessly rehearsed. Rowbart's gung-ho approach to operations on the Subsaharan Africa Desk could not have been more different. My shallow cover op was a typical example of a hastily mounted operation launched with great fanfare and then allowed to quietly disappear when the anticipated results didn't come through right away. Rowbart's view was that if you fired enough shots quickly enough you were bound to hit the enemy. 'A sniper's no use if you don't have a target' was one of his less opaque maxims.

Shortly after my conversation with Felicity Macnamara, Rowbart came into my office for some reason and started to moan about Darwyn's lack of respect for authority.

'That bloody man's got an agent in DeSmid's team and he refuses to tell me who it is,' he complained.

'He probably thinks you'll tell DeSmid,' I unwisely responded with a smile.

'And what if I did?' Rowbart snapped back. 'I'm the Desk Officer not Darwyn, it's my decision to make. What the hell is he doing spying on the South Africans anyway? They're on our side.'

'Surely Darwyn's job is to spy. That's what we're here for.'

Rowbart looked at me as if I were mad. 'That's garbage. I've told Colin Asperton that Darwyn should be disciplined. Whoever is selling us South African secrets could be selling them to the Russians as well, DeSmid ought to be told.'

'You can't seriously mean we should betray one of our own sources,' I protested.

'Sources! What do you mean sources? You make Darwyn sound like some self-righteous journalist. If he's identified someone in DeSmid's team who is willing to betray his own country we should tell DeSmid. That's what we would expect our allies to do if the boot was on the other foot. Do you think the South Africans would ever spy on us?'

I didn't answer that but Rowbart wouldn't let the matter

drop. 'Come on Dylan. We're talking about the defence of the free world here. Nobody spies on their own side.'

'Pollard,' I suggested. The American Jonathan Pollard had just been sentenced to life imprisonment after the FBI had discovered that he had been spying for Israel while working for US Naval Intelligence. 'When the FBI started getting close to Pollard the Israelis tried everything to protect their man but you're happy to throw Darwyn's agent to the wolves.'

'That's totally different. Pollard was on an official Mossad mission. Darwyn has just found some *chop* with access who's willing to sell secrets for a few rand.'

It was a distinction I didn't see. And although Rowbart used the dismissive South African term '*chop*' we didn't actually know what sort of person Darwyn's informant was.

'How do you know John Darwyn hasn't managed to find an anti-apartheid idealist in DeSmid's office?' I asked.

'Oh give me strength. You sound like an editorial in the *Guardian*! We're not talking about idealists. We're talking about the card carrying Communists who control the ANC. Darwyn has someone inside the ANC. If that's where he's been getting South African military plans it means the ANC themselves must have someone in DeSmid's office. We need to find out who it is and tell DeSmid.'

Rowbart seemed to be daring me to disagree. I wasn't about to do so.

He was right about the ANC and the Communists. The South African Communist Party were dangerous, hard-line Stalinists who had supported the Russian invasions of Hungary and Czechoslovakia and were now cheering on the Red Army in Afghanistan. 'But is it really possible that they've got somebody inside the South African high command?' I asked. 'Isn't it far more likely that John's found his own source in DeSmid's team?'

'How the hell would he do that?' demanded Rowbart. 'I sometimes wonder what you're doing on my Desk.' Without waiting for a response he strode out of my office having forgotten whatever he came in for.

Darwyn might not be willing to disclose his sources to Rowbart but he certainly seemed to have got the message that Rowbart wanted to be kept fully informed of whatever intelligence he had picked up. A couple of days later he sent Rowbart a long and detailed report on a planned South African paratroop mission called Operation Mango.

I later realised that it was the failure of Operation Mango as much as the failure of Operation Argon that led to Adam Joseff's murder.

# PART 2

# JAMBA, ANGOLA, 21 NOVEMBER 1987

A lot had changed since the Democratic International two years previously. One of the men behind the Jamboree, Oliver North, was now facing prison for his part in the Iran-Contra affair. But on the ground Jamba still had a makeshift quality about it. The airfield's dirt runway had portable runway lighting but the approach path still came in dangerously low over the trees. Three years later a CIA flight carrying arms from Zaire would crash when approaching at night at the very low altitude needed to avoid enemy radar.

The aircraft that stood at the end of the runway belonged to what in the business was known as a 'CIA proprietary', an air charter company only indirectly linked to the Agency.

Bob 'Kipper' Vogel lifted the Lockheed L100-20, the civilian version of the military Hercules, off the runway and headed northwest. He had been assured by Robbie Perez that there were no government troops within 200 miles of the UNITA base but he knew that if she were wrong they would be operating as close to Jamba as possible in the hope of finding a nice juicy target like him. It was too risky to try spiralling up to an altitude where a Russian-made man-portable surface-to-air missile couldn't reach him, so he just prayed. He wanted out of Angolan airspace as soon as possible. You never knew when the CIA's intelligence might be proved wrong and an enemy MiG jet might suddenly appear out of nowhere. He kept just above the trees until they were safely inside Zambia and he could relax.

The four turboprop engines strained to pull the aircraft up to cruising height and Vogel turned north. The Zambians were no friend to the CIA but he was confident that nobody was going to scramble from the Zambian airbase at Mumbwa far to the east at this time of night.

'Here we go,' he said to his co-pilot. 'Next stop Kamina.' He looked down at the unremitting darkness below. 'We should make better time than we did coming down. No cargo this trip.'

'Just this,' said the co-pilot gesturing to the metal box behind them. 'Wonder what's in there.'

'Better not to ask,' Vogel replied. 'Wake me up when we reach Zaire.'

Vogel was joking, he knew he had to keep his senses alert for the whole flight. Just north of Kayombo, Angola jutted out eastwards and he didn't want to drift too close.

'African frontiers are insane,' Vogel announced. 'Why the hell didn't the Portuguese learn to draw straight lines and right angles?'

He was right about the crazy frontiers but was blaming the wrong nation. It was British politicians, bribed liberally by Cecil Rhodes, whose zigzag lines had stopped the Portuguese advancing across the Zambezi valley.

'We're doing well,' his co-pilot observed. 'We'll be in Kamina right on time, just like you told Perez.'

They had passed Mwinilunga, near the point where the frontiers of Angola, Zambia and Zaire come together, when the explosion came.

The side of the plane disintegrated behind the cockpit

with metal shards blasted in every direction. A wing spiralled off. What was left of the fuselage and everything inside it hurtled towards the ground below.

# X

I remember exactly how the news that a CIA proprietary had been shot down reached me. Julia had had an exceptionally busy week. Richard Mendale was in Washington and Adam Joseff in Taiwan, both apparently forgetting that the next *Exodis Bulletin* was due out in a matter of days. Julia eventually wrote most of it at our kitchen table after Eveline had gone to sleep. We were both determined that work would not disrupt our plans for the weekend. Theoretically I was on call that weekend but I was confident that even if the third world war broke out I would not be required. Clive Shelton, a long-standing executive officer, was on duty at the Subsaharan Africa Desk. He was one of those people who believed that life would be much simpler if his nominal superiors just stopped interfering. Desk Officers were barely tolerated, Deputy Desk Officers were simply ignored. By mutual agreement he was usually given the weekend shifts.

On Saturday morning Julia and I decided that a lie-in was called for but our daughter refused to cooperate. I pulled myself out of bed, took Eveline downstairs to find her a snack and then tried to find toys she would agree to play with before switching on the 'electric nanny', forever grateful to whoever had invented Saturday morning children's TV. Eveline snuggled into me making it almost worthwhile being woken early. Having been on daughter-duty on Saturday it should have been my turn to lie in on Sunday morning but we had agreed to meet friends in Chipping Norton for lunch and a country walk. We left London early and were approaching Oxford when I was startled, and Julia amused, by a novel sensation: my newly issued pager had started to vibrate in my trouser pocket. In those days only the official cars used by senior officers had carphones fitted.

We found a phone box and I called Century House.

'What's up?'

'Bit of a flap,' announced Shelton. 'We can't get hold of John Darwyn in Pretoria. He's not answering his phone. Rowbart told me to call you, he thought you might have another number for him.'

I hadn't. 'Why does Turk want him?'

'An American plane has been shot down. Frank Cato, the CIA Africa Director, is here. Do you know him?'

'Yes, I met him in Jamba.'

'Well he arrived from Cape Town this morning. Went straight to his hotel and discovered a message about a proprietary carrying UNITA diamonds being brought down. He called Turk and they're in the conference room now. Cato was due here tomorrow to see Colin Asperton, apparently.'

Shelton managed to make 'apparently' sound like a personal insult, as if someone had dared set up a meeting without telling him. I didn't know about it either.

'What happened to the plane?'

'That's what we're trying to find out. The Americans don't know. Rowbart thought Darwyn might have more info. He was there when the last lot of diamonds were lost. But we can't find him. Apparently he's got one of these pager things but they don't seem to work too well down there.'

'Well I can't suggest any other way of contacting him. And I doubt if he knows any more than the Americans. Does Turk want me to come in?'

I could feel Shelton's disdain down the phone. 'He hasn't suggested that. I warned him that you wouldn't be able to help.'

I left it at that. The next day I discovered that Darwyn had eventually picked up Rowbart's message but hadn't heard about the plane's loss. He had been working on what turned out to be his report on the planned Operation Mango. Rowbart told him to concentrate on the missing plane. How had the Soviets discovered its route?

I had hoped to take the Monday off but one of the monthly 'catch-ups' that Colin Asperton had with each of his Desk Officer teams was in the diary. I was owed leave but attendance was virtually compulsory. Julia was visiting a prospective client in the Isle of Man with Sir Jonathon Craverse and had volunteered me to be one of the parents accompanying a school trip to the Natural History Museum. I had to be at the school by 1.30. The catch-ups rarely lasted more than an hour and so I was confident that would not be a problem. It was Eveline's first term at 'big school' and I didn't want to let her down.

Although the Subsaharan Africa Desk was focused almost entirely on the forthcoming visit of Salvador Pinheiro, Rowbart found time to call John Darwyn again before the catch-up demanding to know precisely what had happened to the American aircraft. The truth was that nobody knew as the plane had come down in one of the most inaccessible parts of the planet. But Darwyn was happy to supply theories.

His favourite theory was based on the date. The plane

had gone missing on 21st November. Almost exactly two years before, on 25th November 1985, South African Recces had crossed into Angola with a Russian-made SA9 infrared guided surface-to-air missile they had captured from Angolan forces. The Recces had used the missile to shoot down an Antonov An-12 transport plane belonging to the Russian airline Aeroflot fifteen minutes after it had taken off from Cuito Cuanavale. All twenty-one on board were killed. It was the largest Russian loss of life in the war. The downing of the American aircraft now, said Darwyn, was a clear message from the Russians to leave civilian planes alone. Although, he admitted when Rowbart pressed him, neither the Russian Antonov nor the American Lockheed were truly civilian aircraft despite their civil markings.

Darwyn conceded that Robbie Perez in Jamba had dismissed his theory out of hand. She was convinced that an Angolan jet fighter had happened upon the C130 purely by chance and decided to attack. That was not completely implausible. A few months later the Cuban pilot of an Angolan MiG-23 fired two heat-seeking missiles at a twin-engined executive jet peacefully flying over southern Angola. (The Hawker Siddeley 125 jet turned out to be carrying the President of Botswana to a conference in Luanda. One missile hit an engine causing it to fall off and then incredibly the second missile locked on to and destroyed the same engine as it fell to the ground. Demonstrating extraordinary skill the British Aerospace co-pilot who had just delivered the HS125 managed to land the aircraft safely.)

Rowbart wasn't convinced by either theory. To him the truth was self-evident. The Soviets were out to disrupt UNITA's ability to procure modern weapons. Therefore the loss of the diamonds was down to them. They must have known exactly what was on the CIA flight and somehow had obtained the precise flight plan as well. There was a security leak at Jamba. Darwyn, he instructed, must insist on a proper enquiry. Darwyn replied that, as this was an American operation at a UNITA base subject to South African security, MI6 wasn't in a position to insist on anything. That was not the answer Rowbart wanted.

Consequently Rowbart was not in a good mood when he, Felicity Macnamara and I trooped into the small meeting room next to Asperton's office on the dot of ten o'clock. As usual Asperton kept us waiting.

Normally Rowbart did all the talking with Asperton confining himself to occasional words of encouragement, the drawing of often irrelevant parallels and the proffering of superfluous advice. Turk started with the news of the downed plane. Asperton's response was to remind us that the Russians had shot down a Korean jumbo jet over Siberia four years earlier, before adding the gnomic advice that 'We should consider the lessons learned from that.' Turk wisely ignored that remark and started to explain why the loss of the diamonds was so important. Unusually Asperton cut him off.

'Turk, we are all agreed that UNITA is providing an invaluable corrective to other forces in Southern Africa. Clearly they can only continue to do so if they are properly equipped. The loss of the diamonds will hinder them in that regard which is something the Americans need to resolve. But we have other priorities.'

Asperton lapsed into that tone of condescension that he always used when telling us something we already knew. Felicity Macnamara described it as his portentous pontificating.

'The balance of power in the region is not moving in the direction which we had hoped for. Nevertheless we must recognise realities and consider our priorities. The objective of Her Majesty's Government is to ensure a peaceful resolution to the conflict in Southern Africa. It is the considered view of our Ministers that at present the best hope of such a resolution lies with talks Mr Crocker, the United States Assistant Secretary of State, is currently holding with the parties involved. We must therefore use our best endeavours to ensure those talks succeed.'

'You think the Soviets want peace?' demanded Rowbart.

'What I think is irrelevant. And in any case it's not the Soviet intentions in the region which are the issue; it's the Soviet presence in the region. What we all want is the Cubans out of Angola. I must repeat: our Ministers' view is that Chester Crocker is the best hope of achieving that objective. That's why this week's visit of Senhor Pinheiro is so important.

'Our Ministers believe that externally conditions are now propitious. We are expecting President Reagan and Mr Gorbachev to sign a treaty limiting short and intermediate range missiles in the very near future. It is clear that Gorbachev has no desire to keep spending money, not to mention Russian lives, propping up regimes in Africa. And of course Castro cannot afford to keep his troops there without someone else paying. Consequently something on their side has to give. At the same time we must remember that there is a US presidential election in less than twelve months and since Congress passed the Anti-Apartheid Act last year none of the candidates will want to appear to be endorsing apartheid. The White House cannot continue supporting the Pretoria regime unless it can demonstrate that change is starting to happen.'

Rowbart glowered at this but said nothing and Asperton continued.

'There must be a peace agreement in Southern Africa; the issue is getting the two sides, the Angolans and South Africans, to sit down together and agree what everybody else has agreed: the Cubans leave Angola in return for the South Africans leaving South West Africa.'

'And why would the South Africans do that?' demanded Rowbart. 'Every day there's another terrorist attack inside South Africa. If we lose South West Africa the terrorists will be able to move their bases further south, closer to South Africa's borders. We're just going to make things worse.'

'Well of course any agreement will have to include assurances that both the Angolan government and the political parties in what we must now call Namibia will no longer allow terrorist camps and terrorist training in their territory.'

'Assurances we all know will be worthless,' responded Rowbart, more in resignation than in anger.

'Turk we do not make policy. Remember that.'

'Of course I remember that. We all know what's happening down there. At some point South Africa will have to give ground unless the regime in Luanda collapses of its own accord and let's not forget that might happen. There are always feuds going on inside the Angolan politburo.'

'Perhaps. But there's no sign that anyone is about to attempt another coup. Pinheiro's security police have made sure of that. As I said, our Ministers believe conditions are propitious for an agreement but of course there are dissidents: in both Angola and South Africa. Important voices objecting to any kind of negotiation with the enemy. President Dos Santos appears to be edging towards compromise but as you say his politburo is not united. Which brings us to Salvador Pinheiro. He could be the key to pushing the President further in the direction we want. That's why his meeting with Foreign Office colleagues is so important.'

Asperton looked towards Felicity and me. 'There is however a new development which Turk apprised me of only last evening. I asked him to keep the matter to himself until I had a chance to discuss it with colleagues which I have done this morning. It is, we have concluded, very good news. Just as opinion in the Angolan Cabinet is divided so some of the South African cabinet are more inclined to compromise than others. Some still believe a military solution to the country's problems remains appropriate. Others are beginning to realise that with only the Israelis willing to continue supplying modern armaments their armed forces cannot maintain their current remarkably successful record in the Border War.'

I had no idea what he was getting at. What was the new development Turk had 'apprised' him of?

Asperton nodded towards Rowbart. 'Turk informs me that a man we know well, Colonel Hendrik DeSmid, intends to be in London at the same time as Salvador Pinheiro and has suggested a private meeting be arranged between the two of them. That would be, shall we say, intriguing. Nobody should get their hopes up, DeSmid won't be in a position to commit to anything. But Turk tells me he has said that nothing will be off the table.'

That surprised me. 'Including the South African nuclear programme?'

'Including that. The programme is we know rudimentary but the Angolans, and of course the Russians, want it dismantled.'

It wasn't that rudimentary, I thought, the South Africans had been cooperating very closely with the Israelis. Just one nuclear bomb would be enough to make neighbouring countries think twice before pushing Pretoria too hard.

'If DeSmid is willing to talk about that Pinheiro might be willing to listen,' continued Asperton. 'And of course Salvador Pinheiro is not just the head of the Angolan security police but more importantly he is a key member of the politburo of the Angolan Communist Party. Consequently,' he added with a knowing smile, 'his views are accorded greater respect than are those of the security services in this country.'

As if on cue at that moment Asperton's secretary came into the room and passed him a memo. After reading it he announced that Senhor Pinheiro had just agreed to the meeting. He explained that both parties were insisting on complete secrecy and a meeting at the Foreign Office in Whitehall was therefore ruled out. Instead it was suggested that they should meet at Hanslope Park, near Milton Keynes, in six days' time.

Asperton was right, a meeting between Pinheiro and DeSmid would indeed be intriguing. They were both powerful figures behind the scenes and for Crocker's plan to work it was precisely men like that who had to be brought together. Making sure their meeting was a success was now our priority. Nevertheless when the catch-up was over and we were back in his office Rowbart immediately returned to the subject of the downed CIA plane.

'Something stinks down there. The Soviets always know what we're doing. Argon, the raid on the harbour at Moçâmedes, the last diamond convoy ambushed and now this. There's a leak and it's not coming from some disgruntled black at the bottom of the pile. I'll get the Americans to start a proper enquiry. There can't be many people who had that flight plan.'

I nodded and left, I wanted to drop in at home to grab a sandwich before going to Eveline's school.

Darwyn's report on Operation Mango must have arrived just as I was leaving the building. When I saw the report the next day it read like a *Boys' Own* adventure.

The 'Parabats' Darwyn explained were among the most successful of the South African Special Forces groups operating deep inside Angola. Operation Mango would see them doing so again, parachuting down at night some 200 kilometres inside Angola. Three companies from 1 Parachute Battalion would land and then march, fully loaded, for fifty kilometres before setting ambushes on the road north from Cuvelai to Cuvango. They would be dropping in the region of Cassinga which happened to be the site of the most famous Parabat operation of the whole war.

As I read the report I realised that the paratroopers would already be at the Ondangwa Air Force Base in South West Africa close to the Angolan border. They would spend the day resting and making their final preparations. Fourteen hours from now, after their final briefing and last minute checks, they would board their C130 transport and Operation Mango would be live.

We learned a few days later that although the Parabats had landed nearly six kilometres from their planned dropping point they had successfully reached their target before dawn and set up their ambush. But the convoys they had expected to attack did not materialise. Instead there were a few indecisive skirmishes before the paratroopers had to trek back south to be helicoptered out. Operation Mango was a failure.

By the time we heard that our minds were elsewhere: Salvador Pinheiro had landed and plans were in hand for his meeting with Colonel DeSmid.

Other than meeting Foreign Office officials on Friday morning and DeSmid before flying home on Sunday, it seemed Pinheiro was devoting all his energies to shopping and his daughter's twenty-first birthday on Saturday. To my surprise his itinerary didn't appear to include a visit to the Angolan Embassy in Dorset Street and, although the Angolan Ambassador would accompany him to the Foreign Office, the Sunday meeting would be just Pinheiro and DeSmid.

Hanslope Park, the venue for that meeting, is one of the least known parts of what was once described to me as the country's 'Security Landscape'. Her Majesty's Government Communications Centre, HMGCC, is funded by the Foreign & Commonwealth Office, like the much larger GCHQ in Cheltenham. It had been chosen for the meeting solely because it was both secure and obscure. The boffins there are responsible for designing and supporting secure communication systems for the government. Pinheiro and DeSmid would certainly not be seeing anything of the work of HMGCC. And the boffins would see and hear nothing of them. Both men would be bringing their own sweepers, technicians who would ensure that nobody, least of all the perfidious British, would be able to eavesdrop on their conversation.

The Angolan security police chief arrived at Heathrow from Lisbon on Thursday. This was a private visit but given the sensitivities involved the Foreign Office were anxious to ensure that nothing untoward occurred. Pinheiro had brought his own security, two muscular Africans in loose-fitting suits. He demanded that they be allowed to keep their weapons with them but, as was almost invariably the case, this was refused. Only American Secret Service agents accompanying the US President were allowed to carry arms in London when outside their own embassy. Instead the DPG, the Metropolitan Police Diplomatic Protection Group, was providing around the clock cover with armed officers.

Pinheiro was not happy with this arrangement and it was soon obvious he was used to getting his own way. Hanslope Park, he announced, was completely out of the question. He had been shown the planned itinerary and it involved two ridiculously long car journeys before his flight on Sunday morning. He needed to go home as soon as the meeting was over and he would charter a jet to take him back to Luanda from a military airfield close to central London. He would meet DeSmid there. It turned out that he was talking about RAF Northolt and plans for the Sunday meeting were rapidly changed.

The peculiarities of intra-agency protocols meant that my Service had no direct involvement in the first three days of Salvador Pinheiro's visit. We were included in the plans for the final meeting only because DeSmid's initial feelers had been put out to Rowbart who successfully argued that this entitled us to what he called a watching brief.

As Colonel DeSmid was a senior member of an allied service Colin Asperton had felt duty-bound to entertain him during his stay in London. Somehow he had managed to get two tickets for *The Phantom of the Opera* for Mrs Asperton and Mrs DeSmid while he, Rowbart and I had dinner at the Athenaeum. Felicity Macnamara was down at Fort Monckton.

At the last minute Mrs Asperton was suddenly indisposed.

'Does your wife like musicals?' Asperton asked me. I knew Julia would jump at the opportunity providing she could find a babysitter. I needn't have worried about that.

That evening the taxi dropped us off at the Royal Over-Seas League where the DeSmids were staying. Colonel DeSmid I had met in Jamba: a tall man around fifty with a rugby player's physique and the deep tan of those who spend most of their life outdoors. His wife was younger but with the same straight back if not the same tanned skin. In England she might have been described as horsey and I wondered how she would get on with Julia.

The colonel and I walked down to the Athenaeum deep in shallow conversation. He strode along as if on a route march, raising his hand imperiously to slow an approaching car as we crossed Pall Mall. He appeared to be someone who both literally and figuratively spent his life marching. He was, I suspected, a man who did nothing without a purpose.

Colin Asperton was a practised host but the dinner was not particularly relaxed. We avoided all mention of why DeSmid was in London but it was difficult to keep the conversation off the Border War completely. DeSmid's son, I learned, had been a Parabat and had been wounded while landing near the Culonga River in Angola. 'The enemy were using ZPU-2 14.5mm anti-aircraft guns,' the colonel reported, as if that explained what had happened, 'and Frick got hit. Nothing serious but he won't be jumping out of planes again soon.'

'You must be very proud of him,' commented Asperton.

'Of course. He was awarded the Honoris Cruz, the Cross of Honour.'

Towards the end of the meal when DeSmid had stopped singing the praises of South African wine and we had moved on to brandy he asked me what I thought of the Democratic International at Jamba. I made the mistake of replying that having spent four years on the Defence Intelligence Staff I was not impressed by UNITA as a military force.

Rowbart started to disagree angrily but DeSmid waved him aside. 'UNITA are savages, but they're our savages. And Thomas is right. We can't rely on them. So far this month the Cubans have landed 15,000 new troop reinforcements in Angola and that includes some very experienced pilots. They will completely control the skies and we can't beat them with UNITA and our own Special Ops.'

'So you'll have to pull back,' I suggested. 'Give up Namibia. Bow to sanctions and start dismantling apartheid.'

DeSmid shook his head. 'You sound just like my wife.' His smile was belied by an edge to his voice. Sounding just like his wife was clearly not something he appreciated. 'We're not talking about apartheid. You English think it's all about the blacks. But look at our Special Ops troops in Angola. The

Recces, Parabats, 32 Battalion, the best soldiers in the world and half of them are black.'

'With white officers,' I interjected.

'Black and white working together,' DeSmid continued as if I hadn't spoken. 'That's the future of South Africa. But it will take fifty years to get there, probably a lot more. It took the white man centuries. You can't rush these things. The country's simply not ready for this one man one vote nonsense. Remember the Dutch arrived in the Cape before the Zulus. The white man built this country and now Mandela wants to take it away. If we lose Angola completely the terrorists and the Russians will take over in Windhoek and then they'll come for us. Whatever it takes that has to be stopped.'

Before I could respond Asperton fired me a dirty look as if I had started the conversation. He announced that while this was a fascinating subject he would have to draw the evening to a close. It was time for him to tend to his wife. I had better do the same.

I hoped Julia had enjoyed Mrs Asperton's theatre tickets. She had.

'Michael Crawford's voice is quite amazing,' she told me when I arrived home. 'And Rosemary DeSmid was absolutely charming.'

'No awkward political discussions?'

'No, not at all. Rosemary says she always avoids politics when in England, she has relations here including her daughter. We talked about theatre, she was here in the summer and agreed that Judi Dench's Cleopatra was just brilliant. And of course we talked about our families. She would love to meet you, she seems to imagine that British

130

Intelligence is full of gentlemen spies. I suspect her husband has told her far more about what he's doing here than he should have done. You know her son Freddy was injured in Angola?'

'Yes her husband mentioned that. He called his son Frick, he's obviously very proud of him.'

'And so is his mother. She just wants the Border War to end. She's a war child herself, born in Gloucestershire. Her parents emigrated as soon as the war was over, to avoid the rationing Rosemary says. They settled in Port Elizabeth where she met Hendrik DeSmid. Bowled over by a handsome young officer. She was sixteen when they met and eighteen when they married.'

'I wonder what her parents thought of that. He must've been seven or eight years older.'

'That's just what I asked her. Looking back Rosemary is sure her mother would have preferred a pukka English gentleman but she didn't say anything at the time. Life might have been different if she had. Apparently her mother was very English and Hendrik was an Afrikaaner of course. But he had played rugby for the local team, the Crusaders, and that was enough for her father.'

DeSmid had clearly been a determined young man and that had not changed. The next day he dismissed any suggestion that he might need the sort of security Pinheiro demanded. The South African would drive to RAF Northolt with only Turk Rowbart and his sweeper.

The security for Pinheiro was more complicated. He would be accompanied by his sweeper and both of his bodyguards, one of whom would act as his driver. Two Diplomatic Protection Group officers would lead the way in an unmarked car, the usual red DPG vehicles were considered far too conspicuous.

When I left the office on Friday evening everything seemed to be going according to plan. Turk had disappeared to a meeting at the Ministry of Defence after lunch and when Felicity Macnamara returned from Fort Monckton she joined him. They hadn't reappeared by the time I left. Pinheiro's meeting at the Foreign Office had apparently been 'fruitful' and he had departed for Harrods before meeting his daughter for lunch.

When the doorbell went at 9.30 that Friday evening my first concern was that the noise would wake Eveline. Only when Julia opened the door to find two strangers standing in the pouring rain, one waving a warrant card, did it occur to either of us that something might be wrong.

'Mrs Dylan?'

'Yes.'

'Is your husband in? He's wanted at his office. Right away.'

I heard Julia ask 'What for?' as I came to the door.

'I can't say ma'am.' And then to me. 'If you could accompany us sir. We wouldn't want to keep Mr Brasenose waiting.'

Behind me I could sense Julia's startled reaction. She knew Justin Brasenose but she also knew that he had moved on to the Cabinet Office Joint Intelligence Committee. If he was sending policemen to knock on our door this was serious. What the hell was happening?

It felt like I was being arrested.

# XI

We were in a meeting room on the top floor of Century House. Outside the storm was still beating against the windows. I wondered if the tape recorder would pick up the sound of the rain.

I hadn't seen Brasenose for more than two years, since he moved from Century House to the Cabinet Office.

I remembered sitting in his office drinking Lagavulin and discussing Adam Joseff's plans for Exodis. The most obvious change in the man since then was an increase in his shirt size. Brasenose had always been a big man but when I first met him more than a decade earlier he might have been described as sleek: sturdy would be the most charitable description now. His exquisitely tailored suit could no longer hide an incipient paunch. Life in the Cabinet Office was obviously to his taste, quite literally. Brasenose liked his food.

Within the Service he was no longer fully regarded as 'one of us'. I had heard Asperton bitingly remark that in moving closer to the intrigues of Whitehall and Westminster Brasenose had replaced service to Mars the god of war with service to Janus the god of the two faced.

'Sit down Thomas.'

Brasenose sat across the table from me, beside him a man I didn't know and who hadn't been introduced sat pen in hand. Perhaps someone was worried that the rain would make my words on the tape inaudible.

'Sorry to seem so formal but there's been an incident. I wanted your input.'

'What sort of incident?'

'We'll come to that. I have a few questions first. Last Monday. Care to take me through the day?'

'Last Monday?' I couldn't remember anything suspicious happening but clearly something had caused tremors strong enough to reach the Cabinet Office. 'Nothing special happened. Colin Asperton had his monthly catch-up. Then I left early, I had to look after my daughter.'

'A little more detail perhaps. Let's start with what time you left home.'

'Eight o'clock.'

'Your wife can corroborate that I assume.'

'No. Julia had already left.'

'Can anyone else corroborate?'

'I dropped my daughter with a friend at exactly eight, as arranged. She took Eveline to school for me.'

'And when was that arrangement made?'

And so it went on.

I had worked closely with Brasenose over the years and I knew that when he said detail he meant detail. He had once interviewed me after an aborted mission in Poland and it was the closest to an interrogation I had experienced outside the training sessions at Ford Monckton. This time he took me through Monday morning in painstaking detail, all the time posing his questions in a tone of mild disbelief.

'And you didn't visit the gents even once?' he asked at one point.

'I don't think so. Do you remember every pee you take?'

He allowed himself a weak smile. 'Just trying to get the full picture. Now you say you left here at around 11.45 and took the afternoon off. You do that often?'

'No.'

'You agreed it with Turk in advance?'

'No. It didn't seem necessary for a few hours. There was nothing in particular happening in the office, nothing that Felicity couldn't cover.'

Brasenose raised an eyebrow. 'An American plane had been shot down and Salvador Pinheiro was about to arrive.'

'True. But there was nothing I could do about either.'

I wasn't going to let him get me rattled but I was getting tired of pointless questions. I knew Brasenose well enough to be blunt. 'What's this about? You didn't call me in because I may have taken some time off without getting the right signature first.'

Brasenose merely continued as if I hadn't spoken. 'Let's move on to the afternoon shall we? What did you do when you left here?'

His questions became ever more detailed. He wanted evidence. Had anyone seen me arrive home or leave again? Who could confirm the time that I had arrived at the school? Who else was on the trip? Who was in charge? Would she confirm I was with the group the whole time? Anyone else? Name? Address? The man beside him scribbled madly. Who had Julia visited in the Isle of Man? When had that visit been arranged? Who could confirm that? When had the school trip been announced? When had I volunteered to accompany the children?

'Let's take a break,' he suggested at last. The other man

left the room and Brasenose stood up and looked out over London.

'You know we'll check everything you've said?'

I didn't reply.

'What will we find?' he asked.

'You'll find everything I said stacks up. Perhaps then you'll tell me what this is all about.'

For a moment he didn't reply. 'Yes I'm sure everything will, as you put it, stack up. But we need to be certain.'

'Has someone made allegations about me?'

'No, not directly. We're still at a very early stage. But your actions could be interpreted as odd. I don't recall you suddenly taking an afternoon off before.' He returned to the table and sat down. 'The thing is Thomas there's been a leak. From your Desk. John Darwyn sent in a report on a planned South African raid called Operation Mango. There is a suggestion that the Angolans got hold of Darwyn's report. The operation went wrong. The enemy knew the South Africans were coming and cleared out of the way. The paras ended up with nothing to ambush.'

'And you think that was because Darwyn's report had been leaked? Surely it's far more likely that somebody down there got hold of the paras' plans. It's not the first time that's happened.'

'No it's not. The South Africans claim to have a source in Luanda who says Pinheiro has been forewarned about other South African Special Ops. But this time the leak was in London. We know that. With Pinheiro coming to London and possible peace talks in the offing Angola has been moved up GCHQ's priority list. They've been monitoring traffic to and from the Angolan Embassy. Last Monday they intercepted a message from the Embassy to Luanda. It wasn't decrypted immediately and when it was the significance wasn't immediately obvious. The cable contained details of a planned South African parachute drop in the region of Cassinga.'

'Operation Mango.'

'Exactly. Operation Mango. GCHQ assumed the Angolans must have a source inside the South African High Commission in London. After consulting our friends in MI5 and a phalanx of Foreign Office mandarins details of the cable were passed on to Pretoria. That stirred up a proverbial hornets' nest. The South Africans insisted that nobody at the High Commission here knew anything about Operation Mango. The leak couldn't have come from there. In fact they couldn't understand how anyone in London could have found out about the raid. They've tightened security considerably since the Argon fiasco. We couldn't very well admit that our Station Chief in Pretoria had managed to get the details of what was supposed to be a highly secret operation and then sent them here. The upshot is that they demanded that we conduct an urgent investigation.'

'So that's what you're doing.'

'Quite. The obvious first step was to ask who in London might have known about Operation Mango.'

'And the answer was us.'

'Of course. And specifically the answer was the Service's Subsaharan Africa Desk.'

'Or to be even more specific,' I suggested. 'You thought the leak could come from me.'

Brasenose didn't disagree. 'You know as well as I do that field reports are sensitive and access is strictly controlled,' he said. 'We've established that only six people had access, or could have had access, to John Darwyn's report. The Registry clerk who received it, Colin Asperton, Turk Rowbart, his secretary, Felicity Macnamara and you.'

'Except that I wasn't here. The report hadn't arrived by the time I left.'

'In fact it had. The log shows that it was received in Century House at 10:47. You didn't leave the building until 11.45. Your meeting with Asperton finished at 11.30. It would only have taken someone an instant to note down when the raid was going to take place and its targets.'

I couldn't believe it. 'You really think one of those six people is a mole of some kind?'

'That would be the obvious conclusion. But there is a slight problem with that assumption.'

I waited for him to explain but he remained silent. This was unreal. Why would any of us leak Darwyn's report to the Angolans? And something else struck me.

'Why are you telling me this?' I asked. 'Why mention the GCHQ intercept. That's the sort of thing you should be keeping up your sleeve. If you think one of us leaked Darwyn's report you shouldn't be telling us how you found out. You should be trying to convince us you've got a source somewhere, perhaps even in the Angolan Embassy, and that it's just a matter of time before the guilty man, or woman, is uncovered.'

This time a broad smile crossed Brasenose's face. 'I trained you well Thomas. Nobody else asked me that.'

'So I'm not the first to be interviewed.'

Again he smiled. 'No we've seen everyone who had access to that report. One of my people is down in Kent now interviewing Rowbart's secretary. She's the last.'

So that's why Rowbart and Macnamara were needed at the Ministry of Defence this afternoon.

For a moment Brasenose said nothing, his smile disappeared. 'I don't think anyone on that list passed Darwyn's report on,' he said wearily. 'You see Thomas there is a major problem with all of this. As I said Darwyn's report was logged into Century House at 10.47. The GCHQ intercept was at 09.58.'

It took me a moment to take that in. The Angolan Embassy in London had known about Operation Mango before we did. Darwyn's report couldn't have been the source of the intelligence the Embassy had sent to Luanda, unless the monitoring log at GCHQ or the communications log at Century House were wrong. And that was out of the question.

'So how did the details of a raid being planned in South Africa end up at an embassy in Marylebone if it didn't come from that report?' I asked.

'Well the suggestion has to be that someone saw Darwyn's report before it was logged at Century House.'

'But that's impossible,' I objected. 'Security procedures for incoming cables are absolutely watertight. The time in the log is the time it was received and the time it was sent. There's no way Darwyn could have sent the message an hour before we received it. The Angolans couldn't have seen that report before we did.'

Brasenose hesitated just a second and then looked directly at me. 'Turk Rowbart disagrees. He believes there is one way the Embassy could have seen the report first: John Darwyn could have sent it to them. Or he could have sent it to you.'

'That's mad!'

'Is it Thomas?'

He let the question hang in the air before answering it himself. 'Yes of course it's mad. I knew that before you arrived tonight. I could have avoided all this.'

'But process is process,' I interjected.

'No not that. I knew it was mad because I know you. I've gone out on a limb before, you know that, backed my own judgement when people start throwing allegations around.' He was referring to the time the Americans had wrongly accused one of our Station Chiefs in Eastern Europe of being a Soviet agent. 'But people change Thomas. We're still obsessed with men like Kim Philby and Guy Burgess, lifelong Communists who started working for the Russians at Cambridge. But if we've got moles in the Service now they won't be that generation. They'll be loyal, devoted servants of the Service who get turned – blackmailed, bought, betrayed not by ideology but by greed or fear.'

'And you think that could have happened to me?'

He had spoken seriously but there was a flicker of a weak smile. 'Of course not. You forget, I've worked with your wife, she wouldn't let that happen. You're a strong team. But we can't take risks. Go home now. I want everyone in tomorrow. Nine o'clock. It's time to put our heads together.'

He didn't suggest a police escort home and I went out to flag down a taxi. At least the rain had stopped. Streetlights were reflecting back from oil-streaked puddles of water and shop windows stared out at empty streets. There was something almost magical about the city at night but tonight I was feeling oddly introspective. Brasenose's questions had unsettled me. I realised I should have been more upset by the interview than I was, he was questioning my loyalty after all. I should be feeling more involved but in fact it made me feel more detached. I tried to think through the implications of his suggestion that Darwyn might have copied his report to the Angolan Embassy. If that was true it was serious. Darwyn was a widely respected member of the Service, chief of the most important station in Africa. Why would he risk his career? Money, I supposed. Surely not ideology. Could Darwyn be a Russian mole? It seemed unlikely but I realised that I didn't really know what drove the man.

Come to that what drove me? I had now been in British Intelligence for thirteen years and until recently had never questioned what that meant. I had doubts in the early days about whether I was suited for the work but I never had doubts about what we were there for. If there had been any doubts my posting in Moscow would have erased them. Britain and British values were worth fighting for and I was doing my part.

But now? What was the Service doing in Africa?

For Turk Rowbart it was all about preventing the whole of Africa sliding into the chaos that was already apparent in much of the continent. It was about keeping the last remnants of western values and western civilisation alive in South Africa.

For Colin Asperton the issues were less cosmic. He simply wanted what was best for Britain. He accepted the Victorian dictum that 'trade follows the flag' and was determined to ensure the British flag flew high. He was instinctively at home with the values of the Empire and for that reason alone had sympathy and admiration for those Europeans whose ancestors had gone out to Africa and built a way of life that could only be envied.

For neither man was apartheid a moral issue. For Rowbart apartheid was instrumental, for Asperton it was incidental, and for both the end of white rule in South Africa would mean the end of the natural order. In that they surely reflected the viewpoint of the Intelligence Establishment.

I was the odd one out. I hadn't taken part in the anti-apartheid demonstrations at university; if I had done, I thought wryly, the positive vetting when I joined the Defence Intelligence Staff would have been a lot more difficult. But I had shared my father's outrage in 1968 when the South African government cancelled the England cricket tour because of the inclusion of the 'coloured' player Basil D'Oliveira in the English team. For me apartheid and the justification of 'separate but equal' was simply intellectually absurd. I had no objection to working with the likes of Colonel DeSmid to protect my country, but was the Subsaharan Africa Desk really doing that? If the entire Desk took a month off would Britain's security be imperilled? Perhaps I was less upset by Brasenose thinking I might be a spy than by him disrupting the weekend Julia and I had planned by calling me in to Century House the next day.

Julia was more philosophical.

'Thomas you're just having a very early midlife crisis. You really wanted to be back in the field not sitting behind a desk in Westminster Bridge Road. Are you sure it's the values of men like Rowbart and Asperton that are making you dissatisfied with the Service? I remember the Station Chief in Moscow going off on appalling rants whenever the subject of Pakistani immigrants came up but you managed to work with him. The Service hasn't changed. Could it be that you're still smarting from getting the Deputy Saddo role instead of a posting to Berlin or Paris and then having to share it with Felicity Macnamara? Not to mention Rowbart dreaming up that half-baked scheme to have you spy on African students in London.'

Perhaps she was right. But I still felt uneasy. Until now all my time in the Service had been preoccupied with the Cold War, fighting an ideological battle. We cultivated agents by selling them dreams of freedom and the other side peddled dreams of worker solidarity. And in that context I could understand why someone like Philby, still remembered by many in the Service, might choose to spy for the Russians. But the idea that there might be someone anywhere in British Intelligence acting as a mole for the Angolans out of ideological conviction was incomprehensible. Rowbart of course would say that the Angolans were just proxies for the Russians, that whoever had leaked the plans for Operation Mango had been a Communist spy. But if the Russians had discovered the plans they would have passed them straight to the Angolans in Luanda. There was no reason for the Russians to use the tiny Angolan Embassy in London as a staging post.

'Something new has come in,' announced Brasenose, when we gathered next morning.

We were in the same meeting room that I had been summoned to a few hours earlier. Brasenose sat at one end of a rectangular conference table with Asperton at the other. A woman I didn't recognise sat on one side. Brasenose introduced her as Sheila West, a colleague from the Secret Service, what the media called MI5. West apologised that her boss had been called away on another IRA scare. Turk Rowbart had positioned himself next to her leaving Felicity Macnamara and me to sit opposite.

'The message GCHQ intercepted had a codeword at the beginning,' Brasenose informed us. 'Presumably the name of the person or organisation the cable was addressed to. It seems that our American colleagues have come across that designation before. Langley believe it's a personal code for our friend Salvador Pinheiro. In their opinion the cable would have been passed directly to him and not to anyone else, not the army, not the president's office, not anyone.'

'Not the Russians?' asked Rowbart. 'Nothing happens in Luanda without the Russians knowing about it.'

'You're right Turk,' conceded Brasenose. 'I should imagine they are monitoring all diplomatic traffic, but they don't have enough people there to do it all themselves. They will have to rely on the locals to some extent, and that means relying on Pinheiro.'

'But does that mean anything?' murmured Asperton softly.

'I've no idea,' replied Brasenose. 'Probably not. Pinheiro will have someone in the Embassy here and that someone received the Mango plans.'

'But not from us,' Asperton commented. 'Nobody in this room had heard about Mango when the Embassy sent the cable to Luanda.'

Rowbart glanced pointedly at me but said nothing. I wasn't putting up with that.

'You knew didn't you Turk? Didn't John Darwyn tell you he was working on a report when you phoned him before the catch-up?'

'He did, but he didn't say what it was about. I told him to concentrate on the plane that had been brought down.'

'I shall interview Darwyn myself,' said Brasenose.

'You're bringing him here?' Asperton asked. 'Nobody told me that.'

'No, I shall go there. I fly down tomorrow evening. We need to review security, see if anyone there could have seen a draft of Darwyn's report. And I want to know how he obtained the Mango plans.'

'I can go with you,' suggested Rowbart.

'No. The Security Service will assist.'

Having MI5 poking around an MI6 Station was going to ruffle a few feathers but it was not unheard of. The common perception that MI5 operates within the UK and MI6 abroad is wrong, MI5 handles counter-intelligence wherever it appears.

'Let's get back to the matter in hand,' said Brasenose firmly. 'Someone in London is sending intelligence on operations in Southern Africa through the Angolan Embassy directly to Salvador Pinheiro. Pinheiro has an agent here. So it is possible that while he is in London he will arrange a meeting.'

'That would be a massive security breach,' suggested Rowbart. 'The Russians would never let him do that.'

Brasenose nodded. 'Of course you're right Turk. But Pinheiro is his own man. The Russians may know nothing about this agent. And in any case we lose nothing by keeping a close watch on Senhor Pinheiro. It may be that he has already met his agent but I don't think so. There has been another change of plan. Pinheiro has now decided that he doesn't require close protection after all. He is spending today with his daughter and insists the Diplomatic Protection Group officers be stood down.

'Over to you Sheila.' He motioned to the MI5 officer

who confirmed that Pinheiro had decided that he didn't want his daughter's birthday celebrations disturbed by British policemen loitering outside.

'We have of course agreed. The DPG withdrew this morning but we have replaced them with discreet surveillance. That will stay in place until Senhor Pinheiro checks out of his hotel tomorrow morning. At that time the DPG will escort him to RAF Northolt. If anything suspicious occurs we will of course let you know immediately.'

'We need our own people on this,' insisted Rowbart.

Asperton nodded but Brasenose wasn't going to have any inter-agency squabbling. 'The decision has already been made, today's arrangements are in place. Tomorrow is different. I understand you will be taking Colonel DeSmid and his sweeper to Northolt, Turk. I suggest Thomas or Felicity accompany Senhor Pinheiro.'

When the meeting was over Felicity and I tossed a coin. I lost. I would be giving up Sunday morning. Julia was not going to be happy.

The next morning I took the Tube to Lancaster Gate and found the two DPG officers in the hotel lobby, their jackets discreetly buttoned to hide their weapons. In those days they carried Smith & Wesson revolvers. As usual when meeting people outside the Service I had taken one of my fake IDs, this one in the name of Thomas Williams and bearing the Foreign & Commonwealth Office logo with the meaningless inscription Procurement Directorate.

One of the officers introduced himself as Murdoch and cursorily inspected my ID.

'Don't see you buggers at the sharp end very often,' he told me cheerfully.

I said nothing.

'There's been another change of plans,' he continued. 'Pinheiro's daughter is going to drive him. She should be here any minute. We'll lead the way and his goons will follow behind.

'I'll go and sit in the car,' I told Murdoch. 'I don't need Mariana Pinheiro seeing me.'

'Suit yourself,' Murdoch replied, tossing me a set of car keys. 'It's a black Sierra, the number's on the key. We should be out in ten or fifteen minutes.'

The hotel car park only had space for thirty vehicles, all but one occupied by cars considerably more expensive than a Ford Sierra. I sat in the back seat and radioed Rowbart who had told me to let him know when I arrived at the hotel. He had already picked up DeSmid and his sweeper.

'Keep me posted,' he instructed.

He called again half an hour later to check that we were on our way and as he did the two DPG officers appeared.

'Pinheiro's daughter was late,' Murdoch told me. 'Would you believe she said it didn't matter, we could make up time by using the blue light and the siren. I told her speed limits are there for everyone.' His companion grinned at this unlikely assertion.

We waited for Pinheiro's two bodyguards to clamber into a huge black Mercedes before we set off. They were accompanied by a lanky white man who I assumed was Pinheiro's sweeper. Mariana Pinheiro had parked outside the hotel entrance and swung into place behind us as we drove out of the hotel, Salvador Pinheiro at her side. The convertible's roof was up and there was no sign that she noticed me. The black Mercedes brought up the rear.

We turned on to Westbourne Terrace, in some ways one of the grandest of London's mid-nineteenth-century avenues. The majestic Italianate four-storey stucco houses set so far back from the road that they seem oblivious to the four lanes of traffic constantly jolting past. We stopped at the traffic lights at the junction with Cleveland Terrace. An instructor at Fort Monckton had told us never to halt at traffic lights because stopping made things easier for killers and kidnappers. Fortunately that was not a concern in London.

We pulled away from the traffic lights, keeping in the left-hand lane to avoid the traffic turning right into Bishop's Bridge Road and passing the bright red pillar box on the corner of Cleveland Terrace.

As I told the investigation afterwards I observed nothing at all out of the ordinary about the pillar box. Like the two DPG men I hadn't noticed that attached to it was a rectangular metal object painted the same pillar box red. Even if I had seen it I would have paid no attention. It could have been a stamp vending machine or something similar. I certainly wouldn't have imagined it could be a bomb.

# XII

The explosion happened as we started accelerating away from the lights. It came from behind us. The rear window blew in. Shards of glass flew everywhere. The Sierra slewed to one side and hit a car that happened to be beside us.

The police driver, Faversham, seemed to be wedged into his seat but Murdoch was out in a flash running back towards the Pinheiros' car. My ears were ringing. I heard Murdoch shout, 'Come on.'

I tried to follow him but the seatbelt was jammed. I tugged frantically at the buckle and the whole belt came away at the shoulder. I freed myself and ran after him. The passenger door of Mariana Pinheiro's car wasn't there. It had blown right off its hinges and disappeared.

It was carnage. The DPG Sierra was still recognisable but Mariana's Mercedes was in pieces all over the road.

Murdoch shouted again. 'He's alive.' He was pulling Salvador Pinheiro out of the car on to the roadway when the petrol tank exploded. I was hurled to the ground, my face smashing into the tarmac. I heard a scream and looked up to see Faversham, who had managed to extricate himself from the police Sierra, with flames on his arms and chest. He fell and rolled around on the road. I jumped on top of him to try to douse the flames.

Suddenly there was an ambulance and I was being

pulled aside. I was half conscious of one of the ambulance men asking, 'What the hell happened to the car? It looks like a bomb hit it.' It was only then that I realised exactly what had happened. The bomb must have gone off just as the Pinheiros were passing. Then their bodyguards' Mercedes had slammed into the wreckage.

Uniformed police arrived and another ambulance. Salvador Pinheiro had survived but as he was stretchered into the ambulance he looked more dead than alive. He must have been almost alongside the bomb when it went off. Mariana Pinheiro had stood no chance, although whether she was killed by the bomb itself or by the exploding petrol tank I couldn't tell. In fact it was not obvious that the blackened shape where the steering wheel ought to have been had once been a human being.

Neither of Pinheiro's bodyguards had been wearing seatbelts and one in particular was in a bad way. The sweeper travelling with them emerged from the rear seat without a scratch and stood looking blankly around.

I realised St Mary's Hospital was just around the corner. The first ambulance must have been on the spot in seconds. If Salvador Pinheiro lived he would have pure luck to thank.

Murdoch helped Faversham into an ambulance with the two Angolan security men.

'You go with them,' he told me, 'you need to get yourself checked.' I refused. I needed to stay at the scene. I was feeling shaken, had done something to my hand and had a gash on the forehead where I'd hit the ground but nothing serious. I looked down at my suit, that would have to go.

Turk Rowbart arrived with Colonel DeSmid as Faversham was driven away. When DeSmid reached forward to shake hands I realised that I really didn't want to, the palm of my right hand was badly burned.

'You need that hand treated,' Rowbart said. 'I'll handle things here.'

Murdoch, who had already taken charge and didn't need Rowbart's help, put me into a police car without comment. I was driven to St Mary's where it was confirmed I had no serious injuries. I was about to leave with my hand bandaged and a prescription for painkillers 'if needed' when the police constable who had driven me to the hospital reappeared.

Ten minutes later I was facing a pointless interrogation for the second time in two days. I knew Murdoch had already been interviewed while I was at St Mary's. There was nothing I would be able to add to the DPG officers' account. Nevertheless process is process.

'Just take me through what happened,' said Sheila West when she had switched the tape recorder on. The two of us were alone. 'Any detail you can add may help.'

This time the recorder on the table beside me would have no storm to deal with, just the continuing murmur of the traffic on the Westway below us. We were in the now-demolished Paddington Green Police Station, then considered the most secure police facility in London but more importantly just two minutes from Westbourne Terrace and the scene of the explosion.

I had no problem describing what happened when I arrived at the hotel right up to reaching the traffic lights at Cleveland Terrace. After that events were more blurred but I described them as best I could. West probed gently but firmly. Slowly the details came back.

'And did you speak to anyone at the hospital?' West asked when I had finished. 'What did you tell the staff?'

'Nothing. I just said I was passing by when there was a bang.'

'And you used the name Thomas Williams?'

'Yes.'

'Well stick to that. You talk to anyone else?'

'I phoned my wife, Julia. I didn't want her hearing about the explosion on the news. Although I needn't have worried, she was too busy with our daughter to listen to the radio.'

West moved back in her chair and pushed her hand through her short greying hair. A handsome woman I thought. And unflappable. A century earlier she could have been the wife of a colonial governor, calmly supervising the preparations for dinner while outside hostile natives besieged the fort.

'Will Salvador Pinheiro make it?' I asked.

'I'm told the chances are less than 50/50. In any event he'll never recover fully. His daughter died at the scene. You think he was the target?'

'Of course. Who else?'

'I'm keeping an open mind,' replied West. 'Hopefully Forensics will turn up something useful. Justin Brasenose isn't going to South Africa. He wants us together again tonight. At 20.30, Century House. You'll be needed. We'll have preliminary forensics by then. You'd better go home now,' she added with the hint of a smile. 'You can prepare your claim for a new suit.'

In fact I was at Paddington Green for another half an hour while a formal statement was prepared. It was headed 'Statement from Officer C' and I signed the last page Tom Williams. No doubt even that signature would be redacted before it reached the police's own files.

To my surprise I realised it was barely noon when I left the police station. I took West's advice and went home but first detoured past the scene of the explosion. The roads remained cordoned off causing traffic chaos. The police Sierra had been removed but what was left of the two Mercedes was still blocking the intersection between Cleveland Terrace and Westbourne Terrace. The cast-iron base of the pillar box was gaping open. I noticed the passenger door of the Mercedes convertible lying in the road. Forensic teams were on their hands and knees sifting through the wreckage and searching a wide surrounding area. Uniformed police were keeping curious onlookers away.

It seemed obvious to me that Pinheiro had been targeted. It was also clear that there was no way anybody could time the bomb to explode at exactly the right moment. Therefore the bomb had been remotely controlled. We would surely have noticed any wires and so we were dealing with a radio-controlled bomb, not something you could buy off the shelf in London. The bomber must have had a clear line of sight and there were half a dozen places he could have been positioned. On both sides of the road there were parking areas in front of the houses, separated off from the road itself by small hedges. He could have stood there and then walked off towards Paddington Station. Or he could have been parked further back down Westbourne Terrace and driven off towards Bayswater Road.

It only needed to be a small explosion. We were bound to be in the left hand lane, Pinheiro in the passenger seat couldn't have been more than a few feet away. It was a miracle he had survived.

If the explosion had happened just a second or two earlier

it would have been me in the hospital, or more probably the mortuary. I had once before been near an exploding bomb. That one had killed a CIA agent and I still had dreams about it. This time the shock was just as great. My mother once told me that during the Blitz in Plymouth life had just carried on but I never really believed that was possible. Perhaps if you were expecting something like that your reactions were desensitised. But this was London. It was totally unexpected. Although the DPG was there to provide protection I had never seriously thought that protection was needed. We had been pandering to the paranoid fantasy of a police state thug.

On the Tube London life continued as if nothing had happened, although other passengers glanced warily at my scarecrow-like appearance. I should have taken a taxi. The sense of unreality I had felt in Westbourne Terrace returned when I arrived home. Once Julia had checked that I really wasn't badly injured she naturally wanted all the details. I told her everything I knew but the big question remained: who did it? Did the Angolan rebels really have the capability to mount an attack like that in London? They were hardly capable of mounting operations in Angola without American or South African support.

'Poor Mariana,' Julia concluded. 'I didn't warm to her but nobody deserves to die like that, and so young. I must try to get hold of Adam. He will be devastated.'

Adam Joseff had returned from Taiwan and for the first time anyone could remember announced that he needed a holiday. He had left Julia the number of his hotel in Venice but before she could phone he called her. As Julia expected he was clearly shaken. One of Cristóvão Taravares' daughters had come to London for Mariana's birthday party and had given her father the news. He in turn had called Adam. Julia was going to pass the phone to me when I signalled not to and I heard her tell Adam I was not in. Adam was a friend but at this stage I was wary about anyone knowing anything that was not already on the television news, least of all that someone from my Service was only feet away from the explosion.

'Adam's going to come home,' Julia told me when she put the phone down. 'Cristóvão Taravares is travelling and has asked Adam to check that his daughter is OK. Apparently she was quite close to Mariana. I wouldn't have thought Venice was really Adam's scene anyway.'

I tried to turn my thoughts away from the explosion by banishing all thoughts of Westbourne Terrace. The weather was cold but clear and we decided to take our daughter to the local park. Eveline was now five and had inherited her mother's conviction that her bike, like her mother's MG, had to be driven at full speed. As I chased after her I remembered wistfully those days when a walk to the park had merely meant learning through constant repetition, and at inordinate length, that the wheels on the bus go round and round, round and round.

Reassuringly life was returning to normal. Talking about the weather reminded me that Julia's uncle was organising a family gathering in Majorca to celebrate his seventieth birthday. A nice idea but I suspected March was not the best time to visit Majorca. 'Can't you persuade him to try the Caribbean instead,' I suggested. Julia merely laughed.

I told her about Sheila West and we discussed how the appearance of a senior female officer from a rival service was likely to go down in the solidly male sanctums of Century

House. That in turn led us on to the subject of her own career. Adam Joseff had promised her real responsibilities at Exodis but she was working with three very traditional men. When he returned from Taiwan Joseff had passed her a pile of barely legible notes to 'tidy up' before disappearing to Italy. Richard Mendale phoned from Washington to say that he was staying on to give a guest lecture at a security symposium and therefore she would need to rearrange the meeting she had spent two months setting up. And Sir Jonathan Craverse was busy congratulating himself on the assignment he had secured in the Isle of Man by promising a completion date that Julia would struggle to meet.

'They have a lot to learn,' she concluded. 'But I'll whip them into shape.'

That I could believe. Her world seemed suddenly a lot more real than mine. By the time we had put Eveline to bed, grabbed a hurried meal and ordered a taxi the earlier events in Westbourne Terrace seemed quite surreal.

I looked at the clock as I logged in to Century House. It was exactly twelve hours since I had arrived at the Royal Lancaster Hotel for my first, and last, sighting of Salvador Pinheiro.

Brasenose wasted no time on pleasantries.

'Well Sheila, what the hell happened? Who is responsible?'

'We can't be sure. First indications are an IRA splinter group.'

'What!' Asperton couldn't contain his astonishment.

'There was a warning, twenty-four hours before. Using known channels in Belfast.'

'And what exactly did the warning say?' demanded Brasenose.

'The caller claimed to represent a new group, the Six

Counties Liberation Army, and said they would be sending an explosive message to London in the mail.'

'Recognised codeword?'

West hesitated. 'Yes, but not one used for a while. The method is a bit antiquated too. Forensics don't quite know what to make of it. Radio controlled as you know and a type developed by the IRA in South Armagh in the mid-seventies. When Adams reorganised the IRA command structure in 1976 we started seeing it used more widely but it's quite old-fashioned now. We've found ways to jam it but of course nobody was trying to jam anything in Westbourne Terrace.'

'And the explosive?'

'Semtex.'

'That's not antiquated.'

'No the explosive itself is much more recent. Czech-made. We know the IRA received five tons of the stuff from Libya in October last year, but lots of other unpleasant people have it as well. We're guessing that this Six Counties group has something to do with the IRA's old South Armagh Brigade. They were an evil bunch but between us and Gerry Adams we thought their teeth had been drawn.'

'So theory one,' concluded Brasenose, 'Irish Republicans. What do we think of that?'

'Just three weeks ago today the IRA bombed the Remembrance Day service in Enniskillen,' pointed out Rowbart. 'It's got to be possible that they want to bring that carnage to the mainland. A random attack. Pinheiro was in the wrong place at the wrong time.'

'Nonsense,' I responded. 'The bomber must have seen Pinheiro's car. You wouldn't bother with radio control if you didn't care when the explosion happened. It was targeted. This was professional. Painting the bomb casing red and then attaching it to the letterbox, why go to such lengths just to create a random explosion? They could've put a bomb in the letterbox and been miles away when it went off.'

'So what's your theory?' asked Brasenose.

'Someone didn't want Pinheiro to meet DeSmid. I don't know who. UNITA, the South Africans, a faction in his own politburo, the Russians.'

'Why would the Russians want Pinheiro dead?'

'I don't know, that's what we need to investigate. I don't know who planted the bomb or why but it was aimed at Salvador Pinheiro.'

I realised how weak my argument might sound but the idea that this had just been some random act of terrorism simply did not make sense.

Brasenose turned to Sheila West. 'What do you think?'

'I agree with Dylan that using a radio-controlled weapon for a random attack would be unusual. But I don't see how this could have been targeted. The route was only agreed a few days ago. Who knew Pinheiro would leave the hotel at that hour? Who knew which direction he would be driving in? Who knew he would be in his daughter's car? I'm trying to keep an open mind but my money is on this Six Counties group.'

'Well if it is them that's your bailiwick,' replied Brasenose. 'The Home Secretary is already fending off questions about security levels in London, if the press find out we may have had a warning all hell's going to break loose. But at this stage we can't close any line of enquiry.' He looked across at Colin Asperton. 'While Sheila's concentrating on the Irish angle Colin I want your people to work on the assumption Pinheiro was the intended victim. It's now your top priority. Forget everything else, including the Operation Mango leak, I'll deal with that. The Angolans will be jumping up and down at the UN blaming it all on us. We better hope that Pinheiro lives. We're lucky that the car was armour plated.'

Rowbart's gasp of surprise mirrored my own.

'Not armour plated,' corrected West. 'They weren't expecting a bomb. It seems the young lady had some bullet proofing added after the car was purchased. Laminated glass, steel plates in the doors. Waste of time really trying to bullet-proof a convertible.'

'Well it may have saved Pinheiro's life,' commented Brasenose.

I remembered a comment Mariana Pinheiro had made when she visited our house. 'Mariana Pinheiro told me her car was too heavy. I thought she was talking about the steering.'

'You didn't report that,' snapped Rowbart.

'What difference would it have made if I had?'

Before Rowbart could reply Asperton brought the discussion to an end in the traditional civil service manner. 'We'll have a submission for you tomorrow Justin, midday. A piece on everyone who might have wanted to kill Salvador Pinheiro.'

Brasenose nodded. 'I suppose there's no chance someone else was the target. Mariana Pinheiro for example.'

'Unlikely Justin, but we'll look into it.'

We went away to produce the submission Asperton had promised. He and Rowbart decided they would write it themselves and I didn't see it until it had been sent.

Unsurprisingly it contained no new evidence and Asperton was careful not to reach any firm conclusions that might come back to haunt him. Everything was possible but nothing was probable. UNITA had the obvious motive but lacked the expertise. South Africans opposed to the peace process had the expertise but were unlikely to risk operating in London. Infighting within the Angolan regime was possible but why would Pinheiro's opponents stage an assassination attempt abroad? If the Russians had tired of Pinheiro they might relish the chance to embarrass the UK government but there was no evidence that the Russians had tired of Pinheiro, although an operation by rogue KGB elements opposed to Gorbachev's Africa policies could not be ruled out.

The submission then threw in two suggestions I hadn't thought of.

The first was that the IRA were known to have provided assistance to Umkhonto we Sizwe, the African National Congress's military wing. Seven years earlier the guerrillas had carried out their most spectacular attack: blowing up eight enormous fuel tanks at the oil-from-coal refinery at Sasolburg in the Transvaal. Two IRA men 'loaned' by Gerry Adams had carried out the initial reconnaissance. If the ANC discovered that Colonel DeSmid and Pinheiro were meeting to talk peace in London they might have turned to the IRA to stop this happening.

The other suggestion was more intriguing: Marco Mutorwa. The Angolan student was the nephew of a UNITA commander and had been in a relationship with Mariana Pinheiro. That relationship had turned sour but seemed not to have been severed completely. Mutorwa was one of the few people who might be in a position to recognise Mariana and her father and even Mariana's car on a busy street and so would have been able to detonate the bomb at exactly the right time. It was clear to me that Marco could not have planned such a sophisticated attack on his own but Asperton, or more likely Rowbart, had thought of that. UNITA had received training and logistics support from the Chinese, perhaps they were involved.

At the dinner with Cristóvão Taravares Adam Joseff had told me that Mariana's father was worried about his daughter's undesirable boyfriend. I was conscious that I had never reported to Rowbart that the name he had specifically mentioned was Marco Mutorwa. Perhaps Salvador Pinheiro had more reason to worry about Mutorwa's relationship with his daughter than I had thought.

Asperton called me into his office when I had read the submission. He wanted another catch-up, Rowbart was with him. He took my copy of the submission back, security was being tightened now that the horse had bolted.

'My money's still on the Irish,' Asperton said, 'but in case it's not them Turk thought we should pull Mutorwa in. Unfortunately Brasenose wouldn't let us.'

'He doesn't think Mutorwa could be involved?'

'No not that,' Rowbart said in that irritated tone that I had come to realise was his normal way of speaking. 'Brasenose has decreed that all interviews are to be conducted by Sheila West and her team. She interviewed Mutorwa this morning but doesn't think he was involved, even though he had no alibi for when the bomb went off. Said he hadn't got up yet.'

'West's even taken over the Mango investigation,' said

Asperton. 'We've had to fight like hell to get Felicity added to the team West's sent down to South Africa.'

That explained why Macnamara wasn't in the office. As I had met DeSmid I thought it would have been more natural for me to go down to Pretoria. 'I didn't know Felicity had gone down there,' I remarked. My irritation probably showed but Asperton ignored it.

'Turk thought it might be useful to get a fresh pair of eyes.'

'You're too close to John Darwyn,' Rowbart put in.

'I wouldn't say that.'

'You went down to Jamba with him,' Rowbart reminded me. 'You agreed with his conclusions. And you've made no attempt to make him reveal his sources which he ought to be doing as a matter of standard procedure.'

'That doesn't make me a security risk.'

'Nobody's talking about a security risk,' said Asperton quickly. 'Felicity was free and I decided we needed you in case Justin Brasenose changes his mind and lets us have a go at Marco Mutorwa. Bad cop, good cop. Turk interviews him first and then if that doesn't work you might be called upon to play good cop.'

'Perhaps we'll get more out of him than you did before,' suggested Rowbart. 'If we push a bit harder.'

'I pushed as much as you wanted me to push,' I reminded him. 'Operation Studio was supposed to be shallow cover, softly, softly, catchee monkey.'

'But we didn't catch the bloody monkey!' Rowbart stood up and left the room.

'I wanted a quiet word, Thomas,' said Asperton when my boss had left. 'You don't seem altogether happy on the

Subsaharan Africa Desk. The work is perhaps less interesting than your previous roles.'

'Well it's certainly interesting now.'

'Yes that might be true but we mustn't be unduly influenced by what may be a temporary confluence of circumstances. There's been a lot of excitement but the unfortunate incident with Senhor Pinheiro may well be a random act of Irish terrorism. And what Justin Brasenose regarded as a potential breach of security on the Desk over the Operation Mango business no longer seems as serious as he supposed, I understand it is likely that the leak occurred in South Africa. The work of the Desk therefore carries on as before and it is important that the whole team pulls together. Turk is absolutely right that containing Russian ambitions in Africa is crucial to the security of this country. With the Middle East the way it is there must always be a risk to the Suez Canal. If the Reds gain control of the sea lanes around the Cape those risks become intolerable. Everyone on the Desk needs to concentrate on that.'

'I know that.'

'Good. I was sure you would understand.'


'What was he trying to tell you?' asked Julia that evening when I reported Asperton's comments.

'God knows. Asperton can be a pompous arse. I could have been killed by that bomb and to Asperton it was just part of a "temporary confluence of circumstances". I've obviously upset Rowbart, which appears to be an easy thing to do. Felicity tells me that Rowbart is trying to get rid of John Darwyn, he never wanted him in Pretoria in the first place.'

'What's that got to do with you?'

'I don't think it's got anything to do with me. Rowbart just likes doing things his way. Brasenose used to say that in our business we collect thousands of pieces of jigsaw only to discover that when we put the pieces together they don't all come from the same puzzle. The trick is deciding which jigsaw we want to keep. Rowbart doesn't work like that, he decides what he wants the jigsaw to show and then looks for the bits of puzzle that fit.'

'And to extend the metaphor,' said Julia, 'you have to decide whether you're happy with the picture he's chosen.'

'Something like that.'

'Well don't decide today. It's nearly Christmas, let's see what the new year brings.' Then she added encouragingly: 'The way Exodis is going I may need an assistant soon and you could be just the man.'

Despite the accompanying wink I wasn't entirely convinced that Julia was joking.

# XIII

Over the next few days the feverish speculation about the bombing in the press was matched by intense activity by the Metropolitan Police and the Security Service. But the role of my own Service was limited to plaintive requests for relevant intelligence sent to the chief of every MI6 Station in the world. What information I wondered was the Station Chief in Bogotá or Canberra expected to uncover? The main focus naturally was on Pretoria. Felicity Macnamara was told to stay down there to help Darwyn out once West's team had finished their Mango enquiries. I took over her responsibilities in London.

Despite Asperton assuring me that Macnamara had no commitments it seemed that one of her projects, Nighthawk, had suddenly acquired a UK dimension. The Nigerians had recently bought twenty-four Czech-made Albatros jet trainers and were so pleased with them they were considering buying more. That was not good news for us as any Soviet arms sales in Africa were considered dangerous and this sale was particularly worrying as the alternative rejected by the Nigerian Airforce was the British Aerospace Hawk trainer. Clearly a lot of money had changed hands and identifying how much and to whom it had been paid was the top priority of our Lagos Station. Now it seemed one of the key players was coming to London, nominally to promote President

Babangida's privatisation programme, but also we believed to satisfy his passion for gambling.

'If we play our cards right,' Rowbart insisted, oblivious of any potential pun, 'we can surely trap the bastard into something.'

Nighthawk kept me busy and it was Thursday before I learned anything about the bombing that hadn't already been in the newspapers. Rowbart had been fuming about what he regarded as our deliberate exclusion from the investigation and late on Thursday afternoon he and I were invited to the Security Service headquarters which was then in Gower Street. We were shown into another anonymous conference room. Asperton was already there and after a few moments Brasenose appeared with West and one of her team whom she introduced only as Matthew Kelly.

West sat at the head of the table and made clear that this was her meeting. She nodded towards Brasenose, 'Justin has suggested I bring you up to speed with our enquiries but I have to tell you that to date progress has been somewhat limited. Indeed I could say we are little wiser than we were on Sunday evening. You may recall that when Justin pressed me I suggested that early indications ascribed responsibility to an Irish Republican group. That may still be the case but it now seems somewhat less likely.'

'Why?' demanded Rowbart.

'Let us just say that those in my Service with particular experience in this area are highly dubious.'

'So we think Pinheiro was the target,' said Asperton, clearly pleased that his original assumption appeared to have been justified.

'That would seem to be likely.'

'Highly dubious. Likely. What does that mean?' demanded Brasenose. 'Put a figure on it. What's the chance this was Irish terrorism?'

West hesitated. 'There's no supporting intelligence, the IRA have denied all responsibility, the name Six Counties Liberation Army is completely unknown and the codeword used had been compromised, its continued use would be highly unusual. Frankly the whole set-up with the painted bomb casing and radio control is too sophisticated for a random act of terrorism.'

'So less than fifty per cent probability; twenty-five per cent perhaps?'

'Less than ten per cent,' conceded West.

'So it's almost certainly not IRA.'

'Nothing is certain, Justin, you know that.'

'True but we can dismiss the Irish angle for now. Let's move on to the Angolans. What have you found?'

'Well it's early days Justin. Our enquiries are ongoing.'

Brasenose interrupted again. 'We're all friends here Sheila. You know as well as I do that the first twenty-four hours in a murder enquiry are critical. The truth is we're getting nowhere slowly. Now what have we really found?'

West didn't argue. 'We've discovered nothing. The Angolan Embassy have provided nothing. The two bodyguards noticed nothing at the time and nothing suspicious beforehand. According to them Salvador Pinheiro had been acting normally throughout his entire visit. Even changing plans at the last minute and letting his daughter drive him to Northolt was not unusual. Nobody in the hotel saw anything, and nobody in the area saw anything that has been particularly useful. A woman walking her dog claims to have seen a man loitering outside the houses on the opposite side of the street about five minutes before the bomb but can't provide any sort of description except that he wasn't African and he had a brown coat. Of course once the press decided it was Irish terrorism we had lots of sightings of Irish-looking men, whatever that means. The most promising is that a man with an Irish accent and wearing a brown coat and a cap was heard talking to two men in a car outside Paddington Station. But again no useful descriptions, the photofits could fit half the male population of London. One of the men in the car may have replied with an Eastern European accent. Everything else has been a dead end like the woman with an Irish accent who stopped to help right after the bomb went off and then left the scene. We eventually traced her and discovered she's a nurse at St Mary's with no possible connection to all this.'

'You interviewed Marco Mutorwa,' said Rowbart.

'We've interviewed every student on the list you gave us,' West replied, 'starting with Mutorwa. We've interviewed him twice. As we told you on Monday he claims he was asleep at the time.'

'Witnesses?'

'No.'

'Did you search his flat?'

'Not yet, we have him under surveillance. Yesterday Matthew here interviewed him for a second time.'

She turned to the man beside her who spoke for the first time.

'We wanted to follow up some of the points in the Operation Studio reports you gave us. I pressed him about his relationship with Mariana Pinheiro. He became very defensive, said we should ask Tommy.' He glanced in my direction. 'He admitted that he had enjoyed an intimate relationship with the deceased when they were both studying in Lisbon and that she had visited him here. But he insisted that they hadn't seen each other since she came to study in London. I next asked him about his use of the phone box in Byng Place. He was clearly startled by that line of questioning and at first he just stonewalled, simply said he couldn't remember the call you saw him receiving from a call box in Lisbon airport. He was lying of course. And eventually he decided that it didn't matter and opened up.

'He claims he was called by Mariana Pinheiro. At the time she was still in Lisbon. He says she was worried that her father might be intercepting her calls and she didn't want him to discover who she was planning to visit in London. So she told Marco to find a call box and send her the number and a time so she could phone him there when she had finalised her plans.'

That sounded as plausible an explanation as any other. 'Did you ask him why he thought I was a police spy?'

'Yes I did. I've spent twenty-two years in the Service, most of that time questioning people. Mutorwa is not telling us the whole truth. When he's asked a question he wasn't expecting, when there's a sudden change of subject, he slows down. Answers very calmly. He doesn't get rattled, he just pauses. As if he knew that question would come one day and had an answer prepared and is just checking that he's got it exactly right. That's what he did when I asked him about you. He said there were police spies everywhere and that it was obvious you were one because you asked too many questions. I asked who he had discussed that with and he insisted nobody. Nobody had told him and he had told nobody. But somebody told him, he didn't suddenly decide one day that you were a police spy.'

Kelly turned to Rowbart. 'Your report mentions that Mutorwa's uncle is a senior guerrilla leader. That may be but I tell you young Marco is not political. I spend all my time dealing with radicals of one sort or another and he's no terrorist. He's not telling us the whole truth but if he triggered that bomb, which incidentally I think is unlikely, it wasn't for political reasons.'

'He could have been paid,' suggested Rowbart.

'That's possible,' Kelly agreed.

'But who paid him?' asked Brasenose. 'Or was it a crime of passion.'

'Not a crime of passion,' said West. 'This was calculated and well planned. In a matter of days someone found that pillar box and assembled and painted a bomb that could be quickly attached to it. This was cold blooded not hot blooded. Revenge perhaps. Which brings us to Mariana Pinheiro. An interesting young lady and a wealthy one.'

'The benefits of a rich daddy,' Asperton put in.

'Not entirely,' responded Kelly. 'Mariana Pinheiro was clearly keen to make her own way in the world. Tomorrow morning Mr Mutorwa will be interviewed again, but not by us. Not our area of expertise. It seems that in the spring of last year Miss Pinheiro made a rather clever investment on the stock market. As you may be aware a number of people did the same and not perhaps altogether lawfully.'

I caught sight of Rowbart and Asperton exchanging puzzled looks.

'Guinness?' I asked.

'Precisely. Guinness were bidding to buy the Distillers Company and there were a lot of financial shenanigans going on. Some very dodgy characters in the City were up to their neck in them. At one point the Guinness share price suddenly rocketed up. Mariana Pinheiro bought shares at exactly the right time and sold out again almost immediately. She didn't make a fortune, perhaps £40 000, but how did an African teenager living in Lisbon and with apparently no experience on the stock market manage to do that?'

Kelly stopped and looked at us expectantly but none of us said anything. 'Aren't you going to tell us?' Asperton asked eventually.

'I can't. I don't know. But I do know Mariana Pinheiro was in London for just ten days, staying with Marco Mutorwa, and went home £40 000 richer. Our colleagues from the Fraud Squad would like to know how that happened.'

'Thus the further interview tomorrow morning,' put in Sheila West. 'Mutorwa will be picked up first thing and taken to Bishopsgate Police Station. Matthew here will sit in on the interview. We have a warrant to search Mutorwa's premises and unless something unexpected comes up in the interview we will escort him back to his flat and exercise that warrant.'

'We should be there,' said Rowbart. 'We might recognise something.'

'You can rely on us,' insisted West. 'The fewer people trampling around the better. We will bring anything we find back here, including all his papers. You can look at them then.'

Rowbart had to be content with that.

'We've also searched Mariana Pinheiro's flat. We found nothing in the initial search but just to be really sure I sent in a specialist team the next day. There was a little misadventure when we were doing that. Pinheiro had a cousin from Italy staying with her for the weekend, she'd come over for the birthday party. No sooner had my team turned up to search the flat than some chap called Joseff arrived, ex-Defence Intelligence apparently.'

'Who the hell's he?' demanded Rowbart. 'What was he doing there?'

'He said he was a friend of the Italian girl's father. Demanded to see our warrant which hardly seemed necessary in the circumstances. He calmed down eventually and went away. We've sealed the flat off now and you're welcome to go over there. As I say we found nothing there. But we do have an oddity you may be able to help us with. We examined her phone records. We've traced everyone she spoke to in this country. That's turned up nothing. But as I say there is something a little odd. Five very short incoming calls.'

'How short?'

'Very short. All less than thirty seconds. All from different public phone boxes. The first one soon after she moved to London. The last one Monday of last week, 23rd November, at 7.43 in the morning. That one was from Heathrow Terminal 1. We have video tapes from cameras in the terminal but nothing directly of the phone used. No sign of Mutorwa. We're checking every passenger arriving or departing at Terminal 1 about that time, nothing so far. We'll give you the dates and times of all the calls, perhaps they will mean something to you.'

It occurred to me that last Monday's date was certainly familiar, it was the day that Julia had gone to the Isle of Man and, perhaps more importantly, the day Darwyn had sent his Operation Mango report.

'What was Mutorwa doing last Monday?' I asked.

'That's another strange thing. Like I say we checked the video around 7.43 and no sign of him but he was there later. He spent the weekend in Lisbon and arrived back on Monday evening. That's confirmed by the way, no doubt at all.'

'What was he doing in Lisbon?'

'He went to a party,' answered Kelly quickly. The MI5 man then added more reflectively, 'When you're interviewing someone you learn to sense when they're holding something back, perhaps embroidering the truth. He was doing that when I asked about his phone calls. But not when we got on to that weekend. He fell over himself to be helpful. Details of every single minute he was out of the country. And our Portuguese colleagues have made a few enquiries. Everything ties up.'

'As if he was making sure he had an alibi,' I suggested.

'Perhaps,' agreed Kelly dubiously. 'But what for? It's the next weekend he needs an alibi for, when the bomb went off.'

That was true, the only thing that had happened when Mutorwa was in Lisbon was that the CIA proprietary had been shot down and he certainly had not done that.

'Creating an alibi for the wrong weekend might suggest he had nothing to do with the bombing,' I commented.

'How do you figure that out?' snapped Rowbart. 'It suggests Mutorwa is a devious little sod who is up to his neck in something.'

'But he didn't try to set up an alibi for the time of the bombing,' I replied.

'Of course not, he couldn't set up an alibi somewhere else because he was in Westbourne Terrace.'

Kelly intervened again. 'It's not at all unusual that if someone has been hiding something then when they get on to an area where they have nothing to hide they overcompensate with extraneous detail. I don't think we can assume that Mutorwa was trying to set up an alibi in Lisbon.'

We had to leave it at that. I had expected a longer meeting, usually Brasenose dived ruthlessly into the detail. He didn't this time and I suspect that West had been briefing him regularly since the explosion occurred. The meeting had not been for West to brief people but for Brasenose to see how we reacted to her findings and the revelation that Irish terrorism could be discounted. He had a final request to make.

'There's one person's perspective on all this that I'm still a little unclear on. I mentioned it at the JIC this morning and your Chief agreed. I wonder Colin if you wouldn't mind bringing John Darwyn back for a few days. If he returned at the weekend you could have some time with him on Monday and perhaps drop me a note if anything new emerges. In fact,' he added as an apparent afterthought, 'perhaps he could pop into the Cabinet Office on Tuesday, say nine o'clock.'

'Certainly Justin, excellent idea. We'll be there at nine.'

'Oh no need to put yourself out Colin. There's likely to be an early morning Cobra meeting and I could get delayed, I wouldn't want to keep you hanging around. Just tell John Darwyn to ask for me.' Before Asperton could respond Brasenose added, 'And there's another visitor due as well. Salvador Pinheiro's brother-in-law is coming to see him, although the hospital reports that it's still touch and go whether Salvador Pinheiro will live. Martim Vasconcelos arrives on Sunday.'

'I hope we have better security this time,' said Rowbart.

'I understand Vasconcelos is not in the same league as his brother-in-law,' responded Sheila West. 'A Deputy Oil Minister. The Foreign Office have requested no special security measures.'

'On your head be it.'

'If you have any reason to think otherwise say so,' said Brasenose but Rowbart merely shook his head.

After the meeting Rowbart decided that we needed to emphasise that we were not going to be excluded from the investigation. We should therefore take up West's invitation to examine Mariana Pinheiro's flat. As he knew we wouldn't find anything West's team hadn't already *discovered* he sent me.

I spent an hour there marvelling at the contrast with my own student days. The stereo equipment alone must have cost a small fortune. MI5 had left the flat ready to be turned over to her next of kin. Mariana's papers had all been bagged up, taken away, photocopied and then returned. There weren't many, she had certainly not been a conscientious student.

A top of the range leather-bound Filofax ring-binder served as her diary, address book, shopping list and miscellaneous notebook. She hadn't actually used it very much. The only pages that showed real signs of wear were the inserts with London street and tube maps. Most of the diary pages were empty or with a scrawled Christian name. No doubt West's people would have already pored over every page. I looked at the last few weeks. An entry from a week earlier, the day Salvador Pinheiro arrived in London, caught my eye, the single word '*papochka*'. I wondered what West had made of that. Mariana Pinheiro had been born in Russia and so perhaps it was not surprising that she used a Russian word for her father. But *papochka* isn't the usual term for father, it probably best translates as daddy. For an assertive, self-confident twenty-year-old girl to refer to her father as *papochka* implied a degree of affection that seemed to belie her assertion that she was 'not close' to her father.

I noticed something else looking at the Filofax. Next to 21st November, a couple of days before her father's arrival, she had drawn what my old maths teacher would have called a rhombus but what most people would describe as a diamond. That was the day the CIA proprietary had taken off from Jamba on its last flight. I went right through the Filofax to see if I could find any other diamond shapes. There was only one: a diamond had been drawn for 19th November, two days before, but then scrawled through.

I bumped into Asperton when I returned to the office and told him what I had found.

'We must tell Turk,' he insisted, marching into Rowbart's office to announce that I had discovered 'two rhombi' in Mariana Pinheiro's diary. I half expected Rowbart to dismiss the diamond shapes as meaningless but he didn't.

'It can't be a coincidence,' he insisted. 'She knew when that plane was leaving Jamba. I'll bet it was originally scheduled to leave on the nineteenth and was delayed for some reason. I'll check with Frank Cato.'

'You could check with John Darwyn,' I said but Rowbart ignored me, other than to tell me he wanted a written report on my progress with Nighthawk the next day, before I went home for the weekend.

When I approached his office with my report the next

afternoon the door was open and Asperton was standing inside. He beckoned me in.

'Good news Thomas,' he greeted me.

'We've got the bastard,' added Rowbart. 'We've found the radio control for the bomb. In Marco Mutorwa's flat.'

'We found what may be the control,' corrected Asperton. 'It's certainly very similar to radio controls used by the IRA to detonate devices in Northern Ireland.'

'And Marco denied all knowledge of it,' Rowbart continued. 'He hasn't even tried to pretend he used it to control model planes or something like that. The idiot just said he'd never seen it before.'

'Could that be true?' I asked.

'Of course not. He triggered that bomb when he saw Mariana Pinheiro driving past. No doubt at all. The control was under his bed.'

'Why on earth did he keep it? He's had nearly six days to dispose of it.'

'How the hell do I know?' snapped Rowbart. 'Perhaps he was planning another bomb. What's the matter with you? We've got him. West found a map with Mutorwa's fingerprints all over it and a cross right on the spot where that pillar box stood.'

It sounded convincing, perhaps too convincing.

Asperton at least was convinced. 'You will remember Thomas that in my submission to the Joint Intelligence Committee I suggested that Mr Mutorwa was the person most likely to be responsible for the explosion on Westbourne Terrace. That of course was in direct contradiction to our friends from across the river who were clinging to the suggestion that an Irish Republican group might be responsible. My hypothesis would now appear to be confirmed and I'm grateful for the efforts of everyone on the Desk. We should all be proud of our work this week.'

With that he left the room and I was left marvelling that a submission carefully crafted to avoid giving a definitive answer to anything was now being cited as evidence in the constant point scoring between the Secret Service in Gower Street and the Secret Intelligence Service in Century House.

I was still standing by the door. 'Is there anything else?' asked Rowbart.

'The Nighthawk report.'

'Oh that can wait. Mutorwa is our priority. West will have to let us at him now.'

I started to leave but Asperton had been stopped in the corridor by his secretary. He glanced at a slip of paper she passed him and then turned towards us and read it aloud. 'We regret to announce that Salvador Erasmo da Silva Pinheiro, Commissar of Police and member of the politburo of the Communist Party of the People's Republic of Angola, died at seven minutes past four this afternoon in St Mary's Hospital, Paddington.'

# XIV

'You look dreadful,' Julia greeted me that evening.

She assumed I was still feeling the shock of the bomb going off so close to me and that Salvador Pinheiro's death had brought it all back. But that wasn't really true. In reality it was what Asperton would call a confluence of circumstances, epitomised by Asperton himself. His obtuse remarks about my commitment to the Desk still rankled, why couldn't the man just say what he meant? And now the death of two people, one barely twenty-one, was being treated as little more than an opportunity to burnish his own reputation.

There was something deeply unsatisfying about working in an environment where someone as highly educated and clearly intelligent as Colin Asperton devoted so much of his time and effort to what was essentially superficial. I was reminded of a seminar I had attended in my days at the Ministry of Defence. It was at the time of the miners' strike and the Bloody Sunday shootings in Northern Ireland. A senior Home Office mandarin had been asked what was the most serious issue facing the civil service today. She had replied in all seriousness 'the quality of drafting'. Submissions to Ministers, she said, lacked the elegance, elucidation and erudition that were once their distinguishing characteristics. Asperton might well have agreed.

Rowbart on the other hand was from a different tradition:

the can-do task-driven take-no-prisoners school of thinking that was transforming banking and finance but was yet to reach the more arcane corners of Whitehall. He had clearly taken against me, and I still wasn't sure why, but I suspected that he eventually took against most people. Tensions were already starting to creep into his relationship with Asperton. It didn't create an attractive environment to work in.

'We both need to clear our heads,' Julia asserted.

It was one of her favourite phrases and I knew what it often meant: driving down to Cornwall. I wasn't really in the mood for a long drive.

'It's a shame one of Eveline's little friends has a birthday party tomorrow,' I commented, hoping that Julia wouldn't realise I had forgotten the little friend's name.

'It's been cancelled, some sort of bug is going round. Let's go down to Penelowek.'

'Eveline will be awful. It will be 'are we there yet?' every five minutes. She'll demand to be entertained all the way.'

'Of course she won't. We'll wait until her bedtime and just pop her in the car.'

'But it will be well after midnight when we arrive, that's really antisocial. And we don't even know if Anne and Gordon will be there.'

'Oh Aunt Anne said we could arrive at any time. I've got a key. Come on darling, a break from London will do us both good.'

I admitted defeat. If Julia and her aunt had already reached a decision there was no point in my arguing.

'OK, I give in,' I grinned, 'but you can settle Eveline while I drive the first part.'

The last time we had driven down to Cornwall the roads

had been clogged with tourist caravans and farm tractors. Now speeding along the A303 and A30 on a cloudless December night was a pleasure. I could feel myself unwind. Julia had been right.

By the time we reached Stonehenge I had brought Julia up to speed on Sheila West's investigations. I usually found that discussing things through with Julia clarified my own thoughts but this time that didn't seem to work.

'West has ruled out an Irish connection,' I said, 'despite the circumstantial evidence pointing both ways.' Julia smiled, she had been in the Intelligence world long enough to know that the only reason West would rule something like that out was that she had a source in the IRA who had ruled it out for her.

'So Pinheiro was definitely the target.'

'Of course. That was always obvious. Why would the IRA go to all the trouble of making a bomb looking like a pillar box, fitting a remote control, and then just triggering it at random? The question is who knew Pinheiro would be there?'

'And Asperton thinks Mutorwa did?'

'No. He hasn't asked the question. The approach he and Rowbart are taking is find the answer and then look for the proof. And they may be right. West thinks she's found evidence at Mutorwa's flat, but that could easily have been planted. And he can't have done it all on his own. We're nowhere near discovering who helped him and why. We just have to hope that West can get Mutorwa to start talking.'

'So who did know Pinheiro would be driving along Westbourne Terrace on that side of the road at that time in the morning?'

'Well I did.'

'Let's assume it wasn't you.'

'The honest answer is we don't know how many people either father or daughter might have told. Perhaps at Mariana's birthday celebrations the day before.'

Julia considered for a moment. 'That won't do Thomas. That bomb wasn't made overnight. Even the red paint must have taken time to find. This was planned well in advance.'

'But not that far in advance. The meeting with DeSmid was supposed to be at Hanslope Park and if it had been we wouldn't have turned up Westbourne Terrace. The bomb was produced after Pinheiro chose Northolt and somebody reconnoitred the route and realised we would be passing right by that pillar box.'

'But they must have been pretty well prepared. You can't go and buy Semtex off the shelf.'

Julia was right. The bomb was placed at the last minute but the planning must have started much earlier, perhaps before Pinheiro had even arrived in the country.

We relapsed into silence. Somewhere in Devon Eveline woke up and made it clear that nature was calling and 'I'm going to do it now.' After dealing with that she had to be lulled back to sleep with what, for unaccountable reasons, was then her favourite song, 'Lola'. After half an hour repeating 'L-o-l-a Lola' she eventually fell asleep again but it was well past one when we arrived at Penelowek. We crept up the stairs to what was still referred to as Julia's room where the standby cot was waiting beside our bed. Just as welcome were two glasses and a bottle of scotch on the bedside table.

I feared that the Westbourne Terrace bomb would dominate the weekend's conversations but I needn't have worried, Anne Grimspound was not the sort of person to let that happen. Over breakfast she stuck to domestic matters, in particular the implications of her eldest daughter Margaret's announcement that she might not be able to attend Gordon Grimspound's seventieth birthday celebrations in Majorca. Like many American companies the bank she worked for in New York gave its employees ludicrously short vacations and the timing of flights meant she would be flying back almost as soon as she arrived.

After breakfast Aunt Anne insisted on looking after Eveline for the day. 'It will be a treat,' she declared. Despite the biting wind she took our daughter off to explore the rock pools allowing Julia to rescue her MG from the stables. We had an extended lunch in Padstow and returned to Penelowek in time for Eveline's tea. I was surprised to find Adam Joseff there.

I knew that Adam had cut short his holiday in Venice at Cristóvão Taravares' request and gone to see Cristóvão's daughter in London. When she had returned to Italy Adam had evidently come down to his home in Cornwall. He certainly didn't look as if he had just been on holiday. There was a weariness around his eyes and he seemed to have lost weight. I had thought before that he was starting to look his age. Adam was not a big man but he had always carried himself with the rigidly straight back of the parade ground. Now there was a rounding of the shoulders that made him seem less imposing. When he spoke however his voice was as strong as ever.

I was pleased to see him. I hadn't spoken to Adam since our lunch conversation in the pub a couple of weeks before. Although that conversation had not gone well he was a good friend. He had helped smooth out some of my rough edges when I joined the Defence Intelligence Staff and with Exodis he was proving a lifeline for Julia.

Julia had told me about the problems she was having pinning him down recently, with his constant travelling and increasing unreliability when it came to deadlines. Disappearing to Venice without warning had not helped and she hadn't realised he was now intending to spend the next week in Cornwall. But he was still the main reason for the consultancy's success. Julia had shown me the notes he had given her following his trip to Taiwan where the Kuomintang government had recently agreed to allow the opposition to form a legal political party. As later events would show Adam's analysis of the implications was spot on.

'Adam was just telling us about his travels,' Anne informed us before disappearing with Eveline to the kitchen where they had spent the afternoon baking scones.

Julia followed. 'I've heard all about Adam's holiday,' she said. 'I'll be back when Eveline is fed and watered.'

'Can't stay long,' Joseff told Gordon Grimspound, but he was still there when Julia returned. He seemed to have described every canal, church and restaurant in Venice. Julia's uncle was impressed. 'Adam in all the years we've been friends I've never known you take any interest in art or architecture. I had assumed there was a stamp fair in Venice or an old friend you wanted to look up.'

Joseff looked almost embarrassed. 'No nothing like that. I just wanted time to reflect. What are we here for Gordon? What have we accomplished? It used to be so easy. The Nazis were across the Channel. But the war ended more than forty years ago, what have you and I been doing since? Sitting behind a desk in Whitehall propping up a fading empire when we could have been flying to Venice to admire Titian or Tintoretto. The magnificence of the Venetian Empire dazzled the world in its day but nothing lasts. *Pulvis et umbra sumus.*'

We are but dust and shadows. Joseff was the last person I would expect to quote Horace, where had he got that from?

Julia's uncle shook his head. 'That's not you speaking Adam. You've always fought the good fight.'

Joseff looked up and smiled. 'You're right of course. We've all done our duty. But some projects have to remain unfinished. When something utterly senseless occurs, like the murder of Mariana Pinheiro, we're entitled to one small moment of doubt.' He turned to me. 'How's the investigation coming along? She's only been dead six days and the papers have forgotten her already.'

'I don't know,' I replied. 'It's out of our hands.'

'Yes I gather Sheila West is in charge. Has she got the bottle? That's the question.'

'The bottle?'

'To go after the South Africans.'

'You think they planted the bomb?'

Joseff looked at me in surprise. 'Of course they did. Who else? The Angolan rebels couldn't blow up a balloon on their own. But your Service has been in bed with Pretoria for years; if West does find anything she won't be allowed to act on it. Sillitoe's long gone.' He was referring to the refusal of the then head of MI5, Sir Percy Sillitoe, to cooperate with the newly formed South African security service, telling Prime Minister Clement Attlee that such a service would 'certainly be used to keep the black races down'. Times had indeed changed.

'The Pinheiros are history now,' Joseff continued, 'best forgotten. When Cristóvão Taravares gets back he'll have to come and collect Mariana's effects and close up her flat. Then it will be one more cold case for the conspiracy nuts to play with. You wait, you'll be able to fill a book with all the mad theories that will creep out of the shadows: the CIA did it, the KGB, IRA, MI5, the Israelis, the little green men from Mars. But we all know the only ones who will benefit from Pinheiro's death are those who want to derail Crocker's peace mission, the hard-line Boers.'

'Perhaps.' It wasn't a discussion I wanted to get into. 'Cristóvão Taravares won't need to sort anything out. Salvador Pinheiro's brother-in-law Martim is coming over, he arrives tomorrow. I assume he will take the bodies home.'

Joseff said nothing.

'Come on,' said Julia. 'This is all too depressing. It must be time to open some wine.'

Her uncle rose from his seat. 'Quite right. The sun's way over the yardarm. What will you have Adam?'

'Nothing thank you Gordon, I must be off. Things to do, you know.'

Joseff nodded to us and disappeared into the kitchen to bid his farewell to Anne. Then he was gone. It was the last time I saw him alive.

# XV

The loss of the CIA proprietary aircraft, the failure of Operation Mango and even the assassination of Salvador Pinheiro were merely sideshows to something altogether bigger. Between August 1987 and March 1988 a series of military engagements which unfurled around an obscure Angolan town were later to assume mythic proportions. Nelson Mandela would one day hail them as the Battle of Cuito Cuanavale and claim that they represented the 'crushing defeat of the racist army' and a 'victory for all of Africa'. Men who in reality had been miles away would boast of having participated in the greatest tank battle in Africa since El Alamein.

The reality at the time was less spectacular and victory for one side or the other less clear-cut.

For the Subsaharan Africa Desk the fighting around Cuito Cuanavale seemed to rumble on for months like a gathering storm. Almost daily situation reports came in from John Darwyn's team in Pretoria and, usually two or three days later, from Frank Cato's CIA analysts in Langley. They were pored over by ourselves and the Defence Intelligence Staff before contradictory summaries were submitted to our political masters. The DIS saw squadrons of Russian T-55 main battle tanks being decimated by lightly armoured South African Ratel troop carriers supported by a few locally-produced Olifant tanks and told their Minister we could probably sleep safely in our beds. My Service saw the South Africans losing territory in southern Angola and being forced into peace talks that could threaten the future of 'democratic' government in South Africa and by extension, the Foreign Secretary was assured, our own future as well.

The political reality was that the battle did indeed mark the beginning of the end for white South Africa although not because their forces were destroyed, they weren't. But in the battle lines being drawn up across southern Angola it finally became clear to everyone that the sheer size of the Cuban forces and the superiority of the Soviet technology made the eventual defeat of South Africa and its UNITA allies a matter of time. Revolutionary change in that part of Africa was now inevitable.

It was a critical time to be on the Subsaharan Africa Desk. But Cuito Cuanavale and the future of Southern Africa was not the Service's main preoccupation, as I discovered three days after returning from my weekend in Cornwall.

I was summoned to see Colin Asperton. He was seated not at his desk but by a small coffee table. I sat down across the table from him.

'Poland,' he announced without any further introduction. 'The referendum last month was the first election the Communists have ever lost in the whole of the Soviet bloc.' He spoke as if he imagined I hadn't seen a newspaper in weeks. 'It could be the beginning of the end. We need all hands on deck. So good news for you. Time to return to what you know best. I realise Subsaharan Africa is not a natural fit for you. You've never really been happy there and whatever Turk may say he doesn't need two Deputy Desk Officers.'

And so it came to pass that my two years as Deputy Saddo came to an end. My work on the Desk had been exemplary, Asperton assured me, and although there would be no increase in grade or pay this was a good career move. It was time for me to 'rotate' to a more suitable role.

In truth I was happy to rotate, the atmosphere on the Subsaharan Africa Desk had become very tense.

Rowbart was clearly convinced that John Darwyn was leaking his own reports to the Angolans. As far as I could see he had no solid evidence. His suspicion seemed to be based on no more than Darwyn's lack of enthusiasm for the way the war in Angola was being fought. But when I suggested that to Asperton he disagreed.

'Between you and me I put that to Turk. I don't believe that anybody on the Desk here in London leaked that Mango report, in fact I'm not even sure the Angolan Embassy ever saw the bloody thing. Perhaps they got the Mango intelligence another way altogether. Some lefty journalist on the *Observer* who's managed to find his own source down there could have given it to them. Why, I said to Turk, are you so convinced the Angolans are reading our reports? Well it turns out Turk does have evidence. Operation Mango involved two companies from 1 Parachute Battalion. Darwyn's report wrongly said three companies and the cable to Luanda repeated that mistake. Circumstantial of course but I think we do have to accept that the information passed on to Pinheiro came from Darwyn's report. If we accept that nobody here in Century House leaked it then we must be prepared to consider that Darwyn leaked it himself.'

I had been hoping that we had somehow been wrong: that the Mango leak had nothing to do with us and nothing to do with John Darwyn. There must have been dozens of people much closer to the action who knew the Operation was about to be launched and could have got a warning through to the Angolans, although why they would send it via London was difficult to imagine. That now seemed impossible.

'How did Rowbart find out about the error in the report?' I asked. 'How did he know the Operation involved two parachute companies not three?'

Asperton seemed surprised by my question.

'Don't concern yourself with that Dylan. You can leave the SAD behind you now. Go and sort out what's happening in Poland.'

I wasn't going to settle for that. 'Turk must have shown Darwyn's report and the cable from the Angolan Embassy to DeSmid. He would have spotted the mistake. Turk passed a GCHQ intercept and a classified Service report to a foreign intelligence agency, albeit an allied one. Is anything going to happen about that?'

Asperton merely stood up and ushered me out of his office.

If Darwyn found out that his report on Operation Mango had been shown to DeSmid he would rightly have been furious. I knew he was already incensed with Rowbart's behaviour. On the previous Monday the two men had a two-hour meeting from which they both emerged red-faced.

Rowbart had then turned on Felicity Macnamara who had travelled back from Johannesburg with Darwyn.

'I didn't find what Turk wanted,' she told me. 'No evidence that anyone in Pretoria leaked John Darwyn's Mango report and no evidence that he had sent it to anyone in London other than us. And Darwyn still won't say how he got hold of the Mango plans because he says Rowbart would tell the South Africans. DeSmid is up in arms, says he feels betrayed and doesn't want Darwyn back in the country. And to cap it all I couldn't find anything down there to suggest who Darwyn's source might be.'

As Sheila West was still not letting Rowbart interview Marco Mutorwa the only good news for the Subsaharan Africa Desk Officer was that I was leaving the Desk. Having said that when I returned from my meeting with Asperton, Rowbart made a point of calling me into his office immediately and wishing me well in my new post.

'You've done some first class tactical analysis here,' he told me, before adding cryptically, 'but you need to understand strategy in this business as well. That's much easier in Europe than it is in Africa. You might say the issues there are more black and white.' I think he meant that as a joke but you could never be sure with Rowbart.

'I hope you get Mariana Pinheiro's killer,' I said. 'Best of luck with that.'

'We've got him,' replied Rowbart. 'We just need enough evidence to convict him in court. Apparently what we found in the flat and his being the nephew of a UNITA commander isn't enough. Not that it matters. The little sod did us all a favour. Salvador Pinheiro was pure evil.'

'But Mariana Pinheiro wasn't.'

Rowbart said nothing.

The other person who wished me well was John Darwyn. After spending most of Tuesday with Justin Brasenose he took two days leave, quite possibly to avoid any more meetings with Rowbart, but came into the office on Friday. He spent the morning with Asperton, Rowbart and Macnamara engaged in what Asperton called scenario planning, an activity that completely lacked the rigour Herman Kahn had advocated when he introduced the concept to the US military thirty years earlier.

Darwyn popped into my office before leaving for the airport. He had clearly found a decent tailor in South Africa and looked more at home in Century House than he had when he had been based there, but there was still something of the unpolished diamond about him. He was in an odd mood.

'You're off,' he greeted me. 'Wise man. I expect I'll be next, knocking on your wife's door asking for a job.'

'I'm sure she would welcome that,' I said, trying to sound encouraging.

'I suspect not,' Darwyn replied. 'I've already talked to Adam Joseff who keeps telling me it's too early to jump ship.'

It struck me that Darwyn was in a mood that in earlier days would have been called demob happy. It was as if he was distancing himself psychologically from the Service. I suppose I had been feeling a little like that myself until my new appointment had suddenly appeared.

'I'll just have to wait until I'm pushed,' Darwyn continued.

'That won't happen, surely.'

'We'll see. Rowbart's pretty well queered my pitch in Pretoria so something has to happen.' I gave him a puzzled look and he explained. 'Seems I've been doing the job too well. The South Africans don't like it. Not what a declared officer is supposed to do apparently.'

Most Service officers serve abroad undercover. I had supposedly been a Press Attaché in Moscow. But sometimes officers are declared to the host government or at least to their Intelligence agencies. The Station Chief in Washington for example is there to liaise not to spy and is always declared. John Darwyn had been declared.

'Rowbart told DeSmid I'd sent details of Operation Mango to London. DeSmid went mad, demanded to know how I got hold of South African state secrets.'

'Did you tell him?'

'Certainly not. I didn't even tell Brasenose, which of course Brasenose understood. DeSmid is dangerous. I told Brasenose that but he thinks DeSmid has seen the light, understood what the regime down there needs to do if it's to survive. We shall see. Still not your problem any more. We should meet up next time I'm in London, raise a toast to the Jamba Jamboree and all who sail in her.'

I wondered if he'd been out for a liquid lunch but his handshake was firm and there was no hint of alcohol on his breath. I wished him well.

That was my last day on the Subsaharan Africa Desk. A security-vetted language tutor had been hurriedly arranged and I spent the two weeks before Christmas in Ealing brushing up the rudimentary Polish I had tried teaching myself to alleviate the boredom of winter nights in Moscow. That meant I missed the 'Star Chamber' that took place in New York at the beginning of January. I only heard about that later.

It seems that Colin Asperton and Frank Cato had concluded that too many operations were going wrong in Angola. The enemy seemed to know just what was being planned. The South Africans claimed to have proof that Salvador Pinheiro himself had received advance warning of a number of their Recce and Parabat raids, including Argon, Mango and another one called Leeuwyfie. That information could have come from someone high up in the South African Defence Force but Pinheiro was reportedly also given details of the UNITA diamond shipments. Nobody in the SADF, not even DeSmid himself, had access to plans for both the commando raids and UNITA's diamond smuggling. Nor had anyone in UNITA.

The South Africans were pointing their fingers at the CIA and MI6. John Darwyn had acquired information from inside the SADF Special Ops command and was known to have befriended Robbie Perez who had coordinated the diamond shipments. Darwyn and Perez were summoned to New York. There was going to be what Asperton called a Star Chamber, a term which, quipped Felicity Macnamara, signified much but meant little.

I knew nothing about that. My new role officially started on 1st January.

Eighteen days later Julia phoned me with the news that Adam Joseff had been murdered in Antigua.

# XVI

'Adam's dead. He's been shot. In Antigua.'

I had been absorbed by matters Angolan for so long that I thought I had misheard.

'No, not Angola, Antigua,' Julia repeated. 'In the Caribbean.'

We were both stunned. Coming so soon after the bomb attack on Mariana Pinheiro and her father it seemed as if our whole world had gone mad.

Adam was not just a friend. He was someone we had looked up to and admired. I had known him longer than I'd known Julia and he seemed to be a fixture in both our lives. A host of images flooded my mind. Adam in his office tapping on his metal desk with his briar pipe before getting up to scribble in appalling handwriting on his flipchart. Adam in one of the conference rooms staring out over Horse Guards Avenue or Whitehall apparently oblivious to the fractious discussion raging around him and then suddenly interrupting to suggest a compromise where none had seemed possible. Adam returning from a high-level security meeting in Madrid with a postage stamp depicting Alfonso XIII and excitedly showing us how it had been overprinted República Española after Alfonso was forced into exile.

As an old hand in the Intelligence game Adam had trusted no one and believed nothing. He was the ultimate cynic. But on a personal level he had a charm that was touchingly old-fashioned. I remembered him telling Julia in all seriousness that he was sure she would be able to rely on my sense of honour when he discovered that she and I had been booked into a double room on our first operation together. He could also be remarkably generous. As a wedding gift he had presented us with two bottles of 1934 vintage port which must have cost a large part of his salary and which we had still not dared to open.

It was only a few weeks ago that I had seen him in Cornwall enthusing about Venice and quoting Horace, both so out of character that I wondered why I hadn't realised at the time that something strange was going on in his life.

It wouldn't be fair to say that Adam's death was completely ignored by the British authorities. An army colonel from the Defence Intelligence Staff visited the Exodis office the very next day. He spent more than an hour with Julia and Richard Mendale asking general questions about the consultancy's work and taking the occasional note. He explained that there was now nobody at the DIS who had worked with Joseff but the 'former Director General' had still been held in the highest esteem. Mendale quietly pointed out that Adam Joseff had actually been the Deputy Director General. A fortnight later the two Metropolitan Police detectives about to fly out to Antigua spent a day going through Joseff's records at the Exodis office as well as interviewing Julia, Mendale and the new office manager at length. But when their investigations in Antigua were complete it seemed that nothing had emerged that hadn't been in the newspapers.

The most unexpected response to Adam's murder came from Justin Brasenose who invited Julia and me to lunch at the Oxford and Cambridge in Pall Mall. I was surprised to discover that Sheila West was joining us.

'Long time no see,' Brasenose greeted Julia. 'How are you and how's baby Eveline?'

It was typical of Brasenose to remember our daughter's name although he seemed shocked when Julia pointed out that baby Eveline was now five years old and at school.

'How time flies,' responded Brasenose conventionally. That appeared to conclude the social niceties.

'I thought we might have a quick off the record chat about Adam Joseff,' he suggested to Julia. 'I've just seen the Met's report on the enquiries in Antigua. If you will forgive the pun it's rather a rum do. A mugging gone wrong according to the papers but the local police don't believe that any more than we do. You would have thought that the last thing the locals would want is headlines about tourists being mugged but that apparently is better than headlines about gangland executions which is their own theory.'

'They can't be serious,' responded Julia. 'Adam would never have been caught up in that sort of thing.'

'Quite. It's the way he was killed that the locals are fixated on. Two bullets to the back of the head. Mafia style apparently. I wouldn't know about that but I do know that there are a lot of other people who might kill like that, people in our line of business – people Adam would be far more likely to know, people from Angola perhaps.'

That wasn't a line I was expecting the conversation to take.

'Why Angola?' I asked.

'Adam's name has come up in connection with Salvador Pinheiro.'

'In connection with his daughter you mean,' said Julia.

'Perhaps. You tell me. Perhaps you could just take me through what you know about Adam's links with Angola and with the Pinheiros.'

Julia explained that the trading company Mercantaravares was one of her firm's most important clients. Abrahão Taravares, an old friend of Adam's, had introduced him to his son Cristóvão who had then hired Exodis. Cristóvão had later mentioned that his cousin's daughter was coming to study in London and had asked Julia to look after her.

I could feel Julia hesitating at that point, unsure of how much she should reveal to Brasenose. She was well aware that initially I hadn't reported everything to Turk Rowbart. I took over.

'We had dinner with Cristóvão and Adam. It was at the time I was supposed to be a student at SOAS and Adam said there was an SOAS student, Marco Mutorwa, who had been making a nuisance of himself with Mariana. He asked me to keep my eyes open.'

'He knew you were still in the Service? That your postgraduate study was a cover?'

'Obviously I didn't tell him that but Adam was no fool, he must have realised it was likely. Later when I discovered who Mariana Pinheiro was, and that Adam hadn't said anything, I challenged him. He said he had no idea that Salvador Pinheiro was her father.'

'Did you believe him?'

'No. I thought he was playing games.'

'What do you mean?'

'He wanted me to find out if we were watching Mariana. In November he invited me to lunch, it was completely out of the blue. He told me Mariana thought she was being watched and that her phone was being tapped.'

'What did you say?' West asked.

'I told him it wasn't my area and if I was going to get involved it would have to be made official. We didn't speak again until we met in Cornwall after the Pinheiros were killed.'

'Ah yes. We've been trying to trace Joseff's movements over the last couple of months. That would be Saturday 5th December.'

'That's right. Adam had cut short his holiday in Venice and went down to Cornwall for a few days. He came over on the Saturday. That was the last time I saw him. We returned to London on the Sunday.'

'So did Adam Joseff,' put in West.

'Then he must've changed his plans. He had been intending to spend the week in Cornwall,' Julia commented. 'He didn't come into the office until Thursday.'

'You've got a good memory.'

'We had a potential new client. Adam came in to see him.'

'So you don't know why he returned to London on the Sunday.'

'No, why would I?'

'You knew Salvador Pinheiro's brother-in-law Martim was coming to London that weekend?'

'Yes.'

'Did you tell Joseff?'

I couldn't remember but Julia replied to the question. 'Yes that came up. You think Adam went back to London to see Martim Vasconcelos?'

West said nothing but it was obvious what had happened.

'You had Vasconcelos under surveillance,' I said. 'You saw him meet Adam Joseff.'

'Something like that.'

Julia was suddenly defensive. 'Adam was probably just paying his condolences. There's nothing sinister in that.'

'Nobody is suggesting there is,' put in Brasenose. 'It's just odd that Adam's name should pop up. You know he visited Angola in May 1985.'

'That's nearly three years ago,' said Julia. 'It was about his hobby, philately. He told us about it. He was looking for Portuguese colonial stamps, something to do with the Portuguese Congo.'

'Really?' Brasenose sounded sceptical. He obviously didn't know Adam Joseff as well as we did. The idea that he would fly halfway around the world to buy a stamp didn't strike Julia or me as anything out of the ordinary. Brasenose evidently thought differently and I soon saw why.

'We are talking about flying to Angola,' Brasenose emphasised. 'Have you ever been there?' he asked us.

Julia shook her head.

'I've been to Jamba,' I said. 'As you know.'

'How did you get there?'

'Courtesy of the CIA.'

'Precisely. Angola is in the middle of a civil war. And it's a police state. You can't just hop on a plane and fly there unless you know somebody with a lot of influence. You can't even get a visa unless you have a pretty good reason to visit the country and I can't see stamp collecting being that sort of reason. Yet apparently Adam Joseff did just that.'

Brasenose paused and then changed tack. 'Tell me about

Adam,' he said to Julia. 'You worked with him. Was there anything unusual about his state of mind in the months before he died? Anything out of the ordinary in his behaviour. Anything odd about his travel patterns?'

While Julia was answering my mind went back to the meeting Brasenose and I had with Richard Mendale about the time Joseff had flown to Luanda. Mendale had just returned from the South African Military Academy in Saldanha and told us about the plans for the forthcoming Operation Argon. I remembered now that he had also mentioned warning Adam Joseff not to go anywhere near Cabinda. I wondered what exactly Mendale had told his old friend. Had he mentioned that South African commandos would soon be coming ashore to destroy Cabinda's oil storage facilities? What knowledge had Adam Joseff carried in his head when he landed in the Angolan capital?

Brasenose changed tack again. 'You told our colleague from the Met that Adam often gave you a file of notes when he came back from his trips. I wonder if you recognise any of these names.' He took a typed list of about a dozen names from his pocket and passed it across to Julia. She looked at it for a minute before passing it to me. Most of the names looked Portuguese or African. Adam Joseff was the second name on the list.

'What is this?' Julia asked.

Brasenose shook his head. 'For now it's just a list. Do you recognise anyone?'

'Just one. This name near the bottom. I mentioned him just now. He came to see Adam, he wanted to subscribe to our *Bulletin*.'

'Did he subscribe?'

'He hasn't so far. Richard Mendale has been trying to contact him.'

I looked at the name Julia had pointed at, GI Coley.

'I know him,' I said. 'American oilman. He was at the Democratic International in Jamba.'

'A very rich oilman,' said Brasenose. 'Head of a massive corporation. Not the sort of man who makes a personal call on a tiny outfit in London just to subscribe to a magazine. Did Adam say anything about the visit?'

'Not really,' said Julia. 'Coley was only with him for ten minutes or so. Adam said not to put him on our prospect list until he'd seen him again.'

'And did he see him again?'

'Not that I know of.'

Brasenose tried something else. 'Some unusual words have come up during our investigations and I wonder if you've ever come across them, in Adam's notes perhaps. Argon, Leeuwyfie, Mango.'

'No I didn't come across them. Are they South African Special Ops?'

'How did you know that?' snapped West.

'Just a guess. Argon was all over the papers and Justin here summoned Thomas to Century House in the middle of the night to answer questions about Operation Mango. Leeuwyfie's the odd one out.'

Brasenose smiled. 'Leeuwyfie is Afrikaans for lioness, a lion's wifie.' His smile melted. 'You know I can't talk about Special Ops, Julia. We shouldn't be as open with you as we are being. You're not on the inside any more.'

'But you want my help.'

'Which I'm sure as a concerned citizen you are always

happy to provide. Now tell us about Cristóvão Taravares. What sort of man is he? You've been to see him recently.' It was a statement not a question, Brasenose reminding Julia that theirs was not a relationship of equals. He knew more than she did and it would stay that way.

'How did you know I'd been to see him? Am I under surveillance?'

'Of course not. Mr Taravares on the other hand is another matter.'

'You're watching Cristóvão Taravares?'

'Come now Julia, you know better than to ask me that. We're not watching him but obviously a man like that might be of interest to a number of agencies.'

'What do you mean a man like that?'

Brasenose was unflustered. 'Why don't we start with you answering my questions and then perhaps we will come on to yours. Why did you visit Cristóvão Taravares in Trieste the week after Adam Joseff was killed?'

'Because he's a client. Like I said an important client. Exodis was Adam's brainchild. He set it up and got the ball rolling. When people like Cristóvão Taravares think of Exodis they think of Adam, but that's not helpful now. We've built a reputation, a brand if you will, and we mean to keep that going. When Adam was killed we had to move quickly to protect our reputation. We needed to convince our customers that the Exodis service would continue. We have what we call a prospectus, what you would probably call a sales brochure. It had photos of Adam in it so it had to be redesigned. I thought if we could include some quotes from existing clients, perhaps with their photos, that would help reassure other clients. Cristóvão agreed to help. All of us,

Richard, Jonathon and I, went out to talk to our customers, especially those that had been introduced by Adam. I saw Cristóvão Taravares because I'd met him before and I'd done some work for him recently.'

'What sort of work?'

'Nothing of interest to you. He's thinking of buying a company in Belgium. Jonathon Craverse and I did a note on Belgian banks and the prospects for the Belgian franc.'

Brasenose seemed to be satisfied. 'I hope you were successful in retaining your customers.'

'We lost two smaller clients. And a potential one Adam had only just met: the Coley man you were talking about. But the business has held up remarkably well.'

It was my turn to change the subject. 'Any news on the bomb in Westbourne Terrace?'

'Enquiries are continuing,' West replied.

'They don't seem to be very fruitful. According to the papers you're no nearer finding out who did it. What happened to Marco Mutorwa? Last I heard he was the prime suspect.'

West was clearly uncomfortable with this line of conversation and looked around the room anxiously.

'The evidence against Mr Mutorwa was purely circumstantial. His student visa has been revoked.'

I was shocked. 'You mean you've let him leave the country?'

'We had no basis on which to detain him. I believe he is now in Portugal.'

'And what did he tell you?'

'I really can't go into that. As I said enquiries are continuing.'

'Did he say anything about Mariana? What about the business with the Guinness shares?'

'I really can't talk about that,' repeated West. 'It's got absolutely no bearing on what we're here for.'

'Oh come now,' said Brasenose. 'We're among friends and as you say it's not our case. It's got nothing to do with the bomb.'

West still looked unhappy and Brasenose answered the question himself.

'It's public knowledge that there's been an investigation into share ramping in the City. Some very big investors bought blocks of Guinness shares in a coordinated attempt to ramp up the share price. They were successful. Our colleagues traced the purchase of one of those blocks of shares back to a trading company in Italy, Mercantaravares.'

Julia interrupted. 'You can't seriously think that Mariana Pinheiro was involved in that sort of thing. She was a kid.'

'Good grief no. We're talking about millions of pounds being spent to influence the share price. Mariana Pinheiro's deal would have had no impact whatsoever. No what we think happened is that somehow she found out what her cousin Cristóvão was doing and decided she could make a few pennies by piggybacking on his scheme.'

'So it really has got nothing at all to do with Adam or anything in Angola.'

'No nothing at all except that it does show that Mariana Pinheiro was closer to Cristóvão Taravares than we may have thought.'

'It might also suggest that she wasn't too scrupulous about how she made money,' West suggested.

'And did Marco Mutorwa tell you all this?' I asked.

'No he didn't. He denies knowing anything about Mariana's share dealing despite the fact that he's admitted he spent every minute of the day in her company when she visited him in London. He also says that he has never met Cristóvão Taravares and knows nothing at all about him. Talking of which we would like to know more about that gentleman. That's one of the reasons we're here. Anything Julia can provide to flesh out the picture as it were would be much appreciated. If you do see him again we would quite like to know more about his travel plans, future and past. He was in Windhoek in November for example, I would like to know why.'

'When in November?' I asked.

'On a day you may remember,' Brasenose replied. 'Monday the twenty-third. The day John Darwyn sent the Mango report to London.'

I tried to see a connection but failed. Taravares had nothing to do with Operation Mango and nothing to do with John Darwyn,

'Are you suggesting that Taravares might have landed in Windhoek and somehow managed to get hold of a copy of the report Darwyn had just written in Pretoria, eight or nine hundred miles away, and then phoned the details through to someone in London?'

Brasenose's expression gave nothing away. 'No I'm not suggesting that, although actually Darwyn was in Windhoek that day. But he sent us the report before he left Pretoria. By the time he reached Windhoek the Angolan Embassy here had got hold of the details of Operation Mango and cabled them to Luanda. So you're right, the leaking of Darwyn's report is nothing to do with Taravares turning up in Windhoek. It's a bit of a coincidence though: Darwyn and Taravares being in an out of the way part of Africa on the same day. What were they doing there? Darwyn was there to meet Frank Cato to discuss the Americans' plane getting shot down. Why was Taravares there?'

He looked at us as if expecting an answer. There was nothing we could say. 'There's something else,' Brasenose continued. 'You'll remember that on the nineteenth Mariana went to a phone box near Tottenham Court Road and received a phone call from someone in another London phone box. She then called Taravares in Trieste. Well it looks as though the moment Taravares received that call he made arrangements to jet off to Southern Africa. If Taravares being in Windhoek at the same time as Darwyn and Frank Cato turns out not to be a coincidence I'm willing to bet that it's got something to do with whatever Salvador Pinheiro's daughter said to him in that call. That's why anything Julia can pick up about that trip might be useful.'

Julia nodded obligingly although it seemed to me that it was unlikely that she would be able to find anything. I was wrong about that. Julia being Julia I was hardly back at Century House before she phoned with the information Brasenose wanted.

'Cristóvão Taravares was in Windhoek to refuel.'

'How on earth did you find that out?'

'I phoned him and asked, luckily he was in the office.'

'Really? You just phoned and asked him and he told you?'

'That's right. I said we were doing a report on business prospects in Namibia and had heard that he had recently been there. I asked if he had any advice to offer our clients. He apologised that he couldn't help because he'd only been there for half an hour. He had been in Johannesburg on business and was flying home via Cape Verde. His Learjet apparently has a range of 4000 miles so he needed to stop somewhere on the way and his pilot chose Windhoek. Like I said he insisted that they were only on the ground for half an hour.'

'It's possible I suppose. It must be nearly 4000 miles from Windhoek to Cape Verde so it would still be quite a risky flight. There must be places on the coast he could have chosen to refuel, Walvis Bay perhaps, that would have given him more of a reserve. Do you believe him?'

'No I don't.' Julia had clearly been mulling over that precise question. 'First why give me so much detail? Why not just say he wasn't there long enough to be able to help? I asked a straightforward question. Why trot out all that guff about his aircraft's range? Second as you say the route he suggests is just odd. If you want to fly back to Europe via West Africa you have to stop somewhere and a former Portuguese colony like Cape Verde is probably a more natural place for Cristóvão Taravares to break the journey than Nigeria or Ghana. But why choose that route in the first place? Especially when you're flying near a war zone on the Namibian–Angolan border and then over ocean. Why not travel up through East Africa? And if you think about it he couldn't have spent any time at all in Johannesburg. He was in Trieste a couple of days before. I asked him what he was doing down there and he said that he was looking at a potential new coffee supplier. But they don't grow coffee in South Africa.'

'So what do you think all that means?'

'I think it means that Cristóvão Taravares has been sanctions busting. He was carrying something that he didn't want seen by inquisitive customs officials in somewhere like Nairobi or Lagos. Cape Verde is not too worried about boycotting all things South African, it's the one place South African Airways flights are allowed to land without hindrance on the way to Europe.'

Julia was almost certainly right. Cristóvão Taravares didn't seem the sort of man who would worry about such trivialities as United Nations sanctions. He was carrying contraband of some sort, but was he carrying it to South Africa or from South Africa or both?

It wasn't until that evening that Julia and I were able to discuss everything that Brasenose had told us over lunch. We decided we hadn't actually learned very much and what we had learned had been depressing. Brasenose had said he wanted to talk about Adam Joseff but he hadn't said anything that might suggest he was actively looking into Adam's murder. It seemed obvious that Adam Joseff had been deliberately targeted in Antigua but nobody seemed to be doing anything more about it. Similarly the Pinheiros had been deliberately targeted but the only suspect had been allowed to leave the country.

'She sat right there,' said Julia, pointing across the table. 'Mariana Pinheiro was our guest and now she's dead, just like Adam. Surely somebody is going to do something.'

'But who?'

The answer to that question was totally unexpected, not least to the person concerned. The first step in unravelling the mystery of Adam Joseff's death was taken not by anyone with any sort of official role but by a man who liked to describe himself as a retired old sea dog: Julia's uncle Admiral Lord Grimspound.

# XVII

When Julia's Aunt Anne told us that plans for her husband's seventieth birthday celebrations had changed we were happy to go along with them. Spending Easter in the Caribbean rather than Majorca sounded very attractive, the extra cost of the flights would be balanced out by the absence of hotel expenses.

Anne Grimspound used to declare that every family had one black sheep. In her case it was her younger brother Richard. After an undistinguished spell in a distinguished regiment Richard had left the army and discovered his true vocation selling cars. He found success in a world more impressed by his expensive clothes than his expensive education. It was the mid-1960s and British motor manufacturers watched disdainfully as the first Japanese cars started to arrive. Anne's brother saw things differently and took on every imported car franchise he could find. Twenty years later he retired a very rich man with a new wife and a new yacht. He named the yacht *The Ark E-Type* which he asserted was suitably picaresque. *The Ark E-Type*, he told his sister, would be in Aruba at the end of February and she would be doing him a favour if she and Gordon sailed it to Antigua while he spent a month or two in California.

The plan therefore became for Anne and Gordon to collect the boat in Oranjestad and, accompanied by two old friends from their Navy days, sail slowly via St Kitts to Antigua. In Antigua they would say goodbye to their friends and say hello to chaos as their daughter Susan and niece Julia arrived on board with husbands and children. Their other daughter Margaret would fly down from New York for a couple of days over Easter so the family could be together for Gordon's birthday.

It sounded like a good plan and the prospect of visiting the island where Adam Joseff was shot seemed just an unfortunate coincidence. It wasn't seen like that by everyone.

Sometime in March I received a curious phone call from Justin Brasenose. Would it be possible to meet up in the next week or so? Perhaps after work. And if Julia were free that would be even better. He had something to show us. It really wouldn't take very long.

Julia was as intrigued as I was and we arranged to meet the following week. I had imagined a drink in a quiet pub or perhaps at his club but Brasenose said he really couldn't get away. We should meet, he said, at 'somewhere neutral'. That turned out to be at the anonymous three-storey brick-built block that served as GCHQ's London offices in Palmer Street behind St James's Park Tube station. The ground floor of the building was stone clad with its windows blacked out to stop pedestrians walking along the pavement outside glimpsing the secret world inside. Brasenose was using a small meeting room on the first floor; on the other side of the wall behind him people were carrying on their normal lives over a drink at the next door Adam and Eve pub.

'You're off to Antigua,' he started.

'That's right,' I said, assuming he was making polite conversation.

It was Julia who responded with, 'How did you know that?'

'It's my job to know. Why Antigua?'

'It's my uncle's birthday. He's borrowing his brother-in-law's boat.'

'You're not planning a little private enterprise investigation into Joseff's death?'

I was shocked. 'Of course not.'

Brasenose looked directly at Julia. 'And what about your uncle Lord Grimspound? Is he planning anything?'

Julia just shook her head, she looked as bemused as I was.

Brasenose nodded. 'You won't find anything. The Met were very thorough. And I certainly wouldn't advise you to go poking around. But I know you. I've worked with you both remember. If there's some hunch you haven't told me about, if Gordon Grimspound knows something about Joseff he doesn't want to make public, if there's something you think we've all missed I want to know about it. Anything you come across in Antigua you tell me and in return you can have this.'

He passed across a brown A4 envelope. Inside was the Met Police report on Adam Joseff's murder.

'As I said I really don't think you'll find anything but Joseff was killed for a reason and if it was anything to do with his old life or with the Pinheiros we need to know.'

It was my turn to nod. 'I understand but honestly our going to Antigua is just a coincidence.'

Brasenose started to get up, the meeting was over, but Julia wasn't finished. 'Is there anything else you can tell us? Those names you asked me about last time, who were they?'

Brasenose pushed his chair back without answering

Julia's question. When he spoke again there was a surprising hint of melancholy in his voice.

'Adam Joseff was a good man but our business is full of good men lying in unmarked graves with nobody ever knowing how or why they died. What I do know is that Joseff travelled to Angola the day before Operation Argon, he befriended the daughter of the head of the Angolan security police and when that man died he rushed up from Cornwall to meet another senior member of the Angolan regime. What I don't know is why and I don't like questions just left hanging in the air. And that's happening far too often these days.'

He seemed to be looking through us as he spoke. 'The Intelligence services are overwhelmed. Nobody knows what the IRA will do next. Gadaffi is shovelling arms to every nutcase who comes calling. Gorbachev has changed the rules of the game in Eastern Europe, Poland could blow up at any minute, Czechoslovakia and – unbelievably – even East Germany could follow suit. Crocker might really be able to achieve something in South Africa if we can all just keep the lunatics at bay. And God knows what will happen when the Russians pull out of Afghanistan as they surely must. The consequence is that we're now content to let our parochial questions just hang in the air. Mariana and Salvador Pinheiro are murdered on the streets of London, the main suspect is allowed to leave the country and the case is consigned to our too difficult list. Adam Joseff is murdered and we put it on the same list. Somebody in London feeds South African secrets to the Angolans so there's a Star Chamber in New York and when that produces nothing John Darwyn is persuaded to resign, Robbie Perez is sent to Alaska and finding out what really happened is put on the too difficult list.'

As I no longer had any involvement with the Subsaharan Africa Desk that was the first I had heard about John Darwyn having retired.

'That's not how Intelligence is supposed to work,' Brasenose continued. 'Our job is to find pieces of a puzzle and if they don't fit together keep on looking until everything fits, we don't just throw the first few pieces in a drawer and forget about them. You asked me what those codewords were and where the list of names came from. You know what the codewords were. As you guessed they were South African Special Ops and we think they were all leaked to the Soviets. The Angolans were prepared for those ops and for the two diamond shipments that were lost. That's what the Star Chamber was supposed to get to the bottom of. Were Darwyn or Perez somehow involved in those leaks?'

'So you thought Perez might have somehow passed things on, presumably through her brother in London.'

'Perhaps through her brother. Cato was always nervous about her just because her family came from Cuba. The Americans had this crazy idea that they could persuade Cuban pilots to defect. Whenever Cuban jets came into radio range of Jamba the Americans would get on to their radio frequency and Robbie Perez would try to coax the pilots to change sides. Cato thought she might be passing on messages that way. He had the calls taped but didn't find anything suspicious. Then when John Darwyn came to see me in London he claimed that one of his sources was Perez.'

'And you told Cato?'

'Of course I told him. The Americans are our most important allies. Perez knew all about the diamond shipments, in fact she seemed to be the only one who knew the details of both shipments, but she knew almost nothing about the Special Ops that were apparently leaked. We couldn't find anybody who could have been responsible for all of the alleged leaks. That's why Colin Asperton and Frank Cato decided to clear the decks, move everybody who might have had access as far away from Southern Africa as possible.'

'And what about those names you showed me?' Julia asked.

'That was a list of people who went to see Salvador Pinheiro's brother-in-law Martim Vasconcelos at his hotel when he was in London. The only names of interest are the two you spotted: Adam Joseff who visited him on the Monday morning and GI Coley who visited him two days later.'

At the Democratic International GI Coley had been parading around as the great champion of democratic freedom fighters but I remembered Robbie Perez telling me dismissively that he was backing Jonas Savimbi and UNITA solely in order to get his hands on the oil concessions after UNITA's victory. Coming to London to pay his condolences to the Deputy Oil Minister of the government Savimbi and UNITA were determined to destroy suggested that Perez was right, his loyalties were flexible. It occurred to me that GI Coley had done something else in London on that visit.

Julia had been thinking the same thing. 'So Coley visited Vasconcelos and then came to our office to see Adam and discuss the possibility of subscribing to our *Exodis Bulletin*. What was that all about?'

Brasenose simply shrugged his shoulders. 'Another question to leave hanging.'

With that the meeting really was over.

The report Brasenose had given us was much longer than I expected with a thick wodge of photocopied attachments. Julia and I read through every page before setting off for Antigua. We learned very little new. At one stage the two British detectives had clearly thought they were on to something: three tourists who had arrived on the day after Joseff but who could not be found and according to the local Immigration authorities had never left the island. When the Hampshire police checked the home address of two of them, Mr and Mrs Murray, it transpired that they had left on a friend's yacht and flown home from Barbados. The third, a Mr Newman, was different: the home address given to Immigration did not exist and apart from the airport arrival record there was no trace at all of him ever being on the island. Not only that but a quick call to London revealed that the passport used was fake.

'That's the only anomaly they found,' said Julia disappointedly.

'And it gets us nowhere,' I agreed. 'Probably some drug smuggler with a bag full of phoney passports.'

I took the report into Century House before we left for Antigua and locked it safely away.

Julia's aunt and uncle had collected *The Ark E-Type* from Aruba and after two weeks gentle sailing south had dropped their friends at the sailing mecca of English Harbour in Antigua a couple of days before we arrived. There they had collected Susan, her husband and daughter and set sail again. When our plane landed we took a taxi across the island to Jolly Harbour from where we could see St Kitts, Nevis and Montserrat on the horizon. The Grimspounds had arrived that morning. Once aboard we cast off but moored not far away off Five Islands.

The unexpected meeting with Brasenose had unsettled me and I wondered if Gordon had chosen Jolly Harbour because he wanted to visit the Morning Star Nelson museum on nearby Nevis or because it was near to the villa where his friend Adam Joseff had been murdered. If that was the reason it struck me as oddly macabre.

It was while we were sipping rum cocktails and watching the glorious sunset that Gordon mentioned his old friend.

'You know I'm Adam's executor,' he started. 'The poor chap had no family. He's left his stocks and shares, his house in Cornwall and flat in London to the Army Benevolent Fund. He's left all his personal belongings to Anne and me. That specifically includes the stamp collection, I assume because Anne was always kind enough to pretend an interest in them. Anyway I've had a letter from a lawyer named Cartwright in St John's, here on Antigua, saying that the authorities have released Adam's personal effects to him as he was Adam's lawyer on the island. I'm collecting them tomorrow morning. St John's is on the other side of Five Islands.'

'Adam had a lawyer here?'

'That's exactly what struck me. Why on earth would Adam have a lawyer in a place which to the best of my knowledge he had never visited before?'

'There's only one way to find out.'

'I shall see them tomorrow. I thought you or Julia might like to come with me.'

Julia decided she would stay on the boat with her aunt and cousin, pointing out that the nearby beaches were far more suitable for Eveline than a musty lawyer's office. My offer to be the one to stay behind with Eveline was turned down with a smile.

Richard Cartwright's office was on Newgate Street below St John's Cathedral. He proved to be a short, bespectacled, white man of advancing years and we were shown into a room lined with law reviews of a similar age. There was no sign that six years of Antiguan independence had caused him to update anything on his shelves. He treated Julia's uncle with that odd obsequious familiarity that the English middle classes so often demonstrate if they ever encounter a member of the House of Lords.

After Cartwright had expressed his shock at Adam Joseff's murder and informed us that 'Nothing like that has ever happened on the island before' Gordon got down to business.

'I hadn't realised that Adam had a lawyer in Antigua,' he started but Cartwright interrupted immediately.

'Not lawyer really. Kindred spirit. We met at a specialist auction in London seven or eight years ago. Philately, you know. We both wanted the same items, what are known as Ultramar, the early issues made by the Spanish for their colonies of Cuba and Puerto Rico. My particular interest is stamps of the Caribbean. Adam's interest was early Iberian, so we overlapped a little. There were three lots that we both wanted. It seemed silly to bid against each other so I bought two and Adam the third. We got to talking after the auction and I said if he ever came to Antigua he should come and see my collection.'

'And he did so?'

'A couple of years ago I received a phone call saying he

was on the island and we arranged to meet. That would be around the middle of 1985.'

'Did Adam say what he was doing on the island?'

'Just a short break for the sunshine. He wasn't here for long on that occasion, it's far too hot in summer. I was surprised when he phoned again just after Christmas to say that he was coming to the island again and was looking for somewhere to stay, not easy at that time of year. He said he had a particularly difficult report to write and needed somewhere secluded. Just for a week or two. The local agencies he had contacted hadn't been able to help. I happened to have a client whose mother had just died. My client was planning to sell off her villa and contents when the estate was wound up but at the time it was unoccupied. Adam agreed right away, didn't even query the rent. When he arrived he came in here to sign the necessary papers but it's a bit of an exaggeration to describe me as his lawyer. Naturally when he was killed I made myself known to the police and told them as much as I knew. And I repeated it all again to the Scotland Yard detectives.'

Cartwright produced a medium-size suitcase, all that Joseff had left behind on the island. 'The police gave me this. There's nothing of interest in it, I'm really not sure it's worth you taking home. I assume you already have a set of his house keys. No papers. I thought the police may have found the report Adam was talking about but it appears they didn't.'

'And you don't know if Adam was doing anything else on the island, other than writing a report?' Gordon asked.

'No.'

'He didn't mention seeing anyone?'

'No. He was different this time. When he came the first time he was sociable. We had dinner together. I showed him my collection. I have some really quite rare examples. This time he just wasn't interested. More than that he was positively disinterested. He said he might sell his collection and give the money away. I said if he did that I would buy his Spanish Ultramar examples. He replied that was unnecessary, he would give them to me. I asked if he would like to join Francis and me for lunch but he said no, he had to concentrate on his report.'

'Frances is your wife?'

'Oh no I'm not married. No Francis Banerjee. Charming man, came here from Trinidad thirty years ago when they opened the bank next door. Francis was the manager until he retired last year. Like me he is a keen philatelist. He has a wonderful collection, British Empire 1910 to 1952.'

I wondered idly why pick such random years but Gordon nodded sagely. 'George V and George VI.'

'And Edward VIII,' Cartwright insisted. 'Very rare some of them. Francis tried to buy an Australian twopenny scarlet when it came up for auction but it went for a ridiculous sum. But he did have an Edward VIII example Adam was very interested in, a British definitive overprinted Morocco Agencies with the value in Spanish currency.'

I marvelled at the ability of grown men to become so passionate about little pieces of paper; even as a child stamp collecting had never held any attraction for me.

'But you don't think Adam saw Francis Banerjee this time?' Gordon asked.

'I know he didn't. I asked Francis. Like me Francis was shocked. He'd done some business with Adam on his first visit and thought he was a jolly good chap.'

'You mean they had traded postage stamps?'

'No no, nothing like that. Banking business of some kind.'

Gordon's ears perked up at that. 'Could Adam have had a bank account here?'

Cartwright shook his head. 'I shouldn't think so. What would he want that for?'

I already knew the Met Police had checked all Joseff's bank accounts but Gordon wasn't satisfied.

'It would be good to make sure. I wonder if Mr Banerjee would talk to us.'

Cartwright's face broke into a broad smile. That would be no problem at all he assured us. 'I'll phone Francis now and see if he's free today.'

He was free and when, an hour later, we arrived at the small restaurant Cartwright had suggested it was obvious that the two men were regular, perhaps daily, customers. The proprietor, a jovial black woman with a long skirt in dazzling turquoise and yellow, insisted on rearranging the tables so that Cartwright and Banerjee could sit in their customary seats with us beside them.

'Lord Grimspound will sit next to me,' announced Francis Banerjee in a voice loud enough for the rest of the room to hear.

Cartwright and Banerjee could have been twins were it not for the colour of their skin. Both were small men going bald on top, slightly stooped, with identical tortoiseshell-framed spectacles. Both wore suits and ties despite the heat outside. Banerjee sported a garish red and blue silk handkerchief in his suit pocket.

After the initial introductions Gordon plunged in. 'I

worked with Adam for many years, he lived not five miles from me in Cornwall, we saw each other regularly and yet you know he never once mentioned visiting Antigua. What on earth do you think he was doing here?'

That was obviously a subject that Cartwright and Banerjee had pondered over many a lunch since Adam's death. They produced a variety of unlikely theories.

'I don't think he was the man his killer was after,' Banerjee eventually concluded. 'It was his friend.'

'His friend?'

'Yes, the man with the bank account.'

Slowly the story came out. On his first visit Adam had arranged for Banerjee to set up a bank account, but not for himself, for a friend. Adam had his friend's passport and a power-of-attorney registered in London appointing Adam to act for him. It was all above board.

'And what was the name of the friend,' Gordon asked but at that Banerjee drew a line. 'I can't tell you that milord, that's bank business, confidential.'

'Can you tell us anything at all about him?' I asked.

'I really am most terribly sorry. Even the police will have difficulty finding details of the bank's clients. You could try to go to the bank yourself but I can assure you my successor will reveal nothing about the account holder. He is a very serious young man.'

'Adam's friend?'

No, not Adam's friend, my successor is a very serious young man. No Mr Joseff's friend was not young. Although,' Banerjee laughed to himself, 'he was not an old man either.'

'Not old?'

'No not an old man.'

I realised that Banerjee was not really laughing, the expression on his face was closer to a smirk, as if he could see a joke that would be invisible to everybody else.

And suddenly it hit me. I knew who the account holder was. I had seen the name in the Metropolitan Police report, the name they had found in the Immigration arrivals records but not in departures, the name on a fake British passport: not an old man but a Newman, Ronald James Newman.

I put the name to Banerjee and his smirk vanished instantly.

'How did you know that?'

'You just told me. Not old you said. Now tell me, what was the account used for?'

'I cannot divulge any information. You must approach the bank.'

We tried to persuade him to say more but without success. He bridled when I suggested that the bank would be upset with him if they learned he had given us confidential information. He insisted he had not done so and Richard Cartwright would confirm that he had never mentioned the name Newman. We must go through official channels. We had to leave it at that.

After returning to the boat Julia, Gordon and I examined the suitcase Cartwright had given us. I think we had all been hoping that it would produce some sort of clue that the police had overlooked, a diary perhaps or a letter hidden in the lining of the suitcase. But there was nothing. We discussed what we had learned in St John's. The fact Joseff had opened a bank account in a phoney name was certainly interesting but it didn't take us much further forward.

It was too late to call England that day but the next I

phoned Brasenose at the Cabinet Office. He wasn't there but I left a message simply giving the name of the bank and suggesting he might look into an account in the name of Ronald Newman. That afternoon Gordon's daughter Margaret arrived and we set sail.

For the next week we enjoyed the sun and sea and tried to forget about Adam Joseff although in the back of my mind there was the hope that Brasenose would have found out more about Adam's secret bank account. When we dropped Margaret back at Jolly Harbour I tried to call him but he was now apparently on holiday himself. On a whim Julia and I left Eveline with the others on the boat and hired a taxi to take us to the villa where Adam's body had been found. Anne Grimspound was not impressed.

'Such a morbid thing to do. What on earth do you expect to see? It might have been better if poor Adam had been on the jumbo jet that crashed in the sea last year.'

At the time that remark seemed insignificant. I vaguely remembered a jumbo jet crashing in the Indian Ocean but it had nothing to do with Adam Joseff.

The place Adam Joseff had rented hardly justified Cartwright's description of it as a villa. The single storey building was far from palatial. Two or at most three bedrooms and certainly no swimming pool. The house was painted green with white windows and doors, a far cry from Adam's cold stone home in Cornwall. Bougainvillea tumbled along one wall. A sign outside bore the word Four but it was difficult to see why. There seemed to be no other homes anywhere near. We were some way from Jolly Harbour, halfway up one of a ring of hills thick with vegetation. The road here had been little more than a track.

The mystery was not only why was Joseff killed here but what was he doing here in the first place? I didn't really believe the story he had told Cartwright. Antigua gets very busy at that time of year but to suggest that he couldn't find a room anywhere was stretching credibility. And Julia was adamant that he hadn't been working on any report for Exodis. Was he just looking for sunshine? The view out to sea was spectacular but there were equally attractive vistas closer to Jolly Harbour and the beaches around it. Why agree to somewhere so far from any amenities?

We returned to the boat having learned nothing.

On our last day we moored *The Ark E-Type* at English Harbour as arranged with Anne's brother. I called Brasenose's office again and this time there was a message. Mr Brasenose would be grateful if I could breakfast with him at the Oxford and Cambridge at 7.30 the following Monday, my first day back at work.

Breakfast with Brasenose would prove to be a turning point. I would never think of Adam Joseff in the same way again.

# XVIII

Brasenose had been hoping that I would be able to provide more information about Ronald Newman and was clearly disappointed when I couldn't. After speaking to the Antiguan authorities he at least had something to report. The bank had confirmed that a man calling himself Newman had arranged an appointment with the manager the day before Joseff was killed but had not turned up. The bank had also revealed that the only activity on Newman's account were six deposits each of US$40000 received from a bank in Switzerland. The trail stopped there.

'What's curious,' said Brasenose, 'is the dates at which some of those payments were made. You remember that I mentioned to Julia the names of three South African Special Ops: Argon, Leeuwyfie and Mango. According to DeSmid Salvador Pinheiro had been forewarned about all three and possibly a lot more. The account in Antigua was opened three months after Operation Argon and the first deposit was made a week after Operation Leeuwyfie. The second deposit was made a week after the ambush of the diamond shipment. Two of the other payments were also made within days of South African Special Ops that somehow went wrong. The final payment was made on 27th November, right after the Angolan Embassy cable about Operation Mango and a week after the CIA proprietary was brought down. That's just too much of a coincidence.'

Brasenose looked at me and I knew just what he was thinking. If Adam Joseff had set up a bank account under a pseudonym into which he received payments coinciding with failed South African Ops the money could only be coming from the Angolans or their backers, the Russians. But that was unthinkable. Adam was simply not the sort of man that would sell his country's secrets for money. And in addition he didn't have the information to pass on. There had to be another explanation.

'It gets worse,' said Brasenose. 'I've spoken to Richard Mendale at Exodis. He's looked at Adam's travel schedule. Adam visited South Africa immediately before one of those Ops went belly up and again immediately before that first diamond shipment was ambushed.'

'And you think he flew back to London and contacted the Angolan Embassy. That would have been pretty risky, he must have known that they would be on GCHQ's listening list. And what about the other Ops when he hadn't been anywhere near South Africa. Operation Mango for example and the shooting down of the CIA proprietary. Wasn't he in Taiwan then?'

'Yes he was, I've checked.'

'So it's all pretty circumstantial.'

'No Thomas that's not what it is. The pieces we have are starting to fit together. There are pieces missing but the pieces we have suggest that Adam Joseff had started to work for the Angolans or the Soviets. And that he wasn't working alone. Someone else was involved in gathering the intelligence he passed on. Remember someone else accompanied him to Antigua.'

'Why do you say that?'

'Because Joseff used his own passport when he reached the island but somebody else arrived using the Newman passport.'

'His killer?'

'Perhaps.'

I still wasn't convinced about any of it but other pieces were clicking into place in my mind. Adam wouldn't have risked contacting the Embassy directly but he didn't have to. He had a ready-made courier who could visit the Embassy at any time without anyone asking questions: Mariana Pinheiro. That's why he wanted to know if we had her under surveillance. And it explained those odd telephone calls she received. When he had information to deliver he would phone her from a phone box and arrange a drop. In fact he probably wouldn't risk passing on papers or anything physical that might be traced back to him. He would just make a short call as a signal that he had information for her and she would then go out to a prearranged phone box, call him and he would tell her when and where the South Africans were planning something. She would then pass the information on to her father through the Embassy, perhaps making a cryptic note in her diary like she did with the diamond symbols I had found.

It made sense except that we were talking about Adam Joseff, a man I knew and trusted. More than that, a man I admired. A man who wouldn't sell himself for US$40 000. The Met Police file had included a financial report. Adam Joseff was not rich but he was comfortable, and his tastes were not expensive. He spent money on his stamps but even there it often cost him more to travel to the stamp fairs than he spent once there. It was then that more pieces clicked into place and I realised what must have happened.

'I must make some phone calls,' I said to Brasenose. 'I think I might know how this whole thing started.'

Brasenose didn't press me. 'Just keep me informed. And Thomas this is all between you and me. At the moment enquiries into the death of Adam Joseff are purely a police matter. The whole point of the Joint Intelligence Committee is to ensure that different parts of the Intelligence community don't go haring off on private missions that have nothing to do with our national priorities. If I'm to investigate Adam's death officially I need more than what you call circumstantial evidence. If we can prove that the money in that bank account came from Angola that might be enough. If we could discover how Joseff found out about the plans he seems to have passed on that would be a major step forward. What we really need is to find a link between the murder of Adam Joseff and the bombing in Westbourne Terrace, if there is a link. Just saying that Joseff and Mariana Pinheiro knew each other isn't enough. I'm going to speak to John Darwyn again,' he added as an afterthought.

As soon as I got back to my office I phoned Julia's aunt. If my suspicions were right she held the proof. We spoke briefly and I promised to call again that evening.

Julia had announced that morning that she would be late home as she and Richard Mendale had a meeting with an Australian client. I had felt sorry for her until she added that the meeting would be over dinner at the Hilton on Park Lane.

Our new au pair collected Eveline from school and when I arrived home she was putting her to bed without any of the fuss that inevitably accompanied bedtime when I was in charge. I always enjoyed playing games with Eveline when I got home but as Julia remarked the inevitable result was that I wound our daughter up when she should be winding down.

I phoned Julia's aunt who now had the answer to the question I had asked her earlier.

'You were right,' she announced. 'I found the little album, the one Adam called his stock-book. There were seven stamps in it. The two he showed us and five more. All the same design but different colours and values. Is it important?'

'It could be. It could mean that none of us really knew anything at all about Adam.'

When Julia came home she couldn't wait to tell me that the Australian client was so pleased with the work done by Exodis that he had invited her to give a presentation to his senior management team in Melbourne in August. That was much better news than my own: that Adam Joseff had almost certainly been spying on behalf of Salvador Pinheiro.

Julia didn't believe me.

'Let me take you through what I believe Adam has been up to,' I said. 'If I'm right it started with Dona Ana's stamp. You remember he bought that from Abrahão Taravares. And it was stamp in the singular when we heard the story from Cristóvão. Somehow when Adam showed it to us in Cornwall it had become two stamps. Where did that second one come from?'

'He said it also came from Abrahão.'

'He did but was that true? I think Abrahão only had one stamp. There was a set of stamps, Adam told us that, and that set belonged to Dona Ana. I think that for some reason she gave one stamp to her son Abrahão but the rest she gave to her daughter Joana.'

'Mariana's grandmother.'

'Exactly. When Joana died the stamps would have gone to Mariana's mother and when she died in Moscow they would have passed to her husband Salvador Pinheiro. I don't suppose he paid much attention to them. But Abrahão had mentioned to Adam that there had been a whole set of these stamps. He must have said that if anyone still had them it would be Salvador Pinheiro. He may even have offered to contact Pinheiro on Adam's behalf. We have to remember that Abrahão knew something about Adam's background, after all the key selling point of Exodis was all those supposed insights gathered from the secret world of British Intelligence. When Abrahão told Pinheiro about that Pinheiro must have been sufficiently curious to arrange for Adam to come to Luanda. Adam wanted to buy the stamps but Pinheiro didn't need the sort of money Adam could offer.'

'And so,' said Julia, reading my thoughts, 'you think the conversation must have moved on to what Adam could offer instead.'

'That's right and what Adam could provide was intelligence on a raid the South African Recces were about to make on the Cabinda oil facilities. A raid Richard Mendale purely by chance had mentioned to Adam the day before. I expect Adam thought a one-off warning in exchange for those stamps was a price worth paying, after all he had never felt any loyalty to South Africa.'

'But Salvador Pinheiro wouldn't see it like that,' Julia interrupted again. 'If you're right he had found an informant and he had something the informant wanted. So he must have said to Adam I'll give you one stamp for the information on Operation Argon but I'll need more if you want the rest of the set. And so Adam passed on more and ends up with the stamps my aunt has now found in his collection, perhaps with more to come. And Adam mentioned that there were documents as well, he would have wanted them.'

'That's right. He passes plans on to Mariana who passes them to her father and for each Adam gets a stamp.'

'You make it sound like a supermarket loyalty scheme, buy from us and we'll give you Green Shield Stamps.'

'But it was like that. The one thing we all believed in, Adam's loyalty, he sold to the Soviets.'

I expected Julia to argue but she didn't. 'I don't suppose Adam thought of it like that. He was just swapping something with another collector. After all he was a thoroughly decent man.'

'We want to think so Julia, and maybe it used to be true. But he got sucked in. He wanted the whole set of those stamps. They were unique. It became his project and Adam never dropped a project part way through. It became an obsession. If he really was dealing with Salvador Pinheiro that's unforgivable. Pinheiro was an appalling man and Adam knew that. You can't sup with someone like that however long your spoon.'

'But we sup with Savimbi.'

'That's different.'

Julia didn't respond to that. 'I can't believe Adam was like that but it does make some sort of horrid sense. There are still some loose ends,' she commented, 'like the timings. In some cases he was in London or Taiwan when the operations were being planned, how did he find out about them?'

'Perhaps someone brought the plans to him in London.'

'Perhaps. But who? The really big question remains,' Julia

pointed out. 'When he was in South Africa who gave him Special Ops plans? He couldn't have just landed in Jo'burg, phoned up some old contact and asked what Special Ops were up to or when UNITA were moving their diamonds. He had to have help.'

I agreed. 'But Brasenose says that no one person had access to all the information that was apparently passed to the Angolans. Adam must have had a network operating inside South Africa.'

Julia and I looked at each other and I could sense we were both thinking the same thing. There was no way Adam Joseff could have organised a spy ring in South Africa. He had been out of the business for far too long and, as he himself had admitted, he had no experience of operations in Southern Africa.

'He must somehow have found a way to tap into an established network,' I suggested.

Julia shook her head. 'Whose network? If the Russians had a network of agents in place Pinheiro wouldn't have needed Adam.'

She was thoughtful for a minute. 'Aunt Anne made a funny remark the other day which I didn't really understand. I think I'll give her a call, she'll still be up. You go to bed, I'll be there soon.'

When Julia eventually climbed the stairs there was a wry smile on her face. 'I may have an answer to one of our problems. Can you remember before Christmas a jumbo jet crashed into the sea? It was in all the papers. Everyone was killed. I remember thinking how terrifying it must have been for the poor souls on board. The other day Aunt Anne mentioned it and remarked that it was lucky that Adam hadn't been on the plane. I wondered why she said that. Was it just because she knows Adam flies a lot or something more specific? Anyway it turns out that Adam was at Penelowek when the story came on the news and he mentioned that he'd been on the same flight a week earlier.'

'So?'

'So the crash was in the Indian Ocean. It was a South African Airways flight and of course with the sanctions there aren't many places that still allow South African planes to land. It turns out it was the weekly flight from Taiwan.'

'You think Adam flew from Taiwan to Johannesburg, somehow found out about Operation Mango and almost immediately flew off to London to drop in at the Angolan Embassy. That can't be possible.'

'Why not? Adam lived on planes, he wouldn't be phased by flying from the Far East to London via South Africa. And now with Exodis paying he always travelled first class.'

'But Brasenose said he checked that Adam was in Taiwan when the CIA proprietary crashed and the Mango plans were leaked.'

'Are you sure? Why don't you check with Brasenose?'

I did so next morning. Brasenose sounded fairly confident that Julia's theory wouldn't fit but he promised to check.

He called me back three hours later. 'You were right. Joseff came back from Taiwan via Jo'burg. What's more you'll remember Mariana Pinheiro received a phone call that morning which we traced to Heathrow Terminal 1.'

'We checked the video recording to see if we could pick out Marco Mutorwa.'

'That's right. We've looked again and found Adam Joseff.'

That I thought was typical of Adam. He wouldn't risk

using the phone at the terminal where he arrived so he would go to Terminal 1 thinking that if Mariana Pinheiro's phone was being tapped nobody would link the call to someone arriving on the other side of the airport. He was right, we hadn't.

'If Adam did stop off in Johannesburg that would still leave a couple of leaks that we can't link to him,' I added. 'Payments received into that Antigua account when he was nowhere near South Africa. What about what they called Operation Leeuwyfie? Adam was definitely in London then.'

'Perhaps,' Brasenose replied, 'but you know this is all terribly old-fashioned. If somebody down there was passing him secrets why didn't they just use the phone? Why did he have to fly from Taiwan to South Africa? It's not as if Salvador Pinheiro wanted to see actual documents, he just wanted to know where the next raid was going to be and when.'

I knew just what Brasenose meant but I also knew Adam. He prided himself on keeping up with the times but he had learned his tradecraft long ago. 'Adam wouldn't risk incriminating himself by receiving a call from an agent in the field if there was the slightest chance that his agent might have their phone tapped. We'll have to dig deeper.'

Brasenose agreed. 'I've been doing exactly that. There's another possibility. For some of those leaks the agent could have come in from the field, he could have come to London. Operation Leeuwyfie for example. Adam Joseff was certainly here for that but he wasn't the only one.' Brasenose paused and I knew he was preparing to drop a bombshell. 'John Darwyn flew into Heathrow on leave just thirty-six hours before Leeuwyfie went live.'

There was a silence on the line. Brasenose expected me to be surprised by the mention of Darwyn's name but I had already made the link. If Adam Joseff had a source in South Africa who was able to pass on the contents of John Darwyn's secret cables what was more likely than that it was John Darwyn himself? No wonder Adam Joseff had been keen that Darwyn stayed in Pretoria rather than join Exodis. Could they have been in it together, Joseff seduced by a few pieces of gummed paper and Darwyn by dollars in an account hidden in the Caribbean? I didn't want to believe that of either man.

'What does John Darwyn say?' I asked Brasenose.

'That's a bit of a problem,' he replied. 'Nobody seems to know where he is. After the Star Chamber in New York Darwyn called the Establishment people here in London to arrange the details of his departure, pension and all that sort of stuff. Then he signed the papers they sent over, told everyone he was going to retire to Florida and disappeared.'

# PART 3

# NONSUCH BAY, ANTIGUA 17TH APRIL 1988

When Mary Fisher inherited $300 000 from a distant cousin she had never met she and her husband Randall gave up their teaching jobs in Halifax, Nova Scotia, took their ten-year-old daughter Candice out of school and set off to see the world. They bought a thirty-six-foot yacht with cutter rig and mobile staysail, which they were assured was ideal for cruising, from the Morris yard in Maine and headed south.

The Fishers were pleased with their new boat, it was small enough to be easily handled but fast enough when the winds were right. By April they had reached the Leeward Islands and after exploring French culture and cuisine in Guadeloupe they set sail for Antigua. The *Nimble Justine* could carry a lot of sail when the wind picked up but that day the winds had fallen away and they relied on the three cylinder twenty-eight horsepower Volvo engine to take them in towards the shore of Nonsuch Bay.

The family moored their boat offshore and looked for somewhere to set up a barbecue. There were hardly any suitable spots. Most of the shoreline consisted of limestone cliffs or rocky outcrops, all covered in dense vegetation. Mary spotted a small stretch of flattish land. That would have to do. She and Randall began to prepare the barbecue and sent Candice to start digging a pit close to the water to bury their rubbish. Instead the child discovered that someone had been digging there before her.

As the police pointed out later the bay was not an obvious place to dispose of a corpse if for some reason it couldn't simply be dumped in the sea. Whoever had hidden the body had found one of the very few places in the area in which a grave however shallow could be dug. Its attraction had presumably been its isolation. It was miles from anywhere. There were no roads or paths that might bring anyone to the spot. The body had clearly been brought by sea. Had the killer or killers been able to dig a foot or more deeper the remains would have done exactly that – remain. Instead Candice let out a scream as her spade uncovered a hand and was still sobbing inconsolably when the police arrived. Fortunately the child was back on the boat, now moored well away from Nonsuch Bay, when the police uncovered the rest of the body and for the second time in less than four months the island's sole pathologist found himself reporting that the cause of death was two 9mm bullets fired from close range.

# XIX

'How was it discovered?' Julia asked when I told her that an unidentified body had been discovered in a shallow grave beside the sea in Antigua. Justin Brasenose had phoned to give me the news.

'A Canadian family happened to moor up nearby for a barbecue and their little girl found it.'

'That must have been a horrid shock for her.'

I agreed. 'It was in a place called Nonsuch Bay which we must have sailed right past a couple of weeks ago. The way Brasenose described it whoever buried the body had found the only piece of bare, soft ground along that stretch of the coastline.'

I didn't really remember the bay at all, there was nothing there. It was long before construction of the hotels that dominate the bay today.

'The obvious question is why bury a body there?' I said.

'Well you've just said that it sounds like the only suitable place on the bay.'

'But why bury the body? The killer must have taken it there by boat, why not just chuck it in the ocean?'

'If they had done that it could have floated anywhere. It might have been found the very next day.'

'So why not weight it down with something? They were on a boat. There must've been ropes and anchors and so on they could have used.'

Julia had far more experience of boats than me. 'I think you'll find that any ropes and anchors on a boat will be there for a purpose,' she said with a smile. 'You wouldn't want to throw your anchor away. It seems to me that from the killers' point of view it must have seemed a pretty sensible option. But of course they were looking at it in entirely the wrong way.'

'What do you mean?'

'Well they were looking for an isolated spot where there was open ground close to the sea, big enough to bury someone and preferably flat. They thought that nobody else would come searching for a body in a remote spot like that. But of course what was good for burying something was also good for setting up a barbecue. There was probably nowhere else that the Canadians could go ashore for that.'

Julia was right but I still wasn't convinced that it would not have been much easier to dump the body in the sea. Unless the victim had been shot on the boat the killers must have carried the body on board. In that case why couldn't they collect something to weigh the body down at the same time and then let the sea dispose of the evidence for ever?

At the end of the call Brasenose had asked me to meet him at the Cabinet Office at 8.30 the next morning.

'Why does he want to see you?' Julia asked.

I had been asking myself the same question. The fact that another body had been found in Antigua was interesting but there was nothing I could do about it and I had other priorities. A low level agent I had been handling at the Polish Embassy had suddenly been called home. The recall might be good news, the man had apparently been promoted, but passing him on to a new handler in Warsaw would need to be cautiously managed.

'Any idea who the dead man is?' I asked when Brasenose had seated himself behind the enormous desk in his equally large office.

'That's why you're here,' he replied. 'I wasn't completely frank with you on the phone. We know exactly who the man was. His passport was found on the body. In fact both his passports. One was in the name of Ronald James Newman.'

'The fake passport Adam Joseff used to open his bank account?'

'That's right. Although fake may be misleading. The passport blank is perfectly genuine. It's one of ours.'

'You mean it's British?'

'No I mean the blank was ours, it should have been in a safe in Century House.'

'That can't be. Joseff never had that sort of access.'

Brasenose held up his hand. 'We'll come to that later. It's the name in the other passport that's important. That's the genuine article. And that name is John Lloyd Darwyn, until a week or two before he died our Station Chief in Pretoria.'

Brasenose paused to let me take in what he was saying. 'You realise this rather changes things,' he eventually commented unnecessarily. 'There are now of course national security implications: we must consider the possibility that John Darwyn may have been selling secrets to the Soviets or at least to the Angolans. And that raises all sorts of additional questions. If he was, when did that start? When he arrived in South Africa or much earlier when he was here? How was he recruited? And was he acting alone? Of course we may be wrong but irrespective of that Darwyn was still on the payroll when he was killed. The Secret Intelligence Service has lost a senior officer and we need to find out why. In normal circumstances investigating the death of one of its own would become the Service's top priority but there is a complication here. Who would lead such an investigation?

'Darwyn was the Deputy Saddo for many years and received excellent reports from both the then Saddo and from Colin Asperton. Colin then posted him to the most sensitive Station in the region over the objections of the new Saddo, Turk Rowbart. That was unusual. Then when questions arose about sensitive information reaching the Angolans Colin arranged a Star Chamber in New York. John Darwyn was killed almost immediately after that Star Chamber; it is not unreasonable to suppose that the two events are connected. Did he say something in New York that led to his death or, just as plausible, did his killers believe he had said something? The Star Chamber proceedings therefore need careful review. Colin clearly played a key role in those proceedings.'

Brasenose paused as if he were about to impart something vaguely distasteful. 'We all have the greatest respect for Colin but clearly an investigation into this business cannot be left in his hands.' Brasenose managed to convey a note of regret I was sure he did not feel. 'The JIC has therefore agreed that someone with a sound understanding of the Service but currently outside its remit should head up the investigation.'

'You?'

'Quite. Such a decision has the potential to ruffle a few feathers inside the Service especially as Sheila West will be brought in to coordinate enquiries. And the JIC of course does not have the resources itself for such an investigation. Consequently it has been agreed that resource from within the Service will be temporarily assigned to my team for the duration of the enquiry. That means you Thomas, you're off the Op in Poland as of now. Felicity Macnamara will also be seconded to my team. She and Sheila West will go over everything Darwyn has done since the day he joined the Service. I want to know about anything that might connect him to the Angolan regime or to Adam Joseff. As for you it's time to pack your bags and get on a plane.'

'Where to?'

'I'm not sure yet. Portugal, Italy, Antigua, Angola, Namibia. I think probably Alaska.'

I thought he was joking but he wasn't. 'I want someone to have a quiet chat with that Agency woman from Jamba, Robbie Perez. She can't be happy to have been shunted off to some frozen outpost on the Bering Strait. Perhaps she'll open up about her conversations with John Darwyn in Jamba. But that's not the only reason for seeing her. The file report on the Star Chamber is utterly bland but something must have happened in New York and I'm hoping Perez will tell us.'

'Shouldn't we start with Asperton and Rowbart? They were there.'

'Oh we will, but that's my job. I'm seeing them both here this morning. You find Perez. Read the Star Chamber file report first.'

The Star Chambers of the Intelligence world share little more than their name with their Tudor predecessors. There are no formal procedures and the term itself is used so infrequently that what one Service refers to as a Star Chamber may bear no resemblance to what another Service might expect. The objective of this Star Chamber, Asperton explained, was to 'resolve certain lacunae in the dissemination of Angolan related Intelligence'. This was to be done by what anyone other than Asperton would have simply described as a meeting: a one-day gathering at the CIA's New York Field Office in Manhattan. The Field Office at that time was located in the World Trade Center or, as Asperton insisted on writing, the World Trade Centre. This from a man who had once famously had a report on Canadian separatists retyped in order to insert the accent in Québec.

I could see why Justin Brasenose thought the Star Chamber file report was unlikely to be helpful. I had expected a summary of the proceedings, perhaps even a transcript, and as a minimum a description of the conclusions. Instead the file consisted solely of a list of participants and a report from the South African Directorate of Military Intelligence dated two days before the New York meeting. The participants were listed as Asperton, Rowbart and Darwyn from our side, Cato and three other Americans including Robbie Perez, and, I was surprised to see, the South African, Colonel DeSmid.

The South African report seemed to have acted as an agenda although it was merely a long list of 'Potential Incidents'. The incidents were mainly Special Operations that had not gone according to plan, starting with Operation Argon and ending with Operation Mango. The list included the two intercepted diamond shipments.

In their report the South African DMI described what information they thought might have been leaked in each incident along with what external personnel had access to that material. By external I assumed they meant anyone outside the South African Defence Forces but it soon became apparent that what it really meant was British or American. The only external names mentioned for the diamond shipments for example were Perez and Darwyn, although there must have been a score of UNITA guerrillas with knowledge of the plans.

Beside each incident was a code for 'source' which answered one of the questions that had been bothering me. How had DeSmid been able to identify which operations had been leaked to the Angolans and which operations had simply gone wrong? It became clear from the report that most of the supposed leaks were simply guessed at. All but four had the codes C or IC. A footnote explained that C meant Conjecture and IC Informed Conjecture, which I took to mean that C was a guess made after the operation to explain its failure and IC a guess made during the operation by those who were face to face with the enemy. Operation Mango had the source GCHQ which was self-explanatory.

That left three others: Operation Argon, Operation Leeuwyfie and the first diamond shipment with the code GIC. For a moment I thought that was another sort of conjecture but a glance at the footnote quickly corrected that. GIC meant that the source DeSmid was relying on to tell him that the Angolans had been forewarned about Argon and Leeuwyfie and the diamond shipment was the American oilman GI Coley.

I was astonished but it only took a moment to realise why it made sense. Coley had some sort of relationship with Salvador Pinheiro's brother-in-law, Angola's Deputy Oil Minister Martim Vasconcelos.

Somebody had leaked operational intelligence to Salvador Pinheiro. Pinheiro would jealously guard that source, never admitting his or her name to anyone. But at the same time might he not occasionally let it be known that he had a source? After the failed raid on the Cabinda oil tanks might he not boast to his inner circle that he had foiled the raid, that one of his spies had forewarned him? Or did he mention it to his daughter Mariana and might she have boasted about it to someone, her uncle perhaps, Martim Vasconcelos: the Martim Vasconcelos GI Coley had visited in London. The oilman and the oil minister. Robbie Perez had warned me that Coley was supporting UNITA not out of idealism but because he wanted access to Angolan oil, why wait for a UNITA victory if the governing regime's Deputy Oil Minister could be bought?

I could imagine a sequence of events. Salvador Pinheiro and Martim Vasconcelos meet up at some family event and the subject of a recent clash in southern Angola comes up. Pinheiro mentions that the South Africans had come off worst because he had been forewarned of their plans. A few weeks later Vasconcelos is at an oil industry conference somewhere and over late night drinks he and Coley are discussing the Border War when Vasconcelos mentions a recent South African raid that the Angolans had beaten off. My own brother-in-law was responsible for the victory, boasts Vasconcelos. If Coley reported that to someone like DeSmid it wouldn't take long to identify the place and the date and work out that Vasconcelos must have been talking about Operation Leeuwyfie.

Perhaps Vasconcelos had also boasted that his brother-in-law was responsible for thwarting the infamous South African raid on the Cabinda oil facilities, the one where the raid commander was captured, and that his brother-in-law had ambushed an enemy diamond shipment.

The more I thought about it the more likely it seemed. DeSmid had claimed he had a source who confirmed that the Angolans were being forewarned about South African operations. I had assumed he meant he had a spy in the enemy's camp. But in fact there were only three 'Potential Incidents' that his source had identified. One was Argon which had been all over the papers. One was Leeuwyfie. And the other was wholly exceptional, a diamond shipment. It was easy to imagine all three coming up in a casual conversation between Pinheiro and Vasconcelos and Vasconcelos repeating the stories a few days later to GI Coley. This wasn't some sort of sophisticated espionage operation in which DeSmid had a spy in the Angolan camp. It was just a one-off passing on of gossip. DeSmid's evidence was just hearsay. No wonder he hadn't been able to discover where Pinheiro's intelligence was coming from until GCHQ had stumbled across the Operation Mango plans being sent from the Angolan Embassy in London.

DeSmid's source was an opportunist buttering up both sides in a war that for him was not about ideology but about oil. He had visited Vasconcelos in London not to offer condolences on the death of his brother-in-law but to establish whether the murder of a senior politburo member might signal any changes in the balance of power inside the regime. Were Coley's friends, men like Vasconcelos himself, likely to gain power or lose power? Who was now worth bribing? Adam Joseff had visited Vasconcelos to offer condolences but not GI Coley.

And then it struck me. That's not why Joseff had been there either. Pinheiro had been slowly feeding those bloody stamps to Joseff one by one in exchange for information. And when he was killed Joseff's first thought would have been what will happen to the remaining stamps? When we told him Pinheiro's brother-in-law had arrived in London he rushed back from Cornwall to see him. But how would Martim Vasconcelos react? Would he dismiss Joseff as some sort of madman babbling on about postage stamps and spies or would he take him seriously and realise there was something there he could make use of? Either way if he mentioned Joseff's visit when GI Coley came to see him a few days later the American oilman would have paid attention. We knew that he then rushed off to see Joseff, claiming he was interested in subscribing to the *Exodis Bulletin*.

As Brasenose would say the pieces were starting to fit into place but the big questions were no closer to being answered. Adam Joseff. John Darwyn. Salvador Pinheiro. Mariana Pinheiro. Four people murdered. Who by and why? Was there even any connection between the murders in Antigua and London? And did I really need to go to Alaska to find the answers?

In normal circumstances if we need something from the CIA we ask. The Joint Intelligence Committee meets every week and the CIA's London Chief of Station always attends. But Brasenose wanted any approach to Robbie Perez to be more discreet. The Americans had moved on since the Star Chamber and wouldn't want any of the discussions there reopened. Whether there had been an Angolan spy in our midst was no longer relevant. The two main suspects had been taken off the pitch and in any case the game had changed. The daily bulletins from the battles around Cuito Cuanavale made clear that winning the war was impossible, the game now was winning the peace. In 1962 the CIA had tracked the movements of Nelson Mandela allowing the South African police to arrest him. Thirty-five years later

Mandela was negotiating with government ministers and foreign dignitaries from his prison cell and the American-led Crocker peace process was in full flow. There was already talk of some sort of signing ceremony, perhaps in London. The Cubans would leave. The South Africans would give up Namibia. American diplomacy would have triumphed. It was time for the exploits of people like Robbie Perez in Jamba to be written out of the history books.

I wasn't sure that I entirely believed the explanation Brasenose gave for not using official channels. One thing I had learned about him was that although he would painstakingly assemble a theory detail upon detail he wasn't afraid to ignore it completely if his instincts told him to. One of his pet phrases was that 'Intuition is the chaperone of Intelligence'. Somehow he had an intuition about Robbie Perez, that she knew more than she had let on and that she would not respond well to an official approach. Her name had apparently come up in his discussions with John Darwyn and I wondered what exactly Darwyn had said about her.

I spent most of the day trying to track her down. All I knew is that after the Star Chamber she had been posted to a CIA facility somewhere in Alaska. Our Washington Station were unhelpful and my mentioning that this was a JIC matter probably didn't help.

'You want us to ask Langley about the whereabouts of one of their agents without telling them why?' demanded the Deputy Station Chief incredulously.

'Not exactly. You can tell them why just as long as it's not the truth.'

He eventually came back to say that the only Perez the Station could identify in the Agency was a signals specialist based in Colombia. They did fax me copies of the Perez entries in the telephone directories for area code 907, Alaska, and various codes which they told me 'more or less' covered the Washington area. There were a surprisingly large number of Perez entries in Washington, not so in Alaska. There were however a surprisingly large number of CIA outposts in Alaska keeping an eye on the Russians next door. I imagined Robbie Perez guarding the Trans-Alaska Pipeline from the sort of attacks she had organised in Angola.

Given the nine-hour time difference with Alaska I left the office early in order to spend the evening on the phone from home.

'Make sure you keep a record of your calls,' Julia told me, wagging her finger and grinning. 'You can claim for them all.' I laughed; Julia knew that the civil servant in me would be sure to keep meticulous records.

There were limits to what could be accomplished on the phone but if Perez had moved to Alaska as we had been told she didn't seem to have registered with a phone or utility company, bought or rented a house or joined any of the obvious social outlets. As always with Americans I was astonished by their open and welcoming response to anyone with a British accent asking utterly implausible questions. Even a local chapter of the National Rifle Association was happy to try to put me in touch with one of their members whom I claimed to have met on safari in South Africa.

By ten o'clock I was ready to give up. It was no easier to find a named CIA agent in America than I hoped it would be to find a named MI6 officer in Britain. It was only when I woke up the next morning that I realised that there was a much simpler way to find Robbie Perez. I had allowed myself to be sidetracked by Brasenose mentioning the posting to Alaska.

Robbie Perez had told me that her brother, Larry, lived in London. There couldn't be many people named Larry Perez in London. I struck lucky on my very first call and in a way that was totally unexpected.

A male American voice answered. 'Larry Perez.'

'Good morning. I'm trying to contact Robbie Perez.'

Before I could say anything more I was interrupted. 'Sure. I'll pass you over.'

# XX

The next voice was Robbie Perez sounding exactly as she had in Jamba. 'Who is this?' She didn't sound as if she really wanted to know.

'Thomas Dylan. We met in Jamba.'

At first I thought she wasn't going to respond.

'Am I under surveillance?' Perez asked.

'Of course not. I just wanted a chat.'

'How did you know I was here? I only landed yesterday.'

'I didn't know. I was phoning your brother to try to find out what had happened to you. I thought you were in Alaska.'

She clearly didn't believe me. 'Yeah. Sure you did,' she replied, meaning the exact opposite. 'You wanted my address so you could drop by next time you're vacationing in Anchorage. And what a surprise you find I'm right here on your doorstep. What do you want?'

'Just to chat.'

'You said that. What about? I'm not in the business any more.'

'A chat about old times. A few loose ends we'd like to explore.'

'We?'

'You know who I work for.'

'Of course. If there are any loose ends as you put it why don't you ask John Darwyn? He knows everything that's going on down there. I'm out of it.'

I hesitated a moment. 'That's difficult,' I said, 'John is not around any more.' Perez didn't say anything. I wasn't getting through to her but I wasn't sure how much to tell her. Darwyn's murder hadn't hit the press yet. I decided that if I wanted her cooperation there was no point in holding back.

'John is dead. We've just found his body with two bullets in it.'

'Jesus. I didn't think that sort of thing happened over here. Is that what you want to talk about?'

'Yes, sort of. Could you come in to Century House today?'

I could sense Perez shaking her head. 'I'm out of this business. I call on you, Frank Cato hears about it and I'm dropped right back in.'

'How about a drink then or lunch?'

'I'm having lunch with my brother.'

'It's important Robbie.'

She wasn't convinced. 'What's your number? I'll call you right back.'

To my surprise she phoned back almost immediately. I had expected her to consult someone in the Agency before speaking to me again but she hadn't had time to do that. 'We're going to a Palace. Hampton Court Palace. Do you know it?'

'Yes.' We had actually taken Eveline there not long ago. The King's Apartments were still being restored after the disastrous fire a couple of years earlier but Eveline had been fascinated by the Hampton Court Maze.

'Good. Apparently there's a pub right opposite that you can't miss. We'll find a table outside. Twelve-thirty. You can buy me a beer and a ploughman's sandwich. Larry says that's what you guys eat over here.'

255

She put the phone down. I hoped there was only one pub there, I vaguely remembered a large white place opposite the Palace. Julia and I had planned to spend the afternoon in Kew Gardens. That would have to be postponed.

'Perhaps,' Julia responded, 'there may be time for Kew after the pub.'

'OK but I've no idea how long the chat will go on. Perhaps you should go on to Kew and I'll meet you there.'

Julia gave me a funny look. 'No. I'll be with you.'

'You're planning on coming to the pub?'

'Of course. If there's anything we can learn about Adam's death we should both be there. And if this woman is taking her brother you can take your wife. In any case,' Julia added melodramatically, 'you're not having dates with unattached women on your own, anything might happen.'

'Robbie Perez is not like that.'

'It's not her I'm worried about.'

Julia's aunt always seemed shocked at the apparently pointed comments Julia and I aimed at each other. What we regarded as friendly banter Aunt Anne regarded as mildly bad form. Now I must have reacted the same way.

'I was only joking,' Julia responded when she noticed my reaction. She gave me a reassuring peck on the cheek. 'I'm not suggesting other women would find you attractive.'

I chose to ignore that. 'What about Eveline?' I asked. In those days children under fourteen weren't allowed in pubs.

'We'll stay outside. It's a lovely day, I can take her for a walk if necessary.'

The pub was easy to find and Robbie Perez was already there when we arrived, seated at a table outside. She looked just as she had at Jamba: no make-up or jewellery, dark shirt and camouflage pants. She had at least replaced her jungle boots with battered trainers. Beside her was an exceptionally tall man with the same slightly sallow complexion whom I assumed to be her brother. With them was a much shorter woman, an inch or two shorter than Robbie Perez herself and considerably lighter, who proved to be her brother's girlfriend. All three were drinking Guinness and all three needed their glasses refilled. After the introductions I went inside to buy a round leaving Larry and his girlfriend trying to engage Eveline in conversation. When I returned they had succeeded and Eveline was demanding to know why they 'spoke funny', a remark that seem to embrace both Larry's American accent and his girlfriend's distinctive Dublin diphthongs. Julia was trying to explain that we all had accents while Robbie Perez stood by silently with an amused and slightly superior expression on her face, an expression very similar to the one she had bestowed on me when we first met in Jamba.

'My brother tells me that what you English call pub grub is godawful but we have to try it. After that Larry and Clodagh might go for a walk and we can have your little chat.'

Conversation over lunch could have been stilted. Larry Perez seemed to be the strong silent type and his sister was no better but Julia and Clodagh made sure there was hardly a moment of silence. Clodagh it transpired was a nurse now working at the hospital where Eveline was born. This seemed to create some sort of bond between the two women. I was surprised when Julia explained why she was now unable to have any more children, a subject we usually avoided, especially when Eveline was nearby.

The only potentially awkward moment came when Julia mentioned that she worked for a strategy consultancy.

'I thought you were Defence Intelligence,' interrupted Robbie. 'I'm sure that was in the file on Thomas I was shown in Africa.'

'I used to be,' replied Julia. 'I was persuaded to retire. Like you I believe.'

Robbie turned to her brother. 'Why don't you and Clodagh take Eveline to the Palace and go find a throne. We'll catch you up.'

Eveline jumped up, pulling Julia to her feet.

'Won't you stay here?' Robbie said to Julia. 'This is supposed to be unofficial.'

I thought Eveline would object but she grabbed Clodagh's hand and pulled her new friends away to show them Hampton Court Maze. Julia sat down again. Robbie Perez glanced around to make sure no one was within earshot.

'For the record this is just a casual conversation. I happened to bump into Thomas Dylan and his wife on a day out and we exchanged a few words. Nothing more. Now tell me. What the hell is this all about? What happened to John Darwyn and what's it got to do with me?'

'We don't know what happened. His body's just turned up in the Caribbean but he must have been killed within days of your Star Chamber in New York.'

Perez snorted at that. 'Star Chamber my ass. More like *Wheel of Fortune* on TV. You think you'll see the missing letters uncovered one by one when instead wham it's all over and it's on to the next show.'

'You'll have to explain that.'

'Have to explain? I don't have to explain anything. I'm pulled out of there before anything even kicks off, get sent down to Langley to sit on my ass for two days and am then told there's this fuckwit job for me in Juneau, Alaska. Alaska for Christ's sake. Jamba to Juneau. You explain that.'

She glared at me as if I were somehow responsible. Neither of us spoke until Julia broke the silence.

'Are you saying there wasn't a Star Chamber? You and John Darwyn were just summoned to New York and told you wouldn't be going back?'

'Something like that. I don't know about John. We were on the same flight back from Jo'burg and we were both expecting to attend this crazy Star Chamber thing. I was sure it would be a complete waste of time but John was all fired up about it. He was really looking forward to it. But something changed. He was staying up in Midtown someplace but when I arrived at the World Trade Center the next morning I saw him by the elevators. He was arguing with someone. Real heated stuff. The other guy had him by the arm.'

'Did you recognise who it was?'

'Not at the time, the guy had his back to me. I just registered tall, well dressed, my age maybe. I thought he might have been called Joseph.'

My head shot up. 'Why do you say that?'

'They were shouting. One of them shouted something that sounded like Joseph. But that wasn't his name.'

'How do you know?'

'Because I was introduced to him later. When the meeting started. He's one of you guys by the name of Rowbart.'

'Turk Rowbart? Are you sure?'

'Of course I'm fucking sure. He sat right opposite me.'

'I mean are you sure he was the man you'd seen earlier. Tall, well dressed. It could be anybody.'

Perez gave me a look that would have frozen the Atlantic. 'For Christ's sake what business are we in? If I say I recognised him I recognised him.'

'OK. Then what happened?'

'When John saw me coming he pulled his arm away. This man Rowbart seemed to be threatening him. John responded with something about Reagan.'

'President Reagan?'

'Well that's the only Reagan I know. Anyway Rowbart took the elevator and disappeared.'

'John didn't follow him?'

'Not right away. He was shaken. You know, real shaken. Like he'd seen a ghost. Said he'd be up in a minute, he needed to go outside and get some fresh air. Christ we'd just got in from Africa and in New York it's snowing. What'd he want fresh air for?'

'So you left him there and went up to the Field Office.'

'That's right. And just sat there. DeSmid came in looking for John and then disappeared. John didn't appear for another ten, fifteen minutes. He still looked grey and he didn't wanna say anything. He'd been so bullish the day before but now he didn't even talk about the weather which I thought was a subject you English always wanted to talk about. I remember I got pissed off and tried to find somebody who could tell us what was happening but just got ushered very politely back into the room. Meeting was supposed to start at nine, it was gone nine-thirty before everyone else came in. They had obviously been in a huddle together somewhere.'

'So then the inquisition started?'

'Well I expected it to. I thought we'd be pulled apart on the rack before being burned at the stake. But no nothing. I've been to bloodier tea parties. Frank Cato gave a little speech welcoming everybody to New York, telling us all how important the day was and urging everyone to be totally open. We weren't here to assign blame but to find the truth. Asperton replied by saying exactly the same in an English accent. Then DeSmid went through his list and everybody denied passing anything to anyone and that was it. It was all over in an hour. Cato told me to wait there and everyone else left.'

She hesitated for an instant. 'That's the last time I ever saw John Darwyn. Soon after that Cato's assistant came in and said the meeting would reconvene in an hour. So I went downstairs to the underground shopping mall but I don't like shopping so I came back and sat in the room reading the *Wall Street Journal*. Finally Cato comes in on his own and tells me that DeSmid thought I'd passed on information about Special Ops and the diamond shipments to Darwyn and that Darwyn had then passed the information on to the Soviets. It was crap. I told Cato he couldn't possibly believe such bullshit. Cato said it didn't matter whether he believed it or not I was a security risk and the South Africans wouldn't accept me going back to Jamba. The choice was resign or be reassigned. That was it. Like that Meryl Streep, Robert Redford movie I was 'Out of Africa'. After nearly twenty years with the Agency I could go. I said I wasn't going and two days later was told next stop Alaska.'

'So then you decided to resign,' I said.

'No I went to Alaska, to Juneau. Godawful. Nothing

there. Just sitting at a desk. The operational highlight for those guys was to cross over into Canada where it's still legal to go shooting polar bears. It wasn't any good for me. I lasted ten days then hopped on a plane back to Washington. I told Cato to reassign me to a proper post. He refused so I quit and here I am.'

I was bemused by what Robbie Perez had said just as I had been reading the official Star Chamber file report. A Star Chamber is supposed to be a big deal, an occasion for high drama. This one had resulted in two of the leading characters, Perez and Darwyn, losing their jobs. Sparks should have been flying but whatever action there may have been had taken place entirely off-stage. Cato and Asperton carefully set the scene but then moved straight to the denouement. Darwyn itching for a fight capitulated in the wings. Rowbart lost his script. DeSmid read nothing but his script and Perez had an insignificant bit part.

Whatever had passed between Rowbart and Darwyn by the elevators had changed the day's dynamic completely.

'You heard nothing else from John Darwyn?' I asked.

'Nothing at all. Like I keep saying I'm out of it. There's plenty of security work around. I just don't need any of that political bullshit. I'm off tomorrow.'

'Tomorrow?'

'Yep tomorrow I'll be in Beirut, this is just a stopover to see Larry. Beirut's where I'm figuring on basing myself now. I've got contacts there. That's where the action is. And I don't have to give a damn about Uncle Sam and Frank Cato and Jonas Savimbi and all those assholes in Langley.'

She stood up.

'Wait a minute Robbie,' I urged. 'There's more I really

want to know. What happened to John Darwyn? What can you tell us about him? Apparently he announced he was going to Florida to retire and just disappeared.'

'I've no idea why anyone would kill him. There's nothing I can tell you.'

'But what was he like Robbie? What happened to him in South Africa? Do you believe that he admitted passing secrets to the Russians? Did he really say you were involved?'

'How the hell would I know? Nothing makes sense. Like the idea Darwyn would want to retire in Florida, that's the last thing he would ever do. I've had enough. Like I said I'm off, I'm out of it. Come on let's find your daughter.'

'Five minutes Robbie. Just give me five minutes, I have to know about John Darwyn. We trusted him. We believed in him. Did he really sell us out?'

It was too late Robbie was walking away. Julia ran after her and when I caught up with them Julia had the American by the arm. 'This is personal Robbie,' she was saying. 'It's not just John Darwyn. A friend of ours was killed at the same time. A man named Adam Joseff. Someone I've known for years. A family friend. I have to know why he was killed and who killed him. And somehow it's all tied up with John Darwyn but we just don't seem to know what sort of man Darwyn was. What was going through his head?'

Robbie Perez just pushed her away but Julia continued. 'I don't understand your world. I don't understand what drives people like you and Darwyn. I don't understand what our friend became mixed up in. What drives you people?'

At that Perez turned around and looked straight at Julia.

'It's simple. We're patriots. John Darwyn was a patriot. I'm a patriot. My parents came to the United States from

Cuba to escape to freedom. I was proud of them, they were proud of their new country. They taught me to fight for what's right. Dad taught me to shoot. I joined the Agency as a twenty-year-old. They sent me to Vietnam as a secretary in the Station in Saigon. I stayed there and towards the end the Agency used me for one or two jobs they thought would be too risky for a man. The military say there were no women in combat roles in Vietnam. The Agency say they had no women in the field. But they had me. And you know what, I enjoyed it. I enjoyed the thrill. I enjoyed the action. I enjoyed the secrecy. I knew things nobody else knew. The Agency made me special and when Vietnam was over they sent me into the field again. I was the token woman. Of course I knew what was happening, all those two-faced men bitching about me behind my back and leering at my ass. But when they came on to me they soon realised it wasn't like Mae West, I wasn't pleased to see them, I was the one with a gun in my pocket. And finally I was sent to Jamba, Chief of Base. Probably someone's idea of a joke. Send the token Cuban-American to fight the Cubans. But now I was calling the shots. I'd made it. But made it to do what? To fight for freedom? To defend democracy? To help one bunch of lunatics massacre another because some asshole back in Washington has decided that today's flavour of the month is UNITA and Jonas Savimbi? But I ploughed on just like Darwyn. We both knew it was crap but we were both professionals. We both loved our countries right or wrong.'

Robbie turned to me. 'Darwyn came to see me in Jamba. It was just before that first diamond shipment was ambushed. We talked about the diamonds. Somewhere out there some poor sods had been breaking their backs digging for those diamonds just like generations of slaves had done before them. And more poor bastards had carried them down to Jamba to be loaded on a plane to Zaire so they could be swapped for yet more guns. And all along the way people will be getting a cut. Savimbi. Nambala. The officials in Zaire, they will all get their cut. Then when the diamonds get to Belgium the dealers in Antwerp will take their perfectly legal commission. And the jeweller in New York would take his perfectly legitimate mark-up so that some fancy woman on Broadway who's never had to work in her life can make a splash at the opera. And then of course the guys supplying the guns would get their money, the guys in France or Israel or God knows where. Everybody would get a cut except for John and me, the people who make it all possible, who provide the protection. But I didn't sell out.'

She was almost daring me to contradict her but I believed her. 'But did John Darwyn sell out?'

'I don't know. He was a funny guy. You know he changed. That first time I met him with Thomas in Jamba he was a typical Brit. Cold and smooth at the same time. What can I say? He pretended to be the little guy but he didn't really believe it and he made sure you realised he didn't mean it. He was always saying sorry for no reason. You English say sorry too often I told him. And you Americans don't say sorry enough he shot back. He was always like that, kinda superior. For example he liked the blacks, really liked them but the way mothers like their children. He used to talk about countries in Africa as if they were still colonies. He treated Americans like they were children too. Superior, like I said, that's the word.'

She paused for a moment as if deciding what to say. 'He

was good you know, he could fit in. I didn't think that at first. At Jamba when I met him he came across like one of those old Africa types you find at the Mount Nelson in Cape Town, moaning about the good old days in Rhodesia. But he got on with everyone there, better than you did Thomas. When he needed to he could play a part. On the plane coming over to New York he was preparing for battle in the big city. Smart suit and aftershave. Perhaps everything was a pretence. Perhaps there were lots of John Darwyns and he woke up each day and played a different one. You know he was really close to Colonel DeSmid, right from that time meeting him in Jamba. How was that possible? DeSmid's practically a Nazi. What the hell. What do any of us know about anybody else? What do I know about you, what do you know about me?'

She turned back to Julia. 'That's all. There's nothing else to say. I'm sorry about your friend. I'm sorry about John Darwyn. But I can't tell you why they were killed. I don't know. I've got to look after myself now. I've gotta think about my future. Maybe Beirut is the answer. Maybe I just give it all up. My father was so proud when I got that job as a secretary with the Agency. He thought that was all I needed. I was doing something to repay our family's debt to the country that had adopted us and now I should go find a man, settle down and raise children who would be the sort of proud Americans that Larry has turned out to be. Maybe I'll do something like that, without the children of course. If Beirut doesn't work out Larry wants me to come here. He thinks he can find a job for me in his bank. A nice safe job doing something where I'll never have to carry a gun again. Who knows he may be right, I'm getting a bit long in the tooth for this game. Perhaps I'll come knocking on your door Julia, strategy consultancy might be just perfect, if I can figure out what the hell it is.'

For the first time that afternoon she smiled. 'Can you see me as a strategy consultant?'

'Well I certainly couldn't see myself as one,' replied Julia smiling back. 'But who knows? Look me up when you come back.' She reached into the enormous handbag from which she usually took the colouring book and crayons needed to keep Eveline quiet. Instead she pulled out a crumpled copy of the Exodis prospectus.

'This is who we are. The friend I was talking about set the consultancy up. He's left a hole that no one person is ever going to fill.'

We queued up and entered the Palace grounds. The renovation works after the fire in the King's Apartments were still not complete. We had no trouble finding the others and when Eveline saw us she ran to Julia to impart the news that where Larry lived in America there was a much, much, much bigger park where Mickey Mouse and Donald Duck lived. We had to go and see it. While Julia explained that we were not likely to visit Disneyland soon, and that it was a long way away, I noticed that Robbie Perez had stopped behind us. I turned and she was looking at me with a mystified expression on her face.

'What's this?' she said as I approached her. The smile had gone. She waved the Exodis prospectus in my face. 'What does this mean?'

'It's what Julia does,' I said. 'That's her business, Exodis.'

'But what's it got to do with our operation in Jamba?'

I shook my head. 'I don't understand. Nothing.'

'Come on Dylan what's Exodis got to do with the proprietary that went down?' Perez was angry now.

I shook my head again, I still didn't understand what she was talking about.

'You want me to spell it all out?' she demanded.

'Yes. I think you should.'

'There was a diamond shipment being flown up to Zaire, you know that. The plane crashed. That was the second shipment we'd lost. The first got ambushed by the Cubans and Angolans on the way to Jamba. We never figured out how that happened. This time Cato decided we needed a proper inquest. We all met up in Windhoek three days after the proprietary went down. Frank Cato brought some big cheese over from Langley. I was hauled in from Jamba and Lusiano Nambala came down to represent Savimbi. The South Africans were there and John Darwyn was there. Like I was telling you John had been in Jamba when the previous diamond shipment was ambushed. Frank Cato had gone nuts about that. I wasn't supposed to discuss diamond logistics with anyone, not even MI6. So from then on I made damn sure that John Darwyn wasn't told anything about diamond shipments but Cato didn't believe me. I don't know how Darwyn got invited to the debrief this time, he turned up with DeSmid. Cato was pretty pissed off to see him but of course he couldn't say anything in public. Later he accused me of having given Darwyn the flight plan which was nonsense. Of course the flight plan didn't matter but at that time we still thought the plane had been shot down.'

'What do you mean you still thought the plane had been shot down?'

Perez looked at me in surprise. 'Well it wasn't shot down,

was it? They found the wreckage eventually up near Moxico Province. Dangerous area that, more landmines than people. Not much safer on the Zaire side of the border and almost impossible to reach by land. Anyway it wasn't shot down. Someone had put a bomb on the plane.'

That was news to me and I wondered if the Americans had told Colin Asperton. Probably not, better to blame a Cuban MiG than their own security.

'Anyway he was there, in Windhoek.'

'John Darwyn? Yes you said that.'

'No not John Darwyn. This man in the pamphlet. He was at the airport where we had the debriefing. Good looking guy, distinguished.'

I saw what she was looking at. It was the photograph of Cristóvão Taravares.

Now I understood what she meant. I had momentarily forgotten Brasenose telling us about Taravares being in Namibia.

'Yes he was there,' I confirmed. 'We knew that. It's a chap called Cristóvão Taravares. He's a major client of Julia's but he was also a distant cousin of Salvador Pinheiro. He was close to Pinheiro's daughter and when the Pinheiros were murdered in London we investigated the family and discovered this man had recently been to Namibia. Naturally we were suspicious but it turns out he just stopped to refuel on the way from Johannesburg to Cape Verde. Apparently he wasn't on the ground for more than half an hour or so.'

'That's not true.'

'What do you mean?'

'I saw him there. We were just going to start the debrief when an executive jet lands. That doesn't happen all the time in a place like Windhoek. It's not much of an airport. I noticed it had an Italian registration, I hyphen something, that really is unusual. After we'd finished some of us went to the bar. The man in the photo was there, on his own. Like I say good looking, and he knew it. I thought maybe he was something to do with Frank and had been waiting for our meeting to end but he didn't speak to any of us. He finished his drink, got up and left. Twenty minutes after that the Italian plane took off. That jet was at the airport for far longer than half an hour.'

We looked at each other without saying anything. Robbie was still suspicious and I couldn't blame her.

# XXI

That evening Julia and I puzzled over what it all meant. Robbie's parting shot about seeing Cristóvão Taravares in Windhoek was unexpected but not perhaps as mysterious as it first seemed. He was clearly not there just for refuelling. Either he was delivering something or picking something up or both. The most likely explanation was that he was engaged in some form of sanctions busting and that his presence in Windhoek at the same time as the enquiry into the crashed plane was a coincidence. Almost as soon as we had articulated that theory we dismissed it. It was simply far too much of a coincidence. That meant that Taravares' presence at the airport had something to do with the meeting that was going on there. In some way he was connected with the CIA proprietary being shot down, or as we now had to think of it being blown up, or else with Operation Mango which had been happening at the same time. Both the plane crash and the Operation took place before he landed in Namibia and so it seemed impossible that he could have had anything to do with passing the details of either to the Angolans.

If he wasn't directly spying for the Angolans could he nevertheless have been working for them? Perhaps he had been delivering some sort of reward to whoever had leaked the details.

'Or could he,' asked Julia, 'have been collecting something connected with one of the operations?'

We had both reached the same conclusion: the diamonds.

'It's the only thing that makes sense,' I agreed. 'Someone put a bomb on that plane not to stop the shipment reaching Zaire but to cover up the fact that the diamonds were never on the plane in the first place. What the American pilots thought they were transporting was not diamonds but a bomb.'

'So the key question,' suggested Julia, 'is who had access to those diamonds before they were loaded and who also might be connected in some way with Cristóvão Taravares.'

'And the answer to that,' I added, 'surely lies in the phone call Mariana Pinheiro made to Taravares from the phone box in Byng Place. Somebody phoned her in London and told her when the shipments were going to take place. She then called Cristóvão Taravares who shot off to Windhoek to wait for the diamonds to arrive so he could take them back to Europe. And she also made a note for herself in her Filofax.'

Julia completed the chain of thought. 'And the person who contacted Mariana to tell her when the diamonds were going to be shipped out was Marco Mutorwa, the nephew of Lusiano Nambala, the man responsible for the security of the diamonds in Jamba.

It suddenly all seemed very obvious. Nambala had somehow swapped the diamonds for a bomb, had the bomb loaded on to the plane and then brought the diamonds down to the airport in Windhoek where he was attending the enquiry into what had gone wrong. Taravares turned up in Windhoek and waited in the bar at the airport until the meeting was over. Then Nambala had the diamonds loaded on to the Italian jet and off they went.

It was all very neat. It also explained why we hadn't been able to work out how John Darwyn and Adam Joseff had discovered the flight plan for the diamond shipment and passed it on to Salvador Pinheiro in Luanda. They hadn't. Perez had told Darwyn about the first diamond consignment, the one that had been ambushed before it reached Jamba, and Joseff had passed the details on to Pinheiro. But Darwyn hadn't known anything about the second shipment and nothing was ever passed on to Salvador Pinheiro. Stealing the diamonds was Mariana Pinheiro's exercise in private enterprise. She and her friend Marco wanted their own source of funds. Mariana wouldn't need to rely on her father when she wanted a flashy new sports car. Marco wouldn't be reliant on the generosity of an erratic guerrilla leader whom he didn't appear to like very much and who in any case might not be around for much longer. They just needed a couple of people with no scruples to help them out and they found them in Cristóvão Taravares and Lusiano Nambala.

I looked forward to explaining it all to Justin Brasenose. Another piece of the jigsaw had fallen into place. A picture was starting to take shape but, I realised, it wasn't the picture I was looking for.

Understanding what had happened to the diamond shipment got us absolutely nowhere in terms of finding out who had murdered Adam Joseff and John Darwyn or the Pinheiros. It may have even taken us further away. If Marco Mutorwa was working with Mariana Pinheiro to help steal diamonds and ship them to Europe why would he be involved in her death?

The whole business with the diamonds was really a sideshow. The murders of Joseff and Darwyn had not been the result of Lusiano Nambala putting a bomb on a plane in Jamba. They had stemmed, I felt sure, from something that had happened in New York.

The story Robbie had told us about the Star Chamber seemed so odd that I wondered whether she had made some of it up. Had Darwyn really met Rowbart outside the World Trade Center and been left looking like he'd seen a ghost? What had apparently upset him so much? And why had the Star Chamber itself effectively evaporated. If Robbie was to be believed the Star Chamber simply didn't happen. Which at least would explain why the file report was so thin. But this was supposed to have been a rigorous enquiry into potentially serious security lapses. For it all to be cancelled at the last minute made no sense. And for Darwyn to then quietly choose to resign was incomprehensible, although, I reminded myself, the last time I had seen Darwyn I had described him as demob happy.

It wasn't until I was seated in Justin Brasenose's office the following Monday that more of the pieces started to slot into place. Brasenose had greeted me with the comment that he had expected me to be halfway to Alaska. I knew that wasn't meant as a joke as he was clearly not in the mood for humour. Although I had worked closely with him in the past I couldn't remember him arriving in the office in such a foul mood. Something must have gone badly wrong over the weekend, I thought. I was wrong: things had gone wrong before the weekend started.

'Something stinks about that Star Chamber,' he announced before I had time to sit down. 'Nothing about it adds up.'

'That's what I think,' I agreed but Brasenose clearly wasn't interested in whether I agreed or not.

'Really, that's what you think. Well frankly I don't care what anybody thinks. Thoughts are two a penny. What I want to know is what actually happened. I spent the whole of Friday with Colin Asperton and then with Turk Rowbart and I phoned Frank Cato in Langley. And I don't believe a word any of them said. It's mad. We're all on the same side. We all know the rules. What are they all trying to hide and from whom? Colin and Turk I might understand. They don't want some superannuated Whitehall mandarin coming back and telling them things wouldn't have been done that way in my day. But Frank Cato I've known for years, since my time in Washington. Why can't he give me a straight answer? Why did he post Perez to Alaska? What had she done? Do you know what he said?'

I could guess but it was wiser to keep quiet until Brasenose had finished. I shook my head.

'He said she was responsible for that plane disappearing with UNITA's diamonds on board. Now you tell me is that likely? If she'd given the flight plans to the Angolans that's treason. What would Cato have done in that case? She wouldn't just get reassigned somewhere else. I pressed him of course but he told me to leave it alone, forget about the flight plans, forget about the plane altogether. She was responsible. Case closed. Now what the hell does he mean by that?'

'It means the Angolans didn't have the flight plans and they didn't shoot the plane down. There was a bomb on it. And as Robbie Perez was responsible for security at Jamba he's pinning the blame on her.'

Brasenose didn't argue, he just looked at me. 'Are you sure?'

'Yes.'

275

Most people would have asked me how I knew but not Brasenose, that question would come later. He was working through the implications of what I had said in his own mind.

'You mean Cato has discovered that the plane wasn't shot down and hasn't told us. That's bloody ridiculous. But it could be. If the security in Jamba is so weak that the enemy can get right up to an American aircraft on the ground and put a bomb on it without anybody noticing Frank would indeed be more than embarrassed. The crew of that Lockheed were Americans.' He shook his head. 'That's just typical.'

He didn't say typical of what and in any case it didn't matter: what he had suggested isn't what had happened. I jumped in before he could say anything more.

'Cato thinks somebody breached his security,' I said, 'but he's wrong. The Angolans didn't infiltrate that base. Nobody was trying to stop the diamonds reaching Zaire. The diamonds were never on the plane. The bomb was in the container that was supposed to hold the diamonds.' Brasenose was silent and so I told him what I had really wanted to tell him when I'd entered his office. 'I've spoken to Robbie Perez.'

His head snapped up at that.

'You've what?'

'She was in London on Saturday. En route to Beirut. I spoke to her.'

'And she told you someone swapped the diamonds for a bomb?'

'No, she hasn't put the pieces together yet. That's what we've worked out.'

Brasenose's eyes narrowed. 'What do you mean we've? Who's we?'

276

'Julia and me. We talked to Perez together. It was Julia who managed to make her open up. Perez is one very angry woman. She wouldn't have talked to anyone in the business.'

He pushed his chair back and looked me in the eye. 'I think you'd better start from the beginning. How did you find Robbie Perez?'

After I had explained Brasenose made me recite the conversation with Perez almost word for word. He interrupted only to question whether I was repeating exactly what the American had said. 'Don't elaborate,' he insisted at one point.

'Are you sure Perez didn't say who accompanied her to the airport bar in Windhoek?' he asked later. 'You should have pushed her on that. Can we be sure it was Nambala, not say Darwyn, who passed the contraband on to Taravares before the jet left?'

When I had finished Brasenose at first was silent before asking simply, 'Do you believe her?'

'Yes I do.'

'I hope you're wrong. Because if you're right Turk Rowbart and Colin Asperton have a lot of questions to answer. Let's take a walk, clear our heads.'

He said nothing as we left his office and went out into St James's Park. It was a fairly typical April day, the sort of day to wear a coat on the way to work but leave it in the office for a stroll in the park. I waited for Brasenose to start.

'As I told you I spoke to Cato, Asperton and Rowbart on Friday. Let me tell you what they said. Perez was right: the New York meeting was nothing like a real Star Chamber. And that started the evening before. Asperton had supper with Cato and DeSmid and DeSmid suddenly announced he had found out who had been leaking South African secrets to Darwyn. It was one of his staff, he said, but he wouldn't give them the name. Said it was sensitive and he would deal with it when he got home. The important thing was that they shouldn't push Darwyn in the Star Chamber. If Darwyn realised his source had been uncovered then he could pass on a warning which was the last thing DeSmid wanted. Asperton thought that sounded reasonable and agreed not to ask too many questions the next day.

'The way Colin Asperton tells it they were all prepared for a real Star Chamber, although I'm not entirely sure what he means by that. Certainly aggressive questioning, every possibility explored, nothing held back. Perez was also right that the meeting didn't start on time. Rowbart and DeSmid were delayed. And when the meeting did start there was no aggressive questioning and people certainly seem to have been holding back. Colin had expected Rowbart and DeSmid to lead the charge but apparently neither of them said very much. And Darwyn was almost silent. None of them came up with any fresh ideas. John Darwyn couldn't think of any way that anyone in South Africa could have seen his cables to London but equally couldn't suggest any way they could have been leaked from Century House. The whole meeting was over almost before it started. And then Rowbart and Darwyn grabbed Asperton and Darwyn announced he wanted to resign with immediate effect.'

'Just like that?'

'Exactly, just like that. Colin says he was astonished but also I suspect relieved. DeSmid had already made clear that he didn't want Darwyn returning to Pretoria. And Rowbart didn't want him back in London because he thought Darwyn had leaked his own Operation Mango report.'

We turned on to the bridge over the lake and Brasenose fell silent.

'It's all wrong,' he said at last. 'The champagne's popped and then we're served beans on toast. We know secrets are being leaked to the enemy. The Operation Mango intercept proved that even before DeSmid told us GI Coley had somehow confirmed it. So something is seriously wrong somewhere. People are angry. Rowbart wants Darwyn out. Darwyn according to Perez is flying to New York itching for a fight. DeSmid is throwing a fit because he thinks Darwyn has suborned somebody on his team. Cato has just discovered a bomb has been placed on one of his planes and is looking for somebody to blame. And on top of all that we have the unsolved murders of Salvador and Mariana Pinheiro. And yet when the time arrives for a showdown everyone just steps away. Nothing came out of that session that we didn't know about in advance. Cato and Asperton spout their little homilies and then sit back to watch. Rowbart doesn't dig. Darwyn, far from fighting to protect his reputation, meekly resigns. Did he strike you as the resigning type?'

'No,' I had to admit. 'And if Darwyn had wanted to resign he wouldn't have done it on the spur of the moment. He would have prepared for it, gone to London and resigned formally. He wouldn't have sprung it on people after a meeting like that and just buggered off to Florida.'

'So something unexpected must have happened in New York to make Darwyn decide to resign. What?'

'The argument with Rowbart that morning by the elevators?'

'Perhaps. Describing it as an argument might be a bit strong. It could only have lasted a matter of minutes or even seconds. What could Rowbart have said in that time?'

'We should ask him,' I suggested.

'Oh I will. If Perez is right and one of them mentioned the name Joseff that, as the Americans say, is a whole new ball game.'

'Joseff and Reagan,' I pointed out.

'I think we can forget Reagan,' said Brasenose with a wry smile. 'I can't see the President of the United States being personally involved in this. Although it could be that somebody has been doing something they wouldn't want to be public knowledge. The White House and Congress haven't always agreed on policy in Southern Africa. It's quite likely that Frank Cato's been up to things that President Reagan might approve of but which strictly speaking break the sanctions set by Congress.'

I let that go. Even if Brasenose were right why would that matter to Rowbart or Darwyn? 'There's another question you might ask Rowbart,' I suggested. 'Why didn't the meeting start on time? You said Rowbart and DeSmid were delayed. Delayed doing what? Perez saw Rowbart arrive, what was he doing after that which caused the meeting to be put back?'

'That had occurred to me,' Brasenose replied. 'Rowbart led me to believe that he was delayed by the weather, but it would appear that isn't true.'

'And why did DeSmid go looking for Darwyn before the meeting? And did he find him?'

'Colonel DeSmid is the one man in all this business I haven't been able to speak to yet. We need to play this carefully. If Rowbart and DeSmid are keeping anything back

I don't want them talking to each other before we can find out what it is. I'll set up a call with DeSmid and then Sheila West can interview Rowbart at the same time. See if they tell the same story.'

'I could interview Rowbart.'

'No Thomas. There's the issue of hierarchy, you're technically a grade below Rowbart. And in any case I want you kept out of this for the time being. If Rowbart is up to something we might need to put you back on his Desk for a while to try to find out what's happening. I've got another job for you. I've said before that there are still too many loose ends hanging around. We've let matters drag, far too little action far too much inaction. We need to go back and start again on the two sets of murders. I shall ask West to trawl through Joseff and Darwyn's entire lives, I want every possible connection between them uncovered. When have they ever met? When have they even been in the same place at the same time? And I want you to go through all the police files on the Pinheiro murders. What have we missed? Like you say if you're right about Mariana Pinheiro and Marco Mutorwa being involved with the diamonds going missing why would Mutorwa kill her?'

'You still think he did?'

'I'm not sure I ever did think that. Leaving the bomb's radio controller in his flat was too stupid for words and far too convenient for us. But then I'm not sure about him and Mariana Pinheiro stealing the diamonds either. It's a clever theory but entirely circumstantial.'

Brasenose checked himself, stopping suddenly to look at me. 'No,' he said. 'Not entirely circumstantial. You remember you found a diamond shape scribbled in Mariana Pinheiro's diary on the day the plane disappeared. There was a similar diamond mark two days earlier but crossed out. I checked with Frank Cato. The flight had been scheduled for the earlier date but was delayed. There's no doubt that's what those diamond marks in her diary referred to. I took that as evidence that Mariana Pinheiro had been instrumental in passing the flight plans on to her father. But if the plane wasn't shot down that makes no sense.'

'She wasn't telling Salvador Pinheiro in Angola when the flight would take off, she was telling Taravares in Trieste when Marco Mutorwa's uncle would steal the diamonds.'

'You could be right,' Brasenose conceded. 'You may need to track young Marco down and have another word with him. And we might ask your wife to do a bit more digging on what Mr Taravares has been up to. In fact I have a better idea: I'll ask our colleagues in Rome and Lisbon for a little help, ask them to make enquiries about Taravares and diamond smuggling and not to be too discreet about it. Get him rattled.'

'You might talk to the Belgian authorities as well,' I suggested. 'That's the natural place to sell diamonds and Taravares asked Julia to do some background checks there.'

We returned to Brasenose's office and his assistant arranged for me to spend the rest of the day at New Scotland Yard looking through files on the Pinheiro assassination. I could almost hear a sigh at the other end of the line: the police team's work had been painstakingly detailed and they would have known that the chances of me finding anything new were infinitesimal.

The police and the Security Service had collected an enormous amount of material all carefully catalogued and boxed up. Reading through the transcripts of the interviews the team had conducted took me not only the rest of the day but most of the next morning as well. By the afternoon I was confident that there was nothing more worth reading. Only one large file remained and that was the one including my own witness statement. Out of interest I read through my own words.

I had given a very long statement. It struck me that I had mentioned Rowbart a lot, his radio calls to me and his appearance right after the explosion. Perhaps because the conversation with Brasenose had left me puzzling over the actions of Rowbart and DeSmid in New York it suddenly occurred to me that there was something odd about their actions in London. They had arrived on the scene remarkably quickly but in itself that was not surprising. Rowbart had told me on the radio that he had already picked up DeSmid and his sweeper and they were now on their way to Northolt. They might well have been close enough to hear the bomb going off. I read through the statements that Rowbart and DeSmid had given. They described what they had found when they arrived on the scene and their impressions were exactly the same as mine. But there was something missing.

I looked for the statement from DeSmid's sweeper. It wasn't there. In fact there was no mention of the sweeper in either Rowbart or DeSmid's statements. What had happened to him? I hadn't noticed anyone with them when they arrived in Westbourne Terrace but no doubt I had other things on my mind. Perhaps DeSmid had sent his sweeper away when he saw Mariana Pinheiro's car blasted apart. But if that were the case the sweeper would still have been a potential witness and there was no sign that Sheila West's team had interviewed him. It seemed more likely that the sweeper had been dropped off before Rowbart and DeSmid got there. On reflection that seemed a strange thing to have done. It meant that they had heard the bomb and before driving to investigate decided that they would no longer be going to RAF Northolt and therefore didn't need a technician to sweep the meeting room.

I looked through the evidence catalogue. There was an exhaustive interview with Pinheiro's sweeper, who had been in the car right behind Mariana Pinheiro's Mercedes when the bomb exploded. But I could find no mention of DeSmid's sweeper, not even his name. If DeSmid had brought him from South Africa arranging an interview now would be time consuming but I had nothing else to report back to Brasenose.

First I needed a name. If the sweeper had stayed at the Royal Over-Seas League like DeSmid I might be able to find his name and his home address. That didn't work but it occurred to me that there was another way to find what I wanted. I called Brasenose's office and asked his assistant to contact RAF Northolt and get hold of the security details of all visitors expected at RAF Northolt on the morning of the planned meeting between Colonel DeSmid and Salvador Pinheiro.

Brasenose had arranged to call DeSmid in Pretoria at four o'clock and Sheila West would be interviewing Rowbart at the same time. The three of us were due to meet up at five o'clock to compare notes. I would have nothing to say.

I was just about to pack up when Brasenose's assistant phoned back. 'The security logs have been faxed over from Northolt. Will you look at them later or should I fax them on to you now?'

I was impressed that she had been able to obtain the logs so quickly and it seemed churlish to suggest they could now wait on her desk. 'Send them over please.'

I regretted saying that almost immediately as I then had to find the number of the nearest fax machine but ten minutes later the list of pre-authorised visitors with their documentation was in my hand. I noticed that Mariana Pinheiro had been added hurriedly at the bottom of the list with her passport number and the instruction. 'Not to proceed beyond reception.' For everyone else the authorisations included a photocopy of their passport or ID card.

There were two South Africans on the list. Hendrik Andries DeSmid looked up unsmilingly from a passport photo clearly taken some years ago. The other belonged to a man I had never seen before, his sweeper. I saw the first line of his name, Michael Desmond, and then stopped in shock. The surname below in capitals was a very familiar one, although not in this context nor with this spelling. It was the name John Darwyn had shouted angrily at Turk Rowbart in New York: Regan.

# XXII

I put the fax in my briefcase and hurried out into Victoria Street trying to remember exactly what Robbie Perez had said about the altercation in New York between Darwyn and Rowbart. She said they had been standing by the elevators and Rowbart had been holding Darwyn's arm. She thought Rowbart might have been threatening the other man. Darwyn pulled his arm away and shouted something about Regan but what about Regan she hadn't heard. Rowbart had spun around and got into the elevator perhaps because of what Darwyn had said or perhaps because he had seen Perez approaching or perhaps just because the elevator door had opened and other people were getting in.

By the time I had crossed Parliament Square the beginnings of an idea were forming in my mind and by the time I arrived at Brasenose's office I had convinced myself that I knew just what had happened in New York.

Waiting for the fax had made me a couple of minutes late and West was already there.

'Good of you to join us,' said Brasenose. It was clear that his mood had not improved much since this morning. 'Sheila and I have just been discussing what our friends Rowbart and DeSmid have cooked up for our delectation. Not good news.'

'And it's going to get worse,' I interrupted. 'I've found something.'

Brasenose might have taken offence at being interrupted but instead responded sarcastically, 'Do tell.'

'I've found Regan. He was DeSmid's sweeper.'

It was West who responded first. 'Who's Regan?'

Brasenose started to ask a question of his own but changed his mind and instead answered West. 'According to Perez when Darwyn and Rowbart had that row in New York Darwyn said something about Regan. I didn't mention it to you because I assumed he was referring to President Reagan.' He paused. 'It seems I was wrong. Let's just take this step by step. Thomas, tell us what you've found.'

When I had explained there was a moment of silence before Brasenose asked me the obvious question, 'What does it all mean?'

'It means that Regan is someone Rowbart and DeSmid know well but they don't want us to identify. They told him to scarper as soon as they discovered a bomb had gone off and kept any mention of him out of their statements. I don't know who or what he is but I think Darwyn found out and perhaps was planning to bring his name up at the Star Chamber. At the same time Rowbart had come across the name Joseff and perhaps linked him to Darwyn.'

'Rowbart denies that completely,' interrupted West. 'I've just interviewed him. He says Perez must have misheard. Nobody mentioned anyone called Joseph.'

'But your theory,' Brasenose said to me, 'is that Rowbart had a secret he didn't want exposed, something about this man Regan, and Darwyn had a secret he didn't want exposed, that he'd been passing information to Joseff. So they both agreed not to reveal what they knew at the Star Chamber.'

'Something like that. The key question is what did Darwyn discover about Regan?'

'We'll come to that,' responded Brasenose. 'As I say let's take this step by step. Perez says that when Rowbart and Darwyn were arguing one of them shouted the name Joseph. As Sheila points out Rowbart denies that. But suppose it's true and you're right that Rowbart had found out about Darwyn feeding information to Joseff. How could he have discovered that? When Sheila told us about Adam Joseff turning up at Mariana Pinheiro's flat after the bombing Rowbart had no idea who he was. By the time he reached New York he apparently knew all about him.'

I had already worked out how that happened.

'GI Coley,' I said. 'Adam Joseff paid a call on Salvador Pinheiro's brother-in-law Martim Vasconcelos in London. Two days later GI Coley did the same. We don't know what Joseff and Vasconcelos discussed but knowing Adam he was probably after the remaining stamps in the set. If Joseff hinted at his arrangement with Salvador Pinheiro and Vasconcelos repeated that to Coley you can be sure Coley would have relayed that back to DeSmid.'

'Plausible,' admitted Brasenose. 'So Rowbart knew what Darwyn and Joseff were up to but he agreed to keep quiet about it because Darwyn had something on him, something to do with Regan. Where your theory falls down is that Rowbart and Darwyn weren't keeping quiet. When Perez saw them they were screaming at each other.'

'But that was before anything kicked off. I think Darwyn and Rowbart met by accident going into the building and one of them started mouthing off about what they had found, probably Rowbart. He revealed that he knew Joseff and Darwyn were working together. That must have been a hell of a shock to Darwyn and he responded in kind: he brought up Regan's name. That's what Perez heard. Two very angry men.'

'So what happened next?' West asked. 'They certainly weren't shouting at each other when the Star Chamber started.'

'I think we can explain that,' responded Brasenose. 'Let's think about what happened between the time Perez saw Rowbart and Darwyn arguing and the Star Chamber starting. Remember the Star Chamber didn't start on time. Rowbart and DeSmid asked for it to be delayed for half an hour.' He turned to me. 'As we agreed Sheila and I asked both Rowbart and DeSmid what the delay was for. DeSmid told me he couldn't remember, he thought perhaps Turk Rowbart had a call to make. He also said he couldn't remember going to look for Darwyn but if he had it was probably to advise him about the delay. Basically he tried to play dumb, but he's not dumb.'

'Whereas Rowbart on the other hand,' put in West, 'tried to be clever. Before he said something about the weather but this time he claimed Mrs DeSmid, who had come to New York with her husband, was feeling unwell. He said Colonel DeSmid had wanted to check she was all right before leaving the hotel. I suspect he made that up on the spur of the moment and assumed he could get DeSmid to back him up later, not knowing Justin was talking to DeSmid at the very same time. He also denied there had been any altercation with Darwyn.'

'I think it's pretty clear,' said Brasenose, 'that Thomas is right. Rowbart bumped into Darwyn in the lobby and couldn't resist telling him his time was up, he knew all about Joseff. Darwyn struck back by saying he knew something about this man Regan. Whatever it was that Darwyn had discovered DeSmid and Rowbart certainly didn't want it revealed so DeSmid went off to find Darwyn and cook up a deal, silence in return for silence.'

'But what did Darwyn know about Regan?' West asked. 'That's the real question. If Thomas is right and Rowbart had somehow discovered that Darwyn was passing secrets to Joseff why didn't he unmask him as a traitor? What was so secret about Regan that both Rowbart and DeSmid were happy to let Darwyn just retire quietly?'

I looked at Brasenose. There was one very obvious answer but I didn't want to be the one who said it.

Fortunately Brasenose had got there at the same time. 'There is one scenario that fits the facts but is just too absurd to contemplate,' he said, standing up. He turned to look out of the window with his back to us. 'Regan wasn't brought to London to sweep a meeting room for bugs. On the contrary he was brought over to make sure the meeting didn't happen at all. He was here for one reason only: to assassinate Salvador Pinheiro. DeSmid never intended to negotiate with Pinheiro, his plan all the time had been to kill him.'

'And Rowbart must have known all about it,' I added.

Brasenose shook his head. 'That's inconceivable. A British Intelligence officer condoning a bomb being detonated on the streets of London. It's just not how things are done.'

But even as he said it I could sense that Brasenose was realising it was not inconceivable. Everyone could see South Africa was losing the war. I could imagine Rowbart thinking something had to be done. Killing Pinheiro would not only take out a key player but serve as a warning to the rest of the regime. It might even destroy the power balance within the Angolan politburo and then anything might happen.

'What do we do now?' asked West.

Brasenose spun round, his voice firm again. 'I consult. We are talking about a senior member of the Secret Intelligence Service conspiring with a friendly power to murder a guest of Her Majesty's Government. That is more than sensitive. If I had to predict my JIC colleagues' reaction it would be that they will require a lot more evidence before they believe anything like that. We have much more work to do. And may I remind you also that our initial objective was to find out who killed John Darwyn and why, but what we appear to have done is move in the opposite direction. If we are right then two months ago when John Darwyn left New York and agreed to retire quietly he stopped being a threat to anyone. So why was he killed and by whom?'

Brasenose has always had an extraordinary ability to snap from one persona to another. He had suddenly changed from reflective colleague to imperious mandarin.

'There's a lot to do. I will get on to our people in Washington and have them track down Darwyn's movements after he left the Star Chamber. If he really travelled to Florida the FBI should be able to help. We're assuming he travelled to Antigua on the Newman passport but I'll have that checked. Sheila, I want you on Regan. We have his passport details. I want to know as much as you can find without alerting Rowbart or DeSmid. The next time we talk to them I want us to be thoroughly prepared and them to be thoroughly unprepared. Let's see what they say when we spring the name Regan on them. See if we can do anything with Regan's passport photo. And I think we've got enough to put a tap on Rowbart's phone.'

'And surveillance?'

'Not yet. We're treading on dangerous ground already. MI5 tapping the phone of an MI6 officer is somewhat problematic. But we have to do it. There is something wrong inside Century House. Why didn't anyone there realise that the Newman passport Darwyn was using was one of their own? The police investigating Joseff's murder would have contacted the Passport Office with the passport name and number. In turn the Passport Office would have realised they hadn't issued it but they would also have recognised that the number was one of ours. There are standard procedures for that sort of thing. They must have alerted someone in the Service. What happened then? Or rather why didn't anything happen then? Look into that too Sheila. And find out where Rowbart was when Darwyn and Joseff were killed. Did he come straight back here after New York or did he decide to take a holiday in the Caribbean.

'Next there's the issue of GI Coley. When I spoke to DeSmid just now he mentioned he had left New York after the Star Chamber to go game fishing with Coley. Is Coley involved in all this and which side is he on? He was at the Jamba Jamboree and he's pumped money into UNITA. But he's clearly also got contacts in Luanda. My reading is that he's a pure opportunist. He wants to find a way to get a piece of the action in Angola.'

'You think Coley's mixed up in Darwyn's murder?' I asked.

'Probably not. I just don't like him. It's always dangerous when these American billionaires start playing international politics and end up funding someone's private army. Look at what's happening in Afghanistan. No he's not a priority but I'll put out some feelers. Joseff and Darwyn are the priority. And that's where you come in Thomas. You're off to Cheltenham.'

'To GCHQ? Why?'

'Perhaps to GCHQ. But perhaps not. We've been trying to establish links between Adam Joseff and John Darwyn.'

'And GCHQ have found something?'

'No, nothing to do with our friends at GCHQ, just old-fashioned police work. We've looked at both men's credit card statements. Joseff didn't use his much but Darwyn put everything on his. The one thing they both used their cards for was petrol. Two days before Christmas they used their cards at almost the same moment and not very far away from each other: Joseff at Michaelwood Services on the northbound M5 south of Gloucester and Darwyn on the A40 approaching Cheltenham. Darwyn had arrived at Heathrow the day before and picked up a hire car. He dropped it back there on Christmas Day.'

'That was a long way to come for such a short visit,' commented West.

'That's right and it seems to have been entirely personal. He didn't even notify Century House he was in the country. The odd thing is neither man used their cards for anything at all for the next twenty-four hours, it's as if they deliberately didn't want to leave a trace. Did they meet? If so where? The M5 and A40 meet near Cheltenham but GCHQ have no record of either man making any contact with them. So if they were both in the Cheltenham area what were they doing there? It's too much of a coincidence to think they just happened to be there at the same time.'

'But they could have been going somewhere else,' I pointed out. 'If they'd both been going to say the middle of Wales they might have gone that way. Perhaps we're distracted by the coincidence of them being so close to GCHQ.'

'True,' said Brasenose. 'But we've got to start somewhere. According to the chaps who understand these things if you look at where they next bought petrol on their cards, and assuming they didn't buy any petrol with cash in the meantime, neither man went more than twenty or thirty miles north of Cheltenham before turning round and heading back south or east. And the next purchases were the following day so both men must have stayed overnight somewhere.'

He looked directly at me. 'You did well spotting the missing sweeper. Now do some lateral thinking in Cheltenham.'

I left with no idea where I would start. Perhaps I had left my lateral thinking skills at home. In that I was almost right; it wasn't my lateral thinking that was needed but Julia's, as became obvious the next day.

I picked up my fake Metropolitan Police warrant card, warned our contact in the Gloucestershire Constabulary that I would be on his patch and spent the next day visiting hotels in and around Cheltenham; there were a lot. In the village of Painswick a hotel manager thought she might have recognised the photo of Adam Joseff but wasn't at all sure. She was much more confident when I mentioned his limp. Joseff had stayed there using the name Joseph Williams. She remembered him because he had lost his credit card but fortunately carried cash and paid in advance. I copied down the London address he had given although undoubtedly Joseff had invented that as well. The manager was certain of one thing: her guest, who stayed one night, was on his own.

I checked in with Brasenose at five. 'Stay down there,' he instructed. 'Try restaurants, see if there was a booking for Joseph Williams.'

Sheila West's enquiries he told me had been more productive. As we already knew Regan was in London on the day of the Pinheiro murders but she had discovered that he had been there for two weeks before that and had stayed for ten days after. Long enough to plan the bombing and then to plant the radio control on Mutorwa afterwards and mark a cross on a map he happened to find in Mutorwa's room. What really put the cat among the pigeons was that West had also engaged in lateral thinking; she had contacted the Antiguan police and discovered that Regan had been there at the time Joseff and Darwyn had been killed. He had arrived on the island from Miami the day after Adam Joseff, which was two days before Darwyn arrived. He left again the day after the two men were killed.

That, I realised, was the first direct evidence linking the Pinheiro bombing with the murders of Joseff and Darwyn. A man who had not figured in the police investigation in either London or Antigua had actually been on the scene in both cases.

'We need to find him,' said Brasenose, 'but that's going to be impossible as long as he stays in South Africa and DeSmid is protecting him.'

'Which he will because Regan must have been working for DeSmid.'

'We need to start again on the Antiguan murders. What

was Regan doing there and was he with anyone? The more I think about those murders the less I understand, they simply don't stack up. For one thing Joseff is shot and his body left for whoever comes along to find but Darwyn is buried where nobody is ever expected to find him. Why?'

'And why,' I asked remembering the questions Julia had raised, 'bury him at all? Why not tie a weight to the body and dump it in the sea?'

'Which is what the killer must have done with Darwyn's possessions. Joseff's belongings were all there with the body but we've never found anything connected to Darwyn. He arrived at the airport with luggage but it wasn't with the body and it wasn't with Joseff. The killer must have dumped it somewhere. If the body hadn't turned up we wouldn't have known he had ever been on the island.'

'And if the passports hadn't been buried with him nobody would have known even if the body did turn up.'

'That's true. Like I said it doesn't stack up.'

'Unless,' I said thinking aloud. 'The killer didn't want anyone to know Darwyn had been killed at the time but might want it to be known at some point in the future. If for example the police uncovered something embarrassing about Joseff's murder the killer might reveal the whereabouts of Darwyn's body to distract them.'

That sounded pretty weak but Brasenose did not dismiss it out of hand. 'Or perhaps,' he suggested, 'at the right time the killer digs up the body as a warning to others.'

That also sounded weak. I would try out both theories on Julia later when I phoned her but I knew what she was going to say, 'farfetched' would be her most charitable description.

In fact when I phoned home to say I would be in

Cheltenham for at least another day Julia had something else to say.

'I'm joining you.'

'What!'

'Well you could at least sound pleased. The au pair will look after Eveline so tomorrow we can have a romantic night in a nice hotel.'

I was of course pleased but I wasn't sure others would be. 'I don't think Brasenose will be too keen on that,' I suggested.

'Well perhaps he should be. I think I know why John Darwyn was in Gloucestershire.'

I was amazed. 'Why?'

But Julia refused to say anything more. 'I could be totally wrong which would be very embarrassing. I'll tell you after lunch tomorrow. Say five o'clock at your hotel.'

'That's a long lunch.'

'Oh Cheltenham has some lovely shops. If I'm right I may celebrate by buying myself a dress for the summer.'

'And if you're wrong you may console yourself by buying two dresses.'

'If you insist darling.'

I spent the next morning showing Joseff's and Darwyn's photos to dozens of people around the area but I had nothing to report when Brasenose paged me.

'We're going to have to release details of John Darwyn's death,' Brasenose told me when I called him. 'The Antiguan police can't go on saying they don't know the identity of the corpse discovered in Nonsuch Bay when there were not one but two passports found with the body. I'm hoping the story won't be picked up over here but you never know. Just be careful when you show his photo round.'

'I will. Anything new at your end?'

'Just one bureaucratic foul-up after another. We've discovered that Darwyn flew from New York to Miami the day after the Star Chamber but we still have no idea what he was doing down there. He flew out of Miami to Antigua five days later. Would you believe that he got on a plane in Miami using his own passport with the US entry details in it and got off in Antigua using the Newman passport. Nobody checks arrivals against the passenger lists. That system will have to change. There's another more sinister bureaucratic snafu in Century House. The Passport Office copied the police enquiry about the Newman passport to the Registry who checked to see which Desk had requisitioned the blank passport. Surprise, surprise it was the Subsaharan Africa Desk so the Registry simply forwarded the enquiry to the Saddo.'

'And Rowbart replied saying everything was above board?'

'No if he'd done that we'd now have him. He didn't do anything. The enquiry was simply binned and nobody followed it up.'

I could believe that. Century House was a long way from the slick, well-resourced, high-tech headquarters of the James Bond films, which is one reason why those at the top of the Service were so keen to move us out of the building. Although that, I reflected, wouldn't stop what Brasenose called bureaucratic snafus.

I had only just put the phone down when the pager went again. Brasenose had apparently forgotten something, I thought, but this time it was Julia. She had sent an unfamiliar number which when I called proved to be a restaurant I was planning to visit later that afternoon. The woman who answered was expecting me and summoned Julia to the phone.

'You'd better come here,' Julia said without preamble. 'Don't ask why, just hurry.'

Fortunately I was only ten minutes away.

Julia hadn't told me who she had been meeting for lunch but there was really only one person it could be. When I entered the restaurant another chair had been drawn up at the table where Julia was sitting with Rosemary DeSmid. Mrs DeSmid rose uncertainly to greet me.

'Your wife tells me you might be able to assist me in contacting a friend of mine, John Darwyn.'

# XXIII

I sat down, unsure what to say. How much had Julia told Colonel DeSmid's wife, indeed how much had John Darwyn told her?

'Is John a close friend?'

'He is. Close enough for me to know that he works for the same organisation as you. Where is he?'

'And where do you think he might be?'

She looked at me unsmilingly. 'Let's not play games Mr Dylan. If you know where he is tell me.'

I had to make a decision. If she was involved in Darwyn's death she would already have known the answer. If she wasn't involved what harm could there be in telling her?

'I'm afraid he's dead Mrs DeSmid. His body was discovered last week, in the Caribbean. He had been shot.'

Her expression tightened. 'Did my husband kill him?'

That was not a question I had expected and she must have seen the look of surprise on my face.

'Why might you think that?' I asked.

'I believe my husband suspected an improper relationship between myself and John Darwyn.'

'And did he have reason to suspect that?'

She drew herself upright before answering. 'That is not a very discreet question Mr Dylan.'

'This is hardly a time for discretion,' I replied, perhaps too sharply.

For a moment neither of us spoke.

'That's enough Thomas,' said Julia gently. 'You're upset you've lost a colleague, Rosemary is upset she has lost a friend.'

As I believed it highly likely that John Darwyn had been selling secrets to the Angolans I wasn't sure that describing me as upset entirely captured my feelings.

I looked across at Rosemary DeSmid and realised that she was holding herself together with difficulty. There were no tears but the knuckles of her left hand were white as she gripped her fork above an empty plate.

'I'm sorry,' I said. 'I didn't mean to cause offence.'

'No offence taken. It was my silly question. Of course Hendrik could not be involved in John's death.'

She paused again, keeping all emotion out of her voice 'I knew something had happened. When the body of his friend was found in Antigua and John didn't try to contact me it was obvious that something had gone terribly wrong.' She stopped again, before briefly looking away. 'John wouldn't tell me about the mission he was on, just that it wouldn't take long.' She turned back to me. 'I realise that yours is a dangerous world, men die. In Africa I could understand that. If John had been sent to Angola or Mozambique then of course his life would have been in danger. But in the Caribbean. What sort of mission was he on in the Caribbean? He was about to retire. Why send him into danger?'

I tried to make sense of what Rosemary DeSmid was saying. What had Darwyn said to her that had made her think he was going on some sort of mission?

I noticed that Mrs DeSmid was wearing no wedding ring. I tried to remember if she had one in our previous meeting in

London but I simply hadn't noticed. No doubt Julia would have been able to say. How close was the relationship between Mrs DeSmid and Darwyn? It was difficult to imagine that it was, in her word, 'improper'. Neither fitted easily into the usual picture of red hot lovers. Darwyn I would have thought was a confirmed bachelor and Rosemary DeSmid seemed far too proper to jump into bed with a passing stranger. When she said that he had told her he worked for the same organisation as me I hoped he had meant the Foreign Office; if he had really told her that we both worked for the Secret Intelligence Service that would have been an extraordinary breach of security. That was the sort of secret that shouldn't even be shared in bed.

As with Robbie Perez, it was Julia who found the way forward and she did so the same way: by stressing her personal loss.

'You mentioned the death of John's friend in Antigua. I presume you were talking about Adam Joseff. I didn't know Adam was John's friend but he was certainly mine. More than that. He was both an old family friend and my boss. He set up the firm I work for. His murder remains unsolved. I don't think the police have any idea who killed him or why.'

'The newspapers said it was a mugging,' interrupted Mrs DeSmid.

'That's right they did. But the discovery of John's body has changed all that.'

I still didn't know how much I could trust the woman sitting across from me. Julia seemed to have no such doubts but I was more cautious. I certainly wasn't going to tell her that we thought John Darwyn had been supplying Adam Joseff with information which Joseff then passed to the

Angolan regime in exchange for money paid into a bank account in Antigua. But she needed to know some of the truth or we would learn nothing ourselves.

I tried to sound sympathetic. 'Mrs DeSmid, Rosemary, I understand you've lost a close friend, like Julia, but I need to explain something. John wasn't on a mission in the Caribbean. He wasn't on a mission anywhere. We don't know what he was doing there but we think it was something to do with his time in South Africa. Adam Joseff had some business links in the region and we think John must have been involved in some way but we need help to find out more.'

A good place to start I thought would be to find out why John Darwyn and Adam Joseff had been in Cheltenham two days before Christmas.

'Did you know Adam Joseff?' I asked.

'No I never met him although John talked about him. I gather Mr Joseff had recently had a bereavement and was seeking a new direction in life.' That was news to me but I said nothing. 'John I'm sure was a great comfort to him. John called me just before Christmas. He knew I was spending Christmas with my family near here. I'd given him their phone number. But I was surprised when he called. It was a difficult period for me as I've just told Julia. John phoned and I was pleased to hear his voice. He said he was in the area to meet an old friend, Adam, and that perhaps I could join them for drinks. That sounded good to me and we arranged to meet that evening. It was two days before Christmas. When I arrived his friend wasn't there. He'd been called back to London John said, would I settle for just him? It was all rather sweet. John already had a table booked at a very nice restaurant and asked if I could join him now that his friend had gone. Of course I said yes. We had a lovely meal. John was such a lovely man. It was odd seeing him in England, he looked so much more at home. And I suppose I was starting to feel the same. It all seemed very natural. John said he might not be stationed in South Africa for much longer and I told him that I wasn't sure I wanted to go back there. Life in South Africa is changing you know, what with the terrorism and the sanctions. And there were all sorts of personal things happening that I'm not going to go into, family matters.'

Suddenly Rosemary DeSmid pulled herself upright again. Her voice took on a strength that hadn't been there before.

'John asked me to spend the night with him. Not directly like that of course, he was far too much of a gentleman, but that's what he meant. I should have been shocked but I don't think I was and I wasn't offended. But of course I had to say no. I was a married woman. As your wife knows Hendrik and I were drifting apart but I had made my vows before God and I intended to keep them. John understood that. He was disappointed of course, sad. I could see that, really sad. He insisted on escorting me back to my daughter's but he wouldn't come in.'

'Was that the last time you saw him?' I asked gently, knowing that John Darwyn had returned to Johannesburg a day or two later.

'Good gracious no. We became lovers. It sounds so odd to say that. So odd and so right.'

She paused as if expecting me to say something but I didn't know what to say.

'I came to England to clear my head. My daughter lives

here and now my son Freddie is talking about leaving South Africa. Hendrik of course is appalled but I know Freddie. He is as pigheaded as his father. He is not going to stay there and watch the country collapse. He's talked about emigrating here to England or to Australia or New Zealand. I knew that he would do it one day. And when he did what would become of me? Alone in a big house with a husband who was hardly ever there and when he was there only wanted to talk about how many terrorists his men had killed on some raid or how successful the next raid was going to be. All our friends were Hendrik's friends. They were wonderful people, our children used to play together all the time, but now the children are all grown up. There has to be more to life than spending every weekend by the pool, drinking too much and wolfing food off the braai. Hendrik's idea of a holiday is Sodwana Bay game fishing. If the wives come to England it's for Wimbledon not the theatre. They spend more time in Harrods than in the museums and galleries. M&S means more than V&A. That's not what I want any more. John was a lifeline. He had travelled the whole world. You know he reads poetry, can you imagine that? We once spent a whole afternoon debating Dickens's use of satire. And of course John understood Africa but it was the real Africa, the Africa that in my little enclosed world I hardly ever saw.

'I had come to Gloucestershire for Christmas, the time of year when Hendrik couldn't imagine any sane person coming to England, to sort myself out, to think about the future. And now John had offered me a way out but I had turned him down. Had I done the right thing? I don't know. My daughter mentioned my evening out to Hendrik. I don't know what she said but he was furious and we had a terrible row. But when he said we would be going to New York for something called a Star Chamber I can tell you my heart leapt. John had already told me that he would be there. Hendrik and I had a dreadful argument before we left, he hadn't told me that his awful Irish friend was coming on the flight with us. When we got to New York I just wanted to see John again. Of course there was hardly any time for that but I knew where he would be staying and so I left a message for him. He called me as soon as he arrived. We had dinner at a little Italian restaurant off Broadway. Hendrik as usual had dinner with colleagues. It was magical. It wasn't furtive at all. Nothing happened then but it felt as though we had crossed a bridge, nothing would ever be the same.

'Hendrik had told me he would be going to Washington after the meeting and was then going game fishing. He also said that I needn't accompany him. The way he put it was that he didn't give a damn what I did. I told John that and after the meeting, while Hendrik was still talking to the Americans, John called me at the hotel. He had to go away on a new mission, he said, and he wouldn't be going back to South Africa. But the new mission wouldn't last long and didn't need to start right away. It was cold and miserable in New York and he suggested that we fly down to Florida, together. And that's just what we did. Now it seems such an adventurous thing to have done. And it was. In fact it was everything it promised to be, John was everything he promised to be. It was idyllic. John was full of plans for our life together. He was going to take a lump sum from his pension fund and buy us a cottage in the Cotswolds. I told him to slow down, I wasn't even divorced yet. It was all a big step for me and I didn't really know John that well. But when

I phoned my son I told him I wouldn't be going back to Pretoria with Hendrik, I was going to live in England. John and I agreed we would meet again in Cheltenham. And that was it.'

Her eyes started to mist over. Julia reached over towards her but she didn't notice. 'John never called. The dream melted away.'

# XXIV

Rosemary DeSmid stood up. 'I need to powder my nose.'

It was the sort of expression Julia's Aunt Anne, Lady Grimspound, would use. In many ways the two women were very alike. The same clothes – smart but discreet. Their manners were cultured but their pearls were not. There was something very proper about the way they carried themselves, for both of them deportment had been an important part of their schooling. As far as I knew neither were great equestrians but they both looked as if they should be. Despite having spent most of her life in Africa DeSmid still had the pale skin of the English Rose. She was perfectly at home among the lunching ladies of Cheltenham.

'You mentioned that an Irishman accompanied you to New York. Can you remember his name?' I asked when she returned.

'Regan. Regan with an E not like the President. An unpleasant man. Uncouth. Untrustworthy, I thought.' There was the glimmer of a superior smile. 'Rather like the President. I don't know what business my husband had with a man like that. On one occasion Hendrik brought him to the house. It must have been a Tuesday because I always play tennis on Tuesdays. But that day I was running late and Hendrik arrived with two men and announced they were going to have a braai. This Irishman, big red-faced fellow and an Englishman the exact opposite, very cultured, very polite. Army I should imagine. He had that bearing you know. I simply could not imagine why three such different fellows should want to socialise together in the middle of the week.'

'Do you remember the Englishman's name?' I asked.

'Not really, Hendrik hurried me out of the house. It was something like Holborn or Hobart. He only came the once. Regan came again one evening just before we went to New York. Hendrik took him into his study. I don't know what they discussed. Hendrik used to discuss everything with me but he's stopped doing that. And Regan was there again waiting to join us at the airport when we left.'

There was nothing more to ask but Rosemary DeSmid had one more thing to say. 'I have no regrets, Mr Dylan, whatever people may think.'

'You have nothing to regret Mrs DeSmid.'

'John was a good man, a loyal man. He was proud of the work he had done for his country and I am proud to have helped him.'

She swept out of the restaurant, head held high.

'What do you make of that?' I asked Julia when Rosemary DeSmid had gone.

'More to the point what do you think of that? I know you Thomas, I know what you're thinking and you're wrong. You're judging John Darwyn too harshly. Rosemary DeSmid fell in love with the real John Darwyn. He was taking money from Salvador Pinheiro but by his own lights he wasn't betraying us. The Service had already betrayed him. And in any case it wasn't our secrets he was selling.'

I didn't see it like that. To explain was not to excuse. Like everyone in the Service Darwyn had sworn to 'be faithful and bear true allegiance to Her Majesty Queen Elizabeth the Second' and he had broken that oath. At the end of the day loyalty had to be unquestioning or the Service couldn't function. Julia, with her family's military traditions, should know that better than most.

I just shook my head and changed the subject. 'How did you know about John Darwyn and Rosemary DeSmid?'

'I didn't really know,' replied Julia. 'It was a guess. But there was something going on with both of them. When I had dinner with Rosemary in London, you remember when you men packed us off to the theatre, it was obvious that her marriage wasn't perfect. She didn't say anything directly but I could tell, just the way she talked about her children and the way she didn't talk about her husband. I remember her saying that her mother had never really approved of Hendrik DeSmid but hadn't said anything, and that if only she had said something life might have been very different. There was more than wistfulness there. And then when Robbie Perez talked about John Darwyn having changed in South Africa even to the extent of wearing aftershave, it struck me that perhaps a woman had come into his life. It didn't occur to me that it might be Rosemary DeSmid until you mentioned the mysterious trip he had made over Christmas, that he had come all the way from South Africa just for a couple of days somewhere near Cheltenham. I knew Rosemary's daughter lived in Gloucestershire and I put two and two together.'

'So it was female intuition.'

'No it wasn't,' retorted Julia angrily. 'It was assembling the evidence and then applying logic. You could've done it yourself if you hadn't been obsessed with Darwyn meeting Joseff.'

I didn't think I had been obsessed but it was not the time to argue. 'Why do you think Adam and Darwyn did meet? Adam hadn't had any bereavement that we know of.'

'Perhaps he had, Thomas. He'd lost his special stamps.'

'You're joking!'

'No, I'm not. Think about it. Adam has spent his life serving his country. Nearly forty years, war and peace. Fighting secret battles in secret wars, every move made in private so that even those in the Intelligence world can't know more than a fraction of what he does. The only place he can stand up and shout about what's he's achieved is in an altogether different world.'

'Stamp collectors?!'

'Yes stamp collectors, philatelists. Don't mock. In that world he can be special, especially when he finds those unique stamps he told us about. But Salvador Pinheiro has them and Pinheiro doesn't want money, he wants secrets. And Adam succumbs. They're not his secrets. Why shouldn't he trade something that has no value to him or to his country for something unique in his other world? He not only succumbs himself he recruits John Darwyn. Darwyn is feeling bitter about being passed over in favour of Rowbart, perhaps by then Darwyn had already met Rosemary DeSmid and was entertaining dreams that were impossible on his salary. John Darwyn was doing what the Service is paying him to do, collecting Intelligence. Some of it, like details of that diamond shipment, from Robbie Perez, but most I suspect from Rosemary.'

'You think Rosemary DeSmid knew what he was doing?'

'She probably knew he was sending reports back to London but I doubt she knew anything about Adam and

Pinheiro. It doesn't matter, we're talking about Adam Joseff. Adam has chosen his road. But then Salvador Pinheiro is blown up. Adam rushes off to see the dead man's brother-in-law to try to buy the remaining stamps.'

'And Martim Vasconcelos laughs in his face.'

'Something like that,' Julia agreed. 'Whatever happened Adam suddenly realised he wasn't going to complete the set, he was devastated no doubt. Especially when GI Coley visits him and tells him he's just been to see Martim Vasconcelos. I don't know what Coley said but I think at that point Adam looked in the mirror and thought what have I done? Am I selling my soul, risking everything for a few little squares of gummed paper? I think he decided to give up. That's why he told that lawyer in Antigua he'd lost interest and would give him those Ultramar stamps. That's what he wanted to say to Darwyn. It's over. And he found Darwyn wanted to say the same thing. Darwyn had found love. All Darwyn wanted was to buy a cottage in the Cotswolds with the money Pinheiro had put into the account Joseff had opened for him.'

'In Antigua.'

'Exactly.'

I mulled over what Julia had just said. She could be right. The evidence fitted. But was it perhaps what we wanted to hear? We had both looked up to Joseff but it seemed even he had proved himself mortal. Incredibly he had sold out. Now Julia was suggesting he might have repented before he was killed. It was tempting to think that was true but Adam was nothing if not determined. We would probably never know what he was thinking when he flew to Antigua. Any more than we would know if Darwyn was driven by love, or by greed and revenge.

We should have got into the car then and driven back to London but Julia deserved a new dress and there was nothing Brasenose could do today with the information Rosemary DeSmid had provided. The idea of a romantic child-free evening in a nice hotel was far more attractive than rushing back to London. Before going to bed I phoned the JIC duty officer and left a brief message for Brasenose saying I had found something important and would be returning first thing next day. It was past midnight when the phone in our room rang. It was Brasenose. He had clearly seen my message I thought. I was wrong.

'We need you here. All hands to the pump. There's been a development.'

'Same here. Did you see my message?'

'No.'

'I've found out why Darwyn was in Cheltenham. He was meeting his mistress, Mrs DeSmid.'

Brasenose didn't respond and I could almost hear his brain processing what I had said.

'That could be interesting. When can you get back here?'

'Around ten.'

'Not before then?'

'We've been drinking, do you want me pulled over by the police?'

'We've been drinking? Who's with you? Not Mrs DeSmid.'

'Of course not. Julia. She was the one who worked out what had been going on between John Darwyn and Rosemary DeSmid. And she got Rosemary DeSmid to open up, and not just about the affair. DeSmid's confirmed that Regan and Rowbart met with her husband a month or so before the Pinheiros were killed.'

'She told you that?'

'Yes. The two of them came to the house.'

'That really is interesting, just what we need.' He didn't expand on that comment, just told me to be in London by 10.30. 'Paddington Green Police Station. The fun's starting.'

He ended the call without explaining what fun was starting.

I soon found out when I arrived at Paddington Green and was shown into the room Brasenose had commandeered.

'Turk Rowbart was arrested at his home at 7.05 this morning,' Brasenose greeted me. 'He's in the cells downstairs while his home is being searched. Then you and I will talk to him. Sheila West is handling Regan's interview.'

'Regan?'

'He arrived from Dublin last night. I'd better explain. Sheila has been busy. When Salvador Pinheiro and his daughter were killed Regan was staying at a hotel in Camden. We interviewed the staff there but you know what it's like. Even in five months staff have moved on and the copy of the passport photo we had was pretty poor. But luckily a woman on the front desk remembered a South African with an Irish accent. She thought that was pretty odd. It didn't really help us much, although if it was Regan it might explain that supposed warning from an Irish Republican group nobody had ever heard of. Anyway it prompted Sheila to ask the Irish to put Regan's passport on their watchlist, and it came up. Three days ago Regan arrived in Dublin from Johannesburg via Amsterdam. The Irish were a bit slow letting us know but yesterday they told us not only that he had arrived but that he was on his way here.'

'So you picked him up?'

'Not right away. We put him under surveillance when he landed. The first thing he did was go to a phone box and call Rowbart.'

'That was stupid. What did he say?' I knew Brasenose had put a tap on Rowbart's phone.

'He didn't say anything. When Rowbart picked up the receiver Regan disconnected. Then he called again, let the phone ring four times and put the phone down again.'

'So it was just a coded way of saying I've arrived. If we hadn't been watching Regan there is no way we could have linked Rowbart to him from the phone intercept.'

'That's right. Although a good lawyer will still be able to claim it's circumstantial and proves nothing. And I've just heard that the search of Rowbart's house hasn't turned up anything.'

'But you've now picked up Regan. What does he say?'

'He's saying no comment to everything. But Sheila is having another go at him. We've had a breakthrough though, it turns out he was in our files under his real name. The man now calling himself Michael Regan is a bomb maker extraordinaire. I'm surprised the Irish didn't identify him themselves. He disappeared from County Armagh eight or nine years ago when the local brigade fell out with Gerry Adams. He called himself Corrigan in those days. We had never been able to pin anything on him. We thought he'd gone to the United States but clearly he ended up in South Africa and offered his services to Colonel DeSmid.'

'And came over here to plant the bomb in Westbourne Terrace,' I said. 'But why's he back now?'

Brasenose merely shook his head. 'Let's hope Sheila can find out.'

That I thought was wishful thinking. Regan would surely be far too experienced to give anything away when West interrogated him again, whatever threats or bribes she might use. It was time to see if Rowbart would react any differently when we sprang the name of Regan on to him.

Rowbart was in an interview room in the basement and jumped to his feet when we came in.

'What the hell is this about? Why is my home being searched?'

'Sit down,' replied Brasenose calmly. 'We just want a quick chat to clarify a few things. Sorry about the warrant for your house. Our friends in the Security Service got a little carried away. You'll be pleased to know that they're out of there now.'

'And did they find anything?' Rowbart demanded, clearly not mollified by Brasenose's conciliatory words.

'No,' Brasenose replied. 'But there are still a few matters outstanding. Let's sit down, the sooner we can get this over the better for everyone.'

Rowbart's gaze turned to me and I thought he was going to question my presence, or perhaps demand a lawyer, but he sat down.

'Am I to assume that our friend Sheila West is simultaneously having a chat with Hendrik DeSmid?' he asked.

Brasenose smiled. 'No she has other things on her plate these days. In fact it is something she seems to have missed I want to talk to you about. What can you tell us about Michael Regan?'

Rowbart's face expressed not even a flicker of surprise.

'Who?'

'Michael Regan. The man Colonel DeSmid brought along as his sweeper for the planned meeting at RAF Northolt. Sheila doesn't seem to have taken a witness statement from him.'

'He wasn't a witness.'

'But you picked him up with DeSmid. Wasn't he with you when the bomb went off?'

'No. We hadn't picked the sweeper up yet.'

I interrupted. 'But you told me on the radio that you had collected DeSmid and his sweeper.'

Rowbart just smiled. 'No I didn't. You must have been mistaken old chap. Perhaps there was static on the radio.'

'So how were you expecting him to get to Northolt?'

'I was going to pick him up of course, but after DeSmid.'

'Regan's hotel was in Camden,' I persisted. 'Why would you pick up DeSmid in central London and then go across to Camden before coming all the way back?'

Rowbart was perfectly cool now. 'I collected DeSmid from his club. The sweeper was taking the Tube and we were going to pick him up at Ealing Broadway.'

If I hadn't heard Rowbart at the time say quite clearly that he had collected DeSmid and the sweeper I might have believed him myself.

'So you hadn't picked him up when the bomb went off,' said Brasenose. 'But you'd met him before.'

Rowbart looked perplexed. 'Actually I'm not sure I had. No need to really.'

'Now you see Turk that's where I have a problem. We've been told you know him quite well. That you and Regan have dined together.'

'No,' said Rowbart forcefully. 'That never happened. Why

would I have dinner with DeSmid's sweeper? I didn't know the man.'

'Not dinner. I didn't mean that. More like a lunchtime barbecue, what I believe South Africans call a braai. You had a braai with Colonel DeSmid at his home at the beginning of November. We now have a witness statement alleging that Regan was there as well.'

'If he was I don't recall talking to him.'

'That's odd because we understand there were only the three of you there.'

Rowbart wasn't going to be thrown. 'Like I told you I never attended a braai with DeSmid and this man Regan.'

'But you've just said you did attend but didn't recall talking to Regan.'

'No. I said I attended a braai but it can't have been the one you were talking about. There were certainly more than three people there.'

'Do you often attend braais at DeSmid's residence?'

'Not often. Occasionally. He is a very sociable chap.'

Neither man spoke until Brasenose broke the silence. 'Come on Turk we know that the braai we're talking about was the only one you've been to at DeSmid's house. But let's move on. Why did Regan call you last night?'

This time Rowbart clearly wasn't prepared.

'What are you talking about?'

'Last night, when Regan arrived in London, the first thing he did was call you. Why?'

'It's not true, nobody called me last night.'

'Really? Not two calls seconds apart? The first of which you answered and the second you just let ring.'

I could imagine Rowbart's brain slipping into overdrive.

'I think there may have been a call but nobody answered when I picked up.'

'And the second call?'

'It rang off before I got there.'

'But you must have been right by the phone. You'd only just put it down after the first call.'

'I don't know. I was busy. Perhaps I had a drink in my hand.'

'But you can't remember.' Brasenose abruptly changed tack. 'Let's go back to the beginning of all this. DeSmid wanted a meeting with Salvador Pinheiro. How did he know Pinheiro was coming to London?'

'I don't know. It wasn't much of a secret. Thomas had reported that the daughter was having a twenty-first birthday party. I just assumed her father would come.'

'So you told DeSmid not the other way round.'

'Possibly. Does it matter?'

'You tell me. I'm trying to establish who suggested that DeSmid should meet Pinheiro. You or DeSmid?'

'Hendrik.'

'So you told DeSmid that Salvador Pinheiro was coming to London and he immediately said he must meet him.'

'Something like that.'

'You must have been shocked.'

'Surprised perhaps. But you know how things are done down there.'

'But I don't Turk.' Brasenose studied the man opposite him for a moment. 'I really don't understand how things are done down there. Everyone I speak to seems to think that DeSmid is totally opposed to any sort of concession to the terrorists. My Foreign Office colleagues were astounded when you came along with DeSmid's proposal. It seems that the South African Embassy here knew nothing at all about it.'

'But that's often the case in South Africa. The military are doing one thing when the diplomats are doing the exact opposite.'

'Yes that's true. But not like that. The diplomats are usually the ones trying to negotiate while the military refuse to believe anything the Luanda regime says. How many times have potential agreements been sabotaged by UNITA or the South African Defence Force mounting some new attack? You must have been suspicious of DeSmid's motives.'

'No I wasn't.'

'You never had any doubts?'

'Like I say I was surprised, nothing more.'

'Surprised but you didn't say anything to anyone.' Brasenose yet again suddenly changed tack. 'Did you meet Regan in New York?'

'No I didn't.'

'But you knew he was there?'

'No I didn't. The only time I've been to New York recently was for the Star Chamber and he wasn't at that.'

Brasenose nodded. 'No of course he wasn't. But he was in New York at the time. And he was in Antigua when John Darwyn was killed.'

Rowbart stiffened but said nothing.

'You know he was,' Brasenose suddenly shouted. 'You know Michael Regan. You know he killed Salvador Pinheiro and you know he killed John Darwyn.'

'I don't know him,' Rowbart replied, his voice rising. 'I've told you I've never met him. And you can't prove otherwise.'

'Oh but we will,' responded Brasenose, leaning angrily over the table towards Rowbart. 'You think you're so clever, you and DeSmid. That if you keep denying everything sooner or later we'll give up. But there is a weak link. Regan will crack. He is in with Sheila West right now. You see we can place him in Antigua at the house where Adam Joseff was killed. I tell you he will crack and when he does Corrigan will take you down with him.'

'And I tell you I've never met Corri—'

He stopped.

'You've never met Corrigan,' Brasenose completed. 'Would you like to expand on that?'

He waited for a reply.

'I've nothing more to say,' said Rowbart eventually.

'You need to think about that Turk. John Darwyn's murder changed everything. A sadistic African secret policeman was blown up in London and the media had a field day, but with the emphasis on day. Who remembers it now? And if anyone does remember it they probably think that the IRA did it. And I can tell you we're happy with that. The sooner it's all forgotten the better. Pinheiro was no loss to anyone and arresting his killers is only going to remind people that he was under our protection and we cocked it up. But John Darwyn is different. We can't hide that and we don't want to. What will it do to the Service's reputation if we just let it all lie? He was one of us.'

'No he wasn't,' Rowbart retorted. 'He'd taken early retirement and with good reason. He and Joseff had been selling secrets to the Soviets.'

'But can you prove that?' Brasenose asked. 'The Star Chamber was inconclusive. You know that, you were there. I'd give a lot for solid evidence that Darwyn was working for the Angolans. But consider one thing, and think carefully about this, if you're right that Joseff and Darwyn were working for the other side who would have killed them? Surely the ones they were stealing secrets from, DeSmid and you?'

'No. You can't pin what happened in Antigua on me. I came straight back here from New York. I was at my desk in Century House.'

'Yes indeed you were. But DeSmid wasn't and he had a special reason for wanting Darwyn dead hadn't he?'

Brasenose looked Rowbart in the eye again. 'We believe John Darwyn was having an affair with DeSmid's wife. So here is the first question: was Darwyn killed because someone thought he was selling secrets or because DeSmid was jealous?'

Rowbart pushed his chair back. 'Where is this going? I don't know anything about Darwyn's death. If Hendrik did it, which I don't believe, would it matter why?'

'Well you see Turk, it would matter. If DeSmid acted alone, a crime of passion, that's sad but it's nothing to do with us, it's not a Security matter. But if Darwyn was killed for some other reason, something to do with the Service, then there would be no reason to suppose DeSmid was acting alone. We would need to find out who else was involved. And we would want to find someone we could take action against because sure as hell we can't expect the South Africans to take action against DeSmid.'

Brasenose abruptly stood up. 'Think about it Turk.'

Without saying any more he left the room with me trailing after him.

'You sounded as if you were offering Rowbart a

deal,' I commented as we returned to the office he had commandeered.

'I was.'

'But what was the deal and why?'

Brasenose turned and gave me the same look he had just given Rowbart. 'Think about it Thomas.'

Then he turned towards the door. 'Time to tour Whitehall, I need to consult colleagues. I suggest we meet back here at eight o'clock this evening.' A few minutes later I saw him being driven away in the back of his official Vauxhall, he had already retrieved the clunky NEC handset from the centre console in front of him.

When I returned to Paddington Green at eight o'clock, having put Eveline to bed and read her the shortest story I could find, Sheila West was waiting.

'Justin Brasenose is downstairs with Rowbart. He's been there for more than an hour, just the two of them. We're to wait here.'

We settled down to wait and West told me about one positive development. The Belgian authorities had already been tipped off by a dealer in Antwerp that he had been approached by Cristóvão Taravares with an offer of uncut diamonds. Taravares had claimed they were from West Africa but he couldn't produce any documentation. The story he had spun is that he was acting on behalf of a coffee grower in São Tomé whom he'd known for years, but he wouldn't name him.'

'Have you told Brasenose?' I asked.

'Yes. He's decided not to tell the Americans anything about the involvement of Taravares in the diamonds yet. He seems to be really pissed off that Cato let him believe the plane had been shot down.'

'If he did tell the Americans it's not obvious what they could do about it,' I commented. 'If Cato tries to get the Belgians or Italians to move against Taravares he would have to admit that the CIA have been helping Savimbi and UNITA run blood diamonds out of Angola in contravention of Congressional resolutions and UN sanctions. I suppose Cato could at least warn Jonas Savimbi that Lusiano Nambala, one of his top commanders, has been stealing from him.'

West grimaced. 'If half of what I've heard about Savimbi is true that wouldn't bode well for Nambala.'

She was certainly right about that. If Cato were to tell Savimbi his diamonds had been stolen by Nambala, the very man in charge of their safekeeping, Marco Mutorwa's uncle would meet a very painful end. Not that many people would shed any tears over that.

I changed the subject. 'How did you get on with Regan?'

'That man will tell us nothing. We don't have anything to link him directly to the Westbourne Terrace explosion. No trace of anywhere he might have built the bomb. No evidence he was ever in Mutorwa's flat to plant the controller or doctor that map. No fingerprints on anything. And we have no excuse to hold him for anything he might have done in Northern Ireland. The most we've got him for is entering the UK on a false passport and if the South Africans turn round and say it's genuine and he legally changed his name from Corrigan to Regan we won't even have that. We should have kept him under surveillance but it's too late for that now. Let's hope Justin can get something out of Rowbart or we'll have to let Regan go.'

'And Rowbart too,' I said. 'Everything we have is circumstantial.'

'That's right,' said Brasenose entering the room. He turned to West. 'Arrange round-the-clock surveillance and then let them both go.'

'You got nothing then,' she replied.

'On the contrary. I've got everything we need.'

# XXV

'DeSmid killed Darwyn and Regan killed Joseff,' Brasenose announced.

I was astonished by his assertion. Clearly so was West. 'Rowbart told you that!' she exclaimed. 'On the record? He will stand up in court and give evidence?'

'There is not going to be any standing up in court. I've given him total immunity.'

'Not for everything,' West insisted. Now she was not just astonished she was horrified. 'Not for the Westbourne Terrace bombing. You can't do that.'

'Actually I can. It's all been agreed. Let me explain.'

'But Rowbart helped Regan set off a bomb right here.' West pointed in the general direction of Paddington Station. 'It killed two people. It could've killed a lot more. Someone has to face justice.'

Brasenose shook his head. 'If you can pin it on Regan perhaps. But you haven't been able to do that. We're not having a serving officer of the Secret Intelligence Service in the dock at the Old Bailey accused of planting a bomb in the middle of London. It just can't be allowed. Now do you want to hear what Rowbart said or not?'

West sat down. 'Yes I do,' she said wearily. 'I don't suppose you recorded your interview.'

'Of course not. The only way to crack this case in my

opinion was by getting someone to confess to something. DeSmid is out of our control. You've tried but failed with Regan. So it had to be Rowbart and the only way to do that was to offer him a deal.'

'What sort of a deal?'

'Like I said immunity from all prosecution in this country. Rowbart will continue in the Service for a period of three months and will then be allowed to resign. His pension rights will be unaffected. There are some tasks I wish him to perform and after that he will go on what we are describing as furlough until the three months are up. During that time he will not leave the country without our permission and he will be available to answer any further questions.'

'And what does he give us in writing?' West asked.

'Nothing. There will be nothing in anyone's files.'

'That's immoral,' West responded, but she knew she was defeated. Brasenose turned to me. 'And what do you think Thomas?'

'It's disappointing.'

'Perhaps. Now let me tell you what he said. He would say nothing at all about the Westbourne Terrace bomb. On the events in Antigua he was eventually more forthcoming, no doubt because he can show that he was in London at the time. He accepted my assertion that we could prove Regan was present in the house where Joseff's body was found. I also told him that the local police had found what may be partial fingerprints on the shoes discovered with Darwyn's body and had sent them to the United States for processing by the FBI. I made it clear that he had better make a deal with me now because if the FBI results proved conclusive I wouldn't need a deal.'

'Were there fingerprints?' West asked.

'Not as far as I know. And we've got nothing to place Regan in Joseff's villa. But as I say Rowbart accepted what I said.

'His story is this. DeSmid discovered that his wife and John Darwyn were lovers and she had been passing Darwyn details of Special Ops. He wanted to confront Darwyn and warn him off after the Star Chamber but Darwyn left New York right away. DeSmid had thought that might happen and set Regan to follow him. Regan reported back that John Darwyn and Mrs DeSmid were in Florida and that Darwyn had booked a flight to Antigua. DeSmid didn't want to confront Darwyn and his wife together. Rowbart claims that DeSmid hoped that if Darwyn just agreed to disappear from the scene she would come back to him.'

'I don't believe that,' I said. 'DeSmid isn't the forgiving type.'

'Perhaps but that's what Rowbart said. The upshot was that DeSmid decided to go to Antigua and confront Darwyn but he didn't want anyone to know that he'd been there.'

'Which suggests that he was planning to do more than confront Darwyn,' suggested West.

'As I say perhaps. The point is that DeSmid wanted to get to Antigua without being seen and he turned to his friend GI Coley whom he knew had some sort of boat in the US Virgin Islands. They were both game fishing fanatics. Rowbart says he doesn't know what DeSmid said to Coley but it must have been persuasive because Coley personally went down to St Thomas with DeSmid and they set sail for Antigua. They got there on the same day as Darwyn. DeSmid went ashore somewhere. Regan was already on the island

and took him to the airport. DeSmid kept out of sight but Regan watched Joseff greeting Darwyn and then ushering him out to a hire car. Regan followed, keeping well back, not least because he had DeSmid sitting in the passenger seat. But Joseff wasn't expecting to be followed. It wasn't a long journey, fifteen minutes or so, before they got on to a road that didn't seem to be going anywhere. Regan apparently dropped really well back then and thought he might have lost his target. But then DeSmid saw Joseff's hire car parked outside a house. They drove on past and were debating what to do when Joseff suddenly came out and drove off.'

'So they went inside?'

'Regan stayed outside. DeSmid went inside to confront Darwyn. Rowbart claims that there was a fight, Darwyn pulled a gun, DeSmid grabbed it and it went off.'

'Twice. It went off twice,' I pointed out sarcastically. 'Once into the chest and once into the head.'

'Rowbart's story,' conceded Brasenose, 'is not without elements of implausibility. But the point is DeSmid just wanted to get off the island, and as soon as possible, but there was a body to dispose of. DeSmid and Regan pulled down a curtain to cover the body, then Regan quickly drove DeSmid down to Jolly Harbour where he could get a taxi back to Coley's boat on the other side of the island. That was the riskiest part, leaving Darwyn's body in the house, but Regan wasn't away for very long. DeSmid had given Regan the gun and told him to go back and shift the body. When Regan returned everything was as he had left it. He put the body in the boot. DeSmid had told him to bury it where it wouldn't be found.'

'And it wouldn't have been found if that Canadian family hadn't turned up,' West commented.

'Hold on. I haven't finished yet. Regan was just about to leave when another car drew up. It was Joseff carrying a load of shopping. Apparently Joseff walked up to Regan with a welcoming smile on his face and then when he got close hit Regan over the head with a tin of something, knocking him to the ground, and ran towards the open front door. Regan realised Joseff must have seen the curtain rail torn down and chased after him. When he got inside Joseff came out of the kitchen and went for him with a knife, slashed him on the arm and started yelling, 'Where's John?' Then Joseff turned to pull open a bedroom door and Regan took out the gun and shot him twice in the back of the head.

'Regan then wrapped his arm in a towel and drove off. Rowbart says he was panicking. He was supposed to dump the body where it wouldn't be found but he didn't know the island, the injury to his arm made heavy digging impossible and he realised he didn't even have a shovel. So he parked the car, bought some bandages and waited.

'In the meantime GI Coley and DeSmid were on their way to Montserrat where Coley's private jet was waiting to take them back to Florida. When Regan phoned them in Montserrat to explain what had happened DeSmid was furious. He insisted that Regan had to find a way to lose the body but refused to come back to help, that was too much of a risk. Regan still said he couldn't do it, especially at night when any light might attract attention. And here we come to the last piece of the puzzle. Coley took charge. He put DeSmid on the jet and said he would himself sail back to Antigua the next day, collect the body and the gun and dump them out to sea. So that's what he did, except that he didn't. As Rowbart said Coley is a devious bastard.'

'Coley saw an opportunity,' I put in. 'He had the dead body of DeSmid's wife's lover and the gun that had killed him, quite possibly with fingerprints on it. One day that might be useful. DeSmid was already right at the top of South African Intelligence. The time might come when Coley wanted something from him. Or perhaps somebody whose help Coley needed would want to find a way to discredit DeSmid. So Coley collected the body, sailed round to an isolated bay, found somewhere he could dig a hole and dumped the body there. Ready to be recovered if needed.'

'Exactly,' said Brasenose. 'Although knowing Coley he wouldn't have done any of the digging himself. One of his crew would have done that.'

He sat back with a satisfied expression on his face.

West still seemed disgusted. 'So we've solved the crime and now we're letting them all go. DeSmid. Regan. Rowbart. Coley. They all just carry on!'

'I understand your frustration,' Brasenose replied, 'but we're not the police. We're not here to serve justice. We're here to serve something far more prosaic, our country. It's not in the country's interest for us to throw mud at ourselves when there is no possibility of ever finding enough evidence to convict anybody of anything, and when Turk Rowbart can still be useful to us.'

'In what way?' I asked.

'In helping bring peace to Southern Africa. UNITA and the South Africans are hailing Cuito Cuanavale as a victory for them but it's not. They can't carry on. White House policy is changing. UNITA has to make peace with the Communists in Luanda. That means Jonas Savimbi must be brought to his senses. Savimbi doesn't trust the Communist regime in Luanda and he's probably right but that no longer matters. Whether the two sides trust each other or not the only way to get the Cubans to go home is a comprehensive peace agreement. Savimbi is blocking that. And he'll carry on blocking it as long as he thinks he'll get support from outside. I spoke to Frank Cato this afternoon. He's going to Jamba to see Savimbi and make sure he understands the new facts of life. But Frank has to show we are all playing the same tune. We'll send someone of course but the South African military needs to do so as well. They need to send someone Savimbi will believe.'

'DeSmid?'

'Exactly. Colonel DeSmid has to be persuaded to go with Cato and talk to Savimbi.'

'And you think DeSmid can be persuaded after everything he's done to stop a deal with the Angolans? He risked organising a bombing in London to stop that happening. That man is convinced the Russians will be in Cape Town tomorrow if we give up in Angola.'

'Well I probably couldn't persuade him,' conceded Brasenose. 'But Rowbart might be able to. If DeSmid doesn't agree Rowbart could make it clear that we would make life very difficult for him. He was in Antigua when his wife's lover was murdered. There's a new paper down there called the *Weekly Mail* that would love a story like that. Anyway that's the deal I offered Rowbart. Total immunity if he and DeSmid join Frank Cato in Jamba and use their best endeavours to persuade Savimbi to support the latest American proposals from Chester Crocker.'

Sheila West clearly remained far from convinced. 'It's been a very long day. I'll leave you gentlemen to your international intriguing. Just remember a young girl was blown up not five minutes from here and you're letting her killers walk free. One of your own officers was killed and ditto. A former Deputy Director of Defence Intelligence killed and ditto again. I hope it's worth it.'

When she had gone I turned to Brasenose. 'You don't believe Darwyn's death was really a crime of passion do you?'

'Of course not. If it had happened as Rowbart described DeSmid would have had no reason to tell him about it. You don't casually tell a colleague you've shot your wife's lover even if it was an accident. And why take a gun if you don't intend to use it? That certainly wasn't Darwyn's weapon, he wouldn't have risked smuggling a gun on to the island.'

I had to agree with that. Darwyn wasn't the sort of man to carry a gun and he wouldn't have imagined he needed one just for a meeting with his bank manager.

'Darwyn thought he was safe. He had his knowledge of Regan as his protection, his bargaining chip. As long as Rowbart and DeSmid didn't reveal that he'd been selling South African secrets he wouldn't reveal that the man DeSmid had taken to London with him was an Irish terrorist. No doubt he rationalised it all to himself. What damage was he really doing by keeping silent about Regan? The Westbourne Terrace explosion was now just a memory, there was nothing he could do to bring the Pinheiros back to life. He would go off to Antigua, recover the money in his Antiguan account, the money he had described to Rosemary DeSmid as his pension pot, and then retire to the Cotswolds and a new life. Angola, Regan, MI6 would all be consigned to history. What Darwyn didn't realise is that Rowbart and DeSmid weren't focused on history, they were planning for the future.'

'That's right,' agreed Brasenose. 'Pinheiro's death didn't cause the Luanda regime to self-destruct as they had hoped. Everything carried on as before. So they had to try again. Plant another bomb somewhere that would do far more damage. And that somewhere,' Brasenose continued, 'is London. That's why the man calling himself Regan arrived last night. The latest US initiative is bearing fruit. Chester Crocker has persuaded all the parties involved to meet at Brown's Hotel here in London, it could be the breakthrough we've all been waiting for. DeSmid and Rowbart intend to somehow stop that meeting going ahead. And that's why they couldn't risk Darwyn changing his mind and revealing Regan's role.

'Not only that,' I interrupted. 'They couldn't be sure that Darwyn hadn't already revealed Regan's role. Not to us but to Adam Joseff.'

The pieces were finally falling into place. For DeSmid and Rowbart Adam was the loose cannon not Darwyn. Darwyn had sold official secrets, he could be blackmailed. He would stick to the deal he had struck. But Adam had done nothing illegal. His business was selling information. He could claim that Salvador Pinheiro was just another client and John Darwyn just another source.

'All that story about Adam being killed because he just happened to turn up was rubbish. DeSmid left Regan on the island to wait for Adam. They meant to kill him.'

Brasenose nodded. 'That's right.'

'So now what?' I asked. 'How do we find out how DeSmid and Rowbart are planning to derail the Crocker peace process?'

'We don't have to. We just have to stop whatever it is

334

happening. We'll find an excuse to hold Regan for a while, send Rowbart out of the country and make plain to the South African government that Colonel DeSmid is no longer welcome here. With Regan out of the way there's nothing more we need to do. Crocker's conference will go ahead. More than that Rowbart will persuade DeSmid to go with him to Jamba and with Savimbi on side Crocker will get the peace he wants.'

'So West was right. Now that we've found all the pieces of the puzzle and put them together, we're just going to put them back into their box and walk away.'

'The Joint Intelligence Committee met this morning,' Brasenose replied. 'The policy of Her Majesty's Government is exactly that.'

# XXVI

Lisbon is one of my favourite cities. I had first visited it at the age of twelve and for the next six years spent part of every summer with my friend Luis exploring its streets and markets, or in the last of those summers looking for Portuguese girls keen to practise their English. For me the city evokes what the Portuguese call *saudades*, something more than memories, longings. Life had been so much simpler then: no secrets to hide, no loyalties to disguise, no moral complexities.

When I phoned Brasenose to tell him I was going to visit an old friend in Portugal I thought he might object, there were still administrative loose ends to clear up.

'Can't it wait??'

'No.'

There was a moment's silence on the line before Brasenose asked, 'You're going to Lisbon?'

'That's right.'

There was a longer pause this time. I could almost hear him thinking. His words when he spoke were unhurried. 'I hear Lisbon can be a dangerous place to visit. I'll signal our Station Chief in case you need anything.'

I had always loved taking a ferry across the Tagus and sitting at one of the cafés sipping the tiny coffees. I would look back at the city skyline and imagine what it must have been like to live there when the Portuguese Empire straddled the world.

It was a particular café I was looking for when I stepped off the ferry now. The Service's Station Chief in the Portuguese capital had not only managed to discover where Marco Mutorwa was living but identified the café where he took coffee each day before setting out for the university.

'Hello Marco,' I said as I sat down at his table.

He looked startled and glanced around as if expecting to see others behind me or perhaps he was just looking for ways to get away.

'I wanted to talk about Mariana.'

'I had nothing to do with that. I've told you everything I know.'

'I know that Marco. I know you didn't kill her. Of course you didn't. You were her friend, a very close friend at one time.'

I thought he was going to protest again but I held up my hand. 'I know who killed her. I know their names. That's what I came to tell you. I thought you ought to know. We owe you that after what you've been through. Mariana was killed by two men called Turk Rowbart and Hendrik DeSmid.'

'I don't know them,' said Mutorwa softly.

'Of course you don't know them. They're renegade Intelligence officers.'

'Whites?'

'Yes whites. Senior people, but absolutely without authorisation. They acted on their own.'

'They're in prison now?'

I shook my head. 'The world doesn't work like that Marco. We know who they are but the police have been warned off. We have an expression in English: don't wash your dirty linen in public. But I wanted you to know.'

We let a moment's silence hang between us.

'I still don't understand Tommy. Why are you telling me this?'

'Because I think you loved her Marco, that's all. She was beautiful and she was special.'

He looked down. 'Yes she was,' he mumbled, 'very special.'

'The way she organised that business with the diamonds, that was special.'

Mutorwa's head shot up, all his suspicions back. I put up my hand again.

'I'm not here about that Marco. That's all over. We know what happened. You and Mariana, probably mostly Mariana, realised that if you could bring together her cousin Cristóvão Taravares and your uncle Lusiano Nambala there was money to be made. Lots of money. Your uncle told you when the diamonds would arrive in Jamba, I assume you've always had a way to contact your uncle quickly. You told Mariana, she told Taravares and he flew down to Windhoek after your uncle had taken the diamonds and replaced them with a bomb. It was very clever. Using those phone boxes for your messages, that nearly fooled us.'

'Are you going to arrest me?'

'Certainly not. You're a man of the world Marco. People change sides. My government's objective now is peace and stability in the region. UNITA losing diamonds that were going to be used to buy more guns is not something that worries us any more. And the Americans don't want to admit that someone could smuggle a bomb on to one of their planes so they've agreed to let Savimbi handle things. But others don't feel that way, men like the ones who killed Mariana. In fact Rowbart will be flying down there tonight. He and DeSmid are determined to see Jonas Savimbi and tell him what you've all been up to, present him with the evidence. They will be in Jamba tomorrow. You should advise your uncle to talk to Savimbi first, before they get there, make his excuses.'

Mutorwa shook his head. I knew what he meant. Nobody made excuses to Jonas Savimbi. If Rowbart and DeSmid said anything to Savimbi about Nambala's role in the loss of the diamonds that would be a death sentence for Marco's uncle. Of course in reality they wouldn't say anything about Nambala's role because neither Rowbart nor DeSmid knew anything about it. We certainly hadn't told them.

I stood up. 'I admired your uncle,' I lied. 'A man of action.'

I would have liked to order a coffee and watch the Tagus roll past. But I had promised Julia that I would only be away for twenty-four hours.

I should reach Heathrow just as Turk Rowbart was setting off for Johannesburg. Tomorrow he and DeSmid would go up to Jamba to meet Jonas Savimbi, although I doubted that Savimbi would be there when they arrived. Brasenose had just told me that Frank Cato intended asking the UNITA leader to show him the troop dispositions around Cuito Cuanavale.

Marco Mutorwa's uncle would be left in charge in Jamba. No doubt Lusiano Nambala would know how to look after the two visitors.

# AFTERWORD

The peace agreement that ends this book did not end the war. The Cuban fighters and Russian advisers withdrew, Namibia achieved independence and apartheid ended but the bloodshed in Angola went on and on. Peace only came when the whole nation was too exhausted to continue.

Ironically it was to be South African special forces that brought peace of a kind. Hundreds of battle-hardened South Africans, out of work after the ANC victory in South Africa, found employment as mercenaries in Angola. Men like Wynand Du Toit, the leader of Operation Argon, returned to fight for the very regime they had been fighting against, hunting down their former allies in UNITA. Only when Jonas Savimbi was killed in a gun battle in 2002 did the war stagger to an end.

There are numerous books, often personal memoirs, about the wars in Southern Africa, and an even larger number of academic articles. Many are heavily influenced by a desire to be 'politically correct' while others strain to justify the unjustifiable. For purely military matters I relied largely on the reporting of Al J Venter.

I have had to take some small liberties with the facts.

For example the last South African parachute action to take place in Angola was Operation Pineapple in June 1988. I have described it reasonably faithfully but in order to fit in with the plot I have moved the timing slightly and rechristened it Operation Mango.

Angola is one of the richest and most corrupt nations in the world. More than half a million people, largely civilians, were killed in the civil war but some people thrived. As I write Africa's first female billionaire, the daughter of Angola's former President and his Russian wife, is being investigated for corruption on a breathtaking scale. She is merely the most notorious example of a phenomenon with which companies and governments in the West and the East have colluded for far too long.

# ACKNOWLEDGEMENTS

This book would not have been started without the support of the team at RedDoor. Enormous thanks to Clare Christian, Heather Boisseau, Anna Burtt and Lizzie Lewis. The finished book again owes much to the technical skills of Carol Anderson and Jen Parker. I also benefitted enormously from the wisdom and encouragement of Andrew Hook of Fiction Feedback.

I have been fortunate to have spent much of my life flying around the world in a time before we all realised the damage we were doing to the environment. That was also before videoconferencing made the absurdity of flying from London to Australia for one short meeting apparent even to me. Some of that travel was for Pearson Education and two of my regular destinations were Warsaw and Cape Town. The former provided inspiration for *Coincidence of Spies* and the latter for this book. I owe a special debt of gratitude to the old Maskew Miller Longman team in Cape Town who helped me understand something of what life must have been like in Southern Africa during apartheid.

Lastly as always I must thank my wife Liz. She has provided unstinting support and even volunteered to accompany me on research trips to Antigua.

# ABOUT THE AUTHOR

After giving up on an academic career, and deciding not to join the government spy agency GCHQ, Brian Landers helped a former Director General of Defence Intelligence and a motley collection of ex-spooks set up a political intelligence unit in the City of London. Out of that experience sprang the character of Thomas Dylan, a novice who over the years progresses through the labyrinthine world of British Intelligence.

Brian Landers has lived in various parts of North and South America and Europe. He has worked in every corner of the globe from Beirut to Bali, Cape Town to Warsaw and points in between, and in industries as varied as insurance, family planning, retailing, manufacturing and management consultancy. He saw the inside of more prisons than most during three years as a director of HM Prison Service. He has a Politics Degree from the University of Exeter and an MBA from London Business School. In his spare time he helped set up the Financial Ombudsman Service, served on the boards of Amnesty UK and the Royal Armouries, and was Chairman of Companies House.

Landers subsidised his university bar bills by writing a column for the local paper and since then has written articles for various journals, newspapers and websites. As a director of Waterstones and later Penguin his passion for writing was rekindled. His first book, *Empires Apart*, published in the UK, US and India, was a history of the Russian and American Empires. His next book was going to be *Trump, Putin and the Lessons of History* but the subject was so depressing that he turned to fiction.

In 2018 Brian Landers was awarded an OBE in the Queen's Birthday Honours.

brianlanders.co.uk

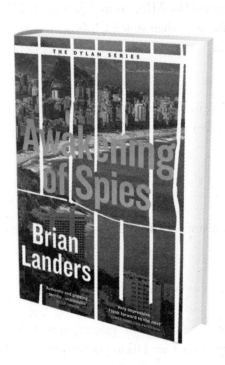

Awakening
of Spies

Brian
Landers

'Authentic and gripping...
terrific... unmissable.'
PETER TOWNEND

'Very impressive...
I look forward to the next'
JAMES HAMILTON-PATERSON

# AWAKENING OF SPIES

Linguist Thomas Dylan is an unlikely spy.

Initially rejected by MI6, his first mission in 1973 is a total failure. But when stolen US Navy secrets appear in Brazil he is sent to Rio de Janeiro: a city of sun, sea and secret police.

As he confronts a brutal military dictatorship Thomas discovers that saving his life is not a priority for MI6 or the CIA.

Who can he trust?

Certainly not Julia French, another novice spy sent to replace him.

Why is Julia lying to him?

This is a twisting tale of intrigue, mystery, romance and red herrings. Can Dylan put the pieces of the puzzle together before it is too late?

John le Carré meets Agatha Christie in the first gripping novel

AVAILABLE FROM ALL GOOD BOOKSHOPS

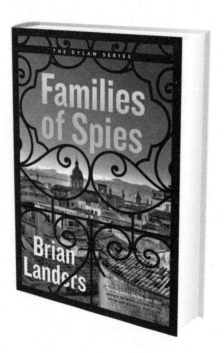

# FAMILIES OF SPIES

Julia Dylan's aunt vanishes while sailing from Kefalonia to Syracuse in Sicily.

Julia's uncle, the head of Defence Intelligence, asks MI6 to investigate but MI6 has higher priorities. The CIA have uncovered a Russian spy at a NATO airbase north of Syracuse.

Julia and her new husband Thomas abandon their honeymoon and join the search. In Syracuse they encounter a suspiciously well-informed detective who is investigating the murder of an Iranian journalist.

Could it all be connected?

And could the connection go all the way back to an infamous Mafia massacre in 1947?

To unravel the mystery of Eveline Sadeghi's death, Julia and Thomas Dylan must not just understand history, but families too, especially their own.

John le Carré meets Agatha Christie in the second gripping novel in the Dylan series

AVAILABLE FROM ALL GOOD BOOKSHOPS

THE DYLAN SERIES
Brian
Landers
Coincidence
of Spies
Brian Landers is the real deal'
ANDREW RAYMOND, AUTHOR OF THE
NOVAK AND MITCHELL THRILLERS

# COINCIDENCE OF SPIES

Winter 1981. Poland is in turmoil.

The Communist regime is close to collapse and the CIA
wants to help it on its way. They ask for MI6
support but insist the local MI6 Station isn't involved.

Why not? Who will they accept?

MI6 agent Thomas Dylan is sent from Moscow. His wife
Julia has witnessed a murder and the
Russian authorities want her out of the country.

But in Warsaw, bullets start to fly.

Two American agents disappear, a terrified Polish sailor
jumps ship in Middlesbrough and a Polish
peasant claims to have found the lost crown of a medieval
king.

In London Julia needs to work out what's happening.

And quickly. Because a KGB killer is on the loose.

AVAILABLE FROM ALL GOOD BOOKSHOPS

Find out more about RedDoor
Press and sign up to our
newsletter to hear about our
**latest releases, author events,**
exciting **competitions**
and more at

**reddoorpress.co.uk**

---

## YOU CAN ALSO FOLLOW US:

 @RedDoorBooks

 Facebook.com/RedDoorPress

 @RedDoorBooks